Tied up in knots . . .

Alex didn't like the way Rush Duncan made her feel or the way he was looking at her now, or more precisely, the way he was trying to look inside her. She wasn't a ten-year-old like Caro whom he could charm with his good looks and his sweet-talking ways.

"I assure you, Mr. Duncan, I'm no longer a child whose heart can be broken by a rambler without roots."

His gaze raked over her. "You definitely aren't a child, Alexandy, but maybe you're worried that your *woman's* heart can be broken by a rambler without roots."

"Spare me," she scoffed. She was determined to show him how little concern she had for his remark.

"The way I see it," he said, "a man can have roots, although they might not be attached to the ground." He patted his chest above his heart. "The roots I'm speaking about are attached here, and they can grow very deep. I've always believed it's not where a man rests his head that makes him a permanent kind of fellow, but where he rests his heart."

Pieces of Yesterday

CAROL CARD OTTEN

JOVE BOOKS, NEW YORK

A QUILTING ROMANCE is a trademark of Penguin Putnam Inc.

PIECES OF YESTERDAY

A Jove Book / published by arrangement with
the author

PRINTING HISTORY
Jove edition / June 1999

The Penguin Putnam Inc. World Wide Web site address is
http://www.penguinputnam.com

ISBN: 0-515-12524-5

A JOVE BOOK®
Jove Books are published by The Berkley Publishing Group,
a division of Penguin Putnam Inc.,
375 Hudson Street, New York, New York 10014.
JOVE and the "J" design
are trademarks belonging to Penguin Putnam Inc.

PRINTED IN THE UNITED STATES OF AMERICA

10 9 8 7 6 5 4 3 2 1

*To my
mother, Ruth Inez Card,
who was my best friend,
and to my
daughter, Christina,
whom I hope can say the same.*

The Memory Quilt

A life;
captured in fabric using wool,
cotton, ribbon, velvet and silk.
Fabric paintings;
clothes hanging on a line, a swing
suspended from a tree.
Houses, buildings, and places no longer standing:
Mountains and rivers — constants
in an ever-changing world.
Joined pieces;
reminders of Grandmother's Flower Garden,
Cathedral Windows, and Feathered Stars.
Stitches;
both running and blind,
complete a pattern — the connecting thread of generations.
The Memory Quilt;
records a life — the passage of time.
                    —Carol Card Otten

Pieces of
Yesterday

Prologue

Harpers Ferry, West Virginia
1860

ESTELLE WILSON STOOD BESIDE the front wheel of the tinker's wagon, her whispered demand desperate. "Get down this minute, Charlotte, or I'll call Pa."

"I'm going, Stella," Charlotte responded, "and you can't stop me. Tyler and me, we're gonna be married."

The man called Tyler sat on the driver's seat beside her sister. With his cap pulled down over his eyes, he appeared indifferent to the argument taking place between the two siblings. His indifference indicated to Estelle that he felt sure of his position in the scheme of things and had no doubts about the outcome.

"Married? You're still wet behind the ears," she told Charlotte. "What do you know about getting married?"

"I'm fifteen," Charlotte answered, "just three years younger than you, so don't go pulling rank on me. Besides, you're getting married."

Frustrated, Estelle sighed. "Three years doesn't seem like a lot, but I've known Herman Paine all my life. You've known Tyler here less than two weeks."

She shot the one in question a look that would have bested most men, but not so this one. Her icy gaze bounced off him like the rising sun's reflection bounced off the surface of the nearby Potomac River. From above the hills that rimmed the river's bank, the fiery ball gilded the green trees with summer warmth, but it couldn't penetrate the cold dread that had settled in Estelle's heart when she considered the journey her only sister was about to take.

She grasped the skirt of her night rail when she wanted desperately to clasp Charlotte and bodily pull her down from the wagon seat. But fearing the use of force would awaken their sleeping parents, she tried instead to persuade the girl to change her mind.

"If you really love him, Charlotte, wait. He'll be back in a few months and then he can court you the way a young lady should be courted."

Stubbornly, Charlotte replied, "I'm not waiting."

Estelle recognized the mulish expression. It was a look she had encountered many times during their growing-up years.

Charlotte entwined her fingers around Tyler's arm. "I'm leaving today. Now. I'm not gonna be here when the war starts. Although folks say a war will never happen, you and I both know it will, especially after John Brown's raid last year and the talk of secession."

"There's been no trouble since the raid," Estelle insisted, "and there won't be any more. Nobody wants to go to war."

"Nobody but Yankees and darkies. And some of the locals. I swear, Estelle, you're supposed to be the bright one. Even your fiancé, Herman, boasts of what he'll do to the damn Yankees if they come sniffing around on Virginia soil."

"Herman does not want a war," Estelle replied.

Her dark-haired pretty sister rolled her blue eyes heavenward. "A lot you know about the man you plan to marry."

"I'm not worried about a war coming or the man I'm going to marry. At the moment I'm more concerned with your future. Please, Charlotte, I beg of you, don't go on this venture that will only lead to the destruction of your good name."

"My good name, Stella, is already sullied. If you must know, Tyler and me, we've been together as man and wife."

"You've what?" Estelle's heart dropped into her stomach. This thing between her sister and this near stranger was worse than she suspected. "Surely you jest. You're but a child, and he's a good fifteen years older. Old enough to know better than to take advantage of a young girl."

Estelle's anger swelled inside her. She lunged toward the wagon unmindful of the noise her tirade would make.

"How dare you take advantage of my sister!" she accused Tyler. "If what she says is true, then you should do the honorable thing and marry her now before the two of you go traipsing across the country together."

"No," Charlotte insisted, "we won't be married here. Pa will never agree to such a match. We'll marry later, on the trail."

Estelle gaped at the twosome. She hoped against hope that this man her sister claimed to love would have a grain of decency in him that would make him want to do the right thing and make an honest woman of her sister. Instead he said nothing as he stared off into space. Her opinion of him sank even lower.

Morning was fast approaching. From a nearby yard a rooster announced the coming day, and the flock of black crows that retired daily to the craggy rocks across the river where they hoteled each night rose into the air. The flock of raven birds obscured the sun as they flapped their wings, rising heavenward.

Estelle considered the feathered cloud of darkness a bad omen. She was so distracted by her grim thoughts that she didn't hear her parents on the porch behind her until her pa shouted an order.

"Get down from that wagon now, Charlotte, and get into the house! No daughter of mine is going traipsing across the country with some footloose peddler with no roots!"

"I'm going, Pa, and you can't stop me," Charlotte responded. "We're going to be married. I'm a woman now." Her voice faltered, and Estelle could see her knuckles had turned white where she clasped Tyler's arm.

"You're no woman, you're nothing but a splittail who's too dang headstrong for her own good. Get down now, gal, afore

I pull you off that wagon and haul you back inside.''

Charlotte nudged Tyler on the arm. ''Go,'' she urged. ''You can't control me anymore, Pa. I'm gonna marry Tyler if it's the last thing I do.''

As Tyler shook the traces, the wagon lunged forward. The bells that hung from the wagon's roof jingled sharply above the noise of the drama unfolding.

''If you leave with that no-good drifter, you'll not be welcome home again.''

Her pa's words chilled Estelle's bones as she ran alongside the moving wagon. ''Please, Charlotte don't do this,'' she begged. ''Wait a few months, and if you still feel the same when he returns, then you can marry him. I'm sure Pa will come around by then.''

''I'm going, Stella. I love Tyler, and he loves me. We're going west together to make a new life.''

Her father followed close behind her now. Estelle heard him yell, ''If you go with this man, gal, you'll be dead in the eyes of this family!''

Estelle gasped. ''Don't say such things, Pa. You know Charlotte will always be part of this family no matter where she is.''

Her father ignored her. ''I mean it, Charlotte, make your choice. It's either us or him!''

Charlotte released Tyler's arm and stared defiantly at her father. ''Then there's no choice, Pa. I'm going with him.''

The wagon picked up speed as they moved up the hill.

''Then begone with you!'' her father shouted. ''From this day forward, you're dead to this family!''

''Please, Pa,'' Estelle cried, ''don't say such things. You know you don't mean them. Go after her, Pa!''

She grabbed her father's arm as he turned and stalked back toward the porch, dragging her along with him as though she weighed no more than a feather. Her mother stood beneath the eaves with her face buried in her palms, her sobs echoing in the empty yard.

''Stop her, Ma! Don't let her go. Make Pa go after her. Don't let him say such things. She's your baby—you can't just let her walk away.''

Her mother looked haggard. She said nothing, but followed obediently behind her husband as he walked into the house.

"Pa, you can't do this! Please, go after her."

Jess Wilson was a stubborn man who expected obedience from both his wife and his children. Charlotte had always been the rebellious one who had fought with her father on every issue. Now it had come to this.

The front door slammed. Estelle, tears pouring from her eyes, turned to watch the wagon that carried her baby sister away. The wagon was nothing more than a watery blur when it disappeared below the rise of the hill. Feeling lonelier than she had felt in all her eighteen years, Estelle whispered to her now absent sister.

"Don't do this thing, Charlotte. Don't set forth on this journey of no return."

1

RUSH DUNCAN ENTWINED HIS fingers with the ten-year-old girl's and smiled down at her. "It's time we go, Caroline," he said. She stood beside him on the stern of the canal boat, watching the crew make their way along the tow path toward the bridge that spanned the Potomac River. "Are you ready?" he asked.

Crossing her stringy arms against her birdlike chest, Caroline set her chin in that stubborn manner that Rush had come to recognize after their long week of traveling together.

"I'm not going," she replied. "I'm happy right here with you. You can't make me go live with some pain-in-the-ass relatives I don't even know."

Rush gulped back a laugh. Caroline Swift might have the face of an angel, but in his opinion, the imp's mouth could use a thorough sudsing. Because it wasn't his place to discipline his temporary charge, he asked instead, "Where did you get such an idea about folks you haven't even met?"

"From you. I heard you tell the captain and his wife that

Alexandria Paine lived up to her name. You said she was a pain in the—''

''Never mind what I said,'' Rush interrupted. He didn't need to be reminded of his response to his old friends' request to deliver Caroline Swift to her family in Harpers Ferry, West Virginia. At the time, he hadn't realized that the sullen, unresponsive child had overheard his conversation. Now he was sorry he had made the comment, and he wished for the child's sake that he could recall it. Since he couldn't, he tried to make light of it.

''You, my young miss, must have misunderstood. My comment to the captain was meant as a play on words. You know, Paine, like pain?'' He arched his brows in jest, but when Caroline didn't take the teasing bait, Rush continued. ''Besides, your cousin and I go way back. The few times I attended school and had the pleasure of sitting behind her, I'd stick the end of her long yellow braid in the ink well.'' Rush laughed, recalling the memory. ''Alexandria Paine didn't appreciate my antics. In fact, she didn't appreciate me at all. Back then she was a bona fide pain in—'' Rush caught himself. ''She whined to the teacher about everything.''

''Yeah. I've known a few whiners, too. In my school, we called them teacher's pets.''

''Teacher's pets. Yep. I presume that is exactly what Alex was, but her mother and father were fine people. They lived in the lockkeeper's house right over there.'' Rush pointed to the white two-story brick structure that sat close to the tall cliffs, several boats down from where they had tied up for the night. ''*Most* of the Paines weren't pains. I'm sure they'll like you and you them.''

''I won't,'' Caroline insisted. ''Besides, I never liked teacher's pets.''

''Why, Miss Caro, as pretty as you are, I can't believe that you haven't at one time or another been some teacher's favorite. In a family of such beautiful and smart women, I assumed such a standing would be automatic.''

Caroline wrinkled her face in disgust. ''I'm not smart. And I sure as hell don't want to be beautiful.''

Rush cocked one brow and studied the child. Although she

was of the age where she was all spidery legs and bony elbows, it was apparent she would one day be a beauty. Not
that she wasn't a pretty little thing now with the mass of black
curls that hung down her back and her deep blue eyes that
sparkled like sapphires when the light caught them right.

He patted the child's head, then pulled on one of the long
black ringlets. When Caroline brushed his hand away, he
watched the straightened curl bounce back into a ring like a
tightly wound spring. He would miss her.

In the last week, they had become companions of a sort.
His own upbringing allowed him to understand Caroline's
frustrations; she was like a piece of flotsam cast into the river
of life with no anchors to give her stability. But she would be
fine once she settled in. The Paines would be more than happy
to take in their orphaned relative. It was time he delivered
Caroline and was on his way north. He had a schedule to keep.

His boat was due to pick up a load of coal in Cumberland,
Maryland, and then transport it back to Georgetown to fill the
hulls of the ships heading abroad. The boats on the C & O
Canal operated from March until December, and Rush had to
compete for business among the other canallers. In the year
or so that he had owned his own boat and mules, he'd built
up a reputation as a trustworthy and dependable man, and he
wasn't about to jeopardize that reputation now.

"You know I can cook," Caroline said, interrupting his
thoughts. "I could live with you. I could cook and be your
housekeeper. I wouldn't be no trouble. I promise."

Rush's heart went out to the little girl. At the moment, she
looked both vulnerable and impervious. He knew how it felt
to be orphaned and homeless. That was why he had to convince her how lucky she was to have family who would gladly
take her in.

"And a fine cook you are, but I already have a permanent
cook. I'm picking him up in Shepherdstown. Besides," he
consoled, "as I told you earlier, the Paines are fine folks.
They'll treat you fairly and they'll love you. More importantly,
they're your family."

Caroline responded bitingly. "I don't have no family.
They're dead. First Pa and John, then Ma." She lifted her chin

a little higher. "Besides, I ain't wanting to live with no pain-in-the-ass relatives."

Rush could have kicked himself for vocalizing his opinions within ear range of the child, but then he hadn't known she had such acute hearing. When he'd voiced his heated opinions to his old friend, Captain Steve, the child had been standing across the deck with Mrs. Steve, out of earshot. Or so Rush had believed.

There was no telling what other expletives the ten-year-old had heard when Rush had first learned what his friend expected of him—a bachelor like himself baby-sitting a young girl. Rush knew nothing about children and didn't want to know about them, but surprisingly enough, once he got over the shock of the captain's request and they had gotten underway, he'd found himself enjoying the child's company.

Not only was Caroline bright, but she was also hard-working. Because his permanent cook had taken sick on the trip south and had to leave the boat, the cooking had been left to Rush. But as soon as Caroline had come aboard in Georgetown, she'd been more than willing to take over the preparation of the crew's meals, and with Rush's supervision she had done a fine job. But a canal boat with four men was no place for a girl.

"Once you get settled in with the Paines, you'll be making new friends and finishing up your school year. You can't have too much schooling, you know?"

"I hate school," Caroline responded. She turned away from him and stomped to the side of the boat.

He followed, stopping behind her. Turning her around to face him, he placed his hands on her shoulders and looked down into her angelic face. "Look, squirt, maybe you and I can make a deal. You come with me to the Paines'. If I'm still without a cook on my way back south, I'll talk to your new family about signing you on as a temporary cook. By then, school will be close to finishing for the summer. Of course, your relatives will have to agree to the arrangement, or we can't do it."

The child looked hopeful. She lifted her eyes to his, and a half smile formed on her lips. "Do you really mean it, Rush?

Do you really want me with you?'' She studied him with the attentiveness of an adult. ''Or are you just saying that so you can be rid of me?''

Damn. Am I that transparent? He had no trouble convincing most females of his acquaintance to give him what he wanted, even if it meant twisting the truth. But then, this young female knew how to get under his skin. Rush found himself not wanting to lie to her.

''Caro,'' he crooned, using the nickname he'd given her, ''these are unusual circumstances.''

Rush had been calling her Caro for most of the week, and the name had stuck. Although he admitted that Caroline was a beautiful name, he thought it more befitting a lady than a ten-year-old girl.

He began again. ''Caro, it's not just a decision I alone can make. You know that, don't you? You also know that I can't fire the cook I have just to give you his job. He has a family to feed.''

''I know,'' she said, her shoulders slumping. ''It's just that—I'm gonna miss you.'' Tears welled in her eyes, but she quickly blinked them back. ''I'll do like you say.'' Her woeful expression was replaced with a belligerent one. ''If you insist, I'll go. Only, if I don't like them, I'll not be hanging around. I'll get me a job as a cook on another boat.''

He watched her move toward the spot on deck where she had left her meager belongings. The kid must be more destitute than he imagined, if everything she owned was in those two burlap bags. One of the bags he supposed held her clothes, the other her needlework that she guarded with her life. During the evenings of the past week, after they had served the crew their dinner, he and Caro had fallen into a routine. He would sit at his desk in the small cabin, working on his accounts, while Caro would sit in his reading chair and perform her nightly stitching.

What little Rush knew about quilting could be held in the thimble that Caro wore on her small finger when she stitched. Since his mother had never had an interest in any homemaking skills, Rush found he derived pleasure from watching the child sew. It was evident even to his inexperienced eye that Caro was adept in her craft.

Rush still puzzled over her strange reaction the one time he had tried to get her to show him her handiwork. She had become almost hysterical, forbidding him to touch the pieced material. He had decided then and there that if she didn't welcome his interest, then so be it. Everyone had a right to a little privacy.

"I'm as ready as I'm gonna be," Caroline said, breaking into his thoughts. In his estimation, she exerted more confidence than a ten-year-old should have.

Rush approached her. "Look, squirt, even if I can't hire you, I'll make you a promise. Every time I pass by Harpers Ferry, I'll drop in for a visit. That way I can make certain the Paines are treating you right."

"You mean it? You'd do that for me?" She threw her arms around his waist. "I'd like that a lot."

A lump formed in Rush's throat, and he blinked back the moisture building behind his lids. "But you've got to promise me one thing."

She looked up at him with adoration on her face. "What's that, Rush?"

"You can't be telling your cousin Alexandria that I called her a pain-in-the—the you-know-what."

"I won't," she promised, her expression taking on a mischievous glow. "But only if you keep your part of the bargain."

She released his waist, and together they exited the boat. Once they were on the tow path that led to the bridge, he clasped her hand. Curious as to what bargain he'd committed to, Rush asked, "What's my part of the bargain?"

"That you'll come see me like you said you would every time you pass Harpers Ferry."

"Oh, my promise? Darlin', you've got yourself a deal." He squeezed her fingers. "You should learn right now that Rush Duncan never breaks a promise to a beautiful lady."

Caroline blushed. "Oh, Rush, I'm not beautiful and I'm only ten years old."

As they crossed the bridge, Caroline's stomach felt queasy.

For the first time ever, she had fallen in love. Rush Duncan
had become her prince. She looked up at him with adoring
eyes and squeezed his fingers tighter. From now on, she would
go by the name he'd given her. From now on, she'd be known
as Caro.

∽

ALEXANDRIA PAINE TURNED THE risen dough into the
prepared pans and stuck them into the oven of her brand-new
Uncle Sam range. She had orders for seven loaves of Sally
Lunn bread. All seven loaves, less the three extra ones she
had made to sell elsewhere, were to be delivered tomorrow
morning to Storer Normal School for the educators' planning
day. No one in town made the crumbly bread as good as
Alex's, or at least that was what the people of Harpers Ferry
claimed.

After giving the pot of vegetable soup a stir, she walked to
the back door of the small house where she lived with her
mother. Picking up the shirttail of her white apron, she dusted
the flour from her hands and stared at the surrounding buildings washed in the lemon light of late afternoon.

A soft breeze drifted through the opening and was immediately gobbled up by the warm air inside the kitchen. The
smell of yeast was strong, sweet. For reasons unknown to
Alex, the scent of bread rising always reminded her of her
father, and a wave of sadness washed over her. It had been
five years since Herman Paine's death, and Alex missed him
as much today as she had on the day they'd buried him in the
graveyard on the hill.

When she saw her mother enter the central yard between
the neighboring buildings, Alex waved. Their house had at one
time been a confectioner's shop and sat at the bottom of High
Street in the middle of the business district. After the flood of
1877, when high water had done considerable damage to the
C & O Canal and had closed the Shenandoah Canal for good,
the owner of the shop had abandoned the building and returned
to his home in Baltimore.

This later ended up being a windfall for the recently

widowed Mrs. Paine and her young daughter, who had had to move out of the lockkeeper's house after Herman Paine's death in 1884. Their family savings had covered the purchase of the house, but not all the needed repairs.

Because the flood had caused extensive damage to the bottom floor of the building, the dwelling had sat empty and in disrepair until the Paines had purchased it five years earlier. The building was safe structurally, although water damage was evident on the first floor. The second floor was unscathed and served as the living quarters for the two women. Only recently had Alex and her mother earned enough money by selling baked goods and produce to begin repairs to the ground floor of the dwelling, and the kitchen was now in fine shape.

Stella Paine mounted the back stoop and preceded her daughter into the heated kitchen. "Alexandria, you do too much. I could smell that bread baking clean across the street. I dare say, a blind man could have followed his nose to our door."

"Smells good, huh?" Alex gave her petite mother a peck on the cheek and pulled out a chair beside the flour-dusted work table. "Sit," she ordered. "Tell me, how were the ladies in the quilting circle? I hope you made my apologies for being absent, but I couldn't refuse the head of the college when he asked me to bake bread for their meeting tomorrow."

"Of course not, but everyone missed you, daughter. They also understand your obsession. It's the consensus of all our friends that you should devote more time to finding yourself a rich husband instead of deriving ways to make money to sock away."

Obsession. Alex ignored the remark. "Mother, really. A husband is the last thing I want. Especially when most of the eligible men in Harpers Ferry have fled for firmer ground, or they are old enough to be buried beneath it."

Her mother harumphed. "There's always the parson. He is certainly interested in you."

"Mother, spare me, please. I'll not be marrying such a bore of a man, and need I remind you that men of the cloth are usually not rich?" Alex grabbed a dishcloth and swabbed the table.

"Don't be blasphemous, daughter."

"I mean no disrespect. I'm only being truthful. Surely you can understand my reaction. Not only is the parson boring, but he is the homeliest man I've ever encountered. A real Ichabod Crane." Alex shuddered when her mind conjured up a picture of the tall, skinny man who resembled the preacher in Washington Irving's *The Legend of Sleepy Hollow*. "You were married to the handsomest and kindest man in the whole county. You of all people should understand how I feel."

A dreamy look settled on her mother's face. "Yes, I guess your father was as handsome as the devil himself and close to being a saint. But times were different then. A girl could pick and choose."

"Mother, honestly. Pick and choose? The war had ended, and so many of the men did not return home."

"But your father did. And don't forget, my Johnny Reb and I were engaged before the war. I was twenty-five when you were born, twenty-four when we married. You, my daughter, are not far from that age now."

"Twenty-two is two years away from twenty-four, Mother dear. A lot can happen between now and then."

"With you, a lot will need to happen. As I said earlier, you work much too hard. At the rate you're going, you'll look like an old hag before you're twenty-four, and then the parson won't even look at you."

"That would be a blessing." Alex rolled her eyes heavenward and took the mixing bowls to the dry sink to wash them. She loved her mother, and they were the best of friends. But her mother and every other woman in Harpers Ferry, both young and old, had made it their responsibility to find Alex a husband. No one wanted to marry more than Alex. Growing up as an only child had made her want to have a large family of her own with many children, but she would marry only when and if she was ready. She'd not marry the parson, or any other man, only for the sake of being married. She would marry a man she loved with all her heart, and of course he would have to be just like her father.

Stella, a dish towel in her hands, came to stand beside her. "Out of necessity, I married late."

A knock sounded on the front door.

"But, Alexandria," her mother continued, "there's no war going on—"

"I'll get the door, Mother."

Alex whipped the cords of her apron free and was already at the arch that divided the front room from the back before her mother could protest.

Today the discussion of the absence of a suitor in Alex's life rankled her. Maybe it was her mother's reference to the ladies of the quilting circle considering her efforts to make money and sock it away an obsession instead of a necessity. Fine words from the ladies who were comfortably placed in the community, all of whom were taken care of by their husbands.

Most of the time Alex could shrug off their comments, recognizing them for what they were. The women were a flock of loving old hens, expressing their concerns over Alex's nesting abilities that they thought were going to waste. But sometimes she wished they could understand that life wasn't as easy for her and her mother as it had been when her father was still alive.

In truth, Alex felt it was her responsibility to take care of her mother. She could only do it by *socking* away every penny she could get her hands on, or pouring those pennies into improvements to the building that would help her with her plan to turn the front space of the ground floor into a quilting workroom. No matter how much she scrimped, there never seemed to be enough money to go around. Just recently, Alex had hung a few of her and her mother's quilts in the windows, hoping to sell them. If nothing else, the touch of color from the quilt designs improved the dingy, water-stained interior that was in much need of patching and painting.

"Bless their souls. They mean well," she mumbled to herself. "But the parson? Heaven forbid that I should become that desperate."

Her thoughts still wrestling with the image of being married to the clergyman, Alex swung open the front door.

Outside, the sun's lemony light was fading to a purplish glow and framed the stranger who stood at the entrance. He was a tall man, Alex noticed, with broad shoulders and a wide expanse of chest beneath his khaki-colored shirt. He was much taller than her five-foot-eight inches because she found that she had to tilt her head backwards in order to look directly into the stranger's eyes. Black eyes, so dark that she suspected that the devil himself could play in their sparkling depths and never be detected.

Alex's voice lodged in her throat when the man said nothing but continued to study her. His gaze slid over her length, making her squirm in spite of herself. He was a looker for sure, Alex thought, a drifter no doubt. A lot of those came and went on the canal.

Alex was about to tell him that the saloon was behind their house on the next street over when she noticed he wasn't alone. Unnerved by his scrutiny and eager for him to state his business and be on his way, she asked with more control than she felt, "How may I help you?"

He said nothing but continued to inspect her.

Thinking he might have seen the confectioner's sign carved in the wooden support above the door, she said, "The sign is misleading, we don't have—sell sweets here."

The man smiled, revealing straight white teeth beneath his bushy, chestnut-colored mustache that was the same color as his hair. "My, my, Alexandy," he said, with his devilishly dark eyes twinkling, "you're about the sweetest-looking thing I've seen in a long, long time."

"I beg your pardon?"

Although his response hadn't been one that Alex expected from a stranger, something about his use of the name Alexandy nagged at her memory.

It was apparent to Alex that the man's overly familiar remark had also gotten the child's attention. The dark-haired little girl no longer hung back behind him. Instead, she sided up to his tall physique and shot Alex a glaring look.

The poor little dear. She must be used to her father's philandering ways, because a philanderer was exactly how Alexander had pegged the man. If his child hadn't been present, Alex would have slammed the door on his handsome face. But because he wasn't alone and her heart went out to the child, Alex kept her temper under control.

"Who is it, Alexandria?" her mother asked, coming to stand beside her in the doorway.

Alex heard her mother's sharp intake of breath, felt her grasp her arm for support.

"It can't be!" she gasped. "Charlotte? Lordy, sister, is it really you?"

2

RUSH WATCHED MRS. PAINE fold like a sail suddenly losing the wind. He raced to catch her. Scooping her up into his arms, he looked to Alex for instructions on where to take her mother.

Alex stood frozen, fear chilling her face. Seconds passed before she jerked into motion. She turned and led Rush through the front room to the back of the building and gestured toward the wooden worktable. "Lay her there," she said.

Behind him, Caroline cried, "I killed her, didn't I, Rush?" A sob clogged her throat. "I didn't mean to."

"Hush, child," Alex admonished. "She's not dead. And you certainly didn't kill her. I suspect she has just swooned. Stay with her while I get the smelling salts."

As she headed for the stairs, she sent Rush a questioning look, then took the narrow steps two at a time.

After Alex's departure, Rush motioned to Caroline. "Come here, squirt." He wondered what kind of horrors the child had suffered if she believed her presence had killed her aunt.

Caroline hung back from the table, making no effort to obey him.

"Please, Caro. I want to prove to you that your aunt is very much alive." He winked at her. "You trust me, don't you?"

The child still remained where she was. Her worried stare shifted from the woman sprawled on the table to the stairs where Alex had disappeared. "She doesn't like me," Caroline insisted.

"Sure she does. Alex is only worried about her mother." Rush patted the edge of the table. "Please, come over here. I want you to see for yourself that your aunt is fine."

A low moan escaped Mrs. Paine's lips.

Drawn to the sound, Caroline left her bags of clothing by the arch and approached cautiously, her tortured expression relaxed somewhat.

Rush took her small hand and placed her fingers on the pulse point of the woman's wrist. "See, your aunt's heartbeat is strong," he assured her. "My guess is she'll be coming around any moment now, and once she finds out who you really are, she'll be very glad to see you."

The woman's eyes fluttered open. She looked first at Rush before her gaze darted around the room. He suspected she was looking for Caroline. When she realized that the child's fingers were pressed against her wrist, Mrs. Paine carefully maneuvered her hand until her fingers were linked with her niece's.

"Honey, I'm sorry I scared you. I know you aren't Charlotte." Pushing up on her elbows, she tried to sit.

"Mother, don't you dare move," Alex commanded from the stairs. Crossing the room, she muscled her way between Rush and her mother.

"Alexandria, I'm fine." When Alex waved the smelling salts beneath her mother's nose, Mrs. Paine turned her head away. "I certainly don't need that. Just help me sit, daughter, so that I may greet our guests properly."

"Guests?" Alex's dark brows shot upward before her dark-brown gaze settled on Rush. "Since I'm at a loss as to whom our guests are, perhaps you can enlighten me, Mother."

Rush *tsk tsked*. "Your tongue is as sharp as ever, Alexandy."

Mrs. Paine chuckled as Alex helped her to swing her legs over the table edge. "I hope you'll forgive Alexandria's manners, Mr.—"

"Duncan," he said. "Rush Duncan."

Still refusing to relinquish the child's hand now clasped between her own, Mrs. Paine studied him. "Why, yes, Mr. Duncan, I do remember you." Eyes the same dark brown as her daughter's held a warm luster. "You filled out quite nicely. But then, you always were a handsome lad."

Rush chuckled. "Thank you, Mrs. Paine." He looked at Alex and grinned. "I don't believe your daughter is of the same opinion." He winked at her and nearly laughed out loud when she sent him a scathing look.

"Don't pay Alexandria no mind, sir. She's smitten with Ichabod Crane."

"Mother," Alex groaned. Her cheeks turned as rosy as the apples piled inside the crockery bowl beside her.

The older woman ignored her daughter's discomfort. "Now," she said, her misty gaze settling on the little girl whose hand she still held. "Why don't you tell me your name?"

Caroline fidgeted beside him, looking almost as uncomfortable as her older cousin. After several tense moments, with all the adults waiting for her to respond, she finally answered. "You're right," she said to Mrs. Paine only, "my name is not Charlotte. She was my mother. I'm Caroline Swift. My friends call me Caro."

She glanced up at Rush, and he grinned at her approvingly. It appeared that Caroline had decided to change her name to Caro. Now was as good a time as any, Rush decided, especially since she was beginning a new chapter in her young life.

"Praise the Lord," the older woman whispered. Her eyes filled with tears, and she blinked them away. "The moment I saw you, I knew. You look just like your mother. It was your resemblance to Charlotte that gave me such a start. That's why I mistook you for her. I'm guessing you're around ten or eleven?"

"Ten," Caro informed her.

"My, my, ten, is it? And what a pretty ten-year-old you are." She stroked Caro's hair. "Your mother's hair was just as curly as yours."

"I know," Caro responded, "we both hated it."

"Why would you hate it? No curling irons for you. You know, it could be poker-straight like Alexandria's."

Caro shot Alex a disapproving look. "I reckon I'm pretty lucky, then."

Above the child's head, Rush's gaze locked on Alexandria's hair. No, she didn't have the midnight cloud of curls that Caro had, but since he had always been partial to blondes, Rush allowed himself to imagine how Alex's thick golden hair would look spread across a pillow—like the gilded brilliance of a sunbeam. The image made him uncomfortably aware of the heat inside the close kitchen. Alex had always gotten under his skin, even way back when, but then he'd assumed it was because she was untouchable. *She still was.* He focused on the conversation taking place between Caro and her aunt.

"Do you know who I am, Caro?" Mrs. Paine asked. "I'm your mother's sister—your Aunt Stella." When the child only nodded, Mrs. Paine enfolded her in her arms and hugged her. After a moment, she set Caro away from her. "And this," she said, looking at Alex, "is your cousin."

"Oh, I know who she is, all right. Rush told me all about her. She's that pain in the—"

"Caro?" Rush interrupted.

Her blue eyes locked with his. She lifted her stubborn chin, and Rush wasn't certain what to expect next. After a moment, she answered. "She's a Paine just like you are."

"That's right," her aunt said, "she's my daughter." She laughed as though she knew exactly what Caro had been about to say.

Whew! Rush relaxed somewhat.

For a moment he thought Caro had decided to break the bargain they had made by telling Alex that he'd called her a pain in the ass. He'd believed earlier that his reference was to be his and Caro's secret. But from the moment they had met Alex at the front door, it seemed that Caro was intentionally antagonistic toward her cousin. Why? Rush wondered. If he lived to be a hundred, he would never understand women. Even Stella Paine surprised him with her next statement.

"I'm sure that a few times in Alexandria's life she's been

known to live up to her name, and then some.''

Everyone laughed but Alexandria.

∞

ALEX SENT HER MOTHER a stormy look before concentrating on Caro. *Cousin?* Not only had they gained a relative whom they knew nothing about until this moment, but the relative was ten years old. Since Alex had grown up an only child, she loved children and wanted someday to have a houseful of her own. But Caro's arrival had raised so many questions that Alex wasn't yet ready to be as accepting of her as was her mother.

The wayward daughter who had run off with a man fifteen years her senior had never been mentioned by Alex's deceased grandparents or her parents. Alex had come by this information after the death of her grandparents, and only then because she had overheard a conversation between her mother and some of Stella Paine's older friends in the quilting circle. Later, when Alex had questioned her mother about her sister, the aunt she never knew existed, her mother told her that her baby sister had died many years ago after she went west.

But now her mother seemed genuinely pleased to have her sister's child returned, accepting her without knowing anything about her—or more importantly, knowing darn little about the man who had delivered her. The same man, she recalled, who at the age of fourteen already had a questionable reputation.

Rush Duncan had been gone from Harpers Ferry for years. Why had he been the one to return her cousin to them? Could he be the child's father? *Impossible.* Rush Duncan wasn't that many years older than Alex.

From beneath her lowered lashes, she studied him. Her mother was correct—the gangly lad she recalled from her youth had certainly filled out quite nicely. Rush Duncan's dark good looks put the few men of her acquaintance to shame. But, Alex reminded herself, looks weren't everything until she recalled the parson and decided looks certainly helped. Where had he been all these years? She pegged him immediately as a wanderer, and she could never be interested in such a man.

Alex stood apart from the threesome, watching the happy reunion. Instead of joining in, Alex felt separated from the others. Questions still plagued her. Why, after all this time, had the child of her mother's sister suddenly shown up on their doorstep? Alex had been of the opinion that no one had heard from her aunt since she left town.

Where was Charlotte now? Alex suspected she already knew the answer to that question and worried that her mother would not be able to accept her sister's death if that should turn out to be the case. Fainting was so out of character for her strong but frail mother, and it had frightened Alex. She wasn't certain how many more scares she could handle.

God willing, she wouldn't have to. Alex breathed deeply, trying to relax; unfortunately, relaxation eluded her. She sniffed and came up short. Something was burning.

"Damn and blast!" Alex ran toward the oven. "My bread."

She jerked open the oven door, and a black cloud of smoke billowed toward the ceiling.

Rush was by her side immediately, shooing her away. "Let me do that," he insisted.

"Thank you, I can do it myself."

But Rush didn't back away. Together they wrestled the hot pans from the oven and placed them on the table. Once the smoke cleared, she saw all ten loaves of bread were the color and the consistency of charcoal.

"You can always use it for fuel," Rush said, his expression amused.

Alex bristled. "I don't think the faculty and students of the Storer Normal School will appreciate eating *fuel* at their luncheon tomorrow."

She felt close to tears, and Rush's smart remark didn't help matters. Her bread was ruined, unfit for human consumption. If she still had enough ingredients left to make more dough, she'd be up all night doing it.

With one finger Rush poked at a charred loaf. "Maybe you can scrape the burned part off."

"Honey," her mother said, "I'm so sorry." She came and stood beside her. "I know you worked all afternoon baking, but I'm sure that Mr. Bodine will understand.''

''Mother, Mr. Bodine was counting on this bread. I gave him my word that it would be on campus tomorrow morning. If I don't deliver as promised, he won't ask me to bake for the luncheon the next time. Besides, we can't afford such waste.''

''Surely what you would have made on these few loaves of bread is not going to send us to the poorhouse.''

''No, Mother, I do believe we'll be spared a trip to such an establishment, but that's not the point. I gave him my word, and I'll not be going back on it. I promised him bread and I'm going to—''

''May I offer a suggestion?'' Rush interrupted.

Alex had almost forgotten his and Caro's presence. After his first suggestion that she sell the bread as fuel, she doubted she'd be interested in hearing any more of his recommendations. She looked at him, then began dumping the burned loaves into the garbage pail before carrying the loaf pans to the dry sink for washing.

He wasn't to be dissuaded, though. Putting his arm around her cousin's shoulders, he said, ''I just happen to know two very experienced cooks who would be more than willing to help out in a crisis.''

''And who might they be?'' Alex asked, not the least bit interested in hearing their identity.

Already she was doing a mental calculation of the ingredients she would need to replace seven of the burnt loaves: flour, milk, shortening, sugar, eggs, salt, and yeast.

She had enough of everything, except eggs and yeast. At this late hour, she couldn't go to the Country Store because it had closed over an hour ago.

''Did you hear that, Alexandria?'' her mother asked, interrupting her thoughts. ''Caro and Rush have offered to help us make the bread. Isn't that wonderful of them?''

Alex felt like telling them it was their fault that she had burned the bread in the first place, but she bit back the retort.

Instead she said, ''You can't be serious.'' She plunged the dirty pans into the soapy water. ''Really, Mother, I'm sure that Mr. Duncan is not a cook. Besides, I just realized I don't have enough eggs or yeast.''

''I am a cook, but not as good as Caro. She's first-rate. If you don't believe me, you can ask my crew.''

''Crew?'' Alex looked from Rush to Caro.

It was Caro who answered. ''Yes, crew. Rush brought me here on his canal boat. When his regular cook took sick, I helped him out. Isn't that right, Rush?''

''That's right, squirt. And a mighty fine help you were.''

Alex watched him pull one of the little girl's corkscrewed curls until it was poker-straight like hers, then he released the lock and watched it spring back in place before he looked at Alex again.

''You willing to give us chefs a try?''

Her mother answered for her. ''Of course she is. I know where we can borrow the eggs and yeast.'' She motioned to Caro. ''Come with me, dear. You can help me carry and you can meet some of our neighbors at the same time.''

''Mother, no. I can borrow the things we need.'' The last thing she wanted was to be left alone with Rush Duncan. ''I wasn't the one who fainted. Maybe you should sit here and rest.''

''I'll be fine, Alexandria. While we're gone, why don't you dish us up some of that soup, and we'll eat before we start baking.'' Before Alex could protest further, the twosome disappeared through the door.

Alex looked at Rush, then toward the sink where the pans soaked. Without a word she found her apron again, tied it around her waist, and hovered near the sink. She felt ridiculous and speechless, although she figured now was as good a time as any to question Rush about Caro.

As though reading her thoughts, he moved toward her. After taking an envelope from his shirt pocket, he handed it to her. ''I was told to give this letter to your parents when I delivered Caro to them.''

The envelope was sealed, but across its front, written in a neat script, Alex saw her mother and father's names. It seemed the sender was not aware of her father's death.

''What do you know about Caro?'' Alex asked, looking into

his black eyes. They twinkled, making her feel very uncomfortable. With more rancor than she knew she should have displayed, she demanded, "And how did you get her?"

"You still don't like me, do you, Alexandy?"

"Would you stop calling me that ridiculous name? And why wouldn't I like you?" She tucked the envelope inside her pocket and busied herself washing the pans. She had learned long ago when you weren't sure of how to answer, it was better to reply with a question.

"For your information, a sea captain friend of mine who sails out of Savannah met my boat in Georgetown and asked me to bring Caro to Harpers Ferry. He knew I grew up here and figured I might know how to get in touch with her relatives."

Alex rinsed the washed pans with clear water. Rush picked up the dish towel and began drying them. His actions surprised her. It seemed like such a domestic act for a man like him to perform.

"You asked what I know about her. Not much, really. All I do know I learned from my friend. He said her family died of cholera somewhere in Nebraska. Caro won't talk about it, but she did admit her ma and pa were dead."

Alex gripped the edge of the sink. "I figured as much." She looked at Rush. "But why—why after all these years without a word would Charlotte choose to send her daughter here?"

"No one else, I guess. Maybe her mother figured it would be better if the child was with her family. It's tough growing up alone."

"It's tough growing up, period," Alex replied. Beside her she heard Rush make a sound of disgust.

"To answer your third question, Alexandy." His voice was filled with sarcasm. "You didn't like me much when we were growing up. Back then, you thought you were better than me, and you still do."

"I most certainly do. . . ."

She stopped talking when her mother and Caro came tromping through the door. "Here are the things you need, Alexandria," her mother said.

Rush looked right through her and gave the twosome a beguiling smile. "It's about time you ladies returned. I'm so hungry I was about to eat this." He held the pan he had been drying close to his mouth.

Caro ran to his side and grabbed it away from him. "Oh, Rush, you're so silly. I know you can't be that hungry."

It was clear the child adored him, but Alex couldn't understand why. Yet she hadn't meant to sound so heartless when she made the statement about growing up being tough. She had forgotten that after Rush's mother died, he had grown up more or less living by his wits. Or that was what her father had said when she used to complain that she was the target of his persistent teasing. What had her father said? *It's because he likes you that he teases you.*

Well, she didn't believe that reasoning for a minute. *Better than he was?* He certainly had his nerve, making such a statement. He didn't know what he was talking about—or did he? Alex searched inside herself. Old resentments, like habits, were sometimes long in dying.

∞

"ARE YOU SURE YOU can manage those loaves without me?" Rush asked.

He and Alex stood at the corner of High and Shenandoah Streets as the early morning sun slid higher in the sky. She was on her way to deliver the bread they had baked during the night to the Storer Normal School, and he was on his way to the canal where his boat and crew would be waiting to get underway.

"I don't recall you complaining about it being heavy when you gobbled down several slices earlier. You said it was as light as a cloud." Alex raised a dark brow. "Now you're suggesting that it's so heavy that I'll be needing your assistance to deliver it." She swung away from him. The basket on her arm would have punched him in the stomach if Rush hadn't jumped back.

"Are you always so amiable in the morning?"

She shot him a heated look over her shoulder. "I'm not usually up all night baking."

"You act like it's my fault that the bread burned." Instead of denying his words, she was as silent as a monk.

Rush had stayed at the Paines' house throughout the long night, not only to help with the baking, but also to help Caro settle into her new surroundings. He had kept the ladies entertained with his sea stories until the wee hours of the morning. Or two of the ladies, anyway. Alex had remained aloof, with her thoughts centered on the task. Until now, he had never suspected that she held him responsible for the fiasco.

"So that's the way the wind blows," he stated. "You blame me because you burned the bread."

Not bothering to answer him, she started up the street.

Dogging her footsteps, Rush was insistent. "Admit it, Alexandy. You think it's my fault, don't you?" He clamped his fingers around her arm before stepping in front of her and coming to a dead stop.

Alex tried to step around him, but he blocked her way. "Don't be ridiculous," she accused.

"I'm not being ridiculous. I'm being truthful. And that's more than I can say for you."

"All right, Mr. Big Shot. You want the truth?" Her face was flushed with anger. "Then I'll tell you the truth. Yes. I think it's your fault that my bread burned." She tried to side-step him again.

"Why? Because I happened to deliver your cousin when it was baking?"

She pondered his question, then tried to muscle her way past him without responding, but he refused to allow her to pass.

"Would you have preferred I didn't bring her to your house, Alex? Your mother seems pleased, even if you don't."

"Don't you dare accuse me of not wanting my cousin. Of course I want her. She seems like a sweet child, and I'm delighted to have her. Although I admit she didn't take to me the way she did to you. Or my mother."

Rush crossed his arms against his chest and rocked back on his heels. "So it's jealous you are, Alexandy." He flashed her his most endearing smile. "I assure you, sugar, there's plenty of me to go around."

This time the basket did hit him in the stomach. "You're impossible, Rush Duncan. I can't expect you to understand. Now if you'll excuse me, unlike you, some of us have to work for a living." With an athlete's gait, she stepped around him.

He watched her for several moments, then followed her.

Rush had been away from Harpers Ferry for years. In fact, in the year or so he'd owned his canal boat, he'd intentionally avoided overly long stops in the area. The place prompted too many painful memories for him to tarry long.

If it weren't for Samson, who owned the saloon on Potomac Street, he wouldn't have stopped at all. But the old man was the only true friend Rush could claim. There were times during the years before he went to sea, when he still called Harpers Ferry home, that he wouldn't have survived if it hadn't been for Samson. Not only had the saloon owner befriended a homeless lad, but he had also given him odd jobs to do and had allowed him to sleep in the saloon's storeroom.

It was from Samson that Rush had learned of the changes that occurred in Harpers Ferry during his absence. One was that Herman Paine had died five years earlier, and his death had evicted the Paine women from the lockkeeper's house on the C & O Canal where the family had lived for as long as Rush could remember. From what he had seen last night of the Paines' current dwelling and the very obvious disrepair of the front room, their life wasn't as easy as it had once been.

Rush ran his fingers through his hair. Hell, for all he knew, Alex may not have had the cash to replace the bread she claimed he'd burned. If so, that would explain her foul mood. He stuffed his hands in his pockets, and his fingers closed around the wad of bills he intended to put in his bank account when he arrived in Cumberland, Maryland—money he'd received from delivering a boatload of coal. The money gave him an idea.

"Hey, Alex, wait," he called, loping to catch up with her. "I almost forgot."

She didn't stop, but kept right on walking.

"Please, I have something else to say. Then I'll leave you in peace."

Maybe it was his admission that he would soon leave her that made her put on brakes. Whatever the reason, Rush didn't care. She came to a standstill. Facing him again, she breathed an exasperated sigh.

Rush removed the money wad from his pocket. When he reached her, he placed it in her free hand. "I forgot to give you this," he said.

She looked from his face to her hand, then back at his face again. Confusion clouded her expression. "What's this for?" The same determined expression that he'd seen on Caro's face appeared on Alex's. "I can't take your money," she insisted, shoving it back into his hands.

"It's not my money," he lied. "It belongs to Caro."

Before Alex could protest more, he stumbled for an explanation, making one up as he went. "That captain friend of mine I told you about. Captain Steve and his wife took up a collection from the ship's crew. Seems our Caro charmed the britches off the sailors of the *Sea Wind,* during their short voyage between New Orleans and Savannah."

A sour expression replaced the determined one on Alex's face, and Rush realized his choice of words hadn't charmed her as he'd intended. "What I really meant to say," he corrected, "was they fell in love with her."

Alex eyed the money. "I still can't take it. . . ."

"You gotta. I sure as hell can't keep it." Her look made him soften his stance. "Look, no one need know about the contribution unless you want them to. It's tough when women have to support themselves. Maybe the three of you can put the money to some good use."

Alex's chin rose a little higher. "We'll not be taking charity, Rush Duncan." She pushed the money toward him again.

"It's not charity; it's a gift." In all his dealings with women, Rush had never met such a stubborn one. But he could match her stubbornness. "My mother, what I remember of her, used to say, 'don't look a gift horse in the mouth.'" Although he never really understood the expression, it seemed like a good argument to use when dealing with Alex.

"I'm certainly not questioning the value of the gift."

"Then it's settled. You'll take the money and use it to help make Caro's life easier." *And you and your mother's as well.*

Alex still hesitated. "I don't know. It seems like an awful lot."

Rush closed his fingers around her hand that clutched the money. Surprisingly, this time she didn't pull away.

"Look, I've got to go. My crew will have the law out looking for me if I don't show up soon." Having run out of arguments as to why she should accept the gift, he said, "If nothing else, the money will pay for the bread I burned."

For the first time since their reunion, she regarded him with amused wonder. The look caused a feeling akin to excitement to pelt his stomach. Gone was the little girl with the long blond braid whom Rush had teased to distraction. In her place was a beautiful woman who at the moment was doing some distracting of her own.

"I gotta go," he said. Such a reaction to Alexandria Paine just wouldn't do. He thought he had outgrown his infatuation with her when he'd become a man. Turning on his heel, Rush almost broke into a jog to distance himself from the woman.

Behind him, he heard Alex call, "Mr. Duncan, it was me, not you, who burned the bread."

Rush smiled to himself.

Sugar, that's not the only thing you so effectively inflamed.

3

AFTER DELIVERING HER BREAD to Mr. Bodine at the Storer Normal School, Alex decided to take a detour to Jefferson
Rock before returning home. She loved the view from the high
summit that overlooked Lower Town, and the place where the
Potomac and Shenandoah Rivers met before passing on to the
sea. The beauty of the place never failed to take Alex's breath
away, and today was no exception. Dressed in its spring finery,
the scene below reminded her of one of those crazy quilts that
had become all the rage in the last few years; a collage of
colors and textures.

Standing on top of the rock named for Thomas Jefferson,
Alex couldn't help but feel a kinship with Harpers Ferry's
earliest and most famous tourist.

Jefferson had described the rivers as a passageway for migration and settlement, and also a place of meeting: the meeting of the Potomac and the Shenandoah; of roads, canals, and
railroads; the meeting of different cultures, and at one time,
the armies of the North and South. The rivers could also boast
the meeting of three states, Virginia, Maryland, and West Virginia.

Not only was it a coming together of places and people from
the past, but also now a meeting place of family who didn't

know each other. And for Alex, the meeting again of a boy she hadn't thought of in years.

She sat on the shale rock. It was a long uphill climb from the town below, and although Alex considered herself to be fit and healthy, the climb had left her breathless, with a layer of perspiration dampening her skin beneath her dress. After she caught her breath, she looked toward the canal and wondered which of the many boats moving along the narrow waterway belonged to Rush Duncan. It was hard to imagine the boy she remembered, the town ruffian, now the captain of his own boat and team.

It disturbed her when she thought of the man who was no longer the pimply-faced lad from her past. All those many years ago he had teased her unmercifully, and it appeared the gadfly had returned to torment her once again.

She decided the life of a canaller probably suited the restless lad she recalled. As a rule, the boatmen were often a rough and rowdy lot. They spent much of their lives afloat, which set them apart from the world of a permanent home and unchanging scenery. She knew she could never settle for that type of life and had vowed long ago that she would never fall for a boatman.

Alex leaned back. Propping on her hands, she closed her eyes. A soft breeze fluttered around her, cooling her heated skin. The early morning sun felt warm against her face. If her mother was here, she would scold her for not taking precautions against the sun, but her mother was home, so Alex could do as she pleased. She sighed and allowed her thoughts to sail free on the wind.

The last twenty-four hours had brought changes into her life—changes that she needed to sort through and decide how to handle. Rush had accused her of not wanting her cousin Caro, but that wasn't true. She did want her. Although there was a twelve-year difference in their ages, Alex believed that Caro could be the sister she never had, or perhaps the child she would never have. But winning her cousin over wouldn't be easy. Caro had been antagonistic toward Alex from the first moment they met.

She sniffed the air. *Spring*. At least the weather was agreeable. For as long as she could remember, this vernal time had been her favorite; the season that budded with new life and a rebirth of the old. She glanced down at the tops of the royal paulownia or princess trees that were named for Princess Anna, the daughter of Paul I of Russia. The trees were putting on a magnificent show with their lavender flowers. Although the species were fairly common along the banks of the two rivers, Alex never tired of their beauty.

Just as she never tired of Harpers Ferry. Although she had grown up in the lockkeeper's house at Lock 33 beside the C & O Canal, she had always considered the town across the Potomac River as her home. She belonged here like the crows that roosted nightly in the craggy cliffs that walled the rivers. It was hard for Alex to imagine being anywhere else, and she wondered how her mother's sister had left all those many years ago without a backward glance. And traveling all the way to Nebraska. To Alex that state seemed as distant as another continent.

Thoughts of her Aunt Charlotte reminded her of the unopened letter in her pocket, the letter that Rush had given her last night and that she had forgotten about until now. Alex pulled out the envelope, causing the roll of money that Rush insisted she take this morning to tumble free. She caught the wad and dropped it into her lap before studying the yellowed envelope and the handwriting across its front. It was addressed to her parents, the contents sealed inside. Her mother didn't know about the letter, but she would be eager to read the missive from her sister. She hoped the contents wouldn't bring on another fainting spell like the one her mother had suffered last night.

The plumpness of the money roll suggested she held a fortune on her faded calico-covered lap. Did she dare count the bills now, or should she wait until she returned home? Good sense told her that such a large sum was best kept hidden. Eager now to count the money and to learn the letter's contents, Alex stood up. Besides, she had lingered far too long. Stuffing both money and envelope back inside her pocket, she headed down the hill for home.

∞

SEVERAL HOURS HAD PAST since the hilltop church in Harpers Ferry could be seen above the treetops. After picking up his cook in Shepherdstown, Rush decided to walk with the mules along the towpath and let his steersman take his place at the tiller of the boat. He wanted to make the town of Williamsport by sunset, where he would tie up for the night.

Besides, the day was too beautiful to glide along on the water when you could walk. Rush enjoyed walking, enjoyed the solitude, and enjoyed the company of his two best mules, Daisy and Petunia. Walking also gave him a chance to study the flora that grew along the path.

Before he'd purchased the *Chuck-a-luck,* Rush hadn't thought much about wildflowers. Flowers didn't grow at sea, and his port calls were too short for anything but drinking and wenching. His interest in wildflowers had grown as he noted the many different varieties that grew up and down the canal. A book on the subject kept him busy looking for and recording the different ones he'd learned to identify. Nights aboard the boat, he had taken to drawing the plants in a sketchbook he kept inside the cabin.

"Who would have thunk it?" he asked the mules beside him. The soft drumming sound of their hooves against the firm ground soothed him. "Me, of all people," he continued, "intrigued by wildflowers of the stemmed variety." Rush laughed at his thoughts. Occasionally wildflowers of the feminine kind were more to his liking. Perhaps he was mellowing in his old age. Not to say that he still didn't enjoy an occasional romp in the hay with a pretty lady. Like Sally from Williamsport. Initially Rush had planned to hook up with Sally, the tavern wench from the Lusty Legs Saloon, when they docked in Williamsport for the night. In the past, he'd shared some pleasant tumbles with her—Sally knew how to please a man both in bed and out.

A ray of sunlight slashed through the trees, gilding the patch of yellow flowers growing on the side of the towpath. Identifying the plant, he said aloud, "Yellow wood-sorrel." The mules ignored his remark as was their custom, but he excused himself anyway. "Be back in a moment," he told the hybrids.

Leaving the side of the plodding mules, Rush strolled over and snapped off several long, slender stalks close to the ground.

"Alexandy," he said with a sigh, the yellow-gold blossoms reflecting against his fingers.

The golden brilliance reminded Rush of Alex's hair. The sunshine color of her long braid had intrigued him even as a lad. Her hair hadn't changed any in the years he'd been away, but the girl he remembered from his past had—she had changed from a pretty girl into a beautiful woman. And just as she did then, she still possessed the fire to heat his blood.

Back then, he'd attributed his attraction to Alexandria Paine as an affliction that all boys suffered when they first came into themselves as men. Considering the intermittent years when he hadn't seen her, much less thought about her, it surprised him yesterday that her mere presence could ignite a flame of yearning in his nether region. Not only had the sun goddess not offered him a kind word, but she had also downright ignored him; yet he'd still been drawn to her.

Rush shook his head at his own stupidity, falling into step again with the mules. "You're too old," he chastised himself, "to still be carrying a torch for the untouchable Miss Paine." Besides, he had vowed long ago to stick with an easy woman like Sally instead of a difficult woman like Alex, who would never be interested in a one-night tumble. A woman like Alex was in for the long haul. Rush would never give his tender heart to a woman. Such an arrangement caused too many complications. There was too much pain involved in the giving.

Furthermore, from what he had seen of Alexandy so far, she still wouldn't give him the time of day. But her young cousin, Caroline, was a different story. Caro, he corrected. Sometime during the last week, the ten-year-old had managed to worm her way into his heart. The reason being, he supposed, that he recognized his past in her present.

He rolled the flower stems between his hands. The gold blossoms blurred together like a sun. A fish jumped out of the canal water, then plopped back beneath the surface just before the bow of the boat passed over him.

"Swim for your life, young fellow," Rush warned, "you don't want to end up as a bigger fish's dinner. Better yet, maybe you don't want to end up being a big fish."

Not like the rest of us, he philosophized. At the moment, he saw himself as an easy target for maybe getting caught by the two women he'd spent the night with—never mind that the night was spent baking bread. The last thing Rush wanted was to have his life complicated by feelings or females. A woman like Alexandy, if she took a notion to it, could reel a man in without a hook, line, or sinker.

Best he stay away from those Paine women, he cautioned himself. Once he made certain that Caro had settled in properly, he would do just that. After all, he had made her a promise that he would visit her again, and he would. Soon Caro would forget all about him, and his and Alexandria's paths would never have to cross. In the meantime, there was warm and willing Sally waiting for him in Williamsport. At the moment, Rush had a sinker that needed a nice, quick plunge.

∞

CARO ROLLED OVER ON her back and opened her eyes. A quick glance around the room and the absence of water sloshing against the hull told her she was no longer aboard the *Chuck-a-luck*. Instead, she was upstairs in her cousin's bedroom, alone in the double bed, lying on a mattress that felt as soft as raw cotton.

Tears filled her eyes as she remembered she was all alone, and a lump formed in her throat. Remembering her promise to herself that she wouldn't cry anymore, she swallowed the nugget of sorrow, stiffening her resolve.

When her folks died, there were weeks when she had done nothing but cry, especially after she had been taken from the house where she had lived most of her life with her family. The same house she had watched burn to the ground because of the sickness that had taken her loved ones.

Caro didn't like to think about those days following her

family's death when no one knew what to do with the orphan. Sometimes she remembered bits and pieces of whispered conversation among the farmers and their wives about honoring her mother's last request. Charlotte had asked them to send her daughter to relatives who lived a long way away from Nebraska.

The next thing Caro knew, she and her few belongings were stowed in the back of an older couple's rickety, smelly wagon, and she was on her way somewhere. The couple had promised the other settlers that they would take her to Saint Louis, whoever he was, then send Caro on to her aunt. But sometime before they arrived at the saint's house, the couple had changed their minds, deciding to keep her instead.

Caro hated the Wormleys—they were old, smelly, and mean. Mr. Wormley used to shout and talk gibberish with the devil, scaring Caro out of her wits. It hadn't taken Caro long to realize why the couple had kept her instead of sending her to her aunt. They wanted a slave to do their bidding, and she fit their need.

Most of those memories were now a blur, except for the day when she had stopped crying after Mr. Wormley threatened to take a horsewhip to her. It was then that Caro had decided not to cry anymore. Or not to cry in front of others. The last thing she wanted was a whipping, or to be called a good-for-nothing orphan, although she reckoned an orphan was what she was. She had decided to run away from the couple the first chance she got, but something happened to change all that.

Caro rubbed her eyes. Sitting up, she slid backward on the bed until she could lean against the headboard. The knobby spools of wood dug into her backbone, reminding her how much she missed the cot where she had slept for the past week aboard Rush's boat. She missed the sound of sloshing water and the feeling that came with floating on the narrow canal. But most of all, she missed Rush. He made her laugh and chased away the sadness. When she was with him, she didn't feel so much like an orphan.

With her finger, Caro traced the design of the quilt that covered her legs. The many colors of hexagon flowers lifted her spirits somewhat, and she allowed herself a wishful day-dream about her ma. Charlotte Swift would have called Caro her ladybird beetle upon seeing her sitting beneath the flower garden quilt. Ladybird beetle was only one of the many pet names her mother had for her, and she smiled at the memory.

Her ma, too, was a quilter, and if all the many pieces of patchwork strewn about the room were any indication, she suspected her Aunt Stella and her cousin Alex were quilters as well. The talent must run in the family.

The quilts Caro and her mother had made, like their house, had been destroyed in the fire, except for the piecework that Caro had hidden outside before their neighbors had fired their house. Sometimes Caro wondered why they hadn't burned her as well, since she'd been exposed to the cholera. If they had, she wouldn't have been left alone and homeless. This thought prompted another one. Why hadn't she gotten the disease when the rest of her family had?

Thinking about it brought on a fresh wave of tears. Her family had been dead for six months now, but she still had moments when she missed them so much that her chest felt as though Tunk Larker had punched her there with his fist, as was his habit of doing every time she shadowed his path.

Caro wouldn't miss the school bully. He was the meanest boy she ever knew. It was a relief to know that she no longer had to worry about Tunk lurking in the tall prairie grass, wait-ing to pounce on her as she walked home from school. Would her new school have a Tunk Larker? Golly, she hoped not. She could easier tolerate her cousin, the teacher's pet, than another bully like Tunk.

Her woolgathering only served to deepen the hole already in her heart, so Caro concentrated on her new surroundings. It was a pretty room and much nicer than the soddie she'd lived in in Nebraska.

She had never lived in a real house with wooden floors or one whose ceiling wasn't made from grass. The wood beneath her feet felt cool as she slipped from the bed and stood. So as not to awaken her aunt, whom Caro believed slept in a room beyond the closed giant doors, she tiptoed to the dresser and mirror before stopping. The large looking glass reflected the image of both her and the room. That they could afford such things, she thought, must mean that her new relatives were rich.

Lacework like flattened snowflakes lay on the polished rock surface of the dresser. On top of the snowflakes sat a brush and mirror with the letters A and P scratched on their silvery surfaces. Her ma had never owned anything as fancy, although Caro knew she loved pretty things. Her gaze traveled over hairpins and ribbons before stopping on an odd-shaped bottle. The light from the window made the clear glass sparkle like sunbeams on a river.

A yellow-green liquid the same color as urine filled the bottle. Now why would her cousin save her own water? The thought made Caro shudder, but then her curiosity got the better of her. She had to know the bottle's contents, if for no other reason than to know if the liquid inside was what it looked like. Besides, one whiff wouldn't hurt her, if she was lucky enough to live through the sniffing.

Lifting the ball-shaped top, she brought the glass stem to her nose and cautiously breathed in. Instead of the odor Caro feared, the scent of flowers whiffed the air. The fragrance smelled like heaven and reminded her of her aunt Stella.

Replacing the bottle in the spot where she had found it, Caro studied a framed picture of a man. Perhaps the man was her cousin's beau, Ichabod Crane, whom her aunt had claimed Alexandria was smitten with. Caro lifted the photograph and stared at the person with the gray hair and beard, and dark, dark eyes. The man was too old to be her cousin's suitor. Reason told her he was Alexandria's pa and her Uncle Herman. Her uncle must be dead like her own parents, since she hadn't met him.

Caro touched the man's face. She knew how it felt to lose your pa, and for a moment she felt a connection with her cousin. But then she remembered the way Rush had looked at Alexandria and how he had told her she was the sweetest-looking thing that he'd seen in a long, long time, and any fellow-feeling she felt toward her cousin quickly disappeared.

Rush Duncan belonged to her!

She returned the picture to its place. When she and Rush had walked across the footbridge leading to Harpers Ferry, Caro had decided, then and there, that someday she was going to marry him. Although he had looked at Alexandria with wonder when he'd first seen her yesterday, Caro reminded herself that earlier he had called her cousin a pain in the ass and said he didn't like teacher's pets. Besides, hadn't he also told Caro that she was beautiful? Because her ten-year-old heart ached with love for Rush, she knew one day he would want to marry her as well.

Lace panels hung across the front windows. Caro crossed the room and peered down into the street. Having lived most of her life, or what she could remember of it, on the flat plains of Nebraska, this place—with its steep hills and tall trees— would take a lot of getting used to. Back home there had been nothing but miles and miles of prairie grass separating them from their closest neighbor. Here, plump hills were lined with two- and three-story buildings so close that she could have tossed a stone across the street and hit the neighboring houses. As she stared out the window at the unfamiliar, she longed to go home, to go back to what was familiar.

Downstairs, a door closed. She listened as footfalls echoed off the wooden stairs. Caro darted back to the bed, hopped in, and pulled the covers up to her chin. Talking with anyone, especially Alexandria, was the last thing she wanted to do. She closed her eyes, faking sleep.

ONCE UPSTAIRS, ALEX SLID the pocket doors that separated her bedroom from the sitting room open a couple of inches. Since her mother's doors were closed, she assumed her parent was still sleeping, but that might not be the case with her young cousin. Children were usually early risers no matter how little sleep they had gotten the night before. Since Caro was in a strange place, Alex suspected she might be awake and not sure what to do with herself. Besides, she would swear that she had heard movement coming from the room when she had first entered the house.

Caro's tiny form was almost lost in the big bed. With the cover pulled up beneath her chin and her mass of black curls spilling over the pillow around her face, she reminded Alex of a porcelain doll.

From where Alex stood, she watched the rise and fall of Caro's chest. The child appeared to be breathing much too heavily for someone who was supposedly in a deep sleep. Recalling exploits from her own childhood, Alex suspected that her cousin wasn't sleeping at all, but only pretending so she wouldn't have to talk to Alex. Well, she decided, it was as good a time as any for the mischievous miss to learn that two could play at her game.

Alex slid the door apart until the opening was wide enough for her to slip through. The doors creaked and groaned in their joints as they moved along hidden rollers.

Once inside the room, Alex glided toward the bed. Her cousin may not have warmed to her immediately, but Alex was determined that she and the child would become friends. After all, they would be living together from now on, and perhaps even sharing the same bed.

Caro lay as still as a mummy, but Alex saw the slightest flutter of her lids. *Just as I suspected—the little minx isn't asleep.*

Alex plopped on the edge of the bed. Faking a yawn, she wiggled unmercifully as she unlaced her shoes and let them drop noisily to the floor before fluffing the pillow and positioning her length next to Caro's. Beside her the little girl still feigned sleep, but beneath her pale lids, her eyes darted like minnows being sought for bait.

''Ho hum,'' Alex said and sighed, propping her hands behind her head. When Caro continued to play dead, Alex flopped from her back to her side, dug her hip into the mattress, then flipped on her other side to face her cousin, but still received no response.

Alex gave the ten-year-old credit. Although she had the face of an angel, she appeared to be as determined as Satan himself to ignore Alex.

Propping on her hand, Alex leaned closer, deliberately allowing her warm breath to flutter the springy curls around the child's face. After several moments of the unavoidable torture, Caro's eyes popped open. Without moving, she stared back at Alex. Then she let out an earsplitting scream and jumped from the bed.

Alex was by her side immediately. "Hush, you're going to wake my mother. I didn't mean to frighten you," she said, hoping to quiet her cousin, but Caro continued her screaming.

A few seconds later Stella appeared in the doorway. When Caro saw her aunt, she flew to the door and threw her arms around her waist.

Alex's mother asked, "Child, whatever is wrong? Did you have a bad dream? Is that what frightened you?" She knelt on the floor beside her niece and cradled her in her arms.

Not giving Caro a chance to answer first, Alex jumped from the bed. "It's my fault, Mother, I scared her. I decided to lay down beside her, and when she woke up and saw me, she started screaming her head off. I guess she's not as fearless as I thought."

Her remark had the desired affect. Caro pushed herself from her aunt's embrace and faced Alex. Her small back stiffened. "I'm not afraid of anything, especially you. But next time you decide to breathe all over my face, I'd appreciate it if you would wash your teeth with some of that flower-smelling water on your dresser."

"What is she talking about, Alexandria?" her mother demanded.

Alex knew it. The child hadn't been asleep when she had come into the room, and she had been up earlier. Alex moved to the dresser and lifted the perfume bottle. Walking toward her mother and cousin, she asked, "You mean this, Caro, honey? This isn't for brushing your teeth, but for making your person smell like a rose."

She pulled the stopper from the bottle and dabbed it against her cousin's nightgown.

The child wiggled away from her and folded her arms against her chest. "Well, I think your breath stinks, and it needs sweetening more than your person. Besides, who cares how a body smells anyway? Bathing once a week is good enough for me."

"Men like it," Alex answered, ignoring Caro's statement about baths.

She and her mother would have something to say about once-a-week bathing, but now was not the time to discuss it. Alex was more interested in her cousin's reactions to her statement about what men liked. No longer did Caro act disinterested, but appeared to be waiting for her next words.

"I understand men like their lady friends to smell like flowers. Isn't that so, Mother?"

Stella Paine looked at her daughter as though she had suddenly taken leave of her senses. Who knew better than her mother that Alex was the last person who cared what any man thought about how she smelled or otherwise—especially the men of Harpers Ferry, and most assuredly the good reverend.

She had owned that bottle of scent for years, and very rarely used it. Her mother's friend had brought each of the Paine women a bottle of the fragrance called Damask Rose on returning from a visit to New York City. It surprised Alex that the perfume still smelled so strong, but her young cousin appeared enthralled with the scented water, and perhaps Alex could use her fascination as a means to get closer to the child.

She thought back to yesterday when she had opened the door to find Rush Duncan and Caro on their doorstep. The child's first sign of belligerence toward her had surfaced when Caro thought that Alex might be demanding too much attention from Rush. When she had assumed he was Caro's father. Was it possible she had misread the reason for her cousin's animosity? Perhaps Caro had a crush on Rush Duncan and didn't want to compete with Alex for his affection.

Yes. That had to be it. Alex recalled a few crushes she'd had when she was her cousin's age. Now that she suspected the reason for Caro's resentment, she would have to find a way to convince the child that she wasn't a threat.

"Aunt Stella," Caro said, lifting her nose from her sleeve where she had been sniffing the perfume Alex had dabbed on her gown. "Is it true? Do menfolk really like ladies to smell like a bunch of damn flowers?"

Her mother almost choked, but she recovered enough to answer. "Why, yes, my dear, I believe most men enjoy women who smell feminine.'' Above the child's head, her mother's gaze locked with Alex's before she turned Caro to face her and brushed the hair from her face. ''I also believe they prefer their womenfolk not to use improper language. A lady should never use profanity.''

''Really, Mother, never?'' Alex returned the bottle to the dresser, then pulled open several drawers and began rearranging their contents. Since she and Caro would be sharing a room, the child needed a drawer in which to store her belongings.

''Never, Daughter,'' her mother confirmed. ''It's time both you girls learned that truth.'' Alex recognized the admonishment, for she had heard it enough about her own slips of the tongue. Her mother asked, ''So how did you two sleep?''

''I never slept,'' Alex responded, walking into the sitting area where she had passed Caro's bags earlier. She supposed her mother had left the luggage there last night when the twosome had come upstairs to bed. She picked up the bags and carried them back into the bedroom, placing them on the bed.

She turned to Caro and said, ''I'll help you unpack. You can store your clothes in the bottom drawer of the dresser.'' She loosened the ties of one of the bags and began to empty the contents on the bed.

''No!'' Caro shouted and ran toward her. She snatched the bag from Alex's hands. ''It's mine. It belongs to me.'' Then, noting the items scattered on the bed, she covered them with her body.

''Of course it belongs to you,'' Alex responded. ''I just wanted to help you put your things away.'' She glanced quickly at the pieces of material Caro gathered into a heap and began to stuff back inside the bag.

''Caro, they look like quilt pieces. Did you make them?''

''It's none of your damn—darn business,'' she answered. ''They belong to me, and you aren't to look at them or touch them.''

''But surely you must know Mother and I are quilters ourselves.'' She motioned to the quilt covering the bed. ''I made that one. We would both love to see your piecework—''

''Nobody touches them but me.'' Once everything was back

inside the bag, she pulled the drawstrings until the top was securely closed. "Only me," Caro reminded her, "and I'm big enough to unpack my own clothes." Taking the second bag, she undid the ties and dumped the contents across the bed.

Alex decided that now wasn't the time to press the child about the quilt pieces. Besides, she needed to speak with her mother alone, show her the letter Rush had given her, and tell her about the money as well.

She placed her hand on her mother's shoulder, but looked at Caro. "You're right, Caro, you are big enough to unpack your things. Mother and I will let you have some time to yourself. When you've finished unpacking, then you can join us in the kitchen for breakfast."

Her mother started to protest, but Alex ushered her from the room, stopping to pick up her shoes. Once in the doorway, Alex turned to her cousin and said, "By the way, anytime you wish to use my perfume, feel free to do so. I'm not much on scents, as you've already discovered. But I'd like you to know that I'm more than happy to share."

From the side of the bed, Caro shrugged her narrow shoulders but didn't respond. As Alex and her mother made their way toward her mother's bedroom, she glanced back over her shoulder. Caro stood in front of the dresser, her gaze locked on the perfume bottle that Alex had returned there earlier.

One step at the time, she reminded herself, smiling. Once inside her mother's room, she closed the door behind them.

4

"DEAR, DEAR CHARLOTTE," STELLA whispered, dropping the envelope and its contents into her lap. With a sob, she buried her face in her hands, and her frail shoulders shook. "If I hadn't feared my father's wrath, I might not have lost all contact with my only sister." The statement was made more to herself than to Alex. "Now it's too late."

Alex knelt on the floor beside her, wanting to comfort her, but uncertain how to go about it. She couldn't imagine the feisty little woman who had been her mother for twenty-two years fearing anyone or anything, but then there was so much about her mother's past that she never mentioned.

Alex could only imagine that her Grandfather Wilson, who had died not long after she was born, must have been some kind of a tyrant in order to banish his willful daughter from their lives forever. Considering the relationship she had enjoyed with her own father, she couldn't comprehend such a punishment being leveled against a daughter.

Unsure of what to do, she finally did what her mother would have done for her if the situation were reversed. She threw her arms around the older woman's shoulders and tried to make her see reason.

"It's not your fault, Mother. Those years were difficult for everyone because of the war. Families from both the North and South were torn apart and never reunited.''

''But if I'd only made more of an effort to find Charlotte. . . .''

''And just how could you have done that? The whole country was in an upheaval.'' She placed a finger beneath her mother's chin and turned her face toward her. ''You mustn't blame yourself. Charlotte could have sent word to you. You were here in Harpers Ferry. You weren't the one traipsing all over the country.''

''Oh, daughter, you don't know how proud my little sister was. She would have died before admitting that she had made a mistake by running off with that tinker. And of course your grandfather, he would never have allowed Charlotte to return home after she defied him.''

Her mother drifted away in her thoughts, then began again. ''Your father, God rest his soul, tried tracing her. It was after the war, after we were married, but the trail stopped cold. It was as though she had disappeared into thin air.''

''See, you did try. It's not your fault that you couldn't find her.''

Her mother dabbed at her eyes with the hem of her dressing gown. ''I shouldn't have allowed her to go with that horrible man. I should have run for the sheriff and had him haul Tyler straight to jail.'' The tears started flowing again, but then they stopped as suddenly as they had come.

''Merciful heavens,'' her mother exclaimed, ''you don't think that our sweet Caro was fathered by that bastard?''

Alex had never heard her God-fearing mother use such language, but until yesterday she had never seen her mother swoon, either.

''Doesn't the letter say who her father is?'' Alex asked.

''It's not a letter at all.'' She thrust the paper toward Alex. ''It looks like some hastily written agreement, signed by a lawyer, I suppose. Both signatures at the bottom are smudged, but one could be my sister's.''

Alex stood. Walking toward the window where the light was brighter, she quickly scanned the document.

In case of my death, my daughter, Caroline Swift, shall be delivered to my sister, Estelle Wilson Paine, and her husband, Herman Paine, in Harpers Ferry, West Virginia.

The two signatures on the bottom were smudged, and one was completely unreadable. The signed document was dated either March 1883 or 1888. The "State of Missouri" was still legible.

She looked at her mother. "Was Tyler's name Swift?"

"All I knew him by was Tyler. A mere tinker, he was. He traveled from one place in the country to the next, selling his wares from his wagon, and defiling innocent young women." Her mother wrestled with another bout of tears. "Merciful heavens. Can you believe I allowed my baby sister to take off for parts unknown with a man whose whole name I didn't know? What could I have been thinking?"

"Mother, please stop blaming yourself," Alex insisted. "You were hardly more than a child yourself. Your father should have had sense enough to find out who his daughter was running off with."

"Alexandria, you don't understand. You didn't know your grandfather."

"Thank God for small miracles. If what I've learned about him today is true, I wouldn't have liked him." She began to pace.

"Or he you," her mother snorted. "I've always thought you had a stubborn streak like Charlotte—strong-willed, defiant, marching to your own drum."

"There's nothing wrong with those qualities. In fact, I always thought I inherited them from you."

"Really?" Her mother looked pleased, more like her old self. She reached out for the paper. "So this tells us nothing about Caro. We don't even know if she has a legal father or if she was my sister's child born out of wedlock."

"She had a father," Alex insisted. "Rush said she told him as much. She said her family—her mother, father, and brother—all died. That's why she was sent here to us. We're the only family she has left."

"But we know nothing about her or my sister. No record of where she's from or where she's been."

"Nebraska. Rush said Nebraska."

Alex felt pleased that she had listened enough to convey this information. If she hadn't been so bullheaded and so angry about her bread, she might have learned more from Rush.

"Nebraska is so far away. It's almost as distant as the moon." Stella Paine's eyes begin to water again. "If only I could have stopped Charlotte—"

"Mother, you must stop this now." Alex knelt in front of her again. "Charlotte is gone. I still don't feel you should hold yourself responsible for something that happened so long ago and that you really had no control over. No matter how much you wish things could be different, they can't. But don't you see, you've been given a second chance, if you want to think of it that way."

"Second chance? Really, Alexandria, you're talking in riddles."

"Caro, Mother. She is your second chance. Charlotte's daughter. Aunt Charlotte must have loved you very much to have entrusted you with the care of her child."

"Oh, my, I never thought about it like that." Her mother's eyes regained some of their usual sparkle. "But I'm old—you know how some days my rheumatism flares up—and I'm helpless as a baby." She looked thoughtful for a moment. "Am I capable of raising a child?"

Alex smiled at her mother. "You raised me, didn't you?"

"Yes, but that was different. Your father was alive. I was young then."

"Your sister must have thought you were capable. And you have me to help you. We'll do it together."

"Oh, daughter, do you think we can?"

"You bet your bloomers I do." Alex reached inside her pocket and brought out the wad of money Rush had given her. "We've got this to help us."

She placed the roll of bills into her mother's lap.

"What's this?" Stella Paine asked. She didn't touch the money, but merely looked at it. "Mr. Bodine must have really wanted that bread to have paid so much for it."

"Mother, this isn't money I received from Mr. Bodine."

"Then where did you get such a large sum? It looks like a small fortune. Did you rob the bank?"

"No, I didn't rob the bank, although I'll admit I've thought about it a few times in the last five years."

"Alexandria Paine, I won't put up with such heathen thoughts. Rob a bank, really!"

"Rush gave it to me, Mother. It's from the men who worked on the ship that brought Caro from New Orleans to Washington. It seemed she charmed the whole crew. They took up a collection for her after they reached port."

Stella finally picked up the money and examined it closer. "There's so much money here." She looked at Alex. "We can't keep this."

"I said the same thing to Rush. He assured me that he couldn't keep it or give it back. The money is a gift."

"A very generous gift. I don't feel right about this. . . ."

"I know, Mother, I felt the same way you did at the time. But Rush was adamant. He insisted he couldn't keep it, that it was for Caro, and we should take the money and use it to help make her life easier."

Alex recalled Rush's argument and decided to use it to help convince her mother they had no choice but to keep it.

"Remember that old adage, 'Don't look a gift horse in the mouth.' I think we should consider that prophecy and use this money to do what we can to make Caro as comfortable as possible. She has no clothes to speak of. And there is still that bag of rags she guards with her life."

For a moment Alex wondered why those fabric pieces were so important to Caro that she forbade anyone to touch them. To Alex the rags resembled quilting squares.

"What is so important about that bag of rags?" her mother asked.

"I don't know, but in time, when she grows to trust us, maybe she'll tell us."

"You're right. We must not force her until she is ready. But the money, we could save it for her."

Save it? Alex rolled her eyes heavenward. If only her mother could comprehend how difficult it had been for her to run their household on the tiny income they produced from selling baked goods and quilts. But she wouldn't worry her with that now.

If her mother would approve of them keeping the money, Alex would use some of it to begin her enterprise. Once her cottage industry turned a profit, she would return every penny of the money she had used and more.

"Well, you think about it, Mother. I'll go and make that breakfast I promised Caro." She stood and turned to leave.

"Alex, wait," her mother called, standing. "You take this. I trust you to use it wisely, just as you've done in the past. You know I have no head for figures. Keeping the household account and making ends meet has always fallen on your shoulders."

She placed the money back in Alex's hand and closed her fingers around the roll.

"You're a wonderful daughter." She walked to the dry sink and poured water from the pitcher into the bowl. "I feel truly blessed this morning. Not only do I have you to love and care for, but also my sister's child, Caro. You're right, Alexandria, I've been given a second chance. God willing, this time, I'll do a better job."

"How about instead of counting on His will," Alex said, reaching the doors and sliding them open, "we go forward with His blessings?"

"Now if he'll just bless us with a husband for you, everything will be perfect."

"Mother. I'm not going to respond to that remark."

The sound of her mother's cheerful laughter followed her through the doors.

∽

THAT EVENING, ALEX RETURNED from downstairs, carrying a tea tray to where her mother and Caro were settled comfortably in the upstairs parlor. Beyond the room's only window, dusk had turned the sky to a deep charcoal gray. A breeze swelled the lace panel covering the narrow opening, wafting coolness into the otherwise stuffy room.

On Hill Street a horse clopped along the pavement. From the kitchen below, the leftover smells of their supper of green beans and boiled potatoes floated upward. After Alex placed the tray on the small table in front of the loveseat, Stella began pouring tea into three china cups.

"So, Caro, dear," Stella said, "what do you like in your tea?"

"Don't like tea," the child responded. Caro sat in the chair beside the loveseat next to a small round table that held the room's only lamp.

My chair, Alex thought, noting that the quilting she had been working on earlier now lay on the floor beside her cousin's feet.

On most nights Alex and her mother usually withdrew to the parlor after dinner, where each stitched and took an evening cup of tea before retiring to their beds for the night. These shared hours were some of Alex's favorites. A quiet time before bedtime; a time that she and her mother devoted to their stitching and to catching up on small talk. It was also a time when Alex let her imagination run free, discussing her dreams with her mother of turning the room downstairs into a quilting workroom to share with her fellow quilters. Now with the money Rush Duncan had given them, Alex's dream was closer to becoming a reality.

"I brought some cookies, too," Alex said. She picked up the dish of sugar snaps and held it toward Caro. The child refused her offer and scrunched up her face in disgust, making Alex question if it was Caro's dislike of tea and cookies or her dislike of her adult cousin that had solicited such a negative response. She imagined it was the latter and hated that Caro hadn't warmed to her as she so obviously had to her mother and to Rush Duncan.

Returning the plate to the tray, Alex picked up her teacup. She took several sips of the warm liquid before gathering the quilting from beside Caro's chair to sit on the settee next to her mother. Alex concentrated on her stitching, deciding it was best to allow her mother to carry the conversation, since Caro seemed so disinterested in anything Alex had to say.

"Come, Caro, have your tea and cookies," Stella urged. She took a cookie, dunked it into her cup, then nibbled the soggy dough. "I know it's not proper for ladies to dunk their food, but it's a pleasure I refuse to deny myself in the privacy of my own parlor.'' Again she dunked the doughy pastry, then took another bite.

From beneath lowered lids, Alex watched her young cousin while pretending interest in the square she was stitching. It was evident that Caro regretted her hasty refusal of the treat when she licked her own lips just as her aunt did when a stray crumb lingered at the corner of her mouth.

Stella reached for another sugar snap. ''Eat, child, please. You don't know what you're missing.''

No longer able to refuse the tempting snack, Caro slid to her knees beside the table. Soon she was slurping tea and dunking cookies along with Stella. Her mother, Alex noted, would never have allowed her daughter to eat in such a noisy fashion, but then, her cousin's circumstances deserved special treatment.

Not only had Caro suffered the loss of her family, but she had also been forced to live with relatives who were total strangers. For the time being, Alex agreed with her mother's decision to overlook the child's manners, believing that slurping and dunking were the least of their worries.

After Caro finished her tea, she left the floor and went to stand beside her aunt. She watched Stella work the needle up and down through the layers of fabric. Once again the child appeared hungry, but this time it wasn't for the taste of tea and cookies. She stared longingly at the quilt square in her aunt's lap, appearing to draw comfort from watching the older woman's busy fingers.

Stella must have noticed her niece's look as well, because she asked, ''Do you like to quilt, Caro?''

Caro nodded her head but didn't utter a word.

''If you're interested, I'm sure that Alexandria and I could find several squares we've pieced that need quilting, or you could work on something of your own.''

The child's face paled. She cut her eyes toward the bedroom, then quickly looked back at Stella.

For such an innocent question, Caro's reaction puzzled Alex. *It's those mysterious quilting squares again.*

Unmindful of her niece's action, Stella said, ''There never seem to be enough hours in the day for quilting, especially

since Alexandria and I have decided to make some quilts to
sell once the workroom downstairs is ready. Would you like
to help us?''

Her mother's admission surprised Alex. Beneath her bed
were at least a half dozen quilts the two of them had discussed
selling. Perhaps this was her mother's way of making Caro
feel a part of their small family by encouraging her to join
them in their endeavors.

Alex lifted a log cabin block from her sewing stack and
handed it to her mother. ''Will this do?'' The square, when
completed, would be a pillow cover. The needle and thread
were still in the pieced work where Alex had left them when
she had last worked on the design.

Stella took the square from her daughter and patted the settee cushion. ''Sit here, Caro,'' she said. ''There is plenty of
room for the three of us.''

Alex scooted sideways so Caro could sit between them.
Once Caro took up the needle, it was clear to Alex that her
cousin was competent. Watching her stitch made Alex want
to question her about her life back in Nebraska, but she didn't
dare. For now she would be satisfied that Caro was sitting
beside her, although Alex knew it was her mother's presence,
not hers, that kept Caro anchored to the loveseat.

Stella continued in a placating tone, ''Alexandria was
younger than you when she first started quilting.'' She stopped
stitching in order to watch her niece. ''I don't believe that she
was as adept with a needle as you are, though.'' Her mother
winked at Alex above Caro's bowed head.

''If my memory serves me right,'' Alex said, ''I think when
I was Caro's age I preferred being outside with Father, following him around the canal or swimming in it.''

She felt Caro's gaze settle on her. Instead of looking up
from her piecework, Alex kept stitching and talking.

''In those days, I was a bit of a tomboy.'' She knew she
had her cousin's attention so she lifted her gaze to Caro's.
''Your Uncle Herman loved the canal, and he taught me everything he knew about it. For that reason, I can understand why
Mr. Duncan is special to you. I'm sure you enjoyed the week

you spent with him aboard his boat, just as I enjoyed the time I spent with my father.''

"Rush isn't my pa, he's—"

"Of course he's not your pa," Stella interrrupted. "Alexandria only meant that she understands how you felt about his leaving you here with us. Isn't that so, Alexandria?''

"That's exactly what I meant.''

Stella set aside her sewing and stood. "I need to make a trip to the necessary so I'll take these tea things down to the kitchen on my way out.''

Once her mother exited the room, an uncomfortable silence settled between Alex and her cousin. How ridiculous—when dealing with the ten-year-old, she found herself at a complete loss for words. Like now. It was apparent that Caro felt the same. This knowledge made Alex more determined than ever to break through the barrier that had them stonewalled.

"Did you enjoy passing through the locks on the canal?" she asked. She hoped the topic would solicit a response from her cousin. When it didn't, she added, "I used to help my father when the boats locked through. If you would like to, we can take a walk over to Lock 33. I'll show you where I lived when I was your age.''

"Rush showed me already," Caro answered, returning her gaze to the material in her lap. Several more moments of strained silence passed before Caro surprised her with a response. "But maybe you could show me where you went swimming. There were no places to swim on the prairie.''

Alex shivered when she thought about the fetid water of the canal that she no longer considered fit for swimming. But Caro didn't need to be privy to those thoughts. Alex was happy that she had hit upon a subject that appeared to interest her cousin. *And there were places on both rivers where they could wade,* she thought.

"Do you swim?" she asked.

"Of course I swim," Caro responded, but she didn't look as confident as she sounded.

"Then we'll go soon," Alex answered.

"Go where?" Stella asked, returning from downstairs.

"Swimming in the canal," Caro replied excitedly.

"Alexandria, you know that water's too nasty for swimming."

Caro shot Alex a reproachful look. Before she could say anything more, Caro jumped up from the couch and stomped toward the bedroom.

"There are places on the rivers," Alex called. Her response fell on deaf ears as she watched Caro disappear beyond the door.

∽

SEVERAL HOURS HAD PASSED since their arrival at Leona Whitley's home, and Alex, Stella, and Caro sat in the parlor with the other ladies of the quilting circle. The group met weekly at different homes throughout Harpers Ferry. As Alex sat with her quilt top in her lap, working on an eight-pointed star she had started quilting several weeks earlier, she only half listened to the conversation buzzing around her.

She hadn't wanted to attend today. She would have preferred staying home and whitewashing the front room, but Alex's mother had goaded her into accompanying her and Caro, claiming Alex should attend because of her cousin and because she had missed last week's meeting because she'd been baking.

The only other children present were Ella Hamilton's two young daughters and one son who were outdoors playing. Shyness had kept Caro inside with the women. She sat in a chair next to Alex, although the cartwheels that Jamie Hamilton was turning beyond the window appeared to hold Caro's interest more than the square of pinwheels she had chosen to bring from home to work on today.

"So, Miss Caro," Rosellen, Leona's sister, said, "what do you think of our town?"

When Caro looked quite uncomfortable and failed to reply, Alex answered for her. "Caro hasn't seen much of our town. She's been busy settling in. Isn't that right, Caro?"

Her cousin nodded her head and gave Rosellen a hesitant smile.

"You'll like it here, I'm sure," Leona Whitley added.

"There are lots of things for youngsters to do, especially if they prefer the outdoors like your cousin Alexandria did at your age." Leona settled her glasses more comfortably on her nose, sending Alexandria a pointed look. "Now she's turned into a proper young woman like the rest of us, but I daresay it was her hooligan ways that kept her from getting a husband."

At the woman's remark, Alex jabbed the needle through the layers of cloth and batting. Calling herself a fool for allowing Leona to upset her, she forced herself to relax, then brought the needle back up through the design with a precision that was as natural as breathing. As a child at her mother's knee, she had learned that every stitch in the actual quilting of a design must be the exact same size. No matter what Leona Whitley said, or thought, Alex had loved quilting in her youth almost as much as she loved it now, but she enjoyed playing outdoors as well. She was about to tell Leona this when her mother came to her defense.

"Alexandria wasn't a hooligan, Leona," Stella said. "She just loved being outside, which is not abnormal for children."

Laughter floated in through the open doors and windows. From her chair, Alex could see the front lawn that sloped like a verdant carpet toward the street. She, too, watched Jamie Hamilton, whom Alex suspected had begrudgingly accompanied his mother and sisters to the meeting. The two Hamilton girls sat beneath a tree, playing with their dolls and giggling as they watched their brother's antics. It was evident that Jamie Hamilton enjoyed acting the clown.

"So tell us about your home in Nebraska, Miss Caro," Leona insisted in her usual overbearing manner. "And tell us about that mother of yours. We remember so little——"

"Leona," Stella scolded, "this isn't the time or place."

Alex bolted to her feet and turned to face Caro, who looked as though she were about to burst into tears. "Come with me, Caro," she said. "I think it's time you join the children in the yard."

Caro seemed as anxious to escape the room as Alex suspected she was. When Alex extended her hand to the ten-year-old, Caro willingly took it. Standing, the child allowed Alex to lead her out the front door and onto the porch.

"Leona, how could you," Alex heard her mother reprimanding her old friend.

"Well, I never meant to upset . . ." Leona's voice drifted into silence as Alex and Caro left the porch and walked into the yard.

With Caro's hand still in hers, Alex stopped several yards away from the tree where the three children now watched them. "You must not let Miss Leona upset you with her questions, Caro. She means well, but she doesn't always think before she speaks. She is sometimes meddlesome, but her heart is in the right place. In time, you, like me, will learn to ignore her remarks."

Caro jerked her hand from Alex's. She looked like a trapped animal unsure of which way to run; back toward the strangers inside or toward the children outside who Alex knew could be more curious and cruel than any adult.

"I want to go home," Caro answered. "I don't want to be here. Your nosey friend makes me sick with all her questions."

"I can understand how you feel. On occasion, she's made me quite ill as well, but she is an adult, and that alone should earn her our respect."

"I don't like her much, either," Jamie Hamilton said, coming to stand beside them. "Miss Leona is always tweaking my ears and nose. She treats me like a baby, but Ma says I have to be polite because she's old."

Neither female had heard Jamie's approach, but Alex was glad for it. His remark, or maybe it was his presence, brought the beginnings of a smile to Caro's sad face. Her cousin relaxed visably.

"Your mother is correct, Jamie," Alex said. "Children must be respectful. In her own way, Miss Leona loves us all."

"Yuck. Who'd want to be loved by her." Jamie made a face. This time Caro did giggle.

"Major Whitley loved her," Alex reminded them, "and her daughter and sister love her as well."

Jamie rolled his eyes toward heaven before he looked at

Caro. "Do you like to play dolls like my sissy sisters, or would you rather play tag?"

"I-I don't like dolls," Caro managed, her reply coming out in a croak.

"My guess," Alex said, "is that Caro is a very good tag player. She's had lots of experience running through prairie grass."

Caro looked at her with surprise that also held an ounce of approval.

"What's prairie grass?" Jamie asked.

"I'll let Caro tell you."

Caro hung back, staying close to Alex's side. Jamie stared at her, waiting for her to answer. Caro, however, spoke to Alex rather than the boy. "Are you sure it's okay if I play outside? Aunt Stella won't mind?"

"Of course she won't mind. You've been quilting with us for several hours. It's time you got to know a few people your own age."

Caro looked as though she wanted to say more, but Jamie tapped her on the arm and shouted, "You're it!" He took off at a fast run, and Caro bolted after him.

Seeing the small glimpse of joy on Caro's face before she dashed off in pursuit of Jamie brought a lump to Alex's throat. That one expression made her wonder how long it had been since her cousin had experienced the pleasure of just being a child. As the twosome darted back and forth across the yard, Alex turned and headed back inside. She took her same chair and was surprised but grateful that the incident with Caro was not mentioned.

It appeared to Alex as the hour progressed that Caro preferred the rough-and-tumble play that she was enjoying with Jamie over the sedentary kind preferred by his sisters. She stopped to talk with the two younger girls, but Alex suspected it was only during time-outs. Not that Alex could blame her. She had been much the same herself when she was Caro's age. Even today, though she loved to quilt, she wished herself home wielding a paintbrush instead of plying a needle.

"So, Alexandria," Rosellen Byer said, breaking into her thoughts, "tell us about this new undertaking of yours. Stella tells us you have plans to turn the front room of your house into a quilting workroom.''

Alex lifted her gaze to meet that of the older woman seated across the room. ''That's correct. That's exactly what I plan to do. I've ordered a large quilting frame from Montgomery Ward and Company that should arrive any day now. The room is big enough to accommodate the frame with plenty of space left over. Now we'll have a permanent place to work on all our bed quilts together. No longer will we have to disrupt each other's households, or husbands, for the putting in.''

''Did I hear you say husbands, Alexandria?'' Leona Whitley raised a silvery brow. ''Is there something you're not telling us?'' The other six women present paused in their quilting to note Alex's reaction.

Alex scanned the room. The women's faces were as familiar to her as her own. She had known all of them for most of her life. Her mother's oldest friends, the two sisters, Leona and Rosellen, along with Millie King, whose husband owned the country store. Ella Hamilton was Millie King's married daughter, and it was her children who were there today. Sena Ford and Lucy Prouty were Alex's childhood friends, and both were now married. Sena was wed only recently, but Lucy, who had been married for a couple of years, was expecting her first child.

Ignoring Leona Whitley's remark while exchanging a look with her mother, Alex continued, ''Not even inclement weather will keep us from our task.''

Would Leona Whitley never tire of her infernal meddling? Alex supposed the older woman meant well, but why had she appointed herself the town matchmaker? Never a moment passed at these weekly meetings that Leona didn't make a reference to Alex's unmarried state, and then give her opinion of how to go about snagging a husband. To hear her talk, one would think she was the only married woman in the universe.

Her younger sister Rosellen had never married, a fact that made Alex wonder how Rosellen had kept from killing Leona over the years. But Leona no longer focused her efforts on her sister; instead, she focused them on Alex, her sole purpose being to badger her friend's daughter into marrying the preacher. There were moments when Alex was tempted to give in just to still the woman's wagging tongue.

Lucy Prouty shifted in her chair and ran a hand over her increasing waistline. "I do so enjoy when we quilt outside on the lawn. I hope this workroom of yours will not eliminate our quilting frolics. It's so much fun to have the menfolk present."

Not yet finished goading Alex, Leona added, "Of course, Alexandria couldn't care less about such frolics. When one doesn't have a man, one doesn't care about frolicking with them."

Alex swallowed her annoyance with the woman and for the second time today acted indifferent to her remark. "If everyone chooses not to use my workroom, that's fine, too. Of course, Lucy, it won't eliminate our frolics. We all look forward to them." Her next statement was directed at Leona Whitley. "I enjoy socializing with my neighbors as much as anyone."

"Harumph!" was the matron's only response.

"I understand you also plan to sell quilting supplies," Millie King said. "I'm not sure my Emmet will take kindly to your competing with his business."

Millie King's husband owned the only country store in Harpers Ferry, and in Alex's opinion, he could use some healthy competition. She wasn't all that impressed with the yard goods he sold.

"Millie, I'll not be selling shovels and feed. The few things I intend to stock certainly won't have much effect on your husband's business. I plan to buy only a few bolts of fabric that will give us all a wider variety of materials to choose from for our quilts. Also, a few notions such as needles, thimbles, quilting hoops, and the like. Mostly items that interest women."

"Emmet carries women's things," Millie added in defense of her husband's business. She sat a little straighter in her chair, and Alex thought she resembled a plump turnip with her spreading stomach and hips visible beneath the purple-red color of her frock.

"Really, Millie," Sena Ford interrupted, "I think Alexandria's idea is wonderful. Since she is a quilter like we are, she has an eye for fabrics. Her quilts are some of the prettiest in town. She'll select fabrics that she believes will look nice made into quilts." Sena smiled at her. "Don't get me wrong, Millie. I'm not saying Emmet doesn't carry nice fabrics in his store, but his taste doesn't always coincide with the tastes of a lady."

"Mother, I agree with Sena," Ella Hamilton said. "Papa's fabrics are nice, but some of them are more functional than pretty. I'm sick to death of dull colors, sick of using washed-out fabrics from dresses I wore ten years ago. Some bright colors mixed in with my patching will suit me real fine." She turned to Alex and said, "I'll be one of your first customers, providing your prices aren't too dear."

"I hope to keep prices low. But who knows, maybe such an endeavor won't work in this town. In order to be successful, I will need to earn the business of the other women in Harpers Ferry as well."

Millie King shook her head and mumbled, "Emmet isn't going to like this."

"Oh, Mother, Papa won't even notice unless you go making a mountain out of a molehill the way you usually do."

Mother and daughter looked as though they were about to argue when Rosellen said, "What this town really needs is a milliner's shop."

"Hats? Emmet carries hats," Millie whined. "Now you all are conniving to steal the bread right out of my mouth and put my poor Emmet out of business."

"Hush up, Millie," Leona said. "You know that is not our intent, but, Rosellen, your idea is absurd. A milliner indeed. You already have enough bonnets in your possession to cover all the heads of the rebel army."

Rosellen Byer glared at her sibling. "Need I remind you, Leona, we no longer have a rebel army. And for your information, I certainly don't own that many hats, and even if I did, it wouldn't be any of your business."

Leona Whitley glared back. "Can't see that all those fancy bonnets you care so much about do you any good. They never got you a husband. Now you're too old to get one and too old to be worrying about what's riding around on the top of your head. If anyone in this room needs a pretty bonnet, it would be our Alexandria.''

"Sister, you can be so tactless," Rosellen snapped. "Unlike you, I never wanted a husband. I suspect when a girl as pretty as Alexandria decides she wants one, she'll have a flock of prospects gathering around her door.'' She paused to catch her breath, then continued. "While we're on the subject of heads, need I remind you you should be more concerned with what isn't inside yours instead of worrying about what's on the outside of mine.''

Touché. Alex hid her smile. *You tell her, Rosellen.*

Everyone who was well acquainted with the two sisters was used to their tiffs, but it always amazed Alex how Rosellen usually bested her sister with words. Maybe it was because Rosellen was the smarter of the two, and Leona was too wrapped up in her own importance to notice.

But if Rosellen's comments bothered Leona, she didn't let on. She delivered her second line of attack, directing it toward Alexandria.

"Why don't you do something flattering with your hair, Alexandria?'' She looked over the top of her spectacles at Alex. "Braids are for youngsters, not for ladies past their prime.''

"There is nothing wrong with my daughter's hair," Stella said, dropping her quilting into her lap.

"I like it this way," Alex said. "It suits."

For as long as she could remember, she had worn her hair in a braid down her back. On the rare occasions she had styled the thick coarse hair into a chignon, the pins had always popped out, leaving her tresses straggling down her back.

Leona ignored Alex's remark. "Need I remind you, my young miss, you are not Annie Oakley. Such a style is suitable for a sharpshooter in a Wild West show, but not for a respectable—''

"Leona," Alex's mother interrupted, "what did you think about Rush Duncan delivering my niece?''

Her old friend hesitated only long enough to gather her thoughts before starting on another tangent. "I think I'd consider myself lucky that she arrived at all. From what I recall about that impudent lad, no girl is safe within a foot of him. Especially after he reached puberty.''

"Leona, you're not being fair,'' her sister criticized. "You know as little about that near-homeless boy as you do about how many bonnets I own.''

"I know what Major Whitley told me.'' She looked indignant and glared at her sister again.

"Mercy, Leona, don't expect us to put much faith in your accounting. You can't remember what happened yesterday much less twenty years ago. Besides, you never even knew the lad. Granted, Major Whitley might have known him, but he's been dead nigh ten years. The way you get your facts mixed up, I sometimes wonder if you remember the major.''

"Of course I remember my own husband, Rosellen. Sometimes you can be so unkind.''

"I'm only suggesting that you don't remember Rush Duncan. But I remember him,'' she added, "from my Sunday school class. He was quite a handsome lad then, and a rascal to boot.''

Leona sniffed. "A boot is exactly what he needed! In the seat of his pants. Back then, and probably now as well. How you surprise me, sister, with your rambling. It was I who taught him in Sunday school, not you. That one,'' she reiterated, "had bad blood. And a person never outgrows bad blood.''

The old dame leaned forward on her chair, and, in a dramatic whisper, continued, "It was rumored that his father was a damn Yankee, but then, with that mother of his, it's hard to tell who his father was.''

Once again, Alex and her mother exchanged looks.

They both loved the two Byer sisters, who were as much a part of Harpers Ferry history as John Brown's raid. But there were times that Leona Whitley needed a good shaking, and Alex would have enjoyed being the one who gave it. A more opinionated woman she had never known.

Stella Paine said, "Well, Caro certainly has taken a liking to Mr. Duncan, bad blood or not. From what I saw of the young man the other day, he went out of his way to make

Caroline feel comfortable and loved while she was in his care.''

"A wolf in sheep's clothing," Leona cautioned, leaning back again.

"Sister, why is it you always expect the worst from men, but yet you're always wanting to make us single women their lambs?"

Leona rethreaded her needle and stuck it back into her fabric. "I was the one who was married, Rosellen. It's only fitting that I should be the one who understands a man's nature."

"Pshaw. You, my dear, only think you understand." Snipping her quilting thread, Rosellen dropped the sewing scissors that hung from her bosom on a ribbon. "I say give credit where credit is due. I agree with Stella. If she believes Mr. Rush Duncan is a gentleman, then who are we to disagree? Caro is her niece. Besides, Stella is a good judge of character."

Leona looked sheepish. "I don't doubt, Stella dear, that you are a good judge of character. I'm only saying that we must defend our daughters."

"Your daughter, Leona," Rosellen quipped, "lives in Philadelphia with her family. She has no need of your protection."

But Rush Duncan did need defending, Alex thought, especially since he wasn't here to defend himself. Although he wasn't on her list of favorite people, she felt it was wrong for Leona Whitley to speak badly of him.

Bad blood indeed!

"Forgive my presumption," Alex said, "but I was always taught that children aren't responsible for the sins of their parents. In my opinion, bad blood is nothing more than hogwash. I'm sure if you and he were cut open and allowed to bleed, your blood, Miss Leona, would look no different from his."

"Well, I never—"

"As my mother said," Alex continued, "Caroline is very fond of him. Considering what we believe she's been through in the last six months, losing her family and all, we're glad that Rush was there for her. He seems truly concerned for Caro's welfare. To me that means a lot."

"Why, Alexandria Paine, I do believe you're smitten with the man."

"Smitten?" Alex rolled her eyes heavenward. "Not hardly, Miss Leona, I have no designs on Rush Duncan. I merely said he has been nothing but kind to Caro."

The expression on Leona's face wavered between doubtful and knowing. "He's not married, is he?" Then she smiled and looked pleased with herself. "Well, then," she said, "maybe you should get to know him better. Although I daresay the good reverend's heart will break if he fancies himself losing you."

"Losing me? I daresay the good reverend never *had* me." Alex struggled to keep her temper. It was time to leave. She stood, and her quilting slipped from her lap to the floor. Leona nudged it with the toe of her shoe. After retrieving the square from the floor, Alex returned to her seat and began gathering up her things. "If you ladies will excuse me, I have work to do at—"

"My, my," Rosellen said, peering past the window and out into the yard. "Who is that fine-looking gentleman talking with your niece, Stella?"

All eight pairs of eyes in the room glanced toward the front yard. The women who couldn't see outside left their chairs and gathered beside the windows to get a better view of the stranger.

Alex's mother was the first to speak. "Why, that's Mr. Duncan," Stella said, pushing to the front of the group. "He promised Caro he would stop by on his return trip from Cumberland."

"My, my, he's so tall," Lucy Prouty squeaked in her little bitty voice.

"And look at those shoulders," Sena Ford added.

Ella Hamilton only sighed.

"I've never seen such a fine head of hair," Millie King added, touching her own thinning tresses.

Rosellen almost purred. "There's something about a man with long, dark hair that could always make my blood boil." She reached for her bonnet that hung on the back of the chair, and after placing it upon her gray head, she began to tie the ribbons beneath her many chins.

Leona nudged her sister affectionately. "Sister, it's not that handsome young man who has your blood boiling but your age."

She turned to face Alex, whose own heart had kicked into high gear on seeing Rush Duncan again. Although Alex hated to admit it, he was exactly how her friends had described him and more.

Leona Whitley's face was flushed with excitement when she threaded her arm through Alex's.

"Why, dear girl," she said, beaming, "I do believe it's time you introduced us to your new beau."

5

"YOU'RE BACK, YOU'RE BACK!" Caro squealed, jumping up and down like a runaway frog.

Upon seeing Rush approach the yard, the girl had run to meet him. "How's my favorite girl?" he asked.

Squatting on the grass beside Caro, he surrounded her waist with his arm. She threw her spidery arms around his neck and squeezed.

A feeling of pleasure warmed Rush's heart, and he wondered if this was how a father felt when greeted by his child at the end of a hard day's work. At that moment he felt a mile high as he lost his face in her wild mop of black curls. Caro smelled as sweet as spring grass with a little West Virginia dirt mixed in.

She stepped away from him only long enough to exclaim, "I thought you'd never get here." Then she charged him again, bumping him from his heels to his seat.

"Hold on there, mate," he teased, his laughter joining with hers. "It's a fine how-do-you-do when a fellow's gal knocks his feet right out from under him."

"Oh, Rush, you're so silly."

It was then that he spied up close the little boy Caro had been playing chase with when he had first seen her in a neighbor's yard. He had stopped first at the Paine residence, and upon finding no one at home, he had left his little surprise for Caro by the front door and decided to take a stroll up High Street. Knowing that Harpers Ferry wasn't all that big, Rush figured the women hadn't gone far and wouldn't be away long. Halfway up the hill, he'd seen Caro playing with this lad.

Rush set Caro aside, blowing her hair out of his mouth and nose, and smiled at the boy standing several feet away, chewing on the end of a long piece of grass.

''Who's your friend?'' Rush asked her.

Caro turned to face the boy, but she kept her arm possessively across the top of Rush's shoulders. ''Him?'' she asked. ''Oh, that's Jamie Hamilton. His mother is inside.'' She pointed to the small house that sat in the middle of the sloping lawn. ''She's at the quilting bee with Aunt Stella and . . . and her.''

''You mean your cousin?'' Rush asked, wondering why Caro's sunny humor of a few moments before had suddenly become cloudy.

''You Caro's pa?'' Jamie Hamilton asked, giving Rush a thorough going-over.

''No, stupid, he ain't my pa,'' Caro answered for him. ''He's, he's—''

''Her friend,'' Rush answered. Caro's jaw snapped shut, and for a moment he thought she might cry.

Women. I'll never understand them. But he didn't have long to ponder Caro's suddenly peculiar behavior because Jamie responded to her earlier put-down.

''I ain't stupid,'' he said. ''A few minutes ago, before he showed up, you liked playing tag with me.'' He slung the piece of grass he'd been chewing to the ground. ''And I ain't so stupid to know I shouldn't have been playing with a stupid girl to begin with.'' The boy turned on his heels and stomped toward the tree where his sisters were sitting.

The moment the boy left them, Caro was all smiles again.

Rush patted the ground beside him. ''Perhaps, little one, it's time you and I had a talk.'' He looked toward Jamie then back to Caro again. ''That was no way to treat a friend. You shouldn't have called him stupid.''

"He's not my friend," Caro insisted, "and he *is* stupid."

She sat beside Rush, her bony knees making humps like a camel's beneath the material of her skirt.

"Well, he appeared to be your friend before I arrived, but I bet you a nickel he isn't anymore."

Rush scratched his head, unsure how to handle what he saw as a delicate situation.

"You know us menfolks," he said. "We've got giant egos. Once a pretty lady like yourself tramples on it, it takes us a while before we come around for more of the same treatment."

Caro's sapphire-blue eyes drilled holes into him, making him feel suddenly inadequate. No longer did he soar a mile high with the birds. Instead, he was down here on earth, groveling along with the rest of the bugs in the dirt.

Her chin inched higher, reminding Rush of how stubborn she could be. "I don't want him to come around anymore," she said, "I don't need him."

"Oh, but you're wrong, Caro. Everyone needs a friend. Would you like to know something else? It would make me a hell—heck of a lot happier if I knew that you had made a few friends here." He propped back on his hands and looked across his shoulder at her. "That way I wouldn't have to worry so much about my best girl in between my visits."

The corners of her bow-shaped mouth lifted into the beginning of a smile. "Oh, Rush, I lo—"

A noisy commotion tumbled across the yard, coming from the direction of the house. Caro jerked her head toward the sound. Rush watched the beginning traces of her smile vanish completely before his gaze followed hers.

"Saints preserve us," he mumbled beneath his breath.

Jumping to his feet, he brushed off the seat of his britches, then preceded to wipe his sweat-dampened palms on his seat. They were under full attack from what appeared to be the petticoat brigade of Harpers Ferry.

As the ladies marched across the yard toward them, Rush was a lad again, fending for himself on the unfriendly streets of the town. He almost bolted, until he received fortification from the girl at his side. Caro looked up at him, then took his hand, entwined her fingers with his, and squeezed.

When the legion of ladies was so close that he could see the whites of their eyes, Rush gave them his most devil-may-care smile.

"Howdy, ladies," he said. "How you all are? I mean," he corrected, embarrassment scorching his face, "how are you?" For a man who prided himself on being a smooth talker, his words had come out as corrugated as a washboard.

The troop of women stopped several feet away from where he stood with Caro. Surprisingly, he was now squeezing the daylights out of her small hand.

The women should have been familiar, but years had turned them into strangers. Other than Alex and her mother, the only one he recognized was Leona Whitley, who appeared to be the band's self-appointed leader. Rush wasn't certain if Alex was a willing participant or if she was just caught up in the tide. A quick glance at her face told him that she was as eager as he was to turn tail and run.

A woman not much taller than Caro pushed past Leona Whitley and Alex, sashaying to a halt only inches away from the toes of his boots. She might have been the shortest among the lady soldiers, but her bearing made up for her lack of height.

"Just look at you, Rush Duncan," she said, giving him a thorough going-over.

Her gaze traveled from the top of his head to the tips of his toes before coming to rest on his face. Rush almost squirmed beneath her scrutiny, but rather than show his embarrassment, he concentrated on her hat. It was the most outlandish creation he'd ever seen, its brim filled to overflowing with an assortment of brightly colored fruit that in his opinion looked more edible than fashionable.

As he stared at her hat, a memory surfaced. He was a boy again, attending Sunday school and listening to a lesson being delivered by a woman similar in appearance to this one. She, too, had fancied bizarre hats. Rush wracked his brain for the name of that teacher, and suddenly it popped into his head.

"Why, Miss Rosellen," he said with a smile, "I see you're still sporting the prettiest hats in town."

He hoped his true thoughts weren't readable, but then he couldn't very well tell her what he really thought about her bonnet. When she warmed him with a brilliant smile, he decided his little lie was worth it, and grinned back at her.

"And you, young man, are still as full of blarney as you were back then. I know what you striplings thought about my hats, not that your opinions were worth a penny. But when you get to be my age, a woman doesn't receive many compliments from such a handsome gentleman, so I'll take your praise as truth." Looking him over again, she said, "You turned out fine, Mr. Duncan, and it appears you have a head full of sense as well."

Rush laughed heartily. "Was that a compliment, or should I be offended?" he asked teasingly.

"What my sister means," Leona Whitley said, stepping forward and dragging Alex with her. "It appears, young Duncan, that age has improved both your looks and your manners, but I bet you're as much of a mischief-maker as you always were."

"There's nothing wrong with a fellow enjoying a good time now, is there, Mrs. Whitley?"

Her hand fluttered against her plump bosom, and she looked at him with wonder. "Well, it's nice to see that you remember my name as well as my sister's."

He rewarded her with a large smile. "I could never forget the major's lovely wife."

Mrs. Whitley tittered. "I was a lovely thing back then, wasn't I? The major always said I was the prettiest girl in all of Harpers Ferry, and, you know, I believe he was right."

Rosellen rolled her eyes heavenward. "Saints preserve us, Leona, the way you do carry on. Would you please allow the rest of us ugly ducklings the pleasure of reacquainting ourselves with this nice young man?"

Leona shot Rosellen a lethal look, but she withheld further comment on the subject. "Allow me," she said haughtily, "to reacquaint you with the others."

As she recited the women's names, Rush nodded and smiled at each lady introduced. When she had finished the introductions, she pulled Alex closer to her side.

"Of course, you've already renewed your acquaintance with our Alexandria. You can't know how pleased we all are that a man has finally seen fit to court her."

Alex gasped and tried to pull her arm free. Her face had turned the same purple-red color of Ella Hamilton's dress, and beside him he felt Caro stiffen. Mrs. Whitley, oblivious to her thoughtless remark, rattled on as though she were talking about the price of eggs.

"Of course, we mustn't forget the reverend. He's had his cap set for Alexandria ever since his arrival a year ago. I don't think he'll take lightly to competition, especially from a rascal like you."

Alex looked at him, her expression furious. In the depths of her dark-brown eyes were sparks as brilliant as fireworks, and Rush expected her to explode at any given moment.

"I-I never. I certainly don't think—" She stopped in mid-sentence as though wrestling with her thoughts.

In all the years he had known Alexandria Paine, he couldn't recall a time when she was at a loss for words. Her continuous babble as a child had on more than one occasion caused him to want to wring her neck, but now it seemed Alexandy had met her match in Mrs. Leona Whitley.

After an uncomfortable moment, Alex yanked her arm from the older woman's grasp. "Mrs. Whitley," she exclaimed, "how dare you suggest—how could you imply . . ." Alex looked toward her mother for help. "Tell her, Mother, that he—that I have no desire to become involved with *him* or—"

"Leona, please," her mother insisted.

"I daresay, Alexandria," Mrs. Whitley continued, "you aren't the first young lady who has been embarrassed when a young man's intentions are made public."

"Hush, Leona," her mother said, "you're embarrassing Alexandria and Mr. Duncan."

This time Alex ignored her mother. "His intentions?" Alex groaned. "He's made no amorous advances toward me, I assure you. Even if he did, they would be useless. I want nothing to do with the likes—"

She caught herself before she finished the sentence, or so

Rush believed. Her response made it clear that Miss Alexandria Paine still thought herself above the likes of him—still thought he was not good enough for the likes of her.

Not that he expected otherwise from the spoiled young miss from his past. Her rejection of him did not rankle him nearly as much as her audacity—that she would express her repugnance to such an attachment not only in front of him, but also in front of the other ladies. It was time he taught Miss Paine a lesson.

Again her mother tried to intercede. "Hush, both of you. This is not the time or place for such a discussion."

Rush watched Leona Whitley puff up like a toad. The woman wasn't about to hush until she was good and ready. "Well, sir?" she said, looking him straight in the eyes. "What are your intentions toward Alexandria?"

"Mrs. Whitley, please," Alex demanded before her gaze found his. "Since she won't listen to me, then maybe she will listen to you. Tell her," Alex said, crossing her arms against her chest, "that I mean nothing to you."

Rush knew he had the power to end this mess here and now. All he needed to do was to admit the truth of Alex's words, then tell Leona Whitley what a meddling old fool she was and to mind her own business. As he stood with all eyes of the attending females glued to him like flies to flypaper, he battled his own devils.

First, he had thought Leona Whitley's remark was uncalled for—the one claiming how pleased they all were that a man had finally seen fit to court Alex. Second, the remark was unbelievable to him. In Rush's opinion, Alex was as easy on the eyes as she had always been, perhaps even more so. What really surprised him was that no man had snatched her up years ago.

Third, he questioned his sanity as to why he cared what the local gossips said about Alex when he had heard her own objections to the possibility of being courted by the likes of him.

But it was his fourth reason, Rush admitted to himself afterwards, that prompted him to respond to Leona Whitley's question the way he did. He enjoyed seeing Alexandy squirm.

He took a certain pleasure in watching the pain-in-the-ass woman finally get her comeuppance. She had looked down her pert little nose at him for perhaps the last time.

"Why, darling," he said, looking straight into Alex's questioning brown eyes and directing his answer toward her. "It was only last week that you and I spent the whole night together, getting reacquainted. I assumed that when I left you, we had an understanding. . . ."

He deliberately let his sentence trail off, expecting the women's gasps, and not surprised that their faces turned as white as the clouds that drifted overhead. Only Stella Paine seemed to find his remark amusing, while her daughter looked anything but amused.

"I think, Mr. Duncan," Alex said, "that you're deliberately misleading these ladies. As you well know, my mother and Caro were with us throughout the night, and it was bed— bread—we were making until sunup."

Her slip of the tongue made him laugh. *Poor Alexandy. I almost feel sorry for putting her in such a position. Almost.* Then he continued with his little show. He thumped his hand over his heart. "Spooning all night, although I would have preferred using my hands."

Caro, at his side, began shaking his arm. He looked down at her upturned face, remembering for the first time since this conversation had begun that there were little ears present. Not only hers, but also those of the other three children who had joined the group standing in the middle of the lawn.

Caro looked up at him and asked, "What does spooning mean?"

"Kissing," Jamie Hamilton answered. "My ma and pa do it all the time."

The ten-year-old's expression crumbled. She jerked her hand free from his and broke into a run.

"Caro," Alex called, turning to glare at him. "Now see what you've gone and done."

Not giving him a chance to respond, Alex ran after her cousin, who was running toward home as fast as her short legs would carry her.

∽

"WHERE COULD SHE BE?" Alex asked herself as she
headed down High Street toward home. She was concerned
for the child, who was still a stranger to the town. For a child
who had grown up on a prairie, this river town could offer all
kinds of threats.

Glancing in narrow alleyways and beneath basement over-
hangs, she looked for Caro's fluff of black hair that would
blend in with the deep shadows, making finding her even more
difficult.

Soon she could see an angled view of their house with its
white blocks that time had weathered to an ivory hue and the
roofless porch that ran the width of the building with its iron
rail that separated from the walkway. Continuing down the
hill, she was able to see the two double windows on each side
of the recessed entranceway. The deep forest-green siding that
encased both windows and doors looked several shades lighter
where the afternoon sun brushed its surface with a golden
glow.

Alex still saw no sign of her cousin as the hill began to
flatten out. No one locked their houses in Harpers Ferry, so
Caro could have gone inside. She looked up at the three windows on the second level which belonged to her bedroom. The
lace curtains hung as motionless as today's breeze. If Caro
was hiding upstairs, the curtains concealed her completely.

Alex shifted her gaze to the gabled sloping roof with its two
dormers off the tiny attic room. *Why didn't I think of it before?*
She knew Caro hadn't enjoyed sharing a room with her for
the past week, and decided that if Caro was in favor of having
her own space, they would make her a bedroom on the third
level of the house. Now the third story was used only for
storage, but it would be a perfect hidey-hole for a ten-year-
old girl. Later Alex would speak to her mother about her idea,
but now she had more pressing matters to attend to. She must
find Caro, and soon.

Dang Jamie Hamilton's big mouth. *Spooning, indeed.* Double dang Ella Hamilton and her husband for calling kissing

spooning, and a triple dang to Rush Duncan for ever suggesting such shenanigans had gone on between them. Alex's lips twitched, and she tried not to smile at the memory of the incident, but unable to stop herself, she finally laughed out loud.

"What a scoundrel he is," she said.

At the time, Alex hadn't enjoyed being the center of Rush Duncan's joke, but admittedly she had enjoyed seeing Leona Whitley's shocked expression on hearing that Rush had spent the night with her. Although she loved the old busybody, she couldn't believe the woman's audacity when she had claimed to the whole gaggle of women present that Alexandria Paine had finally gotten the attention of a man other than the reverend. For once, Leona had been the one shocked instead of the one doing the shocking.

Alex knew her mother would set the wagging tongues to rest with an explanation of what had really transpired on the evening in question. But how could she explain away the damage that Rush's remark must have wrought on Caro's young heart? A heart that was suffering from a bad case of puppy love.

Dang Rush's insensitive hide. He didn't deserve her cousin's hero worship.

Or her good temper, either. Last night and today, Alex felt as though she had made a small breakthrough with her cousin by learning that she and Caro had a lot in common. Her cousin at age ten appeared to enjoy the same things she had at that age: quilting, swimming, and playing boy's games over girl's. She admitted that such small similarities weren't much to grow on, but with a little tender love and care, it was possible that a friendship could sprout between them. Unless Rush Duncan had spoiled everything with his offhand remarks.

Alex was approaching the end of the porch when she saw two tiny feet jutting out from the recessed entrance. Relief washed over her, and she came to a dead stop, using the moment to catch her breath and gather her thoughts. *Thank the Lord I've found her.*

Her heart ached when she heard what sounded like whimpering. *She's crying. Damn Rush and his big mouth.* Most men, she thought, were good for nothing but bringing heartache to women. Alex was glad she didn't suffer from such a complication and vowed that she never would.

Not wishing to send her cousin fleeing again, Alex approached cautiously. She stopped at the tips of the child's feet. Caro sat on the floor with her legs stretched out in front of her, leaning against the front door. Beside her sat an open fishing creel. It wasn't fish that Caro held in her lap; instead, it was a young cat.

"Marmalade," the child crooned, "I miss you so much."

On hearing the exchange, Alex thought the twosome were acquainted, although she had never seen the animal before now. Caro wasn't crying—the low murmuring she had heard was her cousin talking to the ball of ginger-colored fur.

Dropping to the floor beside her, Alex scooted backward until she, too, was leaning against the door. She stretched her legs out in front of her, and asked, "Who's your friend?"

Caro didn't answer, but kept stroking the cat's back. A gurgling purr emanated from the beast, who looked up at Alex through drowsy green eyes.

"I heard you call her Marmalade. Is that her name?" she tried again, but was rewarded with silence. "Do you mind if I pet her?" she asked, certain that Caro would.

When she heard no objections, Alex reached across the child and began to stroke the cat's back. Uncertain what to say, but wanting to say something, she decided to tell her cousin the story about her pet.

"When I was your age," she began, "I had a cat. We were still living in the lockkeeper's house across the river then. My pa gave him to me. Because the cat's fur was the color of snow, I named him Flake."

"Flake's a stupid name for a cat. Sounds more like a horse name."

Well, at least she is listening, Alex thought. The child's gaze never left the cat, but she didn't pull away when their fingers accidentally touched.

Encouraged by this, Alex continued. "Now that you mention it, Flake does sound like the name of a horse. But at the time it was a good name for a snow-white cat."

No other comment was made as Caro continued to stroke the feline and scratch her behind her ears. The cat's purr and the whisper of their combined breathing were the only sounds made on the porch, so when Caro surprised her with a question, Alex almost jumped.

"What happened to your cat?"

"Oh, he hopped a passing canal boat and took off for parts unknown."

"Canal boat?" Caro blasted her with a disbelieving stare. "Cats don't like water. I bet you're making this up."

Alex shook her head no.

"Can't say I blame him," Caro said. "I'd go with Rush if he would let me, but he won't. He said I had to stay with you and Aunt Stella."

Alex suspected as much. There were many times in the past week that she had heard her young cousin extolling the praises of the *Chuck-a-luck,* or more precisely, those of the man who owned the boat.

Caro had made it clear that her sentiments lay with the cat, so Alex didn't expect her next response. "You must have felt awful losing your cat."

Pleased, Alex answered, "Oh, I felt worse than awful. I felt downright miserable. I cried myself to sleep at night for weeks after he left. The summer of his departure, I'd look for Flake on every boat that passed our house. Then one day I saw him."

Caro's eyes got as big around as Dresden saucers when she looked up at her. "He came back?" she whispered.

Alex didn't want to give the child false hopes, but she did want to help her through this sad time in her life. She knew well the pain of losing a loved one. Even today, she still missed her father.

"You saw him? Where?" Caro asked.

"He was sitting on the prow of a passing boat. Like a figurehead he was, sitting as stiff and proud as a carved piece of wood. Our gazes locked for only a moment as the boat passed through the lock, but his look sent me a message."

"Really? What did it say?"

"It was as if he knew I missed him and he wanted me not

to worry about him or feel sad because he was gone. I always felt that if Flake could have told me, he would have said, 'Don't worry about me, I'm doing fine in my new life.' That day I knew I had to let go of him although I wanted to fetch him and bring him back. Sometimes we don't always get what we want, yet we must believe that everything happens for a reason.''

Caro was silent, as though she were pondering Alex's words. *Please don't start crying,* Alex thought, *or turn away. If you do, I'll be bawling with you.*

Caro didn't cry, and she didn't turn away. Instead, she asked, ''Were you still sad?''

''Yes, I was. My heart felt as though it would break when I thought about never seeing that cat again or holding him and stroking his snowy fur. I missed Flake, and still do to this day. But losing him helped me to realize that nothing in life is forever. Our lifetimes are filled with comings and goings. As hard as it is to lose something, or someone we love, we have to believe that the ache will lessen with time.''

Stealing a glance at her cousin, she saw tears forming in her blue eyes. Caro sniffed, then rubbed her nose across the sleeve of her dress. ''I had a cat once,'' she said. ''He went away, too. Do you think that someday my ache will go away?''

Alex wanted to say the right thing. She slipped her arm around Caro's shoulders and hugged her close. ''In time, sweetheart, the ache will dull. It won't go away completely, but it won't hurt as much as it did when it was fresh.''

''I know no cat can ever take Marmalade's place, but do you think I can keep this one, if no one wants her?''

''Of course there'll never be a cat that can take Marmalade's place in your heart, but I bet another cat could make a place of its own.'' She ruffled Caro's curls. ''The first thing we must do is find out who left her on our doorstep.''

''I hate to tell you ladies,'' a deep voice said, ''but that *her* you keep referring to happens to be a *he*.''

Alex and Caro had been so caught up in their conversation that they hadn't heard Rush approach. He stood opposite them on the walkway, his arms propped on the iron rail of the porch.

"I'm the culprit," he said, "who left *him* on your doorstep. I brought that tom for you, Caro, but your Aunt Stella and Alexandy have to approve of your keeping him."

"You brought this kitten to me, Rush?" Caro marveled. She lifted the ball of fur and kissed the cat's pink nose. Then she looked at Alex and asked, "Can I keep him?"

"How can I say no?" Alex asked, laughing. "Yes, my dear, you may keep him, but his care will be your responsibility."

"He's not exactly a kitten," Rush said. "I think he's close to a year old. But he's got a good motor, and he runs well."

"Motor?" Both Alex and Caro asked at the same time.

"Are you ladies deaf? I heard him purring a block away. That was how I found you."

"Oh, Rush, you're always so silly. You couldn't hear him purr that far away." Leaving Alex still sitting on the porch floor, Caro jumped up. Cradling the cat in her arms, she went to stand beside Rush. "Where did you get him? And did you really bring this kitten for me?"

"He wandered onto my boat when I was tied up for the night. The rascal wouldn't leave."

Caro and Alex exchanged surprised looks.

"And, yes, little one," he said, tugging on one of her ringlets. "I couldn't miss bringing my favorite girl a gift when I passed through town."

Caro buried her face in the animal's fur and looked at Rush over the yellow bundle in her arms. "Am I really your favorite girl?" she asked shyly. She looked at Rush, then at Alex, then back to Rush again. "We never did no spooning," she told him.

Alex almost smiled, but instead she kept her expression serious. She was as eager to hear his answer as she imagined Caro was. Let him suffer his own consequences—it served him right.

Rush's face turned beet red. "We most certainly did," he insisted. "Don't you remember how we stirred Alex's bread most of the night?"

"But Jamie, he said—"

"That whippersnapper wouldn't know a spoon from a fork, I'd wager." His dark eyes flashed with mischief when he stole a look at Alex. "I'm real sorry that everyone misunderstood my remark. I reckon I'll have to be more careful in the future with how I express myself."

Alex knew she'd received an apology and a promise that he'd watch his remarks. Her opinion of Rush Duncan rose a couple of notches, and she smiled at him. Caro began chattering like a magpie, so nothing more was needed to be said about the incident.

"You're right, Rush," Caro said. "I almost forgot how stupid Jamie Hamilton is. Oh, yeah, and I almost forgot, thanks for the cat. I'll take real good care of him, I promise. Now I've got to find him a bed."

"He's been sleeping in that creel," Rush said. "If he continues to grow like a weed, I expect he'll not be fitting in it much longer."

Alex watched him, thinking how nice he looked when he blushed. It wasn't often that a grown man blushed, especially one who kept company with the devil. He was more handsome than she remembered him being during his last visit, but that could be because of how he filled out his blue chambray shirt and the denim trousers that hugged his muscular body like a second skin.

Watching him made her heart beat a little faster and a warmth creep into her cheeks. Suddenly she became acutely aware of her own looks and found them lacking, with her faded and wrinkled dress and a hairdo more appropriate for Annie Oakley than a girl past her prime. Not only was she sitting like a brazen hussy on the floor of her porch, her long legs spread out like a spider's, but she was also suffering a tinge of Caro's infatuation with the man.

"I just hope," she said, aggravated with herself for having such thoughts, "that fish weren't sleeping in that wicker before it became a cat bed. If so, we'll have to give him a bath."

Caro buried her face in his fur and sniffed. "Naw, he doesn't stink. If he did, he could use some of our perfume. Now I'm gonna fix him a real bed and make it nice and soft." She turned to go inside.

Alex rose to her feet, smiling to herself at Caro's reference to *their* perfume.

"What are you going to name him?" Rush asked.

"How about Marmalade?" Alex suggested, shaking the dust from her skirt.

"No," Caro said, "I can't name him that. Remember, you said he can't take Marmalade's place." She looked at the cat then back at Alex with a thoughtful expression on her face. "Do you think he could be related to Flake?"

Alex arched her brows mischievously. "Anything is possible. And since he appears to be a canaller like Flake was, who can say?"

Caro pondered her statement and after a moment responded, "I think I'll call him Snow."

"Snow!" Rush exclaimed. "There's not a white hair on that orange cat's body. Why not call him Ginger, or Rusty, or even Sunflower?"

Caro passed Alex a conspiratorial look. "Snow," she said again, letting the word linger on her tongue. "Yep, I've decided. Snow it's gonna be."

Her decision made, Caro slipped through the front door, leaving Alex and Rush staring after her.

6

"SNOW?" RUSH ASKED. "DID I miss something?"

He rounded the opening and stepped onto the porch. Hooking his rump over the iron rail, he stretched his long legs out in front of him.

Standing only inches away, Alex noted the crispy newness of his blue denims compared to the limp oldness of her dress. Only minutes before, she had been considering doing her hair in a more appealing style, and for the first time in years, she was once again contemplating the condition of her clothes.

She suspected that her unaccustomed behavior was brought on by the man beside her. He looked more handsome than she remembered. The afternoon sun limned his brown hair like a halo—hair, she noticed, that had been trimmed into neatness since their encounter a week ago.

Rush waved his hand in front of her eyes. "Alexandy, are you hiding in there somewhere?"

His reference to her mooning brought her back to the present. "I-I once had a cat named Flake," she said, finally answering his first question. "I was telling Caro about him when you arrived."

His dark-brown eyes that today looked the color of bronze twinkled. "And what about this Flake?" He settled more comfortably on the iron rail and arched his brows as though he were amused. "Was Flake also the color of rust, or was he white as his name suggests?"

"Oh, he was as white as snow."

He continued to watch her, making her feel ridiculous for inspiring his ridicule.

She hoped he wouldn't ask her any more questions. Alex wasn't ready to share her story about her runaway cat with him, fearing that if she did she would also have to share her opinion that all boatmen were rootless.

"I heard Caro ask if you thought that Snow and Flake could be related."

"Yes, she did."

"I know she did. I'm asking you, Alex, why would she believe that Snow was related to a cat you must have owned years ago?"

"Because Flake hitched a ride on a canal boat as you said Snow did."

"No kidding?" Rush laughed.

It was a deep, masculine laugh that made his eyes crinkle at the corners, and the heavy brush of hair growing above his upper lip lift at the corners. She watched, fascinated as his cheeks dimpled on each side of his mouth, almost swallowing the edges of his mustache. *Dimples?* Before this moment, Alex hadn't noticed that he also had dimples to earmark his already-good looks.

"All I can say," Rush boasted, "is Flake must have been a good man."

She lifted her chin and met his prideful stare. "Not necessarily," she answered. "His nomadic life almost broke my heart."

"Is that a fact, now?" Rush's mustache straightened, changing into a thick hairy line that reminded Alex of a caterpillar. "Why, Alexandy, I'm learning things about you I never knew before."

"What?" she answered more abruptly than she intended. "That I have a heart?"

Alex didn't like the way Rush Duncan made her feel or the way he was looking at her now, or more precisely, the way he was trying to look inside her. She wasn't a ten-year-old like Caro whom he could charm with his good looks and his sweet-talking ways.

"I assure you, Mr. Duncan, I'm no longer a child whose heart can be broken by a rambler without roots."

His gaze raked over her. "You definitely aren't a child, Alexandy, but maybe you're worried that your *woman's* heart can be broken by a rambler without roots."

"Spare me," she scoffed. She was determined to show him how little concern she had for his remark.

"The way I see it," he said, "a man can have roots, although they might not be attached to the ground." He patted his chest above his heart. "The roots I'm speaking about are attached here, and they can grow very deep. I've always believed it's not where a man rests his head that makes him a permanent kind of fellow, but where he rests his heart."

"Really, Mr. Duncan, such philosophical thoughts from a boatman?"

Alex wondered how their conversation had gotten so personal. It had begun with a cat, and now they were talking about a relationship between a man and a woman.

He sucked in a sharp breath, and his eyes narrowed. "I take it you consider us canallers a rambling bunch incapable of philosophical thoughts."

"I didn't say that, or at least I didn't mean to imply it. I merely suggested that for the most part, canallers don't care about putting down roots."

"Maybe you're speaking of one canaller in particular, or possibly a boy from your past."

"I'm speaking of the boatmen I saw as the daughter of a lockkeeper. You do remember I grew up beside that canal?"

"I suppose your preacher man would better suit a lockkeeper's daughter."

"He's not my preacher man," she quickly responded, "so don't you start on me, too."

She had had enough of this conversation and she turned to go inside, but his fingers locked around her arm, stopping her. He stood so close that she could feel the heat of his body through his blue chambray shirt. To add to her annoyance, he smelled like spring grass mixed with a spicy scent reminiscent of the shaving lotion her father had worn.

His mouth curved into a mocking smile. "I think what you need, Alexandy, is to be kissed by a real man instead of some sissy preacher."

Her temper ignited. "I've never been kissed by that preacher, or any other man—" Too late she realized what she had said. She tried jerking free of his hold.

Alex had been kissed a few times in her lifetime, but none of those kisses had been worth remembering. Yet Rush Duncan was the last person with whom she wanted to share her uneventful past.

He pulled her closer until her shoulder rested in the middle of his chest. She wasn't certain if the thudding she felt came from his heart or her own.

"It's hard for me to believe," Rush said, "that the preacher never kissed you, since I understand he's been courting you for over a year. But I'd swear I heard you say that not only had the preacher failed in his manly duties, but also no other man has had the pleasure of your lips. I think, Alexandy, it's high time you received your first kiss, and I know I'm man enough to deliver it."

Her heart fluttered wildly in her chest. "Don't be ridiculous." Again she tried to yank free. "More importantly, don't you dare kiss me, Rush Duncan."

"Now, Alexandy, don't you remember how all that daring got you in trouble years ago? If you can't remember, I'll refresh your memory. Back then, as now, I took exception to challenges made by pretty girls with long golden braids hanging halfway down their back. Braids, I recall, that always ended up in inkwells, if my memory serves me right."

His face was mere inches from hers, his warm breath brushed fire against her forehead. "Why, Alexandy," he said, "what I really think is that you're afraid you might enjoy being kissed by the likes of me."

"I'd enjoy kissing a snake more."

She pushed against him with her free hand, giving him an advantage she hadn't anticipated. Instead of burying her shoulder in his chest, they now stood front to front, and his other arm encircled her, drawing her closer.

His gaze fell on her mouth. "I can arrange that, too, if it suits you, but I'll—"

"What would suit me is if you would unhand me now. In case you haven't noticed, we're standing beside a busy thoroughfare. It's not enough that you probably ruined my good name with your insinuations among the ladies of the quilting circle earlier, but now you're trying to make me look like a loose woman in front of the whole town."

She tried to kick him, but he dodged the movement with what she believed was practiced skill.

"Please let me go," she begged.

"I like to hear a lady beg." He smiled wickedly and began to lower his mouth toward hers.

Dropping her head, she dodged the inviting lips and glanced sideways. "I believe that is my mother coming toward us."

"Your mother?"

For a moment Rush looked like a kid who was caught with his hand in the candy jar, but he didn't release her. Instead, he twirled around as smooth as a dancing instructor until he faced in the direction she had indicated.

"Why, sugar, I do believe you're right. It is your lovely mother."

His smile changed from mischievous to well behaved, confirming what Alex already knew—a man like him was not to be trusted. She was glad to hear her mother approaching, especially when he dropped his arm from her waist. Yet she wasn't free, because he insisted on holding her hand.

"Mrs. Paine," he said, "our Alex seems to have gotten a hair in her eye. I suppose it came from that cat I brought Caro. I've been trying my darndest to blow it away, but so far I've had no success."

Her eye wasn't exactly where she had the hair, but some things were best left unsaid.

"Well, by all means, Mr. Duncan," Stella said, "don't stop on my account. There is nothing as irritating as having a lash in your eye, is there now, daughter?" She cast Alex an impartial glance before heading toward the doorway. "I take it you found Caro?"

"We did," they both responded.

"How thoughtful of you, Mr. Duncan, to have brought my niece a gift. I'm assuming the cat helped to cure whatever ailed her back there at Leona's. Alexandria, did she say why she ran away?"

Alex turned to face her mother, hoping Rush would release her hand. When he didn't, she moved so that their hands were hidden behind her back. "Maybe it was the excitement of seeing Rush again. She is so attached to him, although I can't understand the attraction."

Her mother shot her a warning look, then smiled up at Rush. "You know my niece adores you, Mr. Duncan, but then, that is not hard to understand now, is it?" She looked at Alex. "I'm assuming Alexandria showed her appreciation by inviting you to stay for supper."

Alex had finally worked her fingers free, and she clawed his hand with her nails. He flinched, but before she could escape, he managed to secure all of her hand in another stranglehold.

"Alexandria," her mother insisted, "you did invite him, didn't you?"

"Mother, I—"

"Yes, ma'am, she did. As I told her earlier, I'd be delighted to join you lovely ladies for dinner. It's not often we canallers get to enjoy a dinner with roots."

"Roots?" Mrs. Paine asked, looking puzzled. Then she smiled. "Oh! I almost forgot about the turnips. I'm so glad she told you what we were having for supper. Not everyone likes turnips, you know, but I fancy no one can cook them like Alexandria. You're in for a real treat, young man." She turned toward the door, then hesitated. "Did you say Caro was inside?"

"Yes, ma'am," Rush answered. "After Alex got the hair stuck in her eye, Caro went inside to find the cat a bed."

"Well, then, if you two will excuse me, I'll go see how Caro is faring."

The moment her mother disappeared through the door, Alex

managed to jerk her hand free. She backed away from him.

"Rush Duncan, you haven't changed one iota, have you? You're still as insufferable today as you were years ago. If it weren't for Caro and her infatuation with you, I'd forbid you ever to set foot in this house again."

"Is that a fact, now? I hope you realize that even if you tossed me out on my ear, I'd be back. Us bad pennies have a way of showing up again and again."

"Indeed."

"So, my dear," he said, examining his hand that had a string of scratches across its back, "what time is dinner? I have a few errands to run before I can sample your wonderful turnips." He dropped his injured hand to his side. "I can't remember the last time I partook of a home-cooked meal."

"I can," she answered sarcastically. "It was a week ago."

"Oh, yes, now I remember. The night we baked bed—bread."

His reminder of her earlier slip of the tongue made Alex blush. If she didn't distance herself from him soon, she might just slip her balled fist into his handsome mouth. But his reminder caused her to remember that he needed to be told about Caro's feelings so as not to cause her any more undo pain.

"Mr. Duncan, I don't know if you're aware or not, but Caro is hopelessly infatuated. I think she fancies herself in love with you. You probably don't realize that it was your earlier remark about spooning—"

"You mean Jamie Hamilton's remark," he corrected.

"Whoever said it, and I think you and I both know who really was responsible, is not important. What is important, though, is that Caro thought you and I had been kissing, and that was why she ran away this afternoon."

His mouth twitched with pleasure. "I'm flattered that one of you ladies finds me dashingly attractive and lovable."

"I'm sure it's only her age," she continued, determined to ignore his jest, "and her circumstances. You've been very kind to her and although you and I aren't exactly compatible, I'm glad that the two of you are."

His expression was no longer full of deviltry, and she felt uncomfortable beneath his serious stare. "Caro, as my mother said, adores you, and she needs all the love she can get from all of us. So if you would, when we are all together, please don't pretend you have an interest in me. When you do, her resentment toward me grows. I do so want us to be friends.''

He was quiet for a moment, studying her face. Even without his teasing smile, his good looks almost took her breath away.

After a moment, he spoke. ''I was wrong the other day when I accused you of not wanting her. You do want her. I could see that when I came upon the two of you earlier, sitting on the floor of the porch. If it will make you rest easier, I give you my word that I'll be on my best behavior at dinner. I'll also try my best not to do or say anything to make her think that you and I are anything but old friends.''

She was so surprised by his remark that she almost kissed him. ''Why, thank you, Rush—Mr. Duncan. You don't know how much I'd appreciate your help in this matter.''

He looked uncomfortable when she praised him. His discomfort seemed out of character for a man who had toyed with her so unmercifully earlier. He started to leave, then stopped, glancing at his hand. ''I owe you for this, Alexandy.'' His teasing manner had returned. ''Although I want it understood that it doesn't mean that when Caro's not around I won't try to finish what I started earlier.''

''You wouldn't, you can't,'' Alex protested. ''I thought—''

''I do so want us to be friends.''

She couldn't believe his audacity. He was using her own words against her. ''You—you're incorrigible,'' she insisted.

''I am at that, sugar. And by the way, I expect you to call me Rush instead of Mr. Duncan. Such an address is too formal for the likes of me.''

''I won't—''

''Oh, you will, Alexandy, if you want me to be on my best behavior in front of your cousin.'' Again he started to leave, but stopped. ''You never told me what time to come for dinner.''

Alex felt like telling him the twenty-fifth hour, but decided that any attempt to dissuade him from accepting her mother's invitation was impossible. ''Seven,'' she said reluctantly.

"Seven it will be. I'm never late for a romantic encounter with a beautiful woman."

"Romantic encounter!" *Did the man have no shame?*

"Would you prefer I call our next rendezvous either heroic, adventurous, mysterious, or idealized?"

"I'd call it detestable," she countered.

He left her then. As he walked toward Shenandoah Street, Alex heard the despicable man laughing.

∽

IT WAS DIM AND cool when Rush walked through the familiar doors of Samson's Tavern on Potomac Street. He allowed the walls to embrace him, hoping that their hold on him would erase the memory of a few moments earlier when he'd held Alexandria Paine in his arms.

The pain Rush now suffered wasn't from the proximity of the woman, but the memory of how good it felt to hold her. He had instigated the embrace to torment Alexandy, but instead he tormented himself. He had been suffering with unrequited lust since the moment he had left her on her doorstep.

"Sammy," he called, on seeing the place empty and believing his friend was in the storeroom. When there was no response, Rush walked across the taproom and bellied up to the bar to wait for Samson's return.

He grabbed a fist full of boiled peanuts from a basket, then swiveled around on the stool and propped his elbows on the edge of the bar's rosin-coated surface. Examining the room, Rush noted the place hadn't changed much throughout the years. It looked the same and still smelled of stale beer, tobacco, and sweat.

Samson's had never been a fancy establishment; it remained rustic and unadorned. It was a saloon a man could visit on his way home from work, or whenever the need struck him. Overalls and boots were as much a part of the standard of dress as were suits and spats.

Boatmen, factory workers, and businessmen sat elbow to elbow around marred oak tables scattered haphazardly across floors covered with peanut shells. Those same men had spit, aimed, and missed the various-placed spittoons. This was a man's domain—no women allowed. There were no barmaids and no paintings of naked maidens hanging behind the bar unless the big bass that Samson had caught and had mounted on a plaque was a female. Maybe, Rush thought, that was why all manner of men gravitated to the place—inside these walls they could simply be male.

The back door of the building banged shut. A man's voice broke out in song, making Rush turn toward the storeroom. He smiled as he recognized both the voice and the tune being sung offkey from behind the petitioned wall.

As the swinging doors swung open, Rush grinned at the burly man who pushed through the opening with a keg riding on his beefy shoulder. A face, much in need of a shave, glanced in Rush's direction. On recognizing him, the words of the song ceased, and the barkeep's mouth broke into a wide grin.

"Well, gol dern," Samson said, hoisting the keg to the rack behind the bar as though it weighed no more than a lady's purse. "I do believe the Bulrush has returned." Samson winked at him, and Rush let the feeling of being home wash over him.

He knew why the older man called him Bulrush; it was because he was known to be bullheaded. Yet every time he heard the pet name, Rush was reminded of the biblical Moses in the bulrushes who had been adopted by the Pharaoh's daughter. In Rush's mind, his own circumstances were not unlike that of the baby's. After his mother's death, Samson had taken him and had saved his life.

"I heard you was in town," Samson said, "and I've been expecting a visit all afternoon." He moved to stand in front of Rush, pulled out a glass from beneath the bar, and plopped it on the counter. "Even made a special trip to the grocery so I could satisfy your thirst." Rush watched as Samson poured the thick creamy liquid into the glass.

"Buttermilk. My favorite. You're too good to me, Samson," he said. Lifting the glass, he brought it to his lips and drank deeply, emptying the contents.

Samson's wide grin grew even wider. "There's more, my

boy," he said, "plenty where that came from."

Rush returned the empty glass to the bar and rubbed his belly. "Right now, I couldn't hold another drop, but I'll take you up on that refill later. Now tell me," he asked, "who told you I was here?"

"Why, my backyard neighbor, of course."

"Backyard neighbor?"

That could only be the Paines, Rush thought. Perhaps he had been mistaken in believing that Alex hadn't warmed to his homecoming if she had already passed on the news of his arrival to Samson. He preened inwardly like a peacock until his old friend's next words took the quills right out of his feathers.

"That little Caro, she sure does believe that you control the sun and moon."

"Caro?" Rush hoped his face didn't show his disappointment on learning the identity of his admirer, although he suspected that if anyone would recognize it, his old friend Samson would. Hoping to camouflage the emotion, Rush made a show of licking the remnants of milk from his lips before he answered, "She's pretty special to me, too."

"Is that a fact, now?" Samson asked.

It suddenly hit Rush where he'd picked up the expression that he'd used on Alexandy earlier. Shucks, he reckoned he'd used those same words most of his life. Without even knowing it, Samson had been more of an influence in the shaping of Rush's personality than either of the two men suspected.

"It ain't that milk that's soured your expression, now is it, son?" Samson's eyes drilled into him as he began swabbing the bar.

"Buttermilk can be pretty sour," Rush countered.

"Not nearly so much as disappointment. Especially if a certain someone doesn't fulfill our hopes."

"You know what I think, old man? I think you sampled the contents of that keg before you brought it in here, and it pickled your brain."

"It ain't my brain that's pickled or me that's in a pickle over a woman. You know, son, even when you were a lad, that little Paine gal had you tied up in knots. Can't say I don't understand why. Back then she was a pretty little thing, and she got prettier as she went.''

Rush almost blushed. ''All I did was come in here for a visit, and what do I get but a lesson of the heart. What do you say we drop this conversation and begin again with a subject we both know something about?''

''I don't mean to preach, but Alexandria Paine is a special gal. If I was a young man in the market for a mate, I'd have snatched her up years ago.''

''You, Samson, of all people ought to know that a mate is the last thing I'm looking for.'' A bitterness that Rush thought he'd buried years ago surfaced like a casket in a flood. ''Love, my good friend, happens only in books. Who better than me knows I'm living proof of such a nonexistent emotion? I'll never give my heart to a woman or accept a woman's for safekeeping. The risk is too great.''

Samson listened, but his gaze never wavered from Rush's.

''One long night and a short good-bye is more to my liking. Now, I'll have another glass of that milk to settle my stomach, and just maybe we can get down to some serious jawing.''

''Lonely is what you are, in spite of your denials. Take it from a man who knows. Waking up every morning to stare at an empty pillow is not a life sentence I'd wish for you. But I can see, Mr. Bulrush, that I can talk until I'm blue in the face, and none of my wisdom is gonna sway you one way or the other. You're as dern bullheaded as you ever were.''

Samson refilled the glass, and Rush picked it up. ''I'll drink to that, old man, and I sure as hell won't deny it.'' He tilted his head back and drank down several gulps. ''Now that the topic is settled, why don't you tell me how you've been besides growing grumpier every day?''

Samson looked affronted. ''Grumpy? You still ain't too old for me to tan your hide, and in case you have doubts, I'm not too old to do it.''

Although Rush was a muscular six-foot plus, if push came to shove, he knew he would be the loser. Although Samson was shorter than Rush, his friend was built like a bull. With a cautionary lift of his hand, he said, ''Neither of us is too old. Heck, Samson, I'm not hankering to put your strength to a test or to argue with you.''

"Good, 'cause I ain't looking to argue either, but I admit I'm glad to see you show respect for your elders. In answer to your question about my health, I'm fine. Just dandy, thank you.'' He wiped the cloth across the surface of the bar again and lifted his bushy brows. ''And curious,'' he added.

Uh-oh, another lecture, Rush thought. ''Curious?'' he asked, ''About what?''

"How did a seafaring fellow like yourself come by Stella Paine's niece?''

Samson looked at him long and hard, as though he expected a confession of guilt.

"It's not what you're thinking, I assure you. I never knew Caro's mother, never even knew Mrs. Paine had a sister until the day my old captain friend met me in Georgetown and asked me to deliver the child to the Paines in Harpers Ferry.''

Samson still skewered him with his gaze.

"Heck, the child came from Nebraska. The kind of ship I sailed on wasn't a prairie schooner. I swear to you, Caro is not my child.'' He shuddered, thinking of such a possibility. "Jesus, Samson, you should know that I'll not sow that kind of seed unless I'm sure I'm ready to be there for the harvest.''

"Stranger things have happened to lads who run away to the sea.''

"If what you're suggesting were true, you realize, don't you, that I would have been seventeen years old? Judging from what little I know about Stella Paine's runaway sister, I'm assuming the two sisters must have been close in age. Maybe close to my mother's age. Besides, I never fancied bedding older women.''

"Shouldn't be bedding any decent woman, old or otherwise, unless you're ready to make a commitment.''

"I assure you, my dear friend, I will heed your warning. Alexandria Paine's virginity is safe with me, if that's what you're hinting at.'' How had they gotten on such a conversation, Rush wondered? ''Besides, Miss Paine made it very clear that she wants nothing to do with a fellow who doesn't even know his own father.''

"She could do worse, you know." Samson's statement had an emotional resonance that lingered between them.

"She could do a hell of a lot better, too. Like that preacher man who fancies her." Rush picked up the pitcher of buttermilk and poured himself another glass.

"Heard tell the feeling ain't mutual," Samson informed him as he began to wipe the rims of nearby glasses with a cloth. "There's something you got to do."

"What's that?"

"You got to find out what happened to Caro's mother when she left here."

"Me?" His question went unanswered, and he wasn't given a chance to say more.

"I spoke briefly to Stella after your visit last week. The same visit that I didn't know you had made until after you were gone."

When Rush tried to protest, Samson waved aside his objection and kept speaking. "She says Caro won't talk about her past. Stella Paine is a good woman who deserves to know about her baby sister. I think not knowing can almost drive a person mad. You should understand that."

Samson was referring to the identity of Rush's father. It was the same discussion that he and the older man had had on numerous occasions and never agreed upon. Rush didn't care who his father was.

"Sometimes, Sammy, it's best not to turn over rocks because of what might be sleeping under them."

"That might be the truth, son, or again it may not. But in this case, I think you should finish what you started."

"What *I* started?" Rush ran his fingers through his hair. "In case you aren't aware of it, I was merely the delivery man."

"The delivery man ought to know what it is he's delivering. That captain friend of yours is in a perfect position to make the proper inquiries. He could hire a detective in New Orleans when he makes that port again. Dern it, I know Stella would appreciate any little thing the two of you might find out."

"Maybe in time Caro will tell her what she wants to know," Rush said, replacing the empty glass on the counter.

"Her niece has only been with them for a week."

Samson went on as though Rush hadn't spoken.

"I've got some money saved, enough for whatever it takes to make inquiries. You send a letter to the captain, or better yet, meet him in Georgetown when he returns. I'd write the letter myself, but you know I ain't all that good at writing letters. But I want to do this for Stella. I need your help."

Rush had never seen his friend so determined. Of course, he would do whatever Samson wanted. The old man had never asked him for anything in all the years he had known him, and this was the one way he could repay him.

Samson left him for the cash register. Once there, he opened it and pulled out several bills from beneath the tray. When he joined Rush again, he thrust the money at him. "Here, take this. There is more where it came from."

"I don't want your money, Samson. I'm not exactly a pauper, you know."

"You ain't rich neither," Samson accused. "You're probably a hundred dollars poorer, if that money you gave the Paines is any indication."

"Money? How did you know about that?"

"I've friends in high places." He looked at Rush knowingly. "No ship's crew took up any collection, neither."

Rush looked away. He couldn't lie to Samson. "They needed that money worse than I do."

"As I said before, you ain't rich." He shoved the bills back toward Rush.

"I'll make a few inquiries," Rush agreed. "I guess there are detectives for such things."

"And you probably won't be rich until I die."

"Die? Now what kind of fool talk is that? First of all, you're too dang mean to die, and secondly, I never knew you were sitting on a gold mine."

"Ain't exactly a gold mine, but I've been saving it for my grandchildren."

"Your grandchildren? You don't have any—"

Rush stopped in mid-sentence. The two men looked at each other across the voluminous quiet. There wasn't a sound inside the saloon but that of the creaking timbers, and perhaps the loud thumping of Rush's heart as the organ threw itself against his ribs.

Rush loved Samson like a father. In fact, he was the only man in Rush's life who deserved such a claim, if indeed Rush was worth the merit. It was apparent the older man also thought of him as his son, but before today he had never heard him vocalize the sentiment.

Rush leaned on the bar and swirled the glass between his hands. If he didn't leave soon, the lump that had formed inside his chest was going to cut off his breathing. He pushed away from the bar, trying for nonchalance. "I'll see what I can do, old man," he said.

His friend's face brightened with a grin. "With getting me some grandchildren?" he asked, the tease back in his voice, "or looking into hiring a detective?"

The old Samson had returned. Rush knew better how to deal with him and asked, "Which do you think?" He moved toward the entrance to the saloon.

"Enjoy your dinner," Samson called.

"My dinner?"

"I understand you're eating with the Paines."

"Is there anything you don't know?"

"Not much," Samson responded with a smug look on his face. "Just remember to mind your manners. If you do, then you might be lucky enough to charm Miss Alexandria as you have charmed the other two ladies of the Paine household. More importantly, I just might get my wish."

"As some famous someone said whose name I can't recall," Rush said over his shoulder, " 'Wishing,' my old friend, is 'the constant hectic of the fool.' "

7

"MOTHER, CALM YOURSELF," ALEX said, watching her mother scurry around the kitchen like an excited mouse.

Stella smoothed out the wrinkles of the damask tablecloth she had placed on the worn wooden table and began to fold the matching napkins into triangles. "It's not every day that a fine young man like Mr. Duncan joins us for dinner."

The same fine young man who resorted to blackmailing me. "He was just here last week," Alex reminded, "but it seems I'm the only one who remembers his visit." Having washed and pared the turnips, she dropped them into the pot, then began making the buttermilk biscuits. "I swannie, you act as though we were entertaining President Harrison himself."

Alex eyed the table skeptically. She couldn't recall the last time her mother had used the few nice linens they still owned. Usually the tablecloth and napkins stayed packed away in the chest upstairs, taken out only for special occasions such as holidays. Next, her mother would be setting out their good dishes and glasses.

"He'll think we're putting on airs," Alex warned her, looking at the fine cloth that appeared out of place in the simple kitchen.

With one hand on her hip, Stella stepped away from the

table to eye her handiwork. "It's at times like this that I wish we still had a dining room. There is no way one can feel refined eating in the kitchen."

"I assure you, Mother, Mr. Duncan wouldn't know refined if it introduced itself to him."

Alex sprinkled flour across the worktable, lifted the ball of dough from the bowl, and slapped it down on the floured surface. She punched the pastry down a few times, imagining it was Mr. Duncan's handsome face, before she began flattening it with the rolling pin. *Not Mr. Duncan. Rush.* She would have to remember to call him that. It was blackmail the blackguard had resorted to, and Alex was at his mercy.

"Daughter, do you have to be so contrary? Although you may not be looking forward to sharing dinner with our guest, there are some of us who are."

Two of you, Alex repeated in her mind.

Stella Paine beat out a rhythm on her lip with her finger. "Do you think I should use our good dishes? They would look so much nicer than this old crockery with its faded design."

"The old crockery is fine, Mother. Mr. Duncan probably eats off tin plates."

Caro appeared at the open back door. "Naw, he doesn't," she said, stepping inside with the orange cat cradled in her arms. "He eats from shiny white plates that reflect your face when you look into them."

Alex exchanged a curious look with her mother. "I suppose his water glasses are made of the finest crystal, too."

"They are," Caro confirmed. "When you hit them with a fork, they ping like a bell."

"Is that a fact, now?" her mother asked.

Instead of answering, Caro held Snow up as high as her arms would stretch and twirled around in a circle.

"Caro," Stella cautioned, "get that cat from over the table." She swished at an invisible hair and said to Alex, "Now I'm sure these old dishes won't do."

"The dishes will be fine, Mother."

Stella looked perplexed as Caro settled on the stool in the corner of the room, cuddling the cat to her chest. Caro's voice took on a dreamy, faraway sound as she continued with her tale.

"Flowers, too—we always had flowers. We would stick them in a white milk jug and place it in the middle of the table. The different-colored blossoms reflected in the jug's surface and looked as pretty as a rainbow."

"Sounds to me like Mr. Duncan set a fancy table aboard his boat. Alexandria, the man has taste."

"We all have senses, Mother."

Stella Paine ignored her remark. "What kind of flowers, Caro? Seems that they would be in short supply along the towpath."

Alex watched her cousin. She appeared miles away; then, realizing the question had been directed at her, she finally answered. "Flowers? Uh, all kinds."

A blush crept into Caro's cheeks, and she looked uneasy. Slipping from the stool, she bolted toward the stairs, stopping only when her aunt asked, "Wouldn't you like to help me set the table?"

Setting the table, Alex thought, looked as though it was the last thing Caro wished to do.

"Do you mind, Aunt Stella, if I go upstairs first and put Snow to bed? He's still not used to his new home, and I don't want him running out the door and getting lost."

Stella smiled. "Of course not, child. I don't know what I was thinking. You tend to the cat, and I'll tend to the table. After all, it's not every day that a girl receives a brand-new kitten."

"Thanks, Aunt Stella. I figured you'd understand. I promise I'll help you tomorrow."

"Don't forget to straighten yourself up before dinner." Stella had gone back to studying the table. "Wash your hands as well."

"Yes, ma'am, I will. I want to look my best for Rush."

Beneath her breath, Stella mumbled, "Alexandria should take such an interest in her appearance." Caro tromped up the stairs. When she was out of earshot, Stella said, "She's such a sweet child."

They were alone in the kitchen. "Yes, she is a sweet child.

I don't know if you've noticed, but she is infatuated with Rush Duncan.''

"Caro?" Her mother looked at her in surprise. "She's but a child.''

"A child who has a bad case of puppy love. I'm sure that is why she resents me. She sees me as a threat.''

"Resents you? Alexandria, you aren't serious? She sees you as a threat?'' The older woman let out a long, audible sigh.

"Mother, listen to me. I do so want Caro and I to become friends, but if she thinks for a moment that I'm interested in Rush Duncan, she will shut me out. I don't want that to happen.''

Stella pressed her hands against her bosom. "Certainly you don't think I'd say anything to her. Heaven knows that nothing would make me happier than for you to become interested in some nice young man, but I'd never suggest to Caro that there was anything going on between you and Mr. Duncan, especially if you think it would upset her.''

Alex picked up a glass and used it to cut circles in the flattened dough. "I assure you there is nothing going on between us, but you should know that Mr. Duncan's remark about us spooning was the reason Caro left Leona Whitley's house in such a hurry.''

"It was young Jamie," Stella replied, "who said spooning meant kissing, not Mr. Duncan. After your departure, he acted very much the gentleman, explaining to everyone that it was all of us making bread until the wee hours of the morning. I daresay, I do believe our friends enjoyed his earlier version about bread-making more so than his latter one.'' Her brow furrowed. "Isn't there anything about him, Alexandria, that makes your blood ripple?''

"Mother, please. We're talking about Caro's feelings, not mine.'' Alex twirled toward the stove, fearing that if her mother looked long and hard at her, she would be privy to information Alex was trying to deny, not only to herself, but also to everyone else. What Rush Duncan did to her blood was less like a gentle ripple and more a breaker crashing against the shore.

"Now where is that biscuit pan?'' she mumbled, bending

down to search the lower shelf, her intention being to distract. After her heartbeat had returned to normal, Alex stood and carried the pan back to the worktable. She began to peel the excess dough from around the biscuits.

Her mother left the dinner table and came to stand beside her. "I hope you intend to freshen up a bit before dinner." She smoothed Alex's hair back from her face as she had done when Alex was a child. "You're a lovely girl, both inside and out, and you have so much to offer a man."

Alex knew her mother meant well. She only wanted Alex to enjoy the same happiness that she herself had enjoyed being married to Alex's father.

"If it will make you feel better, Mother, I will freshen up before Mr. Duncan arrives, but please remember that he is not coming to see me. He is coming to see Caro."

"All right, dear, and I'll keep my mouth closed. Now if you don't mind, I'll go upstairs and attend to my own toilette."

"Mother, there is something else," Alex said, before she got to the stairs. "I don't know about you, but I felt that when Caro was describing dinner, she wasn't referring to the meals she had eaten aboard Mr. Duncan's boat."

"Alexandria, you are so down on that poor man. Is it so hard for you to believe that he might eat on shiny white plates instead of leaves, as you would have us believe?"

"I never said he ate on leaves, but now that—"

"Frankly, my dear, I think the picture the child painted sounds very romantic. Our own table could use some of Mr. Duncan's creativity." This said, she continued toward the stairs. "Is there anything else you wish to discuss before I leave you?"

"No, Mother, I think we've covered everything. You run on and freshen up. When I'm finished here, I'll follow you."

Alone in the kitchen, Alex thought back over Caro's description of dinner aboard the canal boat. Her mother might believe her niece was referring to meals that she had shared with Rush, but Alex didn't believe that scenario for a moment.

China plates, crystal glasses, and flowers? She could better visualize leaves.

What she did believe, though, was that Caro had been describing mealtime with her family back home in Nebraska. And to prove this truth, Alex planned to ask Mr. Duncan about it before he left them tonight.

∽

AT 7:00 SHARP THERE was a loud rap on the front door. Alex started at the sound.

"I'll get it," her mother called, bustling from the kitchen. "I can't imagine why Caro isn't down here to greet Mr. Duncan, but I guess Snow has her occupied elsewhere."

Alex gave the mashed potatoes one last stir. If nothing else, she would give the man credit for being punctual. Not yet ready to face him after this afternoon's debacle, she spun toward the stove and began fussing over the fried chicken.

Her plain supper of turnips and cornbread had turned into a much bigger spread after Rush accepted her mother's invitation to dine. It was apparent that the extra food and its preparation did not matter to her mother, and truthfully Alex couldn't begrudge serving the canaller a home-cooked meal. The money had amply improved their larder. Alex swore to herself that she would remember this good fortune and not allow the man to get beneath her skin.

From the front door she heard her mother's soft laughter, then his much deeper version. She felt an odd stirring of excitement when Rush said something in a husky voice she couldn't quite catch, but then her mother's words chased away the almost pleasant feeling. "I hope you don't mind, Mr. Duncan, but I don't have a white milk jug for this bouquet. I'll find something, though, to do their beauty justice."

He brought flowers, Alex thought.

"A mason jar would be fine, Mrs. Paine."

They entered the kitchen. "Look, Alexandria," Stella said, "Mr. Duncan has brought us flowers. Won't they look nice on our table?"

"They aren't all that special," Rush said, his voice sounding wobbly, as though he were ill-at-ease. "Most folks would call them weeds, but I've become taken by the many wildflowers that bloom along the towpath. I picked these this afternoon when I returned to my boat.''

Stella answered, ''I'm just so amazed by all the different varieties.''

''They won't last as long as yard flowers, but I thought you ladies might enjoy them.''

Wildflowers! A nervous flutter tickled the inside of Alex's chest. What other tricks did the rascal have up his sleeve? Good manners dictated that she look at him and acknowledge his gift, so she turned.

Facing him, her tongue almost tripped on her teeth. ''Good evening, Mr. Duncan.''

Not only had the man beguiled her mother with the flowers, but his appearance was also having the same effect on Alex. Gone were the chambray shirt and denim trousers that he had worn earlier, and in their place a soft, white, cotton shirt and buff-colored pants that fit his muscular body to perfection.

His dark brown hair, tied back at the nape with a piece of rawhide, still held a trace of dampness from a recent washing. In Alex's opinion, the style was both flattering and fitting. He looked devastatingly handsome and very much like a river pirate.

The rich timbre of his voice cut through her thinking. ''Evening to you, Miss Paine.'' Her mother, with her nose buried in the bouquet, didn't see the scoundrel's wink. ''I hope you ladies will do me the honor of dropping all this formality. We've known each other long enough to be on a first-name basis. I'd be mighty pleased if y'all would call me Rush.''

Lifting her face from the flowers, Stella smiled. ''That's a lovely idea. Especially since I suspect we'll be seeing a lot of you in the future. Call me Stella, and you may call my daughter Alexandria . . . I'm sorry, what is that name I've heard you call my daughter?''

''Mother, please. . . .'' Alex felt her face grow warm. Sometimes her mother was as bad as Leona Whitley.

''Alexandy,'' Rush responded with his devil-may-care smile. ''I called her that back when we were no more than sprouts.''

''Then I'm sure Alexandria will be delighted to have you

call her that now. Won't you, dear?'' Not waiting for an answer, she continued. ''If the two of you will excuse me, I'm going to run upstairs and get a vase for these flowers and see where that niece of mine is.''

Rush's earlier threat to finish their interrupted kiss popped into Alex's mind, and she tried to keep her mother from leaving. ''I'll get the vase and check on—''

''No, dear, I'll do it. You tend to the chicken and keep Rush entertained.'' Her mother motioned him toward the kitchen chairs. ''Have a seat if you don't feel like standing. I won't be gone long.''

She started toward the stairs, then stopped. ''Rush, you won't mind holding these, will you?'' She thrust the bouquet into his hands. ''I hate to put them down and have them get crushed.''

Saved by the flowers, Alex thought. At least he couldn't attempt to hold her as long as he was holding the flowers.

Alex couldn't help but smile at the picture he made with the bouquet clutched against his chest—a boy in a man's body. She wouldn't allow her thoughts to linger long on that picture for what it did to her inner calm.

He stared at her. After this afternoon, she didn't trust him as far as she could toss him, and she didn't appreciate being scrutinized like a piece of meat hanging on a hook. ''The wildflowers are nice,'' she said, hoping to distract him.

He winked and grinned. ''I enjoy wild things.''

The cad. Next he'd be telling her he liked his women wild and his whiskey strong.

Hoping to beat him at his own game, she responded, ''I'm not surprised. I never would have believed that wallflowers—I mean, wildflowers—would be to your liking.''

He laughed, a deep, throaty laugh that formed beneath his muscled chest and worked its way up through his tan throat, before splitting his perfectly shaped lips into a heart-stopping grin. He captured her with his eyes. ''Why not, Alexandy, I like you, don't I?''

''I beg your pardon. I'm not a wallflower, Mr. Duncan.''

''That's Rush to you, sugar.''

Not trusting herself to respond, she swung away from him,

showing him her back. With a fork she stabbed at the chicken with more gusto than was called for. *A wallflower, indeed.*

She didn't know that he had rounded the table until she felt him behind her. He wasn't aware of the dangerous position he was in, considering the pronged weapon she held in her hand. In her present mood, she would just as soon use it on him as the chicken, but she didn't want him to bleed all over the kitchen floor.

"Darling, I'm funning with you," he said. His warm breath stirred a loose hair at her nape.

The hair's sudden movement tickled, sending shivers down her spine. Alex slapped at the errant tress.

"Believe me, sugar, there is nothing remotely wallflowerish about you. If anything, Alexandy, I'd have to compare you to a perfect rose."

"A rose?" Rolling her eyes heavenward and brandishing the fork, she turned. "Now I know you do like your whiskey strong."

He looked puzzled. "Heck, most of the time I don't even like whiskey. I'd much rather have a cool glass of buttermilk."

"Humph! Now I've heard everything. I'm sure the only butter that silver tongue of yours comes in contact with is melted before you even get a chance to taste it."

"Why, Alexandy," he said, holding the bouquet of wildflowers against his heart, "it bereaves me to learn that you hold me in such low regard."

She muscled around him. "I hate to shatter your ego, but I don't hold you at all." Tossing the fork to the table, she picked up the biscuit pan and stomped to the stove. She opened the oven door and shoved the pan inside. This done, she faced him again.

He beamed her a tooth-powder smile. "You haven't held me at all, sugar, but I'd wager my last dollar before we're finished that you'll be hard-pressed to turn this silver-tongued devil loose."

"Over my dead body."

"If you like the prone position, I probably could accommodate—"

"I found her," her mother interrupted. They both turned

toward the stairs where Stella stood with one hand resting on Caro's shoulder—Caro stood in front of her on the next step.

"There you are, Miss Caro," Rush said, leaving Alex and walking toward the stairway. He stopped below them, and his next words dripped with charm. "Here I thought you had stood me up for that furry rascal, Snow."

He is as slippery as muck, Alex thought, watching the transformation from debaucher to gentleman before her very eyes.

"My, my, you do look like an angel," Rush told Caro, "and I love your new coiffure."

Caro blushed and looked at her shoes.

It appeared that her young cousin had taken extra care with her hair tonight. Most likely Stella had braided the dark curls into one long French braid not unlike the style Alex usually wore. This new do would also explain her cousin's lengthy absence.

Alex pressed a hand to her own hair. Tonight, because of her mother's insistence that she freshen up before Rush's arrival, Alex had brushed and twisted her straight hair into a fashionable knot at the back of her head. Now she regretted that action. Already the pins were working loose from the thick coil, and she expected that before dinner was over, her hair would be straggling down her back like a brazen hussy's.

"Here," Stella suggested to her niece, "why don't you put Rush's flowers in water so we can put them on the table."

Caro, apparently relieved to escape everyone's close scrutiny, took the vase and the flowers before bouncing the rest of the way down the stairs. "They're so pretty, Rush. I can't wait for you to tell us their names."

"You know their names?" Stella asked, following her.

Using the pump beside the sink, Caro filled the glass container. "Yep," she said, "Rush knows all the names of the flowers. He even draws pictures of some of them."

It was Rush's turn to look embarrassed. He chuckled self-consciously when his gaze met Alex's. "My scribbling," he said, shrugging his shoulders. "A hobby of a sort."

Enjoying his distress, Alex said, "Why Mr.—Rush, you never cease to amaze me. I wouldn't have expected a man with your tastes dabbling in art or drawing flowery pictures."

His expression hardened, but then he softened it with a galvanizing smile. "Why, Alexandy, you'd be surprised what a man with my taste enjoys dabbling in."

Her mother cleared her throat. "Well, now, Rush, I for one would love to hear the names of these beautiful flowers."

Caro, who had finished placing the flowers in the vase, carried it to the table. "I for two would, too." She giggled.

When Caro passed Alex, she got a gust of her cousin's scent. *Roses.* The heady fragrance filled the whole kitchen. *Our perfume,* Alex thought, smiling to herself. She recalled that first day after Caro's arrival when she had told her cousin that men liked their lady friends to smell like flowers.

This, plus what Alex considered small breakthroughs last night and this morning, and also their earlier conversation about the cat, and now seeing Caro's braid, made Alex feel encouraged about their relationship. Perhaps she and her cousin could become friends, and it was this little kernel of hope that made Alex feel suddenly expansive.

Rush Duncan may not have been her most favored person, but it was clear that he was Caro's. All these influences made Alex decide that she would try harder to be more civil to their dinner guest, and so she joined the others now gathered around the table.

"My, how these flowers do smell," her mother said, her arm looped around Caro's shoulders.

Alex stopped at the opposite side of the table from where Rush stood. She was as eager as the others for him to begin identifying the wildflowers.

"You're probably smelling the multiflora rose," Rush told her mother, pointing to several white five-petaled flowers.

Alex supposed the roses he referred to could be fragrant, but their scent couldn't compare with that of the young lady standing beside him.

Next he pointed out a large greenish-purplish petal that curved over a clublike, yellowish spike. "Jack-in-the-pulpit," he said.

Alex's gaze locked with her mother's. "Oh, I do like that one," Stella said.

Alex wasn't certain if it was the flower itself or its name

and its suggested position that inflamed her mother.

Next came the Dutchman's-breeches; the yellow-tipped flowers at the end of the long stems resembled a pair of pants hung up by their legs to dry.

The only flower among the bunch that looked even remotely familiar to Alex was the Queen Anne's lace.

Rush went on to identify several others. With a deep, resonant voice that inspired awe in the onlookers, he named the different flowers as though they were old and dear friends. "Dogtooth violets, oxeye daisies, wild ginger, star-of-Bethlehem."

"I never would have believed so many different varieties grew on the borders of that canal," her mother said. "And to think I lived beside it most of my life."

"And these," Rush added, warming to his topic, "are only a few of the ones that bloom in the month of May. There are many, many more that grow throughout the year."

Even Alex was amazed—not only by all the different kinds of wildflowers, but also by their wild instructor.

She had always loved all manner of flowers like the lavender princess trees that were now in full bloom. Yet what really amazed her was the man who stood at their table, pointing to and naming the flowers as though they were special.

He was an enigma, Alex thought, like a kaleidoscope with its constantly changing set of colors. What kind of man could show compassion to an orphaned child one moment, and in the next be in direct opposition with his own benevolence? A man with a damn-the-world attitude who had succeeded in charming her no-nonsense mother into believing his naivete.

With well-groomed fingers, Rush tended the flowers with a gentleness reminiscent of a father's tenderness toward his new-born babe. For a moment Alex entertained an image of those same well-manicured fingers, touching and caressing her, bringing to bud her own hidden identity.

Mercy! The man even held the power to make one celibate young woman entertain thoughts that weren't so celibate.

"This one," Rush said, directing his words at her and bringing her back from her thoughts, "is one of my favorites. It's called the yellow wood sorrel."

She looked where his finger pointed.

"And why is that?" her mother asked.

Rush's gaze touched Alex's. "Although it is delicate in appearance, its reedy stalks allow it to weather the most difficult storms."

His words, although not directed at her, felt as intimate as a caress. Emotion formed a knot in her stomach, and Alex sucked in a deep breath. Was she imagining it? Was he implying that she was like the reed? And if so, why? What did Rush Duncan know about the storms she had weathered in his absence?

He bent to get a better look at the yellow five-petaled flower. "Not unlike a woman's golden tresses gilded by sunlight," he said.

Alex issued a little gasp. The space between them was marked with tension as Rush blatantly caressed her with his eyes, causing her heart to react. She felt very uncomfortable, but for reasons unknown to herself, she couldn't draw her gaze from his. Her mother broke the spell between them.

"They're all lovely, Rush. While you were pointing out the different flowers, it made me want to capture their beauty in a quilt. What do you think, Alexandria? Should we try making an appliquéd quilt of wildflowers?"

"Whatever, Mother," she answered, feeling flustered. If her mother noticed what had flared between Rush and herself, she didn't let on. Stella's reaction made Alex question if she had imagined it. Oh, how she hoped so. The moment she chanced a look at Caro, however, Alex knew it hadn't been her imagination. Her cousin glared at her with the old resentment.

Alex smiled at her, but Caro didn't return the sentiment, so Alex looked toward Rush for help. It was apparent that he, too, had noticed Caro's angry expression and thought it best to try to erase it.

"This one," he said, drawing everyone's attention to the blue, six-petaled flower with a yellow center, "reminds me of you, Caro, sweetheart. It is called blue-eyed grass. I bet you know why I'm reminded of you every time I come across it."

Caro sighed as though a weight had been lifted from her

narrow shoulders. "I know why," she said, beaming, "because I have blue eyes."

"Exactly," Rush replied. "Although now that I can compare your eyes to the color of these petals, I do believe your eyes are a more vivid blue."

A blush of pleasure tinted Caro's cheeks. "Blue's a prettier color than brown, don't you think, Rush?" She cut her gaze toward Alex.

"Much prettier, darling," he replied.

Her mother hugged her niece while Alex and Rush exchanged relieved glances. "Alexandria," she said, "you never gave me a definite answer about my idea for a wildflower quilt."

"I'm sorry, what was it you asked?" Alex left the table and returned to the stove. Dinner was ready. It surprised her that it wasn't burned, considering everything that had transpired in the last few minutes to distract her.

"Could we do an appliquéd quilt of wildflowers?" her mother asked. "Those native to the area."

"Sounds like a wonderful idea to me. Maybe Rush will loan you some of his scribbling to use as a pattern."

"All of you ladies quilt?" he asked, his gaze settling on the platter of fried chicken Alex placed on the table. "I know Miss Caro does. Aboard my boat on the trip from Georgetown, she kept herself busy quilting every night."

"Caro," Stella called, "come get these biscuits and wrap them in that cloth so they'll stay warm. And to answer your question, yes, we're all quilters. Our Caro is especially talented, but it sounds as though you know that already."

"There's something special about a lady who quilts," Rush said. "I can't imagine how much time it must take to complete a quilt large enough to sleep under."

"Caro's been helping us with our quilting since she arrived," Stella said. "Now if we do decide to do a wildflower quilt, her firsthand knowledge of the wildflowers that grow along the towpath will make it even more beautiful. Isn't that right, Alexandria?"

"It certainly will." She looked at Caro whose gaze was locked on Rush.

"Seems to me that quilting is a skill all ladies should know," Rush said. "I used to mend sails aboard ships. In fact, I met a few sailors who used to enjoy knitting. Since you're so handy with a needle, Miss Caro, perhaps you could teach this old canaller how to quilt."

"Quilt? Men don't quilt." Alex's young cousin looked at her hero as though he had suddenly taken leave of his senses.

"Well, maybe I'll become the first one."

"If that is the case," Stella Paine said, "then you'll be pleased to learn about Alexandria's plans for the front room. She hopes to turn it into a quilting workroom, sell a few piece goods, notions, and some quilts."

"Is that a fact, now?" he asked. "Maybe you should offer quilting lessons to folks. If you decide to, maybe both you and Caro could teach me how, Alexandy."

Teaching Rush to do anything was the last thing Alex wanted to do. "I think not," she said. "As of now, I have no plans to teach quilting. Besides, anyone who frequents my workroom will already know how to quilt."

Caro carried the biscuits to the table. "I'll teach you, Rush. Besides, Alex will be too busy getting her workroom ready."

"Well, that would be mighty nice of you, Miss Caro." Above the child's head, he winked at Alex.

She realized with that wink that he wasn't really interested in learning to quilt, only trying to goad Caro into coming to terms with her past. Alex couldn't fault him for his deceit. In fact, her respect for him inched higher.

Carrying the bowl of turnips to the table, she watched Rush wrinkle his nose. It wasn't hunger she detected in that sniff, but more like a grimace of disgust.

When all the food was placed on the table, Stella told everyone to sit. Rush sat at the head of the table with Alex opposite him. Caro and her mother sat on each side. They linked hands for the blessing, and after grace was said, they began passing the food.

Alex watched Rush from beneath her lowered lashes. He filled his plate with large portions of everything, but took a modest helping of the turnips. At that moment, Alex would have bet her last penny that the scallywag didn't like the vegetable.

Her mother had noticed, too. She picked up the plate of turnips and, using the spoon, placed a comparable portion on his plate. ''Don't be shy,'' she said, ''there's plenty more where these came from.''

''Why, thank you, ma'am,'' Rush mumbled from behind the fat chicken leg he'd just taken a bite of.

''Remember I told you no one makes turnips like Alexandria. Go ahead and try them,'' Stella encouraged.

''Oh, I will, you can be sure of that.'' All three of the ladies watched when Rush lifted a fork full of the yellow-white vegetable from his plate.

On bringing the fork to his mouth, he turned as green as the wildflower stems in the middle of table. It was then that he noticed the three pairs of eyes studying him. His mustache twitched.

''Love turnips,'' he told them. Taking a deep breath and adjusting his lips into a smile, he opened his mouth and emptied the fork's contents inside. The smile remained in place while he chewed and when he swallowed.

Soon after, however, his expression became pained. Beads of perspiration dotted his temple, and his face went from green to bloodless.

''Only problem is,'' he said, gulping out the words, ''turnips don't love me.''

Slamming his hand against his mouth, Rush jumped up from the table and burned a trail to the back door.

8

BY THE TIME THEY had finished dinner, the hour was late, and Stella had insisted that it was time for children and old folks to turn in. Rush had said his good-byes to both females, promising Caro that he would stop in next week on his return trip from Georgetown.

Although Alex felt uneasy being alone with Rush, fearing that he might make good his threat to finish the kiss that he had started that afternoon, she had thrown caution aside. She was determined to learn if the dinners Caro had spoken of with such fondness had taken place on Rush's boat, or if they had been events remembered from her past.

Alex washed the last dish, handing it to Rush to dry and stack with the others on the shelf above the sink. Twice in the last two weeks they had performed this domestic chore together. Her father had often helped her mother wash and dry dishes, but it was not a task that Alex expected from a man like Rush Duncan. But then, he was full of surprises. She never knew what new aspect of his character would be revealed at any given moment.

Like his gift of wildflowers and his knowledge of them. Rush didn't seem to be the sort of man who would take the time to gather a bouquet of flowers for three lonely women.

The gesture had endeared him more to her mother, and although Alex appreciated his thoughtfulness, she was now twice as confused. Maybe her cousin hadn't been talking about home.

Since Caro seemed so set on not discussing her past, Alex had hoped to piece together whatever she could learn inadvertently from her young cousin. Any knowledge of Caro's former life, Alex believed, would make Caro's settling in to the new one that much easier.

Already, because of Rush, Alex had learned that the little girl once owned a cat named Marmalade. Tonight she had also learned that Caro spent time quilting during the week she had been with Rush on his boat. She wondered if he knew about the cherished bag of rags she'd brought with her from Nebraska. There was a reason why Caro kept those quilting pieces a secret, and Alex intended to discover it.

"About—" They both said together, then stopped, embarrassed. Finally, when nothing but silence stretched between them, Rush began again.

"About those turnips," he said. "I hope you don't think your cooking caused my condition. The truth is, I can't stomach those things." His mouth pulled downward at the corners, and he shuddered.

Alex almost laughed, but she held it back, deciding not to let him off the hook so easily. "Why, just this afternoon I believe you told me that it wasn't often that you canallers got to enjoy a dinner with roots."

He looked down at her, and she watched his dimples make deep indentations on each side of his mouth. "You know what I meant, Alexandy, but the truth is, it's my roots that made me unable to abide those nasty little beginnings. When my ma was alive and money was scarce, I ate enough turnips to fill every washtub in Chinatown."

Alex's knowledge of washtubs in Chinatown was sorely lacking, but Rush's indication of how poor he was touched a chord deep inside her. She and her mother had suffered some lean times after her father's death, but growing up, Alex had wanted for nothing, material or otherwise.

"Taking what you just told me into consideration," Alex

responded, "I promise I won't serve you turnips on your next visit."

"Why, Alexandy, are you trying to court me?" His teasing words hung in the heat that had suddenly sprung up between them.

She was uncomfortable with the knowledge that perhaps she'd been presumptuous in assuming that he would eat with them on his return visit.

How was it that he always managed to get her dander up? Of course she wasn't trying to court him. She fought back an angry retort. Alex was determined not to allow him to rouse her to her usual belligerence, so she took a calming breath before answering.

"I heard you tell Caro that you would see her on your way back from Georgetown. If you're interested in a home-cooked meal, it's the least we can offer, considering all that you've done for Caro."

He took a step toward her, and Alex stepped back. As usual, his nearness unnerved her, making her want to escape the kitchen and run upstairs to the safety of her room.

"Before you go," she told him, rounding the worktable, "Caro said something I wanted to ask you about."

"Am I leaving, Alexandy? Shucks, I thought you and I were about to get better acquainted."

Alex's throat felt as parched as a dry riverbed. "Rush, please, be serious. I need to ask you something."

He rounded the table and stopped as close to her as possible without stepping on her feet. "I'm very serious, Alexandy. I'll answer your something, but what do I get in return?"

Nerves fluttered in her chest. She sidestepped Rush and headed for the front room, thinking the closer they were to the front door, the easier it would be to get rid of him once he had answered her questions.

Stopping in the center of the bare room, Alex faced him. "You can have my promise never to serve you turnips again, but only if you'll get me some answers about Caro's past."

As he joined her, there was a stalking, purposeful intent in his gait. "You're the second person today who has proposed such a solution."

"The second?" His statement surprised her. "Who was the first?" she asked. Alex couldn't recall her mother and Rush having an opportunity to talk in private. If it wasn't her mother, who could it be?

"It was Samson, your backyard neighbor. He and I go back a long way. He asked me if I'd do some checking into the why and how of Caro's sudden appearance in Harpers Ferry."

"Samson. The saloon owner? I know he and my mother have renewed an old friendship now that they are backyard neighbors. I see them talking across the fence. But how do you know h—"

"Why, Alexandy, you're not as shrewd as you would have me believe. I thought you knew, sugar. I frequent saloons and other dens of iniquity." He deliberately exaggerated the last three words.

"And—and what did you tell him?"

"I told him I'd think on it. Now, my sweet treat, ask me the something you needed to ask me, because I'm not certain how much longer these history questions are gonna hold my attention, especially with you standing so close to me." He leaned toward her.

His nearness, coupled with his words, made Alex almost forget her question. Finally it came to her. She spilled out the words, backing away from him as she did so. "Do you eat on china plates and drink from crystal glasses?"

"What? Are you funning with me, sugar?" He laughed.

Those husky vibrations sent her pulses spinning and her feet into motion. She stepped away from him again. With each backward step Alex took, he followed with a forward one.

"I tell you what, sugar, if it makes you happy, sure I eat on china plates and drink my beer from crystal glasses."

"And—and flowers? Do you serve them in a white milk jug where their colors reflect like a rainbow?"

An "aw, shucks" look appeared on Rush's face. "Never thought about drinking flowers, but if that's what you like, I'll try it."

He was so close she could see the amber flames from the lamps in the kitchen reflecting in the brown depths of his eyes.

In spite of her present position, disappointment assailed her.

It was true; Caro had been describing dinner on his boat, or Rush had implied it. Implied, not actually said it. Lordy, the man had her so befuddled she wasn't certain what she had asked or how he had answered.

Alex stepped backward again and came up short when she slammed into the wall. The jarring stop made the pins she had been warring with most of the evening pop loose from her hair. The long hank slithered loose from its knot like an exotic snake and swished down her back.

She heard Rush's quick intake of breath as he pinned her against the wall with a hand on each side of her head just above her shoulders. He was so close Alex could feel his body heat through their clothes. Slowly he dropped his hands to her hair and with gentle fingers, not unlike the ones Alex had watched him use to play with Caro's curls, he spread her fallen hair around her shoulders.

The planes of his face looked more angular in the dusky shadows, his chiseled lips more perfectly formed. For a brief moment Alex wondered how it would feel to have his lips pressed against hers. What really surprised her was that she no longer wanted to escape. She wanted to be kissed by this man who was a study in contrasts. Not daring to breathe, she swallowed and stared him boldly in the eyes.

With the pad of his thumb, Rush traced the profile of her face—forehead, brow, cheekbone, lips, chin, stopping only when the line led his thumb to the pulse point behind her ear. Once there he paused long enough to slip his warm hand behind her neck and draw her face closer to his.

Alex felt the silk of his mustache before he brushed his lips against hers. Her senses hummed like a plucked bow string when he increased the pressure of the kiss and pressed her closer to the wall. He smelled like soap, starched shirts, and wildflowers. Before this moment, Alex had never understood how exciting those scents could be, or more importantly, how the combination could take her breath away.

But then she realized it wasn't just the scents, it was the whole. Maybe she was flirting with the devil, but at the moment she didn't care. She wanted to kiss him back. Alexandria Paine had never kissed a man before. Of their own volition, her arms inched around his waist, and she pressed against him. When his tongue prodded the seam of her mouth, she opened it to allow him admittance.

His breath quickened. Or was it hers? She was shocked by her own response, if indeed it was hers. Alex felt so light-headed that she wasn't sure where she ended and where he began. They were meshed together like the front and back of a quilt. She could feel every hard plane of his body as he pressed against her softer ones. He pulled her away from the wall and encircled her in his arms.

"God almighty, Alexandy, you're sweeter than I imagined."

The husky words made chills play tag up and down her spine. He hugged her so close, she thought he might squeeze the breath right out of her, and she wished he would. Just when she thought it couldn't get any better, the flame he had ignited was doused.

He stepped away from her, and she felt as though someone had yanked them apart. Still reeling, Alex blinked. Then she realized Rush had robbed her of the pleasure.

He stared at her long and hard, his breathing mimicking her own shortness of breath. "I'm sorry," he apologized. "I didn't mean to get so carried—oh, hell, who am I kidding," he mumbled, moving toward the door.

Alex touched her bruised lips, unable to move or to think. Suddenly nothing made sense except that Rush planned to leave her. Wanting to say something but uncertain what to say and wanting him to go, Alex uttered the first thing that popped into her head. "The plates, Rush—were they china?"

"Plates?" What he thought of her question was apparent in the withering look he sent her. "Hell, no, Alex, I don't eat off china plates or use crystal glasses. Leaves, sugar, are more suitable for my animal tastes."

The front door slammed, and he was gone.

∞

BY THE TIME HE got to the top of the hill, his anger had cooled. Rush looked down on the grave and wondered how he had found it after all these years. The last time he'd visited the Harper Cemetery had been when they had buried his mother, almost fifteen years ago. He had been twelve at the time; it was two years before he had left Harpers Ferry for the sea.

Crabgrass choked the out-of-the-way spot that had been granted to the misfits of the town; those who were unable to afford a family plot, or those with no funds to be buried elsewhere. None of the graves in this remote corner was marked with marble or granite tombstones, and no epitaphs were inscribed in memory of loved ones. Only a weathered brick with the person's name was etched into the clay surface, standing as a reminder that these grave dwellers were no more in death than they had been in life.

Rush struggled with the heaviness of his thoughts. Usually he wasn't given over to melancholy. But tonight his warring emotions had sent him on a skirmish up this hill, to battle truths that were long ago buried.

He looked down on the town where he had grown up. Home, he thought. Heck, he didn't have a home except for the twelve-foot-square cubicle on his canal boat where he ate and drank from tin utensils instead of china and crystal ones. Rush still hadn't figured out why Alex had asked him such a stupid question when the moment had called for more romantic thoughts. Maybe if he'd answered yes to her question, he would have been more to her liking—not that she seemed all that opposed to kissing him at the time.

Rush ran his hand over his hair. It was like daylight on top of this hill. The grassy knoll that swelled like a matron's plump bosom was caressed by the half moon that shared the velvet sky with a canopy of stars twinkling like jewels in the clear night. From a nearby tree, an owl hooted, and a critter rustled through the grass.

Rush squatted beside the grave where his mother slept. Time had caused a slight indentation in the earth, as though the weight of her problems had followed her to her final resting place.

Lord, Rush hoped not. Life had saddled Eudora Duncan with enough problems on earth. What few memories Rush could recall of his mother were mostly hazy ones, but there had been times in those first twelve years of his life when he had caught snatches of the woman she had been before living had killed her. Those moments weren't all bad, and he supposed she loved him in her own way. Things might have turned out differently for the dark-eyed beauty Eudora had once been if she hadn't borne an illegitimate son, if she hadn't turned to whiskey and then to whoring. His mother's struggle had taught him two things: A person did what she had to in order to survive, holding on to living until it beat her down anyway.

The second important lesson he'd learned from his mother's experience was to keep his pecker away from virgins—ladies like Alexandria Paine.

According to Eudora Duncan, she had been a fine, upstanding miss until the day Rush's father had ridden into her life. He had been a horse soldier, passing through town, when she met him. Much later she learned he was a married man with children, and their brief affair ended as quickly as it had begun. He rode away, leaving Eudora with a broken heart and a bastard son.

To this day, bedding whores bothered Rush. Heck, most of the time he left them alone as well, believing that those so-called fallen angels hadn't fallen from grace because of their own choosing, but because of their circumstances.

On the rare occasions Rush felt a need to relieve his sexual urges, he made damn certain both parties enjoyed the session. Most women whom Rush bedded felt very satisfied with the experience and the sizable sum he left them for their time.

But this particular set of values wasn't helping him at the moment. Alexandria Paine had left him harder than a boat tiller. He enjoyed teasing her, and through the years when he had thought about Harpers Ferry, she had been the sunshine in his dreams, although the girl with the golden hair had been forbidden fruit to a boy whose mother was the town whore. Now fate had made their paths cross once again, and he had taken advantage of the situation; but as it turned out, he hadn't benefitted from the kiss they'd shared. At the time, her lips had felt so damn good he questioned how anything so sweet could leave him feeling so damn low.

Even now, some thirty minutes later, he wanted to head back down the hill and finish what he'd started. He wanted to lay Alexandy down, spread her legs, and bury himself in her fiery crevice and carry them both as high as the moon, but he had to face the truth.

A woman like Alexandria Paine wasn't the kind of woman interested in one night of pleasure. She was a lifer through and through. Her whole persona demanded commitment, and the word "commitment" was not in Rush's vocabulary. *Love 'em and leave 'em* had been the rule he lived by for the most part, and so far it had kept him out of trouble.

Why, then, couldn't he erase the memory of their kiss or the softness of Alexandria's womanly body? Instead he stood on this hilltop with the moon only a touch away, and he was craving the sun.

Disgusted, Rush got up. He had wasted enough time searching for his past at his mother's grave while digging his own: that is, if thoughts of Alexandria Paine were any indication of where he was heading. Love sent a person to an early grave; his mother was dead proof of that. In the future when dealing with Alexandy, he would have to be more like his ornery old self. Heck, his devil-may-care attitude had served him well through the years, and he hoped it would continue to keep a golden-haired angel at bay.

∽

"MERCIFUL HEAVENS," ALEX MUTTERED as she made her way up the stairs, "that devil almost possessed me."

She wasn't certain if hell was wrought with eternal flames, but Rush Duncan's embrace stayed to torment her. He had left her with a fire all over her body unlike any she had ever known.

Reaching the second level of the house, Alex padded toward the small lamp her mother had left burning on the parlor table. Once there, she turned down the wick, making certain the flame was extinguished. Then she allowed her eyes to adjust to the darkness before attempting to move toward the bedroom.

The last thing she wanted was to call attention to herself by tripping. Alex wished only to be left alone in her misery, to crawl into bed and forget about the kiss she had shared with Rush Duncan only moments before.

It was surely the devil's work, she thought, that had made her act like a brazen hussy, returning Rush's passionate advances with a few of her own. Lordy, the last thing she needed was to awaken Caro, feeling certain that the shrewd ten-year-old would know immediately what her older cousin had been up to and dislike her more.

Alex needed her own room, especially tonight. She gave the loveseat a quick glance and contemplated sleeping on its worn surface, but decided its shorter length wouldn't accommodate her much longer height, so she trudged on.

Once inside the bedroom, she saw there was enough light from the moon passing through the lace curtains to allow her to make out the form and placement of the furniture. Looking toward the bed, she noted that Caro appeared to be in a deep sleep.

Good!

It was warmer than usual, and her mother hadn't bothered to open a window. The sooner Alex could rid herself of her clothes, she decided, the cooler she would be. Stopping beside a chair, she slipped off her boots and stockings, then peeled away her remaining garments except for her chemise and drawers. She dropped the bundle of discarded items on the chair before tiptoeing toward the pitcher and bowl on the washstand.

A real bath would have been more to her liking, but at the moment she lacked the energy to drag out the tub in the kitchen and fill it with water. A wet cloth would have to do. She needed to wash away the heat along with any leftover memories of Rush Duncan; like the feel of his lips against hers, the silken brush of his mustache against sensitive skin, or his arms encircling her, holding her close.

Saints preserve me. Even now the contemplation of the last thirty minutes did funny things to her stomach and made her skin flame from the inside out. *Where is that washcloth?* she thought.

She inched toward the washstand, groping in the charcoal darkness for the cloth that usually hung on the rack above the bowl and pitcher. Instead, her feet made contact with water on the floor, and she slapped her hand against her mouth to smother a squeak. After the initial shock of her warm toes swimming in cold water, Alex's second reaction was disgust, believing that Snow had christened the floor and she had the misfortune to be standing in it. Reason told her the puddle was much too large to have been made by a cat of Snow's size. A careful inspection of the area surrounding the washstand revealed that water was sloshed everywhere, and Alex decided that Caro must have spilled it earlier.

Had she tried to bathe the cat? Alex looked toward her bed, straining her eyes to see through the darkness. If the two lumps beneath the cover were any indication, chances were not only would she be sharing her bed with her young cousin, but also with Snow. *Maybe,* she thought, *I should take my chances with the loveseat in the parlor, but for the moment I'll settle on finding the washcloth. Now where is it?*

Alex dipped her fingers inside the bowl, still half filled with water. The liquid felt chilly as she slid her hand beneath the surface, searching for the lost rag. *Ah, there it is.* Lifting the cloth from the water, she wrung it out, then brought it to her face.

She stood for several minutes without moving, her face buried in the damp folds of the cloth. *Heaven,* she thought. Only when she began to rub the rag down her neck and over her shoulders did she realize it wasn't the cotton terry cloth she normally washed with.

Curious, Alex slipped to the window. Once there, she held the rag up to the muted light.

Her heart thumped inside her chest. It wasn't her washcloth. It appeared to be one of the quilting pieces from Caro's bag of rags, the same pieces she'd brought with her from Nebraska but refused to allow anyone to see or touch.

It was too dark for Alex to make out the design, so she spread the square over the back of the chair to dry before moving to the bed. Alex hadn't found the washcloth she sought, but in finding the quilting piece from Caro's past, it had pushed her present problem with Rush to the back of her mind.

Perhaps this latest discovery meant her cousin Caro planned to share a little more of herself with Alex and her mother. Oh, how she hoped so. Encouraged with her find, Alex slipped beneath the covers, easing both child and cat to one side of the bed before she stretched out beside them.

The last thought that flirted with her consciousness before she drifted off to sleep was of Rush. But it wasn't his kiss or his embrace that toyed with her thoughts. Instead, it was Rush's uncanny ability to make a lonely little girl like Caro want to do and be whatever he encouraged. There was no doubt in Alex's mind that such a feat was not the work of the devil, but more the labor of a saint.

9

ALEX AWAKENED TO CURIOUS stares from two pairs of eyes; one the color of sapphires, the other the color of emeralds. The owner of the latter lay upon her bosom, his tiny shoe-button nose mere inches from her chin.

Having grown up hearing the old superstition about cats, "that they would suck the breath from a baby," Alex wondered if that were the case now, if Snow was indeed trying to suck her breath away, perhaps on orders from her young mistress. Yet Caro didn't look all that threatening this morning. She lay on her side beside Alex, her head propped on one hand, studying both Alex and the cat. Last night's braid had been replaced by her usual disarray of black curls.

"Snow's cold," she said. "He's trying to get warm. Your breath warms him."

Wanting to keep the moment light, Alex responded, "I guess it's lucky I took a big swallow of that rose-water perfume before I retired last night. Otherwise he might expire from the smell."

Caro's blue eyes widened, and she shot a look at the dresser where the scent bottle sat. "You're funning with me, aren't you? You didn't drink no perfume."

Rush's expression coming from Caro's mouth made Alex

smile. "I seem to recall a certain young lady once told me I should sweeten my breath with its contents, and since that same young lady is still sitting next to me, I reckon drinking that liquid worked."

Caro sat up. Her nose wrinkled. She looked toward the dresser again, then at Alex, before flopping down on her back. "You didn't drink it. It's the same amount as it was last night. Besides, it costs too much to waste."

"Waste?" Alex faked an insult. Caro appeared to be in excellent humor this morning, and Alex gloried in the moment. "What about me? I might have been the one who was wasted if I had drunk from its contents. Besides, who told you it cost too much?"

Caro regarded her with amusement. "Aunt Stella. She said a lady must use perfume sparingly because it costs too much to waste it."

"I see." Alex imagined it was her mother's diplomatic way of telling her niece that too much perfume was offensive. She wondered if the information was passed on before or after Caro's heavy dousing of the scent last night. "I'd say your aunt Stella passed on some good advice. As she said, using it sparingly will make it last a lot longer."

"Yeah. I never had any bottled scent water before. We always used homemade soap when we bathed once a week."

Caro reached over and stroked Snow's back where he still lay on Alex's chest. The cat's eyes were no longer emerald orbs in his orange face. They were now slanted slits, and his earlier purr had changed to a contented snore.

"Aunt Stella also said a lady should wash more than once a week. You reckon that's true?"

"My mother is pretty smart when it comes to proper behavior for young ladies. On this particular issue, I'd have to agree with her."

"Yeah, I guess so. Since she is my ma's sister, she must be pretty smart."

Alex wondered if she dare mention the patchwork square to Caro or let her cousin tell her about it in her own time. Her cousin settled the dilemma with her next words.

"You found Marmalade, didn't you?"

Alex's gaze followed Caro's, which had settled on the chair where last night Alex had hung the patchwork piece to dry.

"Wow! So that's Marmalade. It was so dark in here when I came to bed, I couldn't see anything. When I found the cloth in the wash bowl, I wrung it out and hung it up to dry."

"Yeah, it's Marmalade, all right. My ma and me—we made him together." Caro slipped from the bed and went to the chair. She picked up the appliquéd fabric and studied it for several minutes. Then, returning to the bed, she brought the still-damp material with her and spread it on the rumpled covers. "See, I'm such a good quilter, I know I can teach Rush."

"From what I've seen of your piecework, there is no doubt in my mind that you could teach him. From the looks of those stitches, I'd say you're a better quilter than I am."

Caro's tiny finger traced the orange outline of the cat. "My ma, she made me sew real even stitches. She always said I was better than she was, but I wasn't." There was a slight hitch in her voice. "My ma could do anything."

"I don't know, Caro. I'd say you're following right in your mother's footsteps. I'd guess both of our mothers were taught to quilt by the same person, which would have been our maternal grandmother."

Caro propped her arms on the edge of the bed and wiggled. "I never had a grandma or a grandpa."

Alex wondered what Caro knew of her grandparents; not that she knew all that much about them herself. She did know that she wasn't particularly fond of their mothers' father, who in Alex's opinion should have stopped Charlotte from running away from home all those years ago.

"We all have grandparents," Alex answered, "but some of us aren't as lucky as those who had the privilege of knowing them."

"You—you didn't know our maternity grandparents, either?" Caro seemed pleased that she wasn't the only one who had missed out on such a relationship.

"Maternal," Alex corrected, "meaning our mother's side of the family. No, I never knew them. They passed on not long after I was born."

"I guess that's why I never knew them, too." Caro bent across the bed and lifted Snow from Alex's chest and moved around the end of the bed.

There were so many questions that Alex wanted to ask her cousin about her family. Apparently Caro hadn't known her paternal grandparents, either and that made Alex more curious about the man who had fathered her, but she cautioned herself to go easy. In time she felt the child would tell her, but for now Alex saw no harm in pressing her about the quilting square.

"Caro, why did you wash Marmalade?"

Her cousin didn't answer immediately. When the silence stretched between them, Alex suspected that Caro wouldn't answer her at all, but as usual, Caro surprised her.

Carrying Snow with her, she moved toward the door. "I thought if what Aunt Stella said was true about bathing, then Marmalade was way overdue for a bath."

The child was too smart for her own good. She started to speak again. "But—"

"I'm gonna go see if Aunt Stella is awake. Snow's hungry. He needs to eat."

"Wait. I'll help you find him. . . ."

Caro had already disappeared into the parlor.

Alone, Alex lifted the square and spread it across her knees. Upon further inspection of the piece, she could see that the stitches were as fine as any she could do herself. The square showed a picture of a fat orange cat leaping through spiky green grass that met a blue cloudless sky.

"A prairie," Alex said in wonder. "The prairie where Caro lived with her family."

She held the material against her chest and hugged it. "I'd bet my last penny that the secret to Caro's past is in the contents of that ragbag. Now, Alexandria Paine, it's up to you to convince your young cousin to show you what other secrets she brought with her."

After this morning's discovery, the idea still seemed monumental, but one she felt closer to conquering.

∽

AS SOON AS RUSH'S boat arrived at the Georgetown terminus, he unloaded his coal, then made inquiries as to which ships were in port. On learning that Captain Steve's schooner lay at anchor on the Potomac River, Rush sent word to his old friend requesting an audience. His request was rewarded with an invitation to dine aboard the *Sea Wind.* After giving his crew the night off, Rush started on his way to meet the captain.

A thick, warm wind blew against his face as he walked along the wharf. During the day, the river would be alive with activity, as ships came and went and people scurried here and there. Dusk brought a different feel to the river. All activity had ceased as though the bustle had settled in for the long-awaited night.

The sound of water lapping against ship bellies, the occasional raucous cry of a seabird, and the muted conversation of men aboard an anchored ship drifted to Rush's ears as he moved along the waterfront.

The river was covered with vessels, creating a forest of masts that reached toward the heavens. Beyond the many blackened silhouettes of ships, the setting sun washed both sky and water in brilliant hues of pink, orange, and red. The harbor smelled of dead fish, rotting vegetation, and river mud. Somewhere among the many vessels, someone was cooking cabbage, and the very distinct aroma made Rush's stomach growl with hunger.

"Thank God it isn't turnips," he mumbled to himself. The thought made him cringe, then smile for the memory it summoned. The Paine women had learned really fast Rush's true opinion of turnips. He imagined he had received his just desserts when those dang nasty vegetables refused to stay down once he'd swallowed them. But there were desserts of another kind. When he considered Alexandy's kiss, Rush felt he'd come out fine in spite of his suffering.

Maybe, a little voice reminded him. *Remember that talk you had with yourself beside your mother's grave. A woman like Alexandria Paine is dangerous, the kind of woman you should steer clear of.*

"I know, I know," Rush conceded, "but a last course as

sweet as Alexandria Paine lingers in the mind long after the tasting.''

The voice insisted, *She's as toxic as poison.*

"But what a way to die," he said out loud.

"You fixin' to die on me, son?" a real voice asked, interrupting Rush's conversation with himself. "Heck, you haven't eaten yet, and it would be a waste of good food."

Surprised, Rush swung around to face the man who spoke. "Why Captain Steve, sir, how long have you been behind me?" He felt his face turn the color of the blood-red sun that had slipped below the horizon only moments before.

"Long enough to recognize a lovesick sea cow when I hear one."

"Do you mean a manatee, sir?" Rush offered his old captain a teasing grin with his insubordinate answer.

"I assume," his friend responded, "a manatee can be lovesick, too, since they are one and the same."

The stocky captain lengthened his short stride, closing the distance between them. Beneath his stubby arm, he carried a bottle. He looked at Rush with twinkling eyes.

"Since my wife isn't with me this trip, I decided I needed a little fortification to get me through the night. Mildred's not too keen on having alcohol aboard ship, but she ain't against me having a little nip now and again. Especially when I'm celebrating." Together they walked along the wharf. "Are you still not a drinking man?" the captain asked.

"I've been known to have a little nip now and again," Rush responded, "especially if I know what it is I'm celebrating."

"Sounds to me like you're smitten with a lady, if that conversation you were having with yourself is any indication. I take it this means you no longer shy away from women."

"Smitten with a lady? Shy away from women?"

They approached the dock where the *Sea Wind* was moored. The captain preceded him across the plank, and Rush followed him.

"Maybe you weren't shy," his friend continued, "but I seem to recall when you sailed with me, drinking and wenching was a pastime you didn't particularly enjoy. You would rather have gone to bed with a glass of milk and a good book.''

''A pastime that kept me out of trouble,'' Rush said lightly. ''Besides, you worked me so doggone hard, I didn't have the energy to drink and wench.''

The captain winked. ''I suppose there was a method to my madness, considering you were the best first mate I ever had. My expert training, of course.''

''Of course.''

Rush followed the older man to his cabin where he opened the door and ushered him inside.

Captain Steve lit a lamp to ward off the approaching darkness. ''Never could understand,'' he said, ''why you gave up the wind in the sails for the bags of wind that pull those sluggish canal boats up and down the C & O.''

The captain's easy humor brought on a comfortable glow, making Rush realize how much he had missed the old salt.

''I don't believe my two mules, Daisy and Petunia, would take too kindly to you calling them bags of wind.''

''You and I both know, son, there are no dumber animals alive than mules. Heck, they don't even know if they're ass or horse.'' The older man shook his large, silvery head. ''When you gave up the sea, it was a waste of good sea legs.''

Captain Steve motioned Rush toward one of the chairs that surrounded the familiar round table. ''Take a weight off,'' he ordered, ''while I muster up some glasses.''

Being inside the cabin, enjoying the easy camaraderie, brought more pleasant memories to Rush's mind.

He sat down. He had spent many enjoyable nights around this table, not only alone with the captain playing chess, but also with his wife Mildred when she decided to cruise with her husband. Rush may not have had much of a family to speak of in those early years of his life, except for Samson, but in the latter years, he had been blessed with good friends; people like the captain and Mrs. Steve.

''We'll eat in a few minutes,'' the captain told him. ''Well, mate, you gonna tell me about this little gal who has you talking to yourself? Sounds like serious stuff to me.''

Nothing would have made the Steves happier than for Rush

to find a woman to settle down with, but since that would never happen, Rush steered the conversation in another direction. "I take it you mean young Caro?"

"Caro? What kind of fool name is that? Leave it to you to find a gal with such a name. Sounds as peculiar as the names of those mules of yours. Daisy and Petunia? Whoever heard of a sailor naming his mules after flowers?"

Rush broke into laughter. "I'm one sailor, or ex-sailor, who happens to like flowers, but perhaps the name Caroline Swift would suit you better."

"You mean my young passenger? How is that sweet child?" The captain returned to the table with two glasses. After setting them down, he pulled the cork from the whiskey bottle and poured them each two fingers full. "My Mildred grew really fond of that little girl on our trip from New Orleans. She would have kept her if she could have. Young Caroline, is she settling in with her kin?"

"Caro's settling in just fine," Rush told him. "The Paines are real nice folks. Stella Paine is Caroline's aunt. Herman Paine, Stella's late husband, was the lockkeeper across the river from Harpers Ferry when I grew up there. Mr. Paine has been dead now for almost five years." Rush shifted, and stretched his long legs out in front of him. "Stella and her only daughter live in a small house in Harpers Ferry now. Both women were delighted to have their long-lost relative returned to them."

The captain cut him a curious stare. "Would this only daughter go by the name of Alexandria?" Not waiting for Rush's response, he walked to his desk and rustled through some papers. When he found the paper he wanted, he returned to Rush's side.

"I guess if her name is Alexandria, that would partly explain this thank-you letter," he said, handing it to Rush. "This was waiting for me when I docked in Georgetown."

The captain sat down across the table. "I may be getting senile in my old age, but I don't recall taking up any collection for Caroline from my sailors. Besides, most of those sons of bitches are too dang stingy to part with a red cent, except for booze or a hot tumble in the hay."

Damn Alexandria Paine for being so damn polite. Rush hadn't expected her to write the captain and thank him.

"You wouldn't know anything about this, would you, son?" He took a drink of liquor, watching Rush above the glass' rim, waiting for his response. "It seems," Captain Steve continued, "that Miss Paine wanted to thank me and my crew for our generosity on Caroline's behalf. She said the hundred dollars was much too generous of a gift, but that they would put the money to good use."

For the second time in the span of the last hour, Rush felt his face burn with embarrassment.

"I'm nothing but an old salty dog soon to be hung up in retirement, but am I wrong in assuming that this Miss Paine is the same young lady you were babbling on so about when I happened upon you on the pier? I believe you called her Alexandy."

The man might be old, Rush thought, but he had the keen sense of a dang bloodhound.

"I seem to recall you saying something about her being sweet and how you enjoyed the tasting." His bushy gray brows bobbed up and down like sun-bleached corks on the water. "I do believe those were your exact words."

Rush ran a finger beneath the rim of his collar that suddenly felt too tight. "I believe, my good friend, you're as senile as you claimed to be earlier. Why would you think I know about such a gift?" He lifted the glass of whiskey and swallowed the contents. The liquor burned a lava trail going down, but its fire gave him an excuse for what Rush supposed was a face two shades redder than his earlier color.

"If you don't know about it," the captain said, pinning Rush with his sea-green eyes, "then I better post a letter to Miss Paine and tell her there's been a mistake. I sure don't know anything about a gift of such a large sum of money."

"You wouldn't do that," Rush said with a nervous gulp, "would you?"

"I will unless you see fit to set the log straight."

"Pour me another round," Rush said, pointing to his empty glass.

The captain slapped his hip. "I knew there was a lady in

your life. Especially now that she's driven you to drink.''

"Hold on a minute, friend. Let's get one thing straight. There is no lady in my life." Rush slipped his hand over the top of the glass so the captain couldn't pour more whiskey. "On second thought, I don't need that." With a hangdog expression, he added, "If you must know the truth, there are three ladies in my life. One of them is young Caro, the other two her aunt and cousin. My first impression of the latter was that those two ladies were damn near destitute and needed that hundred dollars a heck of a lot more than I did."

"That's mighty charitable of you, son, but don't you think credit should be given where credit is due?"

"Alexandria Paine wouldn't have taken the money if she thought it came from me. She's very proud, always has been." Rush's voice softened when he recalled Alex's stance that day in the street when he had tried to give her the roll of bills. "She told me outright that she wouldn't be taking charity."

"Always has been?" the captain asked. "I take it this Miss Alexandria and you are old friends?"

"Not exactly friends. Let's just say I knew her. She and I didn't exactly come from the same side of the tracks."

"Tracks? I thought you said her father was a lockkeeper."

"He was. A good one, too. Herman Paine made a decent living for his wife and young daughter. A hell of a lot better living than the town wh—" Rush caught himself. *That drink of whiskey must have loosened my tongue.* "Than my mother made," he corrected.

Rush couldn't look at his friend. He had never told the Steves about his background, and they had never asked. Rush had decided a long time ago that some things were best left unsaid.

The captain stood, went to the sideboard, and lifted the cloth covering from over two white china plates filled with food. "I suggest we eat this while it's still hot." He carried the dishes back to the table, pulled several pieces of silver from a drawer, and, after handing the utensils to Rush, sat down. "Some of us turn out fine in spite of our upbringing."

Their eyes met, but Rush didn't respond to the captain's statement. Instead, he said, "Eating sounds good to me. I'm as hungry as a whale." He eyed the thick slices of roast beef, the potatoes smothered in brown gravy, and the mountain of green peas. "You still have the same cook?" He forked a mouthful of potatoes into his mouth.

"I'm still married to Mildred, aren't I?" The captain winked at Rush and had a good laugh at his own joke. Between chuckles, he said, "But John cooked this. He sets a fine table, as you already know."

After each man downed several more mouthfuls, the captain asked, "So how do you think I should respond to Miss Paine's letter?"

"Don't. For all she knows, you might never have received it. Besides, I never heard of folks thanking folks for sending them thank-you notes."

"There's a first time for everything. But you should know I feel as malicious as a sea snake, letting that young woman believe that I and my crew were charitable when we weren't."

"Maybe agreeing to help me will help lighten your guilt."

The captain spooned in a mouthful of peas before asking, "How's my helping you supposed to help me?"

Rush pushed back his empty plate and rubbed his belly. "I want to find out what I can about Caroline's background. She refuses to talk about her past with anyone. I hoped you might still have the name of the couple who secured her passage aboard your ship, and an address where they might be reached."

Waiting for the captain to finish his dinner, Rush, lost in thought, picked up a knife and tapped the end against his empty glass—the clear resonant ping sounded like a bell throughout the cabin. After several more moments of contemplation, he continued explaining his reasons for wanting to contact the couple.

"Stella—Mrs. Paine, that is—knows nothing about her sister Charlotte after she left Harpers Ferry nearly thirty years ago. No one had heard a word from or about her until the day I delivered Caro to the Paines' doorstep. I understand Caro is the spitting image of her mother at the same age, because Stella swooned on seeing her for the first time.

"Her reaction shocked everyone, especially Caro. She thought she had killed her aunt."

"I'm sorry to hear that," the captain said. "Such a reception must have scared Caroline half to death."

"I had a hard time convincing her that her aunt wasn't dead, but once Stella came around, she smoothed over the situation."

Captain Steve leaned over the table. Rush noticed the man's upside-down reflection appeared in the now empty plate then disappeared again when the captain pushed back from the table. The image made Rush recall Alex asking him if he ate from china plates at what he believed to be the most inappropriate time. *Women!* He would never understand them, but he didn't have long to contemplate the enigma, because the captain's words brought him back to the moment.

"Surely the child had a letter or papers to explain why, after all that time, she had been left in her aunt's care."

"There was the envelope you gave me that was addressed to the Paines. I gave it to Alex, but she never mentioned its contents to me."

Now that he thought about his last visit at their home, Rush decided he hadn't given Alex a chance to explain. She had said she wanted to ask him something, but the conversation had turned ridiculous when she kept demanding he tell her what kind of plates he ate from.

"It's strange she wouldn't mention the missive," the captain said. "Surely it must have held a letter from the child's mother." He waited for Rush to answer.

"Next time I see Alex, I'll ask her."

"Seeing her, I suppose, is another one of your charitable duties." The captain gave him a sly look.

"I'd like to say I'm just one wonderful son of a gun, but in truth, I can't. I'm doing this for my only friend in Harpers Ferry: Samson. You remember me talking about the saloon owner who took me in after my mother's death? Samson is now the Paines' backyard neighbor. Since he and Stella were both born and raised in Harpers Ferry, their friendship goes way back. He asked me to find out what I could about Stella's sister, Charlotte, and so I agreed to make some inquiries."

"You could hire a detective."

"I will, but first I'd like to have somewhere to start. That's why I wanted the couple's name and perhaps an address."

His friend scratched his head. "I'm sure I've got that information around here somewhere, but it might take me a few days to put my fingers on it. I'm not promising an address, though—not everyone has a permanent one."

"I understand. Anything you can come up with will help. Can you remember anything about the couple?" Rush asked.

"No, not really."

He looked thoughtful for a moment before picking up a meerschaum pipe from a wooden stand that sat in the middle of the table. Pulling out a leather pouch and opening it, he began stuffing the pipe's bowl with tobacco.

"I do recall they were an older couple. I talked to the woman more than the man. The husband looked sickly, or maybe he was just tired from the trip; since I believe they claimed to have come all the way from Nebraska."

After filling the pipe's bowl, he struck a match to the tobacco and puffed a few times.

Rush used the silence to make a point. "Nebraska is a long way from New Orleans. If their intent was to deliver Caro to Harpers Ferry, why would they go to Louisiana? It seems to me the much shorter route would have been overland. Wouldn't it?"

"I can't answer that, unless river travel was easier for them. They could have hopped on a keelboat or a steamer practically anywhere on the Mississippi."

The captain puffed a few more times on his pipe, and the fragrance of cherry-laced tobacco filled the air.

"You know, now that I think about it, that old couple acted uncomfortable, almost nervous, when they gave the child over to my care. They said they had instructions to deliver Caroline to her relatives in Harpers Ferry."

Rush blew out his cheeks. "It still seems dang strange to me that they would take Caro to New Orleans to get her home."

"Could be the couple took her in after her parents died. Maybe they never planned to send her to her relatives. It's not uncommon for childless families to take in orphaned children. Maybe they were relocating in the South. Like I said earlier, the old man looked sick, almost near death. Maybe it was his illness that prompted them to send her back East to her real family. Could be," the captain added, "that they no longer believed they were capable of taking care of her. Perhaps my ship seemed the easiest way to get her home since I was sailing for Savannah, then on to Georgetown."

"If that's the case, if they were drifters," Rush said, "I may never find them."

The captain sucked on his pipe. "In time I would think Caro would tell her aunt and cousin what happened."

"Unless she blocked from her mind the period from when she left Nebraska until the time she arrived in New Orleans. She never mentioned the couple to me. I only know what you told me about her, that her family had died in Nebraska of the cholera."

"That's what the couple told me, and I had no reason not to believe them. Of course, my Mildred welcomed the child with open arms. Caroline looked exhausted when we got her, but she warmed to Mildred after the first few days at sea."

"When I got her," Rush added, "she appeared to have made a full recovery. She was full of vip and vigor, an independent little cuss who to this day doesn't mind speaking her mind. Reminds me a lot of her older cousin at that age."

"Alexandria? The same lady you have no romantic inclination toward?"

Rush ignored his friend's remark, forcing him to continue.

"Caroline changed under Mildred's care," the captain said. "By the time we reached Georgetown, she was chattering like a magpie. She was no longer the same somber child we took aboard in New Orleans."

Rush didn't want to contemplate what horrors Caro might have endured after her family's death. Their deaths alone were a tragedy. It amazed Rush that Caro had survived and appeared to be unscathed from her experiences, for she had been uprooted from familiar surroundings and dragged halfway down the United States by boat with only God knows who.

Rush's interest was really piqued now, since his conversation with his old friend. Not only did he want to find out about Caro's past for Samson and the Paines' sake, but also for his own.

"As soon as you can put your fingers on that couple's name, I'd appreciate it," he told Captain Steve.

"If I can't find where I stashed the information, Mildred will know where to look. When I return to Savannah, I'll ask her about it, then forward what information we have on to you. Anything to help further your cause. In the meantime, could I interest you in a game of chess?"

Rush laughed. "You don't think I came here just for a free meal and information, now do you? I may not miss you, but I still miss our chess games."

The captain stood. Walking to a bookcase, he retrieved the chessboard and pieces and returned to the table. "I reckon I am going soft in my old age because I miss your ornery companionship. Now, before I get too mushy, I suggest we set our minds to some serious chess playing."

Several hours later when they were well into the game, the captain's earlier statement surfaced in Rush's mind, interrupting his concentration. He looked across the board at his old friend.

"Further my cause?" he asked, puzzled.

"I wondered when that particular reference would sink into your thick skull. By now you should know that I'll do anything to get you to settle down with a fine, upstanding lady like my Mildred. Sounds like this Alexandy fits the bill."

"You never give up, do you?"

"Checkmate!" the captain shouted. Having won the game, he grinned knowingly.

The captain's winning the game, coupled with his satisfied grin, was all the confirmation Rush needed.

10

HAVING BRUSHED THE LAST stroke of whitewash on the walls of the front room, Alex dropped the brush back into the bucket, pressed her hands against the small of her back, and stretched. Her spine made short snapping sounds that sounded like corn popping in a skillet.

"Mercy," she complained, "I must be getting old."

She looked at her hands, which were chapped from having immersed them in the lye soapy water. Her shoulders ached, her arms felt rubbery, and her poor feet had rebelled hours ago, expressing repugnance for every extra step she took, every chair she topped in order to reach the ceiling with her paintbrush.

But with the chore now complete, Alex stepped back and admired her handiwork, feeling quite pleased with herself. Before undertaking this project, her only attempt at painting had been on paper with a transparent wash of colors. She had failed miserably in watercolors and soon learned how much more adept she was with a needle and thread. But she had watched her father paint walls often enough. He had made the chore look so easy, but then, everything Herman Paine did looked easy in the eyes of his adoring daughter.

The wall brackets and the large quilting frame she had ordered from Montgomery Ward had arrived yesterday. Tomorrow she would secure the brackets to the walls and begin displaying some of the quilts that she and her mother hoped to sell when they could decide on which ones to part with.

She had also emptied out a chest that she and Caro had found in the attic room, and once she could figure out how to get the cumbersome piece down the stairs, Alex planned to use it to display her yard goods when they arrived.

Upon learning about her quilt workroom, Samson had offered her several spindle-back chairs he no longer used or wanted, along with a long, narrow table that would fit perfectly against the side wall.

The same wall, Alex reminded herself, that the disreputable Rush Duncan had pinned her against on his last visit. Even now she couldn't look at that spot without feeling heat suffuse her body. Earlier she had given that area a thorough going-over with the white paint, hoping to erase the memory completely from her mind.

It hadn't worked. He still intruded upon her daytime duties and trespassed in her nighttime dreams. Thank goodness Caro didn't suspect that Alex spent so many hours thinking about the man her young cousin worshipped. Since the morning Caro had shown her the quilting square of Marmalade the cat, the two girls had become much closer. So much so that Caro had told Alex she preferred sharing her room instead of moving to the attic space when Alex had suggested she could have a room to herself.

Two familiar figures passed by the front windows, and soon her mother and Caro stepped inside the door. "Afternoon, daughter," her mother called, her face all smiles. "This morning Caro met her teacher and some of the children in her class. Since school will be out in less than a week, her teacher decided she can wait until the fall term before she begins."

Alex looked at her cousin who was bent over the paint can, stirring the whitewash with the brush. "I imagine Caro is disappointed about this news," Alex teased.

Caro shrugged her shoulders. "I never liked school back home," she replied. "I reckon it won't be much different here. Never understood why a body has to go to school anyway."

"So the body can learn, silly," Alex replied. "Just think, if you're real smart and do well in school, maybe someday when you grow up you can become a teacher."

"Yuk! I'd never want to be a teacher."

Caro pulled such a sour face it made Alex laugh. "Why, I believe it was only yesterday that you told me you were going to teach Rush how to quilt."

"Quilting's easy, and it ain't nothing like school."

"It isn't easy," Alex's mother corrected, "but you are right, it isn't anything like school."

Caro continued to stir the paint. Both women watched her, expecting further comment on the topic, but none was forthcoming. Instead, she looked up, changing the subject entirely. "Have you seen Snow, Alex?"

"Oh, I saw him, all right. I had to toss the rascal out the back door." She pointed at the floor across the room. "He decided to leave his signature on the wood." Alex walked in the direction she pointed. "I tried to wash those tracks with lye soap, but I was too late. They had already dried. I guess we're stuck with a trail of cat paws across our floor."

Caro skipped across the room to study the tracks. "Snow did that?" She covered her mouth with her hand to smother a giggle. The little cat feet tracked across the room as far as the archway that led into the kitchen.

"Oh, no," Caro exclaimed. "He must have white paws! I better go find him and wash his feet."

"I washed his feet," Alex insisted, "before I tossed him out the door. He didn't go far for all my efforts. Last I saw of him, he was snoozing in a pool of sunshine on the back stoop."

Caro looked toward the back entrance then at the prints again. "I guess he knows his name is Snow." She grinned mischievously.

"I guess he does at that," Stella replied. "A pretty smart cat. He must have gone to school."

Caro shrugged her shoulders again, but the trace of a smile tipped up the corners of her mouth. "Speaking of school, as soon as it lets out today, me and this other kid, we're gonna give our cats a ride in his wagon."

"Does this other kid have a name?" Alex asked.

" 'Course he has a name." Before Alex could say more, Caro dashed toward the kitchen. Alex watched her move to the back door, then she disappeared into the small yard, calling, "Here Snow, here kitty, kitty."

Alex looked at her mother. "Jamie Hamilton," her mother responded.

"*Stupid* Jamie Hamilton?" Alex asked, surprised.

Her mother laughed. "I guess Caro has decided he isn't as stupid as she first believed."

"I'm just glad to see she's interested in someone close to her age. She dotes on Rush so, I was worried she would never make new friends. Now if we could just get her to open up about her past, everything would be perfect."

"Life is never perfect, Alexandria, but I'm a firm believer that time is a good healer. When Caro is ready, she will tell us about her past."

"I hope so, but as you well know, I'm not one with a lot of patience. I guess we have all the time in the world to wait."

"You and I, maybe," her mother said, "but I don't know about my joints. My rheumatism has me feeling as stiff as a board. My old joints have been throbbing like a toothache all day. I only hope they're not predicting rain." Stella moved stiffly toward the stairs. "If you don't mind, I think I'll take a short nap before dinner."

"Maybe a nice warm bath would soothe you. I'll heat water for all of us after supper. Now you go on and rest. I'm going to clean up here and then pull out those quilts we've been storing forever under my bed. After supper, if you feel like it, we'll go through them and decide which ones we want to sell."

"Sell? I hope, daughter, you aren't being too optimistic about selling those quilts. Most folks in these parts make their own. I figure if we sell one, we'll be doing well."

"One's better than none. If we can't sell them maybe we can trade them. And, yes, Mother, I am an optimist."

Her mother shook her head and mounted the stairs. "I hope your tendency to expect a favorable outcome doesn't disappoint you, love."

"It won't, Mother. I just know my workroom will be successful."

After her mother disappeared, Alex turned back toward the front room. Funny, she thought, since her cousin Caro and Rush Duncan had come into their lives, their conditions had taken a turn for the better. Not only had the money Rush had given them turned her dream of a quilting workroom into a near-reality, but it had also eased the burden of making ends meet.

It wasn't Rush's money, but Caro's, she reminded herself. By now Captain Steve and his crew would have received her letter of thanks for their donation. Someday she hoped to meet Rush's good friend and thank him in person, but how she would accomplish this she had no idea. In the meantime, she would just have to try harder to be more tolerant of the man who had brought such favorable changes into their lives, if for no other reason than for Caro and her infatuation with Rush.

And your own.

She would have argued with herself, but she knew the argument was fruitless. For the first time in Alex's life, she had met a man, or met again a boy who was now a man, to whom she was attracted. No matter how much she denied it, the truth was evident in her reaction to Rush's kiss and to his persistent intrusion into her mind. What she would do about the attraction, Alex didn't know. Long ago she had sworn an oath to herself never to fall in love with a rambling man, a canaller like Rush Duncan. More important, she couldn't forget Caro's feelings for him. Although Caro was only a child, her feelings were very real. Competition from Alex was the last thing Caro needed in her already complicated life.

Alex removed the paintbrush from the can and placed it in the cleaning solution. This done, she carried the pails of soapy lye water to the small landing on the back of the house and placed the paint rags in the water to soak. The strong solution burned her chapped hands when she dipped them into the water.

"I'll clean these later," she said aloud, looking around the yard for Caro. Then she heard her cousin's voice. Her question carried to her across the small backyard.

"You think Rush will be back later this week?" Caro asked. Alex looked toward the saloon and saw Caro in conversation with Samson. They stood together outside the storeroom's open door—Samson, Caro, and Snow.

"Hard to tell about that one," Samson responded, "but I suspect we'll be seeing a lot more of him in the next few months."

"You really think so? It's because of me, I bet." Caro hugged Snow to her and rocked the cat like a baby.

Samson laughed. "Probably is, little one." Samson's gaze met Alex's above Caro's head. "It's hard to resist a pretty lady," he said. Feeling Samson's words were meant for her instead of Caro, Alex felt her face grow hot.

Unsure what to do, she whirled around and headed back inside. "Mercy," she scolded herself, "now I'm imagining the neighbors know what's inside my mind. Alexandria Paine, you must stop this fantasizing over the likes of Rush Duncan."

As she headed upstairs to the bedroom, she continued to lecture herself. "Rush Duncan is nothing more than a philanderer. You know his type. No roots, a woman in every canal town along the towpath."

When she finally reached the bedroom, Alex was so disturbed by her thoughts that she flopped down on the floor beside the bed with such a flounce that her skirt swelled around her like a giant pumpkin shell. She beat at the skirt with her hands, trying to deflate it before burying her face in her palms in frustration.

"I could use a fairy godmother," she said. "Instead of making me the pumpkin, she could make me a fine coach to whisk me away from all of this."

Could she be in love? Alex wondered, then decided if this was love, she wanted no part of such torment. More important, she had no time for such an annoyance. She was far too busy getting her workroom ready for use.

She massaged her temples, wondering why she had come upstairs. Then she remembered. "The quilts! I came up here for the quilts."

Reaching beneath the bed, her hands groped for the familiar stack. They had been stored beneath the bed for so long, they would probably need a good washing to get out the dust. Finally her fingers grasped the familiar pile. With a quick tug, then a long sweep of her arm, she managed to move the stack of quilts from beneath the bed.

But the quilts weren't alone. They were accompanied by Caro's bag of rags. Alex's probing and pulling had caused the contents of the burlap bag to spill out onto the floor in a heap, revealing the bag's contents.

She recognized that they were the same quilting squares she had seen the first night of Caro's arrival, only now the pile seemed larger. What she could see of the jumbled mess, Alex recognized the same precise stitching as that of the Marmalade cat. Alex knew she shouldn't touch the squares, that Caro wouldn't approve of her snooping, but Alex's curiosity got the better of her.

One by one, she straightened out the squares, placing them in rows across the floor in front of her knees. Her quilter's eye recognized many of the representational designs used both in the appliquéd and pieced material: birds, flowers, leaves, and stars. There were some pieced in the familiar Wheel pattern, the Wandering Foot, and the Log Cabin. As she ran her fingers over the rainbow-colored designs, Alex felt a connection to the aunt she had never known, not only as a relative, but also as a fellow quilter.

Excitement coursed through her. She scooted backward on her knees as she flattened and straightened each block, imagining the way the finished quilt would look when it was finally sewn together as a whole. She was sure the finished quilt would be a legacy to Caro's past, a precious recording of a mother and daughter's life set in cloth with needle and thread.

The pieces that really thrilled Alex were those with appliqués. One appliquéd square represented a family; a man and woman with their two young girls. One girl's hair was the color of sunshine like her own, the other the color of midnight like Caro's. The foursome stood in front of what looked like a facsimile of Jefferson Rock.

As she studied the worked square, Alex was convinced that the cloth picture represented her mother's family when both sisters were still children. The unfolding of another piece revealed a tinker's wagon pulled by a horse. Alex studied the vehicle. She supposed it was the wagon belonging to the man her Aunt Charlotte had run away with all those years ago—the same man who might be Caro's father.

Anxious to see more, Alex unfolded another square and spread it out with the others. The third one looked like a house built—

"No!" Caro shouted from behind her. "You mustn't touch them!" A startled Snow leaped from her cousin's arms and streaked across the end of the bed and out of the room.

Frozen in place, Alex could only watch while Caro darted around her and fell to her knees and began scooping up the quilt pieces, covering those she couldn't hold with her body. When Alex tried to apologize and help her gather up the strewn pieces, the child became almost hysterical.

"I'm sorry, Caro," she said, trying to calm her. "I never meant to snoop. When I came in here to get the quilts stored under the bed, your bag—the pieces fell out." She placed a hand on the child's back, trying to quiet her. "Please, let me help you pick them up. I'll close my eyes and won't look, I promise. But please, honey, let me help you."

"No. Don't touch them." Fear marked her tiny features. "If you do, you'll die like the rest of them."

"Die? Like the rest of them? No, Caro. Caro, I won't die—"

"You will, you will!" her cousin insisted. Tears began to flow from her sapphire-blue eyes. "Then they'll burn up our house and they'll come and send me away again."

"Caro, honey, no one is going to burn our house." Alex tried to gather the child in her arms, but Caro jumped to her feet, her spidery arms holding as many of the squares as she could against her chest. Terror marked her cousin's features.

"Please, Caro, let me help you." Alex picked up several of the squares that were now strewn about the area in front of her knees. On seeing Alex touch them, Caro tried grabbing them away, which only made her drop the rest of the pieces.

"Don't touch them. You mustn't touch them. I should have left them buried." Caro began to cry in earnest now.

"Buried? Oh, Caro, sugar, you're not making sense. Here, let me help you put them back in the bag."

"You'll get cholera! You'll die like my ma, pa, and brother. Snow will run away like Marmalade did. I'll never see any of you again!" Caro sobbed and sniffed.

Cholera? Burn our house? Suddenly it dawned on Alex what Caro was saying. Apparently the child was revealing what must have taken place in Nebraska after her family had died of cholera. Perhaps neighbors burned Caro's home to the ground to keep the disease from spreading. But why would they allow a ten-year-old to witness such a tragedy?

What should I do, what should I do? Alex felt almost panicky herself. How could she make Caro realize that the squares didn't carry the cholera scourge? *Or, did they?* Her experience with the dreaded disease was nonexistent. *Where's Mother? She would know.*

Alex finally understood Caro's reason for safeguarding the squares—the links with her past. It wasn't that she was afraid to share them with others; it was that she feared that whoever touched them would get the disease. The disease that had killed her family.

Poor baby, how can I tell her not to worry when I don't know for sure if what she claims is true?

Alex took a deep breath. *Think, dummy. Think. What can I do to calm her?*

The square of Marmalade. Caro had washed it. She believed it was safe to handle after she had washed it. *Yes, yes, Caro, honey, you're smarter than I am.* Her cousin had washed the square to rid it of the cholera germs.

Alex jumped to her feet. "Caro, sugar, listen to me. We'll wash these. Just like you washed the square of Marmalade. Then they won't be infected any longer."

Caro continued to sob. She sat on the floor. She had piled as many of the squares as she could beneath her. The others she held in her arms.

"Don't move, Caro, please," Alex pleaded. "You stay right where you are. I'm going to fix everything."

"You can't fix it. No one can!" Caro sobbed. "You're gonna die because you touched them. Snow's gonna run away.

They're gonna burn our house, and I'll have nowhere else to go.''

Alex rushed toward the door. "Don't move, Caro, you hear me? I'll be right back. Trust me, I'm gonna fix everything. You'll see. I promise you, they won't burn our house.''

Alex practically sprinted down the stairs and to the back porch. Once there, she sought out the two pails of soapy lye water. Reaching inside one, she slung the rags that were already soaking in the water onto the floor. Then she grabbed the two pails and charged back up the stairs. Water sloshed, wetting the floor and the hem of her skirt.

Going as fast as her legs would carry her, Alex raced back toward the bedroom. "Look, Caro. See—see what I have. I've brought lye water. The lye soap kills germs. It's better than the soap you used on Marmalade. We'll wash the squares like you washed the square of Marmalade. You'll see, everything will be fine.''

Caro still sat hunched on the floor, her sobs muffled by the squares she held in her arms.

Alex rounded the bed and plunked the pails of soapy water down on the floor beside Caro. "We'll wash them, honey. The germs will go away if we wash them.'' The ten-year-old ignored her and continued to sob into her lap.

"Caro, you trust me, don't you, honey? Please, please let me put them in this water I brought up from downstairs.'' Alex reached for several of the material pieces scattered around her cousin.

"No!'' Caro protested. "Only me, only I can touch them. The cholera didn't kill me.'' Her child's voice took on an almost eerie sound. "I wanted it, too—I prayed it would make me sick so I could die with the rest of them. I didn't want to be left alone—''

"All right, Caro,'' Alex interrupted, "you put them in the water.'' *Lordy, what had the child experienced?* "Just like you did the night you washed Marmalade. Remember, Marmalade was clean after you laundered him.''

Caro looked at the pails of soapy water, then back at Alex.

"Remember, Caro? After you washed the other square, I touched it. It's been days, and I'm still fine. You wash them.

We'll wash them together. The germs will be gone once they're clean.''

Alex held out her hands. "See my hands, see what the lye soap did. It practically washed away my skin, it's so strong." She tried to laugh, but it sounded feeble to her own ears. Alex's hands were red and chapped from having been in the soapy water. Such a little pain compared to what Caro must have suffered. She felt tears gather in her own eyes.

"I promise once we wash the squares, there will be no more germs. Okay? Will you put them in the water, Caro, please?"

Caro sniffed. At least she seemed to be listening. *Dear Lord, don't let us all die of the cholera.*

Alex plunged her hands in the water. "See, I'm washing my hands. I'll wash away all the germs that I might have gotten from touching the squares earlier. Everything is going to be fine, darling. Just put the material in the water."

After several tense moments, her instructions seemed to register. Reluctantly at first, then almost eagerly, Caro began to stuff the pieces of cloth into the water.

"That's a good girl," Alex crooned. "You'll see, everything will be fine."

When all the squares were in the water, Alex swished them around with her hands. The soapy water burned her chapped hands like fire, but the pain reminded her she was alive, that Caro was alive, and she hoped the cholera germs were dead.

Caro dunked her hands in the water, pushing the rags below the surface and making certain they were completely submerged. Their fingers brushed in the soapy water, and Alex found Caro's smaller ones and squeezed.

Again she crooned. "You'll see, darling, we're going to wash away all those germs. Soon they'll be gone forever."

"I-I don't want you and Aunt Stella to die because of me."

"Oh, honey, we won't. You mustn't believe that someone's dying is caused by something you did or didn't do. Our days on earth are numbered from the moment we come into the world—it's God's will that we should live or die."

"But—but my ma, pa, and baby brother. Why did God will them to die and not me?"

"Oh, Caro, sugar, I wish I knew the answer to that question.

Maybe together you and I can discover the answer. I lost my pa when I was seventeen—not nearly as young as you were, but age doesn't lessen the pain of loss. What does make it a little easier is having someone with you who loves you and recognizes the pain you're feeling. I was lucky. I had my mother. You weren't so lucky, but now you have me and your aunt Stella.''

"But what if you get the—"

"It's not going to happen, I promise." She lifted her hands from the bucket and dried them on her skirt. "You know what I think, Caro? I think we both could use a good hug right about now. Won't you come over here and let me hug you?"

The invitation was all the child needed. She threw herself into Alex's arms, nearly knocking her backwards. Alex laughed nervously while regaining her balance enough so that she could encircle Caro with her arms. She rocked and patted as more tears spilled from Caro's eyes, and sobs wracked her thin body. Alex no longer fought her own tears.

She buried her face in Caro's hair. The child smelled like salty tears, lye soap, and rose-water perfume. Her small face fit perfectly in the cradle of Alex's shoulder. Alex gently stroked the mop of curls that felt like satin beneath her rough fingers.

Maybe now, sweetheart, Alex thought as she hugged and rocked, *you can put this whole horrible experience behind you, and we can begin again together.*

11

A SHARP WIND BLEW off the Potomac River, making the squares of quilting flap on the clothesline like flags in a parade. Alex clothespinned the last wet square and stepped back. Her mother, several feet behind her, paced the length of the line, studying each of the squares with awe.

"That poor child," her mother said, coming to a standstill beside Alex. "How horrible that our Caro had to endure such suffering. Not only losing her family to death, but then seeing her home, everything she held dear, burned to the ground right in front of her eyes." Stella Paine shook her head and *tsk-tsked*. "What that child has lived with these last few months is beyond my comprehension."

"Beyond mine as well," Alex responded. "I only hope now she'll be able to put that chapter of her life behind her and begin fresh." Alex picked up the wicker basket and started toward the house. "She was almost in hysterics. I felt so helpless, Mother, I didn't know what to do."

"You handled it fine, Alexandria, although I wish you would have called me." Shaking her head again, Stella preceded Alex up the back steps. "I can't believe I slept through the crisis."

"Now that it's behind us, I'm glad you did."

Alex didn't know whether she should express to her mother that the squares might still be contaminated with the cholera germ or bide her time and wait to see what happened. Surely, she reasoned, after six months and soaking the quilt pieces overnight in the lye-soap water, the blocks would no longer contain the germ. Besides, hadn't she read somewhere recently that cholera was spread by contaminated water? Too bad there was no one in Harpers Ferry she could voice her concerns to without the fear of causing a panic over the still-dreaded disease. She thought of Rush and wished he were here. Maybe he knew about such things.

Her mother broke into her thoughts. "Well, Caro certainly seems to have made a full recovery. Early this morning, she took Snow over to Jamie Hamilton's for his belated wagon ride. She seemed so happy and carefree. It is as though a great weight has been lifted from her shoulders."

"I'm sure it has, Mother. We can count ourselves lucky that children are so resilient." Alex walked into the front room where the brackets she planned to secure to the wall today were piled on the floor. "How's your rheumatism this morning? I hope you're not in too much pain."

With a flutter of her hand, her mother waved aside Alex's concerns. "I'm fine, daughter. Just a little stiff. My aches seem so minor after learning what I have about Caro in the last twelve hours. Do you think once those pieces are dry and ready to be sewn into a quilt top that she will tell us more about her past?"

"I think she will, but if she doesn't do so immediately, we must not press her."

"Of course, we won't press her." Stella ran her fingers along the quilt frame Alex had assembled during the night, which now stood in the middle of the room. "Everything is falling into place, Alexandria—the workroom, Caro coming to grips with her past. I think we're due for a celebration, don't you?"

"Did I hear celebration?"

Both women turned toward the doorway, where Leona Whitley and her sister Rosellen stood. "Are you going to ask us in to view this workroom of yours, Alexandria, or leave us standing out here to be blown away by the wind?'' Leona asked.

Her mother laughed. ''Of course not, come in, ladies.'' She bustled toward them, ushering them inside. A strong gust grabbed the door from her fingers and slammed it shut, causing both women to jump. ''We have so much to celebrate, and I can't wait to tell y'all about it.''

Leona's bulldog jowls fluttered as if they had been stirred by the blustery wind. ''I heard you mention celebration, Stella. Does this mean Alexandria's young man has popped the question? See, Rosellen, I was right. There is going to be a wedding in our near future.''

''Hush,'' her sister reprimanded. ''You promised me that if I'd come over here with you, Leona, you would refrain from badgering poor Alexandria about getting married. We haven't been here five minutes, and already you've gone back on your word.''

This morning Rosellen wore a hat that lived up to its owner's name. Huge pink and red cabbage roses covered every straw inch of the floppy brim. On a larger woman the hat might not have seemed so massive, but on Rosellen's petite form, the size and weight of the creation looked as though it might break the woman's delicate neck. To Alex's amazement, Rosellen's neck remained unbroken, and she carried herself with the same self-possession that she always did.

Alex smiled at the two sisters. ''I'm sorry to disappoint you, Leona, but there is no wedding in my immediate future. And need I remind you again, no young man, either.'' Alex looked to her mother for help.

''Alexandria is right, Leona. We have no call to celebrate a wedding, but we do have reason to celebrate. My niece, Caro, has brought with her from Nebraska a marvelous quilt. As soon as Alex and I can sew the pieces together, we can begin the 'putting in.' '' She tapped the frame with her fingers. ''It will be the first quilt ever to be quilted in Alexandria's workroom.''

The two women clucked like hens. ''Such an event does call for a celebration. We can have a frolic,'' Rosellen said. ''We'll invite the whole town.''

Leona's jowls quivered in excitement. "Right here in this room. Since you face High Street, we'll close off the lower section of the road and have a real party."

"We'll have a picnic supper and perhaps some dancing," Rosellen added. "Do you think we can talk Bowstring and his friends into supplying us with music if we promise them a free supper?"

Bowstring, as he was called by the townspeople of Harpers Ferry, was the finest fiddler in the area. He was nothing more than a hillbilly who lived in the hills on the Maryland side of the river. Whenever the good folks of Harpers Ferry decided to hold a shindig that required music, Bowstring was usually called upon to do the fiddling. He and his friends would have done the fiddling for nothing because they loved music, but if you threw in a home-cooked meal prepared by the best cooks in Harpers Ferry, the little band of musicians gave their all to providing some of the best fiddling available this side of the Mason-Dixon line.

"I'm sure Bowstring would love to come," Leona said, "especially if food is available. From the size of that man, it wouldn't surprise me one whit if the only time he eats is when we feed him."

"Sister," Rosellen scolded, "Mr. Bowstring is merely raw-boned, not starved."

"If you want my opinion, his raw bones are in desperate need of some meat."

"I swan, Leona," her sister replied, "you think everyone who is not as plump as a roasting chicken is suffering from malnutrition. We don't all have to look like you."

"Well, I never." Leona's plump bosom puffed up with indignation. "What is the world coming to when one's only sister compares her to a roasting hen?"

"Leona and Rosellen, stop quibbling this minute," Stella insisted. "One's girth or lack of it is not the issue. Your idea of a frolic is all well and good, but since it will be Caro's quilt that we'll be quilting in Alexandria's workroom, I think we should let the two girls decide whether they are willing to suffer such a large frolic."

"Certainly a frolic isn't cause for suffering," Leona said.

Patting her hair beneath her big hat, Rosellen said, "Every-one loves a frolic. The party will give me an excuse to show off my newest bonnet. I ordered it from a milliner in Balti-more, and it should arrive any day now."

"Since when do you need an excuse to show off, Sister?"

Rosellen shot Leona a scathing look before transferring her gaze to Alex. She, along with the other two women, waited for her response.

Alex hesitated, toying with the idea of the quilting bee. It seemed only fitting to have Aunt Charlotte's quilt be the very first one to be quilted on her new frame and in her workroom. In a way, it would be like a homecoming. Alex could only imagine what the event would mean to her mother and to the success of her cottage industry. It would be a good way to let the townspeople know about her workroom.

"Before we make any plans," she told the three eager women, "we'll have to check with Caro since the quilt be-longs to her." Alex hoped her cousin would agree. "I'll ask her this evening and let you ladies know in a day or two."

Rosellen cupped her hands beneath her chin. "It's been so long since we've had a real frolic, and I know the ladies in our quilting circle will be pleased. May is such a delightful time for an outside party—not too cool and not too hot, but I daresay today is more like March than May, the way the wind is blowing."

"We'll have Mr. Lorber at the paper print up flyers to dis-tribute around town," Leona added. "It's only fitting that I should be in charge of the supper arrangements. Oh, I just can't wait." Her eyes took on a dreamy expression like that of a young girl. "I do so wish the major could be in atten-dance."

"Ladies, please," Alex said. "We must not rush ahead with these plans. Remember, I must check with Caro first. And my room is not yet ready. I still have a lot—"

"Looks fine to me, Alexandria," Rosellen said. She spun around in a circle, taking in the freshly painted walls. "It's a fine room. There is still plenty of space even with the quilting frame taking up the center. And those front windows allow in so much light. It will be wonderful for stitching. You don't plan to cover the windows with shades, do you?''

Alex only had time to nod that she didn't before Leona voiced more plans for the quilting. "I have extra chairs we can use. We'll have that quilt done in no time flat.''

Rosellen continued, "Then when the sun goes down, we can get down to some serious eating and dancing. There is something so romantic about dancing beneath the stars.''

Stella, caught up in the excitement, added, "Alexandria can make her wonderful Sally Lunn bread.''

Leona giggled like a young girl. "Alex and her young man can get down to some serious spooning, too.''

"Leona!'' All three women chimed her name together.

But Leona wasn't to be silenced. "I'm only repeating what that handsome young man told us.'' When everyone present gave her the evil eye, she ignored them, continuing, "Of course, Mr. Duncan must attend the festivities. After all, he is responsible for bringing young Caro home.''

"Mr. Duncan isn't my young man, Leona,'' Alex reminded her for the second time that day, "and he doesn't seem the type who would enjoy such festivities.''

Silently Alex questioned the truthfulness of her words. Rush's interest in wildflowers had certainly surprised her, as well as his devotion to her young cousin. But she wasn't about to praise him in front of Leona Whitley, who would misconstrue anything Alex said and have the couple at the altar before the day ended. "You do realize that Mr. Duncan has a canal boat to run?''

"But a man has to relax sometime,'' Leona answered. "Besides, I've never known a bachelor to pass up a good meal when it was offered to him, or I don't see him disappointing you by not attending.''

"Mrs. Whitley, please,'' Alex pleaded. "You have to understand that Caro has an infatuation with Mr. Duncan. It's very important that around her you don't refer to Rush as my young man.''

"Rush, is it?'' Leona's eyes grew wide, all knowing. Then her hand fluttered to her bosom. "Alexandria, you aren't suggesting that I would do anything to hurt that innocent child?''

"Yes, Sister, we are,'' Rosellen answered for Alex. "If

we're to have this frolic and Mr. Duncan desires to attend, you must promise to keep those lips of yours buttoned. And you must stop badgering poor Alexandria about the man, especially now that you know where young Caro's sentiments lie.''

Looking affronted, Leona grumbled, ''Well, I never.''

''Sister, do you understand Alex's request?''

After several strained moments, Leona responded. ''Oh, very well, but Mr. Duncan must be invited.''

Alex fidgeted. The last thing she wanted was for Rush Duncan to attend the festivities, but then she did have Caro's feelings to consider. ''If we see him again before the party, then we'll invite him,'' she replied. She hoped not seeing him would let her off the hook, but Leona was bent on Rush attending.

''Better yet,'' Leona added, heading toward the door, ''I'll tell the lockkeeper to deliver Mr. Duncan a personal invitation the next time he passes through.'' Satisfied with her idea, she called to her sister. ''Come, Rosellen, we have plans to make.''

Rosellen followed her sister to the door, then stopped. ''As soon as you've talked with Caro and she has made a decision, let us know, Alexandria. We'll not go forward with our plans until we hear from you.''

The sisters disappeared through the door. As the twosome made their way up the street, Rosellen anchored her hat with her hand to keep the wind from lifting it from her head.

Alex was bothered more than she cared to admit by the prospect of Rush attending the planned festivities, especially after their encounter on his last visit. Instead of looking forward to the event, she wished the idea could be blown away on today's wind.

That evening, after supper, when the three women in the Paine household decided to partake of the bath they had missed the night before because of the crisis with Caro, Alex decided she would broach the subject of the quilt with her cousin, but she would wait until the time was right.

The old copper tub had been dragged out of the pantry, and several pots of water had been set to boil on the new range.

When the water was the right temperature, Stella was the first to use the bathtub, then Alex, and now Caro. Surprisingly, her cousin sat in the tub with the sudsy water covering her shoulders, seemingly content. While Alex's mother shampooed her niece's curls, Snow sat on a chair beside the tub, swatting at the many bubbles that floated from the foamy lather on top of Caro's head.

Alex had decided to heat the iron and begin pressing the many quilt squares that she had taken off the line earlier. It was a homey feeling, the three of them together, sharing in each other's ablutions. Having Caro in their lives, Alex decided, was almost as good as having a child of her own.

"But Snow is a boy, Aunt Stella," Caro said. "Do you think he ought to be watching me bathe?"

"I'm sure, Caro dear, that Snow is more interested in playing with soap bubbles than ogling your person. Besides, he would need very thick spectacles to see beneath that film of soapy water."

"Then it would be okay, I reckon, if Jamie Hamilton were here. He's a boy, but he couldn't see my person beneath the soapy water either."

Stella cleared her throat. Her gaze met Alex's over the top of Caro's wet head. From the mouths of babes, Alex thought, and suppressed a laugh.

"I think, child," her aunt answered, "Jamie Hamilton's presence would make it an entirely different situation. Young ladies don't allow young gentlemen to see them in their altogether, or vice versa."

"Why? I used to watch my ma bathe my brother John." Caro lifted her hand from the water, making a pyramid of bubbles on her palm. She blew the suds at Snow, giggling when the white froth stuck to his nose.

Alex's mother rolled her eyes heavenward. "Bathing is different when it's family doing it," Stella answered. "Just like us—we're family so we can share this experience."

"We're all girls," Caro insisted, "except for Snow, and I reckon he doesn't count because he's a cat."

"Yes, we are all girls, and that definitely makes a difference," Stella agreed, "but I'm sure that in time when both you and your brother grew older, the two of you would have become more modest in your bathing habits.''

Caro looked thoughtful.

Alex watched her, concerned over the turn their conversation had taken. Surprisingly, though, Caro seemed to be fine with the discussion and appeared to be satisfied with her aunt's answer.

''I guess I'll never know if we would have become more—more modern.''

''Modest,'' Stella corrected.

While Stella bent to kiss her niece's wet cheek, Alex wondered if she dared to question Caro about her past. Now seemed as good a time as any, especially since Caro had brought up the subject of her brother.

''Would you like to tell us about your brother John?'' Alex asked. She continued to press the patchwork squares, pretending to concentrate on them instead of looking directly at Caro.

For a moment the child said nothing, then she spoke. ''Johnny was three, and he was only a half of a brother.''

''You mean a half brother,'' Alex's mother corrected.

''Yeah, I guess that's what I mean. Me and him, we didn't have the same pa. Same ma, but different pas.'' She reached up and gave her hair a good rubbing before dropping her hands into the water again. ''My ma always said it didn't make no never mind that I didn't have the same blood as Johnny's pa had. She said, Jack loved me just as much as he loved Johnny. Of course, he had me a lot longer than he had my baby brother.''

''How long did he have you?'' Alex questioned.

Caro rolled her eyes toward the ceiling before resting her hand on her chin. ''Most of my life. He 'dopted me when I was not much younger than baby Johnny, before we headed west.''

Continuing to press the square instead of pressing Caro for more details about her past, Alex kept on ironing.

So, Alex thought, the man who had died of the cholera, along with Caro's mother and half brother, had not been Caro's real father. Who had fathered her? Was it the tinker Charlotte ran away with all those years ago?

It appeared that Alex's mother had less patience than she did. "Did you know your real pa, Caro?" she heard her mother ask.

"Naw, not really. I was too little. Ma said he left us 'cause he was a gambling man. You know, he never could sit still."

Alex heard her mother's quick intake of breath. "Where did he leave you?" she asked.

"In a salon."

Stella Paine croaked. "A gambler. In a saloon?"

Alex shot her mother a warning glance. "I think, honey, what your aunt Stella wanted to know was the name of the town where your pa left you."

"A town? I'm not sure. Maybe that's when my ma became a barmaid."

Her mother's face turned as white as a sheet, and Alex feared she might suffer another fainting spell. Alex put down the iron and walked to her mother's side and gently squeezed her shoulder. "Mother, why don't you get the hot water for Caro's hair, and we'll rinse out the shampoo together."

"Good idea, Daughter," Stella responded. Slowly, the color returned to her face. "I'll make sure the rinse water is just the right temperature."

Lordy, it was worse than they suspected, if what Caro said was true. The man who had fathered her wasn't the tinker, but a gambler who lived in a saloon, and Aunt Charlotte was a barmaid.

"I hate rinsing," Caro complained, breaking into Alex's thoughts. "Can't we leave the soap in?"

"If we did that, your hair would look like hay instead of hair. I daresay Rush wouldn't like his favorite girl to have a hayfield growing on top of her head. Yes, we must rinse it." Alex helped her cousin to stand, then folded a clean washcloth and handed it to Caro. "Cover your face with this rag when we pour the water over your hair. I promise we'll be finished in no time."

"I don't suppose Jamie Hamilton would want my hair to look like hay, either," Caro mumbled, placing the rag over her face.

Stella returned with the warm water. "Okay, Caro, are you ready?"

"Hurry, hurry," Caro said, squirming like a worm on a hook when the water was poured over her head.

"It smells like vinegar," Caro grumbled, her face buried in the rag. She squirmed some more. "Just hurry—please?"

"The vinegar will make your hair feel silky," Alex's mother added.

Together, both women massaged the mass of curls until the shampoo was rinsed away.

"At last, we're finished," Alex told her. "You wait while I get something to dry you with."

After helping Caro step from the tub, she wrapped her in a big turkish towel, dried her, then helped her to put on a nightgown. "See, that wasn't so bad now, was it?" Not giving the child a chance to answer, she pulled her close and hugged her. "Mother will brush your hair while I get rid of this bath water."

Alex scooped pails of water from the tub, then lugged them to the back door and tossed the contents outside. When the tub was almost empty, she dragged it to the porch and dumped the remaining water. Her task finished, she returned inside to the ironing board.

Caro now sat on a high stool with Snow in her lap while Stella stood behind her brushing her niece's wet hair. "Caro tells me her adopted father's name was Jack Swift."

For the third or fourth time in the last hour, Alex exchanged another curious glance with her mother.

Spreading an appliquéd square on the board, Alex began ironing it. She recognized it to be the same square she had been looking at last night when Caro had interrupted her. The square was of a house that looked as though it was part of the hill behind it. The dwelling had sprigs of grass growing from its roof and two windows, one on each side of the door. When Alex finished ironing the piece, she held it up so Caro could see it. "Can you tell me about this?" she questioned tentatively.

Caro looked at the square, then quickly glanced away. Alex detected a spark of pain in her cousin's blue eyes, but decided she wouldn't let that look sway her from asking her next question. "Was this your house back in Nebraska?"

After a moment the ten-year-old nodded. "Yeah. It was our soddie." Suppressing a sigh, she stroked Snow's fur.

Alex and her mother watched Caro, waiting for her to continue. When she did, she appeared to gain more confidence in the telling. "The soddie was built from Nebraska marble."

"Nebraska marble?" Alex and her mother questioned at the same time.

Caro giggled at her relatives. "Folks in Nebraska call sod marble. On the prairie, houses are built from sod because there isn't many trees to use for lumber."

"Nebraska marble," her mother repeated. "Imagine that, Alexandria. A house of grass. You realize, Caro, that you've seen things that Alex and I can't even imagine because we've both spent our whole lives right here in Harpers Ferry."

She's probably seen things she shouldn't have seen as well, Alex thought.

Caro puckered her lips. "Yeah, I guess I am smarter than both of you."

Alex smiled and finished ironing another square. "What about this one?" She held it up so both her mother and Caro could see it. This block, too, was done in the same appliquéd technique as the previous one of the sod house.

"That's my ma's milk pitcher," Caro informed them. "When the prairie flowers bloomed, we would pick them and stick them in that pitcher on our supper table. My ma always loved flowers."

It must be the pitcher that Caro had told them about. What had she said? *We would stick flowers in a white milk jug and place it in the middle of the table. The different colored blossoms reflected in the jug's surface and looked as pretty as a rainbow.*

With Caro's last revelation, Alex felt certain that she had been correct in her earlier assumption. Caro had been describing mealtime with her family back home in Nebraska when she had described eating from china plates and drinking from crystal glasses. Feeling encouraged, she asked her cousin,

"Did you make a square showing china plates and crystal glasses as well?"

"Huh?" Caro looked at Alex as though she had suddenly taken leave of her senses.

Her cousin's response made Alex feel ridiculous for having voiced such a question. "Never mind," she said, "but I hope you realize, Caro, that all these wonderful quilt pieces you brought with you from home tell a story—a story about your past."

"I know," Caro answered matter-of-factly. "My ma called it a memory quilt—she said when we finished, it would be the story of our lives." Her expression grew troubled. "That's why I had to save them when—when they burned our house." A shadow of alarm touched her angelic face. "Alex, are you sure it's safe for you to touch them now that we washed them in lies?"

"Lye soap, dear," Alex corrected, smiling at her young cousin.

"Of course, they are safe for us to touch," Stella said, "and don't you let anyone tell you differently."

Her mother's words were meant to comfort Caro, but Alex still wasn't convinced that washing the squares had made them safe to touch.

Later she would ask her mother not to mention Caro's story to the other ladies of the guild for fear that they would believe the squares were still contaminated. In the meantime, she would try to learn as much as she could about the dreaded disease, but she realized that if none of them became ill, that would be the real proof.

Stella came to stand beside Alex at the ironing board and thumbed through the stack of already ironed squares. "Come here, Caro. Tell us the meaning of these other pieces." When Caro approached them still holding Snow, Stella began spreading the blocks out on the surface of the worktable.

"I might not remember everything," Caro said, "but I'll try to tell you what I do."

"A tinker's wagon," her mother said, sucking in her breath. Her hand that covered her bosom shook visibly.

Caro looked at the square for several moments, then said,

"That wagon belonged to my real pa. My ma said they gambled all over in that wagon before they got me from the stork and I grew too big to gamble."

Gamble or ramble? Had Caro confused the two words? "Don't you mean ramble, not gamble?" Alex asked.

"Huh?" Caro considered Alex's question for several moments, then she asked, "Does ramble mean the same as traveling?"

"Yes, it does."

"Yeah, I remember now. My ma said my real pa was a traveling salesman. He wandered all over the countryside, selling stuff from that wagon." She pointed to the appliquéd square of the tinker's wagon.

Stella's expression grew eager. "Your real pa?" she quizzed. "Do you remember his name, Caro?"

"Of course, I know my real pa's name. My ma said although Jack 'dopted me, I should never forget my real pa's name. It was Tyler Moore."

"Tyler Moore," Stella whispered. Her eyes filled with tears, and she blinked them back, hugging her niece to her. "Tyler Moore," she repeated again.

"Aunt Stella, you're crushing Snow." Caro tried to squirm from her aunt's arms.

"Snow? Oh, my word, I'm sorry, Snow. I didn't mean to crush you." She set her niece away from her.

"Can I go to bed now?" Caro asked. "Me and Snow, we're tired. That Jamie Hamilton ran my legs clean off, making me pull him in his wagon."

"You had to pull him?" Alex questioned. "Seems to me, he should have been pulling you."

"I didn't mind. If I pulled him I could keep him away from the other girls."

"You mean his sisters?" Alex, along with her mother, studied Caro, waiting for her answer.

"Naw. They only like to play with their silly dolls. Jamie and I like to climb trees and play chase. When those other girls started chasing Jamie, that's when I decided it was best that I pull him. That way, I could have him all to myself."

"All to yourself," Alex and her mother repeated together.

Alex could see that her mother was also trying to keep a straight face.

"Not all to myself," Caro corrected. "I had to share him with Snow and his cat Minerva."

"I see," Alex responded, shaking her head. It seemed that her young cousin had turned fickle. Not only did she have a crush on Rush, but she also had one on Jamie. This thought reminded Alex that she hadn't mentioned the quilting frolic.

"Come on, child," Stella said, "I'll accompany your weary body to your bed and tuck you in." Her mother took Caro's hand, and together they started up the stairs. "Remind me, Alexandria, to speak to young Jamie for running my niece's legs clean off."

"I'd prefer you didn't, Aunt Stella," Caro said. Her face grew serious. "I kinda liked pulling him."

"Caro, before you go up," Alex called, interrupting their parting, "I meant to ask you something about your quilt."

The twosome paused on the stairs. "I know what you're gonna ask." Caro said.

"You do?"

"Yeah. Miss Leona, she already told me about the quilting frolic this afternoon when I was at Jamie's house."

"She did?" Alex and her mother exchanged looks again, and Alex felt her temper rise. The woman hadn't waited. Some days she felt like wringing Leona Whitley's chubby neck. "What did Mrs. Whitley say?"

"She said we would have a big frolic if I agreed that we could start quilting on my quilt in your new workroom."

Alex slammed the ironing board with her hand, nearly upsetting the iron. "Of all the nerve! I told her—"

"Don't be mad at her, Alex. Besides, she said if I agreed, we could have a big celebration, and I'd get to dance in the street with Jamie Hamilton."

"Then you don't mind? It would be okay with you if we begin working on your quilt after we get it pieced together?"

"If I can dance with Jamie Hamilton. Of course, he said he'd run away from me—that he wasn't dancing with any stupid girl." She smiled knowingly. "I don't care, though. I can run faster than he does, so I'll catch him."

''Then it's all settled,'' Stella responded. ''We'll all have a big time at the quilting frolic.''

Caro yawned. ''Good night, Alex. I'll see you in the morning.''

''Cover your mouth, child,'' Stella admonished. Alex watched her cousin skip up the stairs as her mother followed her.

Alone in the kitchen, Alex shook her head. ''Would that my own love life was that easy. Not that I have a love life.''

She wondered what Rush Duncan's response would be, if she decided to chase him until she caught him. The thought made her laugh out loud.

Alex feared that she might not fare so well against the canaller, considering that she was the one who had fallen all over him at their last meeting. Or so it seemed each time she recalled the heart-stopping moment.

She walked to the archway and stared at the wall where Rush had pinned her with his body. Even recalling the moment now made her knees go weak. If she were smart, Alex decided, she would run her own legs clean off her body—as fast as they would carry her away from Rush Duncan.

12

THE MEMORY OF HIS visit with Captain Steve stayed in Rush's mind on his return trip to Cumberland. So much so, that he had decided to forgo a stop in Harpers Ferry, thus postponing a visit with the Paine women.

Rush knew he was breaking his promise to Caro by not stopping, but chances were the child wouldn't even suspect he had come and gone without seeing her. Besides, if his feelings for Alexandria Paine had been so transparent that his old friend the captain had picked up on them, Rush didn't dare risk anyone else discovering his foolish affections, especially one Alexandria Paine.

It was mid-morning, and a thin layer of mist hung over the craggy rocks to his right and spread like a lady's frothy petticoat over the two rivers. The sun was working overtime to burn off the mist, and the whole river gorge was burnished with a golden haze.

Rush stood at the keel of his boat and waved at his steersman who walked along the towpath beside the two mules, Daisy and Petunia. Soon they would approach Lock 33 at Harpers Ferry. Rush would be the one locking the boat through the lock. He had assigned himself to the task, hoping to avoid the pull to stop in Harpers Ferry that was as strong as a magnet this morning.

Damn, he thought, he must be getting soft in his old age if his feelings for Alexandy had been so transparent that his old captain picked up on them.

Smitten with a lady. ''Never.''

But then Rush corrected his earlier thought. It wasn't that his skin was transparent. Instead, he had thin skin. He had always suffered with what he saw as a troublesome disorder of fragile sensibilities.

After he grew up, he hid those emotions behind a devil-may-care attitude: an attitude that had served him well for twenty-seven years until a certain young lady with golden hair had begun peeling away the thin layers of his defense and making him vulnerable—making him entertain thoughts he had no right to entertain.

It didn't matter who Rush was or what he had become. To Alexandria Paine he would always be the boy from the wrong side of the tracks. Tow tracks, he thought, ridiculing himself. Yes, it was best he had opted not to stop in Harpers Ferry this trip. Besides, he didn't think his libido could take another close encounter with Alexandy.

The lockkeeper's house at Lock 33 appeared in the mist. Rush picked up the conch shell he had brought back with him from a voyage he had taken to the Caribbean when he'd been a sailor aboard a ship. Most boatmen used tin bugles to alert the lockkeeper of their approach or yelled ''Yea-a-a-a-a-a Lock!'' or ''Hey-y-y-y-y-y Lock!'' Rush preferred using the conch not only because of its sentimental value, but also because he knew no lockkeeper could sleep through its prolonged high-pitched sound. The wailing call was especially good when traveling the canal at night.

Rush centered his concentration on locking through the lock. It was a delicate procedure with no margin for errors, and the most demanding part of canalling. His boat, like others, was standardized for canal travel and fit snugly into the locks, with only inches to spare on the sides and with no room to spare at the ends.

"Rudder against the stern," one of his crewmen confirmed from behind him.

With the rudder against the stern, the lock gates could now be closed. Once the boat was inside the lock, the same crewman jumped ashore and turned a heavy rope around the snubbing post to brake and stabilize the craft. If the boat wasn't stabilized, the lock's churning water tended to toss the boat against the delicate masonry walls, or the far gate of the lock. Such a blow could damage or even sink the boat, or damage the lock's masonry.

Steering was an art, and Rush prided himself on his ability. Guiding the keelless, cumbersome, oak-bottomed freight off the levels into a confined space wasn't to be taken lightly. It was said by some to be like submerging a tight-fitting tabletop in a full bathtub without bumping its sides.

Just as Rush took pride in his own ability, he also took pride in his mules, which, in his opinion, were the best of the best. Daisy and Petunia might not be sure of their origins from ass or horse, but they surely weren't as dumb as Captain Steve had implied. Experienced mules like Daisy and Petunia didn't require a driver when snubbing a boat into a lock. Trained mules slacked off immediately. Once they were through the lock, the team would start pulling again with only his whistle for a cue.

Since Rush had decided to change mules at this lock, the other steersman now walked beside them. When the fallboard, which resembled a cleated gangplank, was thrown over the side of the boat when the water inside the lock reached its highest level, a fresh team of mules from the stable in the bow would be herded out quickly to replace Daisy and Petunia. Then the twosome would get to eat and ride for the next six hours.

The two no-name mules that would replace Daisy and Petunia were still new and known as "greenies" among the mule tenders. Thank God the pair had passed the sit-down stage a while back. A "sit downer" often sat down and refused to move. This problem was solved by hitching trained mules to the "sit downer" and dragging it along until it stood. That action alone told Rush a mule couldn't be too dumb if it figured out that standing was more comfortable than sitting down.

The locking-through procedure usually took eight to ten minutes to complete. Rush heard that one crew had set a record of three minutes. He wasn't interested in setting records, but how a lock worked never ceased to amaze him.

"Captain Duncan, hail ye," the lockkeeper called after they had exited the lock. The man pointed to his son who ran along the towpath beside the moving *Chuck-a-luck,* waving an envelope. "I was told to make sure you received this missive when you passed thorough." His words grew fainter as the boat moved up the canal away from Harpers Ferry.

The crew member who had manned the snubbing post during the locking through took the envelope from the lad, then jumped back on the moving boat. He brought it to Rush where he stood at the tiller.

Rush's first thought after receiving the envelope was that something had happened to Caro, and he felt lower than canal scum that he hadn't stopped in Harpers Ferry as he'd promised her he would.

Now it wasn't possible for him to turn around, but if worse came to worst, he could stop farther up the canal and hike back to town.

He tore open the envelope, relief washing over him when he saw that the contents didn't bear bad news. Inside was a printed flyer that read:

A quilting frolic
will be held this coming Saturday
to celebrate the opening of Alexandria Paine's
new quilting workroom and the
reuniting of Caro Swift with her family,
the Herman Paines of Harpers Ferry.
The day will be filled with quilting and socializing.
Dinner prepared by the best cooks in town will be served,
and the day will end with a street dance with
music provided by Bowstring's Fiddlers.
Come one, come all, and share in this wonderful celebration.

At the bottom of the flyer, a personal note had been scratched in a shaky penmanship:

Dear Mr. Duncan,

　　Your attendance is demanded at this event because two young ladies of the Paine family will be gravely disappointed if you fail to attend. We can't have that now, can we?

　　　　　　　　　　　　　　　　Mrs. Leona Whitley

"Damn," Rush muttered, wadding up the flyer and jamming it into his pocket.

That was all he needed, to attend a frolic where in all probability he would be expected to dance with Alexandy. The thought of holding her in his arms again made him as hard as the tiller he held in his hand.

This realization alone was reason for him not to attend. His anger grew, but he directed it toward Mrs. Leona Whitley who, at the moment, he blamed for his present uncomfortable situation. How dare she suggest that his failure to attend would gravely disappoint Alex and Caro.

He wouldn't attend. He could always claim he never received the invitation, but then as closely knit as the residents of Harpers Ferry were, he doubted that anyone would believe him. Least of all, his old friend Samson.

Well, damnation, he didn't see he had much choice in the matter unless work demanded he appear elsewhere. Rush's mood brightened. There was always that possibility.

But then there was Caro, whom Rush knew he wouldn't disappoint. The child had had too many disappointments already in her young life.

He was wrong—the missive did bring bad news. Not life-threatening, but then again, maybe it was. Seeing Alexandria Paine, holding her in his arms, just might prove to be his kiss of death.

⤙⤚

ALEX ROSE WITH THE sun on the day of the quilting frolic. Already it promised to be beautiful; the sun gilded the sky above the horizon with a thin layer of gold, while a soft breeze blew off the rivers, cooling the air to the perfect temperature. Tending to her morning ablutions, she couldn't recall a time when she had been more excited about a quilting.

A glance at her cousin told her the child was still fast asleep, but Snow had vacated his favorite spot at the foot of the bed when Alex got up. Together they readied themselves for the long, festive day. Alex used the tepid water she poured from the pitcher into the bowl, while the orange cat used his sand-paper tongue to wash himself.

Until the moment had arrived to dress for the day, Alex hadn't thought much about what she would wear to the party. In truth, she had been far too busy. Alex, her mother, and Caro had worked diligently throughout the week, stitching the squares of Caro's quilt together so it would be ready for the quilting today.

In spite of their busy pace, her mother had still found time to sew a much-needed dress for Caro. The yellow gingham now lay across the chair where her cousin had left it last night when sleep had finally claimed her. In her mind's eye, Alex could still see the delighted child, strutting around the parlor like a new filly that had just discovered her legs.

Her mother had made the dress from a bolt of cloth that Alex had purchased for her workroom. On seeing Caro's re-action, she knew the decision to use some of the material for her cousin's dress had been the right one. Caro had been so thrilled with the new frock that Alex had trouble holding her tears in check.

What a clotheshorse young Caro had turned out to be. Alex's mother said she had come by her vanity honestly, claiming Caro's mother, Charlotte, had also loved fancy clothes and dressing for parties.

Thinking about the upcoming party, Alex knew there was nothing in her wardrobe that could be considered fancy. Her clothing didn't usually concern her—clothes were merely meant to be functional. But because today was to be special,

Alex wished she had something besides her usual worn dresses to wear.

The pocket doors slipped open, and her mother appeared in the opening. Alex pointed to the bed, then covered her mouth with her finger to alert her mother that Caro still slept. Pulling her wrapper around her, Alex tiptoed across the room to where her mother waited. Once inside the parlor, she closed the doors behind her.

"Why are you up so early, Mother?" she whispered, giving her a light kiss on the cheek. "Today is going to be long and busy, and you would do well to get a few extra hours of sleep."

Stella Paine smiled. "I knew you would be up with the chickens and I wanted to catch you before you dressed." She took Alex's hand and lead her across the parlor and into her own bedroom. "I've got a surprise for you," she said.

The moment Alex stepped through her mother's doors, she saw the dress spread across the end of the bed. It was made from the same gingham material as Caro's dress.

"Mother, you shouldn't have."

"Now, don't you get angry with me," Stella cautioned, "for taking it upon myself to use more material from the bolt. I just figured that you needed a dress as much as Caro did."

Alex walked to the bed and ran her fingers over the sunny fabric. She couldn't remember the last time she had owned a new frock to wear. "Don't be silly, Mother. I'm only concerned for your welfare. Where did you get the extra time to make it as busy as you were with the quilt and then Caro's dress—"

"Don't worry your pretty head about me," she answered, looking smug. "I had the time. In fact, all I have is time. Besides, it is a special occasion. You've worked so hard and done without so many things these past few years."

"We've done without together—"

"Hush, child. You deserve it."

Alex took a quick breath. "It's beautiful," she said. Her eyes begin to water. "I can't thank you enough. But what about you? What are you going to wear?"

"Oh, bother, Alexandria. I've plenty of serviceable things

to wear. No one is going to look at an old widow-woman like me anyway.''

She knew one man who would look at her mother. Samson. He seemed to like talking with a certain widow-woman. Alex turned her face from her mother's to hide her smile. Lately the two old friends engaged in daily conversations in their backyards. Alex wasn't about to mention the frequency of their meetings for fear her mother would believe she disapproved. She was delighted that her mother had found her old friend again.

''As for anyone looking at an old widow-woman like yourself, I hope you won't be too disappointed when no one looks at your daughter, whom Leona Whitey considers past her prime. But,'' Alex emphasized, ''if clothes would make them look, I daresay this dress will turn some heads.''

''You know how much stock everyone puts in dear Leona's prattle. Past your prime, pshaw!'' Her mother beamed. ''I tried to make your and Caro's dresses similar. Your grandmother, rest her soul, used to dress Charlotte and me alike, but we were much closer in age than you and Caro.''

This was the first time she had heard this about the two sisters. Curious, Alex looked at her mother. ''You know, I've never heard you talk much about your life when you were young, before Charlotte ran away. It's as though you didn't exist until you married Father.''

Stella sighed. ''Of course I existed. I guess, Alexandria, I did you a great disservice by not talking about my childhood. I felt so horribly guilty for allowing Charlotte to leave. I shouldn't have let her go. Then when we never heard a word from her, it became too painful to remember our times together as children.''

''Mother, I told you before. You shouldn't blame yourself for something you could not control. Your father let her go. He should have been the one who stopped her.''

''My older, more mature self agrees with you, but back then she was my baby sister. I felt responsible for her because I was the oldest. As children we were inseparable, which is unusual for girls so close in age.'' Her mother paused as though she was trying to sort out her thoughts. ''My parents referred to Charlotte as their stubborn daughter and me as the malleable one. Maybe Charlotte felt she needed to live up to their opinions, and that was why she ran.

"When she left, it broke my heart. There were times following her departure that I actually hated my father for allowing her to leave. Then the war came, and the whole country was torn apart. Ours was not the only family whose loved ones left and never returned. Once your father and I married, the passing years made it easier to pretend that Charlotte was dead. Especially when the efforts he made to find her never came to anything."

"At least we know now that Tyler Moore wasn't all bad," Alex said. "He married Charlotte and gave their child a name."

"Then deserted them, leaving Charlotte to work in a bar."

"Aw, Maw," Alex said, hugging her mother close. "Don't look so sad. Here we've become maudlin when today we should be happy."

"You're right, Daughter, but don't call me Maw." She tried for a lighter note. "I detest that name."

"All right, Mother dear." Alex picked up the dress and held it to her. "Are you sure you weren't the stubborn sister?"

"Stubborn? Me?" She placed her hands on her hips. "Only with you, Alexandria. I have to be in order to keep you in line."

Holding the dress against her, Alex stepped away and twirled. "I daresay Caro and I will be the fairest belles at the ball." In an almost-forgotten dance step, she whirled around the floor.

Stella laughed, swaying in time with Alex's steps. "The moment I saw that daffodil-yellow material, I knew it had to be made into dresses for my girls. And I was right. With your yellow hair you'll look like a sunflower, and Caro with her black curls will look like a goldfinch."

"Mother, really—a flower and a bird?" She took two steps forward and one step back.

"God's creatures, Daughter," her mother called. "There is nothing prettier than nature's jewels."

Alex swirled to a stop in front of her mother. "I think,

Mother-of-mine, that you are the jewel in my crown.''

Her mother's smile broadened.

From the doorway, Caro asked, still half asleep, ''Who is wearing the crown jewels?''

''Last I heard it was Queen Victoria,'' Alex quipped, ''but you and I, Caro, will be wearing the prettiest dresses at the frolic.''

Caro was awake enough now to notice the dress Alex held against her.

''Do you like it?'' she asked. ''I knew Aunt Stella was making us twin dresses. I bet you were surprised.''

''Yes, I love it, and I was surprised. You and me, kid, are going to be so beautiful in our new dresses that we'll charm the britches off everyone attending.''

''Alexandria,'' her mother admonished, ''where did you hear such an expression?''

Then all three of them laughed.

Alex knew where she had heard such an expression, but she didn't dare tell the others. When she thought about the expression's origin, she realized that for the first time since the frolic had been planned, she wanted Rush Duncan to attend. Her impulsive change of mind made her question her motive.

Why did she have a change of heart? Was it because there was something about Rush Duncan that made her want to be attractive and not a girl past her prime?

No, she reasoned, she just wanted to put her new dress to the test.

To charm his britches off?

This last thought made Alex's face burn as though she had sat too close to the fire.

∽

AROUND NOON THE QUILTERS began to arrive. Alex, Stella, and Caro greeted the women as they stepped through the front door.

Leona Whitley, the usual self-appointed leader, led the others around the room, pointing out various things as though it had been her hard work that had completed the workroom instead of Alex's.

Alex only half listened to the matron's chatter when Rosellen stopped in front of them. "Lovely hat," she said. "Those cabbage roses look so real I can almost smell them."

"Why, thank you, dear," Rosellen replied, sniffing. "You know, I do believe you're right." She inhaled again. "I can smell them." Awed by this discovery, she moved, then stopped beside Stella and dipped her head. "You smell them, Stella?"

Alex looked at Caro and winked. Both girls hid their giggles, knowing it was Caro's rose perfume that the older woman had smelled instead of the silk flowers adorning her large hat.

"Alex, you've done a wonderful job," Sena Ford said. She stood with the three other women on the opposite side of the quilting frame.

Leona glanced down at Caro's quilt, which Alex, Stella, and Caro had put in the frame last night. "Are you talking about the quilt or the facility?"

"Why, everything," Lucy Prouty responded in her little-bitty voice. "I never imagined a room used only for quilting. So much light, too."

Ella Hamilton ran her fingers over the few bolts of yard goods Alex had spread out on Samson's table. "Nice fabrics, Alex. I can't wait to get my scissors on that light-green floral."

"Your father has the exact same color in his store," Millie King added. "I've seen it nigh a dozen times."

"Oh, Mother, he does not. Remember, I helped you shelve most of those fabrics, and I've never seen anything close to that color."

Millie King's lips snapped shut so fast they sounded like a cork popping from a bottle.

"I only intend to purchase a small piece," Ella reassured her mother. "That color will look so pretty in those bed quilts I'm making for the girls' room."

"You know," Lucy Prouty added, "I think I would like a piece of that for my baby's quilt as well." She folded her hands affectionately on her increasing stomach. "I suppose greens and yellows are neutral colors, and since I don't know if I'm going to have a girl or a boy—''

"You better have a boy," Leona warned. "Anything else, and that man of yours will send it back. We all know Cal Prouty is looking for a son to help out in that blacksmith shop of his."

Lucy looked uncomfortable. "Why, Miss Leona, my Cal will be happy with any child the Lord sees fit to bless us with."

"Of course he will," Rosellen said. "Don't you pay no mind to my sister. Young people today, Leona, don't breed babies to become drudges."

Turning to Sena, Lucy asked, "What's a drudge?"

"I think, ladies," Alex answered before Sena could explain, "that we should begin quilting now. If we don't get started soon, we'll have accomplished nothing when we stop for dinner."

"Good idea, Alexandria." Rosellen removed her hat and hung the flowery creation on the coat stand that Alex had placed beside the door.

"We have tea and cookies in the kitchen," Stella announced, "and I can also boil coffee if anybody prefers it to tea."

"Heavens, Stella, we just ate breakfast." Leona moved toward them. "Besides, we need to save our stomachs for that wonderful dinner we'll be serving later."

For the first time since Leona Whitley's arrival, she gave Alex and Caro her full attention. "My, my, look at you two. All gussied up in new dresses. Twins, is it?" Leona raised silvery brows and looked at Stella. "Your doing, I suppose."

"Yes," Stella answered. "I made the girls' dresses."

"Your grandmother," Leona told Caro, "always dressed your mother and your aunt in look-alike dresses, although two girls couldn't have been less alike in both temperament and looks."

"I know," Caro responded. "Aunt Stella already told me. Alex has gold hair like Aunt Stella used to have, and I have black hair like my mother."

"That's right, Caro," her aunt answered. The look she sent

Leona told her enough had been said about the two sisters' differences.

"I believe we wore dresses alike as well, Leona," Rosellen reminded her.

"Don't remind me," Leona said. "You were always such a chubby thing that Mother soon discovered we couldn't wear the same styles."

Rosellen looked up her nose at her sister. "I wasn't chubby, merely rounded in the right places. Unlike someone else I know."

"Well, I never." Leona harumphed.

Ignoring her sister's disapproval, Rosellen said, "Stella, dear, the dresses look lovely on both girls."

"One can hardly call Alexandria a girl, but maybe she'll get the attention of that nice Mr.—"

"Miss Leona." Alex shot the older woman a warning glance.

Alex was tempted to take up a needle and sew the matron's lips together if it would keep her silent. She stole a glance at Caro, who appeared unmoved by her remark. Alex relaxed somewhat.

"Why don't you sit there," she said, pointing to a chair, "and Rosellen, you sit here." She pulled out a chair from beneath the quilt frame, deciding it best to separate the two old cats. "Everyone else fill in where you wish."

"Thanks to Samson," Stella said, taking a seat beside Leona, "we have enough chairs. He was more than generous, donating several chairs and that table so Alex could display her yard goods. He hauled that chest down from the third floor, too. If he hadn't, we probably never would have gotten it down the stairs."

"He seems like a nice man," Millie added. "I wonder why he never married."

"I guess he's a nice man in spite of his profession."

"Leona Whitley, there is nothing wrong with Samson's profession," Stella said in his defense. "He makes an honest living and he's highly respected in this community."

"But he sells spirits, Stella."

"He attends church every Sunday. Always helps those less

fortunate than himself.'' Stella's face took on a determined expression. ''If my memory serves me right, I believe the major frequented his saloon on numerous occasions when he was alive.''

Alex silently cheered her mother.

''But—''

''But, nothing, Sister. Stella is right. Samson is a well-respected man in Harpers Ferry, but more importantly, we've not come here to gossip and judge others. We're here to finish this lovely quilt of Caro's.'' Rosellen looked at the fabric in the frame. ''Would you look at that?'' she exclaimed. Curious now, the other ladies focused their attention on the quilt.

''It's a beautiful piece of work,'' Millie King affirmed.

Sena Ford ran her finger over several squares. ''Unusual, too,'' she said, ''the way she used both appliquéd pieces as well as the traditional patch.''

''Fine stitching,'' Lucy Prouty said, leaning as far over the frame as her stomach would allow.

''I love the way y'all put it together, Caro.'' Ella Hamilton smiled at the child. ''One day you'll make some man a good wife with your fancy stitching.''

Jamie's mother couldn't have said anything that would have pleased Caro more, Alex thought. She suspected Ella knew of Caro's infatuation with her young son.

''I daresay, child,'' Leona Whitley offered from her chair, ''this quilt will someday be an heirloom.''

''I know,'' Caro replied. ''It's my legacy from my ma. We worked on it together.''

''Then you are a quilter yourself?'' Rosellen asked.

Caro looked toward Alex for confirmation.

''She's on her way to being a fine quilter. In fact, it was Caro who insisted that the worked squares be joined by sashes and a border.''

''My ma, she wanted it finished that way. She said it would be like looking in a window.''

''Windows to your world,'' Rosellen added. ''How nice.''

All the women clucked their approval.

Stella put her arm around Caro's shoulder. ''Caro has explicit ideas about the quilting. She and her mother had discussed it, and Caro said it was how Charlotte would have finished the bed quilt herself.'' Stella looked at her niece. "Do you want to tell them or do you want me to?"

"You do it," Caro said, suddenly turning shy.

"We are to quilt around the designs. You can see that Alexandria and I already marked the lines with a pencil on each square and also on the sashes and the border."

"So we'll be using the Diagonal Crosshatch design on the background and follow the designs of the blocks."

"Just as they're marked, Leona," Rosellen said. "It will be a breeze to quilt, and when we're finished, it will be even more beautiful than it is already. Caro, perhaps you can tell us what some of these blocks represent. That is, if you want to."

Caro squirmed uncomfortably. "If Aunt Stella and Alex will help me."

"Of course, we will, child," Stella said.

Millie King checked her lapel watch. "Now that we know what we'll be doing, I suggest, ladies, that we get started stitching."

She pulled her chair closer to the frame and took out her needle and scissors. "I don't know about y'all, but I can't wait to hear about this lovely quilt."

13

ALTHOUGH CARO PLIED HER needle with nearly as much deftness as the other women of the quilting circle, it was evident the child would rather have been elsewhere. Alex watched her glance toward the front windows each and every time a body moved past. When Snow took himself out the door to nap in the sunshine, Alex almost told her cousin that she could join him, but the three of them had decided earlier that because it was Caro's quilt and the Paine household was hosting the quilting, it would be best if Caro remained with the other women during the day.

As the afternoon wore on, more and more ladies stopped in at Alex's workroom. Some came not only to help with the quilting, but also to chat and socialize. Since a better part of the day was to be spent on the quilting, it had been decided beforehand that the men wouldn't show up until it was time to close off the street in front of the house where they would begin setting up the tables for dinner. After everyone had eaten, then the dancing would begin.

Stella took over as narrator, explaining to the quilters what she had learned about the squares from her niece. Any woman who spent hours quilting could only admire the work spread out in front of them. Charlotte's love of the craft showed in her attention to details. Oohs and ahs issued from the women's lips as Stella told about each square. During the telling, Caro became so quiet that Alex suspected Snow had stolen her tongue, carrying it outside when he went for his nap.

"That one represents my father, my mother, Charlotte, and me," Stella said, indicating the square with the family standing in front of Jefferson Rock. "And that one," she said, pointing, "I believe is the house we lived in as children. It's a shame the flood of 1870 destroyed it."

"I remember that house," Leona Whitley said. "Goodness, I haven't thought about it in years. How nice that Charlotte captured it in her design. Our family's house was destroyed by that same flood." She looked at all the women. "Harpers Ferry saw a great number of changes after Charlotte left, not only from the war, but also from rising water."

Everyone recognized the square of the Potomac water gap where the Potomac and Shenandoah Rivers came together in the Blue Ridge Mountains.

Guardedly Stella explained the significance of the tinker wagon, telling those who already knew Charlotte's story that Caro's real father, Tyler Moore, had traveled the country in that wagon, selling his wares.

No one mentioned the patch that showed a building with the word "saloon" embroidered above its door. Alex suspected that her mother had forewarned the others, or perhaps good manners dictated they not ask.

"That one there," Stella said, pointing to the sod house, "was Caro's home in Nebraska." She looked at her niece and asked, "What did you say folks called sod on the prairie?"

"Marble," Caro answered with a weak smile. Then she turned several shades of red.

Poor Caro.

Alex, who sat beside her young cousin at the quilting frame, moved her leg close to Caro's, hoping to lend her support. She leaned over and whispered in the child's ear, "Not much longer, honey." Returning her attention to the ladies, she pointed out a square of a small country church. "That is Caro's church back home."

No one asked about the square that depicted the second

family. Like the first one, this one also showed a father and mother. Instead of two daughters standing beside the parents, there was a small black-haired child holding a baby swathed in a blanket.

Not even Leona Whitley, bless her soul, questioned the square's meaning. By now the women all knew Caro's history and didn't wish to broach a subject they assumed might be too painful for the little girl.

There were other squares the group could comment on and did; a square of a Christmas tree, a snowman, a black-haired girl flying a kite, and last but certainly not least, the one of the marmalade cat. Alex and her mother, along with the other ladies, learned from Caro, who suddenly decided to tell them, that the cow and chickens were very much a part of her earlier life.

There were also representational designs that most quilters would recognize: the dove for innocence, the honeysuckle for devotion, the pine tree for fidelity, and the pineapple for hospitality.

Charlotte's quilt told a lot about the person who made it, especially that person's life after leaving Harpers Ferry.

To a quilter like Alex, the triangles, wheels, the Wandering Foot, and the familiar Log Cabin pattern represented migration and movement. Because her aunt had traveled so far away from home, Alex believed that wanderlust was a theme her aunt had chosen to depict in the quilt's design. This gave Alex an insight into the aunt she had never known.

Beside her, Caro giggled. Alex looked at her cousin, then followed her gaze to the front window. Jamie Hamilton, along with several other boys, had their faces pressed against the plate glass. Their warm breath fogged the glass, making their flattened noses and contorted mouths look more like the faces of monsters than those of angelic young boys.

Ella Hamilton jumped up from her chair. The other women laughed at the boys, watching as Ella flew toward the entrance.

"Leave them," Leona called. "They're only having fun."

Ella wasn't about to be deterred. "Jamie, you and your friends get away from that window right now," she warned.

"If you don't, Alexandria will have the whole lot of you washing windows tomorrow."

"Ah, Ma, we're hungry," Jamie groaned, stepping back, his friends following suit. "When y'all gonna feed us?"

"Soon enough. You go help your father set up the tables."

"They won't let us help. Pa said we were in the way." He looked toward Caro, then quickly turned away.

"You go tell Mr. Hamilton if he doesn't allow you boys to help, none of you will get fed."

"Ah, Ma, it's getting late," Jamie whined. "Look, the sun is gonna be down soon."

Millie King glanced at her lapel watch. "Mercy! You know, girls, it's nearly five o'clock."

"Five o'clock? No wonder those boys are hungry." Stella looked at Caro. "Child, why don't you get that plate of cookies from the kitchen and give those starving boys a snack."

Caro looked at Alex. "You heard your aunt," she said. "You've worked very hard today. You look as though you could use a cookie yourself."

Like a jack-in-the-box whose lid had suddenly sprung open, Caro popped up from the table. She hit the kitchen running, grabbed the plate of cookies, then was out the door so fast that it made Alex's head spin.

"Youth," Rosellen said with a sigh.

Ella returned inside. "You two can say good-bye to those cookies."

Stella laughed. "No one else wanted any, and I'm glad the boys will enjoy them. I only hope they don't spoil their appetite for supper."

"Never in a million years," Millie King added. "My grandson inherited his grandfather's hollow legs."

"I guess, ladies," Leona said, pushing her chair away from the frame, "that we should start thinking about serving dinner." Standing, she stretched and hobbled toward the window. "The menfolk are setting the tables on that nice stretch of grass up the street a ways."

Rosellen stood as well. "We didn't finish all of the quilt, Alexandria, but we finished more than half of it."

Chairs scraped across the floor when several of the other women stood.

"I want to say," Rosellen continued, "that the workroom is lovely. Truly ideal for stitching our big quilts together. I'm sure you'll get tired of having us old hens here all the time."

The others agreed.

"Never," Alex insisted. "That's what it's for." She bent forward and examined the project. "The quilting is beautiful. I can't tell you how much the three of us appreciate your help."

"Next time we meet, we'll finish it," Sena added.

"If the good Lord's willing and the creek don't rise," Lucy Prouty quipped.

"Mercy, girl, don't even jest about such a thing," Leona scolded.

"I-I wasn't. I didn't mean—"

"Of course you didn't," Alex assured her. She leaned toward her old school friend and whispered, "You should know by now not to allow Leona's bluntness to bother you."

"Oh, I know." Lucy looked disgusted with herself. "I just don't face off the old dragon as well as you do."

Alex squeezed Lucy's hand and winked. "I've had more practice."

∞

THE SUN SLID BEHIND the mountains, tinting the sky in a palette of rainbow colors before darkness settled over the town. Tablecloths covered the makeshift tables, and candles and lanterns spilled halos of golden light on the centers of the creamy white material. After the meal, the women covered the food to ward off flies and other insects until later when the dancing and frolicking made the merrymakers return to the tables for a sustaining snack.

Bordering the backside of the narrow grassy strip where the tables had been set up, the wall of shale rock beneath Harper House, built by Robert Harper who operated the town's first ferry, was aglow with dozens of candles that some ingenious person had placed randomly on the shelflike fissures. Those candles now winked and glowed like a swarm of summer fire-flies.

Bowstring and his fiddlers were in fine form tonight. They strummed out a waltz, and the music floated on the warm air, mingling with soft conversation and easy laughter. From a nearby tree, a series of reedy spiraling notes that sounded like the song of a woodthrush made Alex wonder if the bird had been imbibing the men's spiked punch. Didn't the feathery creature know that birds weren't supposed to sing at night?

As Alex contemplated this last thought, she considered taking a nip herself, especially if the brew would put her in a more festive mood. What was the matter with her anyway? Good sense told her that she shouldn't be so restless since the day had been so successful.

Not only had those of the quilting circle done fast work on Caro's quilt, but also other women from town had come up to Alex, praising her idea of a women's workroom. Some had suggested that she carry a variety of items such as needlework supplies. Alex had thanked them, promising that she would consider their suggestions.

Because there had been so much enthusiasm for her project, she questioned why she felt so glum. Her mother and Samson waltzed by, and Alex waved and smiled at the twosome. Then Caro sprinted past, chasing Jamie Hamilton across the grass. The lad didn't appear as though he was trying very hard to escape her cousin. Just like a man, Alex thought, running until he was caught. Considering her sardonic reflection, Alex almost laughed aloud. *As if I have so much experience in the ways of the heart.*

A night moth fluttered by her nose and flew toward the flame of a distant candle. Alex exhaled a long audible sigh. Tonight everything and everyone seemed to be drawn to something; the moth to the candle, her mother to Samson, and Caro to Jamie. Even the good reverend, who would normally be dancing attendance on Alex, had been drawn out into the country to comfort one of his grieving parishioners.

Only she was totally alone and not pulled in any direction. Tonight disappointment was her only companion, and Alex wondered how it had come to this when earlier she had believed that the planned festivities held such promise. In her heart, she knew the reason for her discontent, but instead of allowing the reason to surface, she brushed a piece of grass from the front of her skirt.

A lot of good her new dress had done her when there was no one present to admire it or her. Even the reverend would have been a diversion, but no, she wasn't allowed his company tonight, either.

"Sakes alive, I must be desperate," she grumbled, jumping to her feet. "Leona Whitley was right—I'm no longer a girl, but a woman far past her prime. Fuddled, too, if I'm missing the reverend!"

A walk was what she needed, Alex decided. She dodged the street full of swirling dancers until she was on the opposite side. Stepping onto the sidewalk, she realized her black mood had not abandoned her as she had hoped it would. She was thankful she didn't have to explain her absence of dance partners to the ladies of the quilting circle. She had been spared that little discomfort because the women were nowhere in sight.

Later, when the subject of the party came up—as Alex knew it would—her mother would assure her the evening hadn't been a total waste because Alex had danced a few rounds. Only Alex would know differently. None of her dance partners had interested her, and Alex had no doubt that her feelings had been reciprocated.

The few men she partnered had all been canallers, men who had stopped in Harpers Ferry for the night and had come across the river to join in the frolic. Those men had made it clear immediately where their real interest lay. Their idea of a good time wasn't spending the evening with a woman past her prime and drinking spiked fruit punch. They were more interested in fast women and a slow drink of whiskey. Soon they had left the festivities and wandered to one of the few taverns in town that had a ready supply of both.

"Good riddance to bad rubbish," she mumbled. Her comment drew curious looks from a couple she passed.

Tonight most of the buildings that lined High Street were aglow with light. Their owners had purposely left lanterns burning in front windows, allowing their glow to spill over into the street. It was a pretty sight, she thought. The lights from houses and the many candles made the area look as bright as a decorated Christmas tree.

Alex looked toward the strip of sky. A thousand stars twinkled like diamonds. The moon maker had hung a full moon for the occasion, and its pearly glow washed the surrounding mountains and hills with a silvery sheen.

A perfect night for romance.

The thought came unbidden, but with its surfacing, Alex realized why the party held no special magic for her. Of the several canallers she had danced with earlier, the one whose arms she had longed to be in had not made it to the frolic. *Rush Duncan.* When she thought about him, his absence made her sad. Then disgust with herself made her angry.

How dare he not attend the frolic when his presence would have meant so much to Caro. *And me.* She had been dead wrong about him, imagining there was a heart beneath all that muscle and brawn. He was heartless, she decided, and she was glad she had made a vow years ago never to become involved with a canaller. All of them were no-good drifters.

Alex paused as she neared the end of High Street where it intersected with Shanandoah. Bowstring and his musicians stood on a makeshift platform in the middle of the road. Someone in the crowd shouted a request for a polka, and the fiddlers began to pick and bow a lively tune.

Alex watched, unable to keep from smiling and tapping her foot as people skipped by. In the next moment, a man she had never seen before grabbed her and pulled her into the throng of dancers. Soon they, too, were skipping and whirling around the street in time with the music. Alex had always loved the polka. Caught up in the music, she let herself enjoy the dance. Why not? she reasoned. It would probably be her last one this evening.

Her partner was a skillful stepper and very easy to follow. Because the crowd demanded it, Bowstring kept the polka music going at a frenzied tempo. After several turns around the street, Alex's earlier black mood lifted.

Her partner was tall with dark hair and eyes and reminded

her a lot of Rush Duncan. Unlike Rush, this stranger was not given over to small talk and teasing, which suited Alex just fine. It was clear to her that the man loved to dance and only wanted a partner, and she was definitely in need of one. What difference did it make if they didn't exchange the usual small talk? They still could have a good time together.

When Bowstring strummed out the beginnings of a waltz on his fiddle, it was only natural that she should go willingly into the stranger's arms. She smiled up at him, and he returned the pleasantry. For the first time this evening, Alex was glad that she had on a new dress.

∞

AS RUSH ROUNDED THE corner of the building on High Street, the first thing he saw was Alex in the arms of another man. His heart squeezed up into his throat, vacating his chest, and he had to force his feet and legs to continue moving him through the crush of onlookers watching the dancers.

He silently cursed himself for coming, then cursed himself for not getting here sooner. The loading delay in Cumberland made his arrival in Harpers Ferry much later than he had intended. Not only had he missed a fine supper prepared by the best cooks in town, but now another man was holding the dessert.

Earlier in the week, when he had made up his mind to attend the frolic, Rush had found himself looking forward to the affair, and his freshly polished shoes had all but flown across the footbridge from the canal. He'd been filled with pleasure, contemplating the night, but now he wasn't so sure how he felt. One thing for certain—he wasn't prepared for the disappointment and jealousy that he was experiencing on seeing Alex looking so beautiful, and contentedly happy, in the arms of her preacher man.

In her yellow dress and with her sunbeam-colored hair, she was his sun goddess. He watched as the thick braid threatened to slip free of the knot secured at her nape with a yellow ribbon. It was a style Rush hadn't seen Alex wear before tonight, and although the do was becoming, if Alex was his woman, Rush would insist that she wear her hair loose and flowing over her shoulders and down her back—the way it had been the last time he saw her, the same night he'd kissed her.

Just thinking about that kiss made him grow hard with want, a condition no decent man should entertain while observing an angel. Thank God the revelers were more interested in watching the dancers than in watching a frustrated man lose control.

His plans had changed. Now he would put in a quick appearance, say hello to Caro, then leave. No need to hang around when staying confirmed what he already knew. There was nothing for Rush in this town, least of all a certain yellow-haired girl with brown eyes. He stopped behind a group of spectators to speculate and saw no advantage in his staying.

Before tonight, Rush hadn't considered that a parson would offer much in the way of male competition, but then he'd never seen such a well-turned-out preacher. Alex's partner looked more like a man of the world than a man of the cloth. Not only did the good reverend have more than passable looks, but he also had God and an army of angels on his side.

With a bastion like that, where did Rush stand? He grinned in spite of himself. It left him on the opposite side of the pearly gates and slipping fast.

Oh, he imagined that some might consider him handsome; in fact, he'd been told as much on occasion. But unlike the pastor, he had no princely champion on his team. All Rush had was his devil-awful past that he had lived with all of his life, and that was nothing to offer a lady. In Rush's opinion, he had a snowball's chance in hell of winning Alexandy from the preacher.

"Hellfire," he grumbled. "I didn't come here to stage a battle. I came to see Caro and share in a home-cooked meal." Since he'd missed the supper, Rush decided, he would settle on seeing his small friend before he left.

A thrust of energy hit the backs of his knees, almost toppling Rush from his feet. He caught a glimpse of movement over his shoulder, then felt a small hand on his thigh. His attacker swung forward, using his leg as a post, then came to a dead stop in front of him.

On recognizing Caro, Rush laughed. "Hold on there, mate," he said.

Caro, dressed in a yellow dress with her mop of black curls flying around her face like a flustery cloud, looked up at him. "You came, Rush," she said. "I knew you would. It wouldn't have been the same without you. I just told Jamie that the man dancing with Alex wasn't you, but he didn't believe me."

Jamie? Rush smiled at the lad. It was the same boy Caro had been playing with at Leona Whitley's house. Apparently she no longer thought Jamie was stupid if the way she grabbed the boy's hand was any indication.

When the lad tried to wiggle his hand from her embrace, she yanked him forward. "Come here, Jamie. I've got to introduce you." She began the introduction like a proper young lady would. "Rush, this is Jamie Hamilton."

"The stupid one," the lad reminded him.

"Apparently she doesn't think you're stupid anymore." Rush extended his hand. "Pleased to meet you for a second time, Jamie."

"I told her we'd met, but that silly new dress she's wearing makes her think she's got to act like a sissy."

"New frocks have a way of doing that to women, but you gotta admit she sure does look pretty."

"Sorta," Jamie responded when Caro gazed at him with an expectant expression on her face. The lad looked as though he would dart as soon as he had a chance.

Rush returned his attention to Caro. "Seems as though you and your cousin are both spiffed up for this affair." He glanced toward Alex and the man holding her, spinning them like a top around the street. It was evident to Rush that the couple had been dancing together forever, judging by the way they both knew their moves. More to himself than to Caro, Rush said, "Never would have suspected that a preacher could be such a good dancer."

"Preacher?" Caro's gaze followed Rush's.

"That fellow ain't our preacher," Jamie told him. "Tonight's the first time I've ever seen him. I thought he was you."

"That's not your preacher?" Rush asked, looking at the two pint-sized squirts standing in front of him. Earlier, Caro had said Jamie claimed the man dancing with Alex had been him, but her meaning hadn't penetrated his brain.

He asked again. "You mean that man dancing with your cousin isn't the preacher who's been courting her?"

"Heck no," Caro answered. "Aunt Stella said the reverend was called out in the country to attend to his bequeathed."

"Do you mean bereaved?"

"I don't know—I guess I could. Those words sound the same."

"Then who is that?"

Before Caro could answer, Jamie Hamilton yanked his hand from hers and vaulted like a rabbit freed from a trap.

"He's getting away," Caro groaned. Swinging away from Rush, she ran like a fox to catch him. "I'll see you later," she called over her shoulder.

Rush scratched his head. Now both his girls were preoccupied with other men. He was glad that Caro had decided to accept Jamie as her friend, but when he looked back at Alex and her partner, his feelings weren't as charitable.

Now that Rush knew he wasn't in competition with a saint, he put on his best devil-may-care smile. Pushing past the crowd, he headed toward the dancing couple.

There was no law that said a man couldn't cut in on a dance and ask a lady to finish it with him. The way he saw it, the stranger had already had more than his share of Miss Paine's time.

It was Rush's turn to dance with Alexandy. When he thought about holding her in his arms again, his heart tripped faster than his feet, trying to catch up with the moving couple.

14

"MAY I?" RUSH SAID, tapping Alex's partner on the shoulder.

The man look surprised, then reluctant to release her. Rush tapped him again, this time a little harder, and the man finally conceded without a word.

"Don't look so disappointed, Alexandy," Rush said, smiling, although it wasn't the pleasure he expected to feel when he held her in his arms. Alex looked as though she had given up steak for hamburger, and her affront sat in his stomach like spoiled meat.

She watched the man until he disappeared into the crowd, then turned to him, not smiling. He experienced a jealousy so strong that it put him in a foul and belligerent mood. He gave a belittling snort and pulled her hard against him.

Instead of lightly placing his palm just above her waistline, he splayed his fingers against her back and kneaded her warm skin beneath her dress.

Alex's quick intake of breath warned him he was out of line, but what difference did it make? She had made it clear that she would rather be dancing with her ex-partner than with him. She tried to pull away, but Rush held her fast. Assuming his most cocky posture, he said, "Now is that any way to treat an old friend who just wants a turn around the street with a pretty lady?''

When she looked as though she would bolt anyway, he captured her right hand with his left. But instead of holding it at arm's length, he folded it close to his chest, bringing her inches closer than was considered proper for polite dancing.

He dipped his head next to her ear and whispered, ''Don't fight it, sugar. You know you like my arms around you.''

Alex stiffened, anger flaring in her eyes. ''I assure you Mr. Duncan—Rush—that I don't like your arms around me. In truth, I abhor your touch.''

''That a fact? I would have sworn my touch wasn't all that loathsome to you. The last time we were together, it was you who applied a stranglehold on my neck.''

''I never did such a thing.''

''Got the bruises to prove it.'' He grinned. ''Would you like me to show you?''

''You wouldn't dare,'' she quipped, ''but then, maybe you would.'' Suddenly she looked as though she might cry and she tried to jerk away. ''I guess, sir, I had you figured all wrong.''

When her eyes began to tear, Rush felt lower than scum on a rain bucket. Instead of slinging hateful remarks at the prettiest woman at the shindig, he should have been wooing her with pretty words. He had come here tonight specifically to see her, and what had he done? Slung insults at her because she hadn't acted as pleased to see him as his pride wanted her to be. *Fool!*

''Look, I'm sorry, Alexandy. What I said was cruel, uncalled for. I didn't mean to act like such an ass.''

With his apology, her stance softened somewhat, but not completely. When the tune ended, she flouted a victorious expression as if to say, ''It's not my fault that the music ended.''

''Thank you very much for the dance,'' she said. She would have left him, if he hadn't held on to her hand.

''I said I'm sorry, Alexandy. What do you want? Blood?''

A flush touched her cheeks, but she didn't respond. The fiddlers began another tune, and Rush urged her to return to his arms. ''Come on, Alexandy, they're playing our song.''

"Our song?" Her brows lifted, but at least he had her attention.

The strains of "When You And I Were Young, Maggie," flowed around the now slow-moving dancers.

"Please," he said, refusing to release her hand. He deepened his smile. "I really do want to dance with you."

Resigned to her fate, she finally quit trying to tug her hand loose from his. "Only," she said, "if you can explain to me how this is *our* song."

When he saw the beginning of a smile curve her lips, Rush let go of a real hard, solid laugh. "Come here, sugar, and I'll serenade you with the words."

"You sing, too?" Alex rolled her eyes in disbelief. "You're a man of many talents, but this last one I've got to hear."

She allowed him to pull her close. Once she was right where he had wanted her to be all along, Rush began to sing the words softly:

> "I wandered today to the hill, Alex,
>   To watch the scene below.
> The creek and the old rusty mill, Alex,
>   Where we sat in the long, long, ago."

Amusement lurked in her dark brown eyes. "I believe this song was written for someone named Maggie, not Alexandria." She really smiled at him then, and her smile caused a tightening in his cockles, and not the cockles of his heart.

"Just let me finish," he whispered.

He waited to begin singing only long enough so that he would be in time with the music.

> "The green grove is gone from the hill, Alex,
>   Where first the daisies had sprung.
> The old rusty mill is now still, Alex,
>   Since you and I were young."

The fiddlers plucked out the chorus, singing along with their instruments. When they sang Maggie, Rush sang Alex.

> "Now we're aged and gray, Alex,
>   The trials of life nearly done.
> Let's sing of the days that are gone, Alex,
>   When you and I were young."

The song drifted to a close, and Rush twirled them around until the last note no longer lingered in the air.

Appearing dizzy, Alex said, laughing, "I better allow you to lead me to the sidelines—I should say carry me to the sidelines, if that is indeed *our* song."

"Now wait a minute." Rush kept her hand tucked in the crook of his arm while they stood talking. "It could be our song." He winked at her. "Look around you, sugar. We've got hills, and if my memory serves me right, there are still a few rusty mills left out there on Virginius Island."

Alex looked toward the Shenandoah River. "That's all that's left of Virginius Island," she reminded him. "Floods, time, and war have contributed to the demise of our once-prosperous industrial island."

"I seem to recall a grove of trees on one of those hills." Rush pointed to the hills whose peaks were bathed in moonlight. "And we both know that wild daisies grow all over this area."

Alex challenged him. "There is that part of the song about being old and gray. I admit I'm older, but . . ."

Rush began to examine her hair, and she stepped away from him and laughed.

"We did sit together in the long long ago," he reminded her.

"Not together," she corrected. "In school, you sat behind me."

Their gazes caught and held. For several moments neither one said anything; they only looked at each other. When they became aware that they were staring as though they were the only people around, Alex blushed and stepped away.

"Yes, I guess it could be our song," she mumbled breathlessly. Her blush deepened.

"Darling, that color becomes you."

"Then you like my dress?"

"No, I like your blush," he teased.

Then she really turned red. "Oh, I thought—"

"The dress looks real fine, too. In fact, Alexandy, I can't recall a time when I've seen you look prettier."

"Now you're just being polite."

Her brown eyes looked radiant, reflecting the glow of the many candles and lanterns surrounding the area.

"Good enough to kiss," he teased. He stared at her mouth.

Alex fussed with the small buttons on her bodice. "Don't even try it, Rush Duncan. Besides, everyone in Harpers Ferry would see, and then we would be the talk of the town."

"In this town, sugar, I betcha tongues are already wagging. If being seen worries you, though, I'm sure I could find us an out-of-the-way shadow." He made his brows wiggle like a villain's.

Bantering in a relaxed manner, Alex responded, "I wouldn't want to bruise you again."

"I think I could handle a few more bruises, seeing I'd be getting them in the line of duty."

"Duty?" She slapped his arm playfully.

From behind them, a familiar masculine voice spoke. "It appears that the Bulrush made it after all." Then the voice laughed.

Resigned that there was no way to escape his friend, Rush responded, "Samson, you know I wouldn't chance missing seeing your handsome face again." Still holding Alex's hand, he swiveled to face his old friend. On seeing Alex's mother standing beside Samson, Rush immediately released Alex's hand. Embarrassed, he said, "Evening, Stella. It's a fine night for a frolic."

"It is at that, Rush," she answered. Her eyes sparkled the same way Alex's had only moments before. "We're so glad you made it. A few of us," she said as she looked at her daughter, "were beginning to think you wouldn't."

Rush exchanged a look with Alex that said, *So you were missing me.* "I wanted to get here earlier, but there was a delay loading coal in Cumberland."

"Have you eaten yet?" Stella asked. "There's plenty of

food left. We covered what wasn't eaten to keep the bugs off. Alexandria will fix you a plate."

"You're not serving turnips, are you?" He looked at both ladies and grinned.

"No turnips," they both replied.

"Then I just might allow you two to twist my arm. Of course, I haven't eaten since the last time you ladies fed me."

His response seemed to amuse Stella. "It's been that long, has it? Then I suggest that Alexandria get you some food at once. I'd hate to see you pass out from hunger."

"No, ma'am. I mean, yes, ma'am. A plate of food would suit me fine."

As the foursome moved toward the tables, Alex asked him, "Have you seen Caro yet?"

"Sure have. I saw her when I first arrived. I think I've been replaced."

"Not totally," Alex confirmed, "but you may have dropped from first place to second."

"The same Jamie Hamilton whom I assume she's no longer accusing of being stupid."

"One and the same." Her eyes crinkled at the corners. "Last time I saw her, she was running hell-bent-for-nothing to recapture him."

"Uh-hmmm!" Samson cleared his throat.

"Sorry, Stella, Alex," Rush said. "Anyway, he was running away from her, and she was in hot pursuit."

"It's been that way all night." Alex chuckled. "But I don't think he's trying too hard to get away."

"No, we fellows have a way of running until we get caught."

Samson slapped Rush on the back. "Sure do, son, sure do."

Rush wondered why in the devil he had said that. Now both Alex and her mother would think he was trying to get snagged by some well-meaning female when in truth being caught was the last thing he wanted.

Or was it? Maybe a part of him did wish to be caught. Lately his mind had been playing with the image he had always had of himself, and keeping his freedom didn't exactly appear to be his top priority. He couldn't get Alexandria Paine out of his mind, and even Caro had tugged at heartstrings he didn't know he possessed.

Samson draped an arm around Rush's shoulders. "Glad you made it, son," he said, bringing Rush back to the present. "We all are."

I just bet you are, you old coot. It was evident that Samson was still determined to get those grandchildren they had discussed on Rush's last visit. Fat chance of that happening. Or did Samson see something in Rush that he was only now discovering about himself?

"Look who's here," Leona Whitley called. She waved her hand, then beelined across the grass toward them. "See, Rosellen," she announced so loud that everyone within shouting distance could hear, "I was right. It is that nice Mr. Duncan."

He was about to sit down at the table they had reached, but Rush wished he could hide beneath it. "Saints preserve us," he mumbled, but his words came out much louder than he intended.

Alex leaned toward him. "In Leona's opinion, she believes that she's worthy of such public veneration."

"I wasn't calling her a saint, but I could go for public strangulation."

Alex silenced a giggle with her hand. "She means well. You just have to learn to ignore her."

"Ignoring that woman would take a much stronger man than me." Rush pasted his best smile on his lips and turned to face the approaching sisters. "Evening, ladies," he said.

"Evening to you, Mr. Duncan," Leona answered, batting her almost lashless eyelids. "See, Alexandria, I told you that your nice young man would come."

"Sister, please." Rosellen extended her hand toward Rush. On first looking at her, he thought she carried a basket full of roses in her opposite hand, but further inspection revealed she held one of her infamous hats. "It's so nice to see you again, young man. Please ignore my sister."

"Ignore me? Impossible." Leona shoved her chubby gloved hand toward Rush. "After all, Sister, I'm responsible for this lovely party we're all enjoying, as well as for Mr. Duncan's presence."

"We're all responsible for this party, Leona, especially Caro and Alex. I take it that you've been told about Caro's wonderful quilt we ladies worked on all afternoon."

"We haven't had a chance to tell him anything, Rosellen," Stella said. "Rush just arrived, and I've been led to believe he hasn't eaten in over a week." She winked at Rush. "At the moment, I believe he is more interested in food than conversation."

"Nonsense," Leona said. "Never knew a man who couldn't eat and talk at the same time."

Rush wondered if that was like walking and chewing gum.

"You, Stella dear," Leona continued, "just want him all to yourself." She looked from Stella to Samson. "You already have one gentleman paying you court. It's not fair that you should have two."

"Paying me court?" Stella's eyes grew wide. "If I didn't know better, I'd conclude that you've been sipping the gentleman's punch." She handed an empty plate to Alex. "Paying me court, indeed."

"Here, let me do that," Leona said. She snatched the plate from Alex's hands and began serving up huge portions of food. "The way to a man's heart is through his stomach, Alexandria. I imagine you've learned some methods to win a man."

Leona Whitley was insufferable, in Rush's opinion. He couldn't understand why Alex allowed her to say such unkind things, but then he supposed the friendship between Stella Paine and the sisters went way back. Well, his didn't. He, for one, didn't like the way the old biddy continually pecked away at Alexandy, as though she were no better than yesterday's chicken feed.

"Miss Leona," Rush said, "I assure you that Alex doesn't need food to get a man's attention. A man would have to be blind not to recognize her beauty."

His defense of Alex had all four ladies looking at him as though he suddenly sported a halo.

"That's my boy," Samson said to Stella. "Taught him everything he knows."

"Well, Mr. Duncan," Leona responded, "I wasn't saying

that Alexandria isn't fetching, because we all can see she is, especially when she fixes herself up as she has today. Alexandria knows she's like a daughter to me and that I have her best interest at heart. Isn't that right, dear?"

Stella answered for Alex. "Of course she knows, Leona, and so does Rush." Her interference was meant to brook no comment from the two young people. "Hurry, dear friend, and dish up that food. Then us old folks will leave Rush to eat his dinner in peace."

"That's exactly what I planned to do, Stella," Leona answered. "I just wanted to make certain that he got a taste of everything. Men have notorious appetites, don't they, Mr. Duncan? My major, now there was a man who had an appetite." Then more to herself than to those present, she added, "And not only for food."

"Leona, how you do carry on." Rosellen took the plate from her sister's hands and plunked it down on the table. "You sit down and eat, Mr. Duncan," she told him, lacing her arm through her sister's. "The two of us must continue our visiting."

Rush supposed Leona Whitley didn't mean to be cruel and thoughtless with her remarks. If everyone else saw them as harmless, then he should, too. "Miss Leona," he said, "thank you for thinking of me. It's evident that you know how to please a man."

"Why, thank you, sir," she responded, pleased, but then her rounded spine straightened as though she suddenly remembered herself. "Of course, I do, Mr. Duncan. That's why I was the one who married and Rosellen did not." Allowing her sister to lead her away, she called as they departed, "We'll leave you lovebirds alone for now."

"Hee-haw." Samson laughed and would have slapped his knee if Stella hadn't dared him with a look not to do so. Instead, he swallowed another laugh and said, "Leona Whitley is getting battier every day."

"Don't be cruel," Stella warned him. "Beneath all that fodder, there beats a heart of gold. She just likes the persona of a busybody. That way she can disguise her loneliness."

"She been lonely all her life?" Samson asked. "For as long

as I can remember, she's been sticking her nose in where it didn't belong.''

"Samson, you're talking about my oldest and dearest friend," Stella answered.

Samson looked genuinely sorry. After a moment, he said, "You're right, Stella. Forgive me. I promise not another bad thing will cross my lips about the woman, but only if you'll agree to do me the honor of the next dance." He bowed slightly.

Rush had never seen Samson act the part of a gentleman, especially a gentleman who appeared to be courting a lady. Could it be his old friend was sweet on Stella Paine?

"In that case," Stella responded, "I'd be delighted to dance with you."

He and Alex watched the older couple make their way to the street where waltz music floated on the air. Rush looked at Alex, and she returned his look. Then they both laughed, confirming Rush's belief about the couple's budding romance.

Sitting beside Rush, watching him eat, it suddenly occurred to Alex that it wasn't only her mother and Caro who were enamored with a man. As much as she hated to admit it, the moment Rush had appeared tonight, cutting in to dance with her, the evening had taken on a magical glow.

At first she had been angry with him for chasing away her dancing partner. Although she hadn't learned the man's name, the stranger had rescued her from a bad case of the doldrums, and for that she was grateful. He had also been a wonderful dancer, and Alex had been enjoying herself. Only moments before Rush's arrival, Alex had convinced herself that she no longer cared if he came to the frolic or not. So when he did show up, she had been caught completely off guard.

After all, she was supposed to be angry with him, believing his absence would upset Caro. But the moment Rush had taken her into his arms, touched her back like a caress, and later apologized for acting like an ass, Alex had to admit that what she felt for Rush Duncan was unlike any other emotion she had ever experienced.

Never had there been a man who could make her fighting mad and deliriously happy at the same time; or bring her close to tears one moment, then have her laughing joyfully the next. Not only did he make her want to appear beautiful in his eyes, but he also made her want to be a woman not past her prime.

She watched him as he ate. Instead of noticing her or talking, he concentrated on his food, appearing to savor every bite. Leona had been wrong. Apparently Rush was a man who *couldn't* eat and talk at the same time.

Yet his silence didn't bother her. She enjoyed it. Alex felt her cheeks warm as she considered their behavior, sharing a personal but very natural experience not unlike that of a husband and wife. She shifted on her chair, but not enough to break the spell. Watching him made her heart almost stop. He was unequivocally the handsomest man Alex had ever seen.

Again he wore his hair tied back with a strip of rawhide. Even with the distance of their chairs separating them, Alex believed she could smell the sunshiny clean fragrance of his hair. His stark white shirt was open at the collar, revealing a triangle of skin the same sun-browned color as his face and neck. Would his chest be the same bronze shade? Growing up beside the canal, Alex had been exposed to the sight of many a man's bare chest as they worked shirtless on their boats. Therefore, a man's naked chest didn't offend her the way it might someone of a different experience.

She continued to study him. Rush's virile good looks again put her in mind of a river pirate, and suddenly she pondered how it would feel to be plundered by such a man. Having already experienced his kiss and recalling the way it made her feel, watching him made Alex want more.

Merciful heavens! What was she thinking? No decent woman should entertain such thoughts, but then, growing up in a home with a mother and father who were very much in love with each other, she had a good idea what went on between a man and woman. At one time Alex had entertained thoughts of having a similar relationship with a man.

The thought made her heart quicken and her lower stomach burn with an uneasy flame. Now, five years later, Rush Duncan had come into her life, making her contemplate thoughts about the marriage bed.

Lordy mercy! I'm as foolish as a mooncalf.

"Alexandy!" Rush called, drawing her from her thoughts. He leaned back in his chair and patted his stomach, then looked at her with deep brown eyes that appeared more black than brown in the near-darkness. "Where is your head?" he asked.

"My head?" She shook it as though to clear it. "Right here on my shoulders where it has always been," she jested.

He grinned, and his silky mustache that resembled a caterpillar lifted at the corners. "Didn't you hear me? I asked you about Caro's quilt. The one Rosellen mentioned."

"Caro's quilt?" Alex repeated. "Why it's—it's—"

"Rush, Rush!" Caro squealed, ducking between their two chairs. A bright red circle dotted each flushed cheek. "Quick, quick, hide me!" she screeched, giggling. "Jamie's gonna get me."

"Is this the same fellow you were chasing earlier?" Rush asked. Turning away from the table, he cradled her against his side and draped an arm around her waist. "Are you the same girl whom I distinctly recall couldn't talk because this Jamie boy was going to get away?"

Caro nodded her head. "Yeah, I'm the same one." Her blue eyes danced with merriment as she searched the crowd for her pursuer. "I caught him lots of times, but now he's gonna catch me."

"Then why are you running, squirt? I'd think you would want to be caught."

"I do, or I did," Caro stammered, "but if he catches me, he's gonna make me dance. His pa said he'd give him a quarter if he'd dance with me. Jamie wants that quarter for a new slingshot."

"Is that a fact, now? Dancing is not all that bad of a thing, darling," he finally said, "especially if you're doing it with someone you like."

He set Caro away from him, and his gaze touched Alex's. The exchange was like a caress, and Alex found it hard to breathe.

"After all, squirt," he continued, "you and your cousin here are the two prettiest gals at this shindig. You can't blame a guy for wanting to dance with you."

With an air of confidence, Caro responded. "Yeah, I know we are. But—but I don't know how to dance."

Rush stood and reached for her hand. "Then it's high time we remedy that. What if I teach you? Then Jamie can earn his quarter. If you play your cards right, the two of you will be splitting the profit."

"Splitting the profit? What does that mean?"

"It means, little one, that he'll enjoy dancing with you so much that he'll give you half of his slingshot."

"Half of a slingshot? Oh, Rush, you're always so silly. What good is a half of a slingshot?"

Alex rose. She didn't want to miss hearing Rush's explanation.

He repeated Caro's question. "What good is a half of a slingshot? Seems to me it would require that the two of you spend a lot more time together, figuring out how to make the thing work."

He winked at Alex while they moved toward the street.

"We already spend a lot of time together," Caro informed him, "but if we each had a half of a slingshot, Jamie would always be wanting my half." She gave this some thought. "I think I understand. You always have a good answer."

Alex was beginning to wonder if there was anything that Rush didn't have an answer for, or an answer that would satisfy a ten-year-old.

"Rush, do you remember the day you brought me Snow?" Caro asked. "That was the same day I called Jamie stupid."

"Yes, I remember, honey. What about it?"

"You said everyone needed a friend." She jerked on his hand, stopping him.

Alex stopped beside them as Caro cupped her hand over her mouth so only they could hear her words. "He's my boyfriend," she whispered.

"Is that a fact, now?" There was a glint of humor in his eyes. "Good for you, Caro," he said. "Every pretty girl ought to have a young man who's sweet on her."

Caro grinned from ear to ear. "I think so, too, Rush." She looked at Alex. "Since Aunt Stella has Samson, and I have Jamie, we gotta find someone who'll like Alex."

Alex felt the color creep into her cheeks. She wasn't sure if she was embarrassed because of the way her cousin had phrased her statement, or the way Rush was looking at her now. She said the first thing that popped into her mind. "Don't you worry yourself any about me, young miss. I'm just fine without anyone."

Rush's steady gaze bore into her. "Is that a fact, now?" he repeated, but didn't wait for her to answer. Instead, he took Caro's hand and led her out among the other dancers, leaving Alex alone on the sidelines.

Alex wondered as the paired couples passed in front of her why she was so hard to like, so much so that even Caro had implied that finding someone for Alex wouldn't be easy.

"What's he doing to her?" Jamie asked, jerking her from her reverie. The boy appeared several moments after Rush and Caro had left her.

Glad to be diverted from her thoughts, she answered, "Rush is going to dance with Caro."

"She said she didn't wanna dance."

"I guess she changed her mind, Jamie. We girls have a way of doing that."

Lately she'd been doing a lot of it herself; disliking Rush Duncan one moment, then wanting him to kiss her the next.

The street resounded with music, and Alex recognized the tune being played as "On Top Of Old Smokey." Ella Hamilton and her husband, Ham, glided past them. Ham called to his son. "Why don't you dance with Miss Alex?"

Jamie shook his head no and folded his arms across his chest. His parents said something to one another, laughed, then continued moving in the same direction as the other dancers who circled the street.

Were Ella and Ham laughing at her because she didn't have a partner? No, they weren't. It was Caro's remark that had made her so sensitive. Determined to steer her mind from this last thought, Alex looked down at the boy beside her. "Do you know how to dance, Jamie?" she asked.

" 'Course I know how to dance. My ma and pa taught me." He watched Caro and Rush. Now that they had gotten past the basics, they, too, were doing the two-step like the others circling the street in the same direction.

Ella and Ham made another pass. "I'll give you two quarters," Ham called to Jamie above the music.

Heaven forbid. Now Ham was bribing his son to dance with her.

"Two?" Jamie repeated, holding up two fingers. His father winked at him and nodded his head yes before the couple moved on down the street.

"Two quarters," Jamie said. "Wow! That's fifty cents." He appeared to be thinking about the fortune just within his reach. After several moments passed, he turned to Alex and bowed in her direction. "Miss Alex, would you please dance with me?"

Alex wanted to refuse, but how could she? Reason told her that Ella and Ham were only trying to get their son to dance. With anyone.

"Why, Jamie," Alex said, "I thought you'd never ask." She curtsied slightly then took the hand Jamie offered and allowed him to lead her into the street. Soon they, too, were circling the area with the other dancers.

This was the same young man who had learned about spooning from his parents. It appeared that Ella and Ham had also taught him about dancing, for he was quite good for a ten-year-old. When he smiled up at her with his cupid face, she decided that the lad was on his way to becoming a real charmer. It was no wonder that her young cousin was smitten.

Now Alex not only had to worry about her own heart's vulnerability, but she also had Caro to worry about as well. She hoped her mother was capable of looking after herself.

Lordy, Alex thought, was she up to all this courting?

When the song ended, Rush and Jamie joined them, and the two males decided to change partners. She watched Caro and Jamie move shyly together along the street. Caro had come so far in these last few weeks; she no longer was the sullen, quiet little girl Rush had delivered to their door. Her arrival had changed them all for the better.

She looked at Rush to see that he was watching her. "Still fine without anyone, Alexandy?"

His question caught her by surprise, but she quickly recovered and feigned ignorance. "Excuse me?"

"Since your cousin no longer has an infatuation with me, I was hoping I might be of interest to you."

"Of interest to me?" He looked so serious, Alex had to laugh. Then, deciding she would devil him as he'd done to her so many times, she said, using Caro's expression, "Rush, you're always so silly."

He cocked one dark brow. "It's silly I am?" He grabbed Alex's hand and pulled her through the crowd and onto the sidewalk.

Unable to do anything but follow and giggle, Alex allowed him to lead her. They passed the musicians at the end of the street and soon they were on Shenandoah away from the crowd of dancers.

Alex's heart was in her throat, but she finally managed to ask him, "Where are you taking me?"

"I think it's time you learned, Alexandy, just how silly I can be." He took several more steps, then stopped at the corner of a building. "Are you up to the challenge?" he asked, facing her.

He was giving her a chance to back down, but Alex knew that she had been longing for such silliness all night.

Never one to back away from a challenge, she answered, "I am."

Her reply was all the consent Rush needed. Instead of pulling her along as he had earlier, he fell into step beside her and encircled her with his arm.

"Where are we going?" she asked, her response more of a croak than a question.

"To see my scribblings," he answered. His smile was sincere, not his usual pigs-in-clover grin.

Alex took a deep, stabling breath.

"Oh," she said faintly.

As he led her toward the footbridge that crossed the river, she hoped that her decision to follow him was the right one.

15

LEAVING THE STREET BEHIND, Rush led them over the well-worn path toward the footbridge. With his arm encircling Alex's waist, his thoughts also bordered on indecision.

Am I thinking with my head or with what's in my britches? He doubted his old friend Samson would approve of him showing Alex his etchings or, more importantly, his itchings, which was his intention the moment he had asked her to accompany him to his boat.

A decent man wouldn't ask a woman like Alex to compromise herself, but when had he ever conformed to the standards of propriety? If anyone saw them together, her reputation would be ruined. What then? Would he be willing to marry her when he had vowed long ago never to marry? Was the pleasure of taking Alexandy to his bed worth the risk involved?

She stumbled. While steadying her, his fingers accidently splayed over the side of her breast. That one touch made him feel as though he'd been struck by lightning, and his body grew hard with need.

Hell, yes, it was worth it. If Alex was willing to compromise herself, then he was willing to spend a lifetime in hell to experience the little bit of heaven he believed awaited him in her arms. Maybe it was like Samson had said. Maybe Alexandria Paine had always had him tied up in knots. If this was true, then Rush felt tonight was as good a time as any for him to seize and hold her. A smart man knew to strike when the iron was hot.

They were on the bridge now, and Alex slowed her pace. Sensing her nervousness, he stopped, pretending interest in the scenery.

"Beautiful night," he said, pulling her closer to his side. He propped his free arm on the rail, and together they stared out at the confluence of the two rivers.

Without the brightness of the many candles and lanterns in town, a milky darkness surrounded them. The water below the bridge looked like silver ribbons swirling around black rocks. A metallic glow plated the surrounding hills, while patchy clouds scuttled across the moon's surface.

A soft breeze lifted a strand of Alex's hair that had worked its way out of the confining braid. In the moonlight, its golden color looked like a silken skein. The scent of roses and woman enveloped him, making his heart thud against his ribs.

Pulling her closer, he said, "I predict we'll have rain tomorrow."

"Rain?" Alex shifted, putting air between their bodies.

Talking about the weather wasn't exactly his idea of a romantic conversation, but with Alex he needed to tread lightly before getting down to the serious stuff.

He pointed at the moon with its circle of light. "The ring around it suggests we're in for some wet weather. It was raining in Cumberland when I left."

Alex's gaze followed his finger. "Maybe it does mean rain, but to me that big old moon looks like a white china plate filled to overflowing with mashed potatoes."

"China plate?" Rush dropped his hand. "What is it about china plates that fascinates you? Every time we're together the subject comes up." *And always at the most inopportune times.*

He jostled her in his arms. This time she didn't try to get away, but turned to face him. "It's because of what Caro said right after her arrival. Oh, Rush, you won't believe the change in her since your last visit."

"What does Caro have to do with china plates?"

"Lately she has revealed so much—"

Rush pressed his finger against her lips and regarded her thoughtfully. "I can tell that she has settled in just fine as I knew she would, but you have my curiosity aroused. What about the plates, Alex?"

"Oh, yes, the plates. Not long after Caro's arrival at our house, she began reminiscing about Nebraska. Since she had always refused to talk about her past, her revelation took me by surprise. She began to describe mealtimes back home, suggesting they ate from white china plates that were so shiny they could see their reflections in the surface, drinking from crystal glasses that pinged like a bell if they were hit with a fork. . . ."

Her voice trailed off as though she wasn't certain how to continue.

"What else?" Rush asked.

"Flowers. Caro said they had flowers they would place in a white milk jug in the middle of their table. She said the different-colored blossoms reflected in the jug's surface and looked as pretty as a rainbow."

Alex's gaze returned to the moon.

"Is that all?" When she didn't answer, he said, "I still don't understand what Caro's mealtime experiences have to do with me. The last time you and I were together, you asked me if I ate from china plates and drank from crystal glasses. Why?"

Alex seemed miles away. He placed his finger beneath her chin and turned her face toward his. "You're not telling me everything, are you?"

"It's nothing, really. That was before I got to know you, but I didn't believe for a minute that you ate from—but then, you brought us the wildflowers, and I was really confused."

Suddenly her meaning sunk in. Rush let his breath out slowly. "I think I understand. You didn't believe that someone like me would be cultured enough to eat from china plates and drink from crystal glasses, is that it, Alexandy?" His mood veered sharply to anger.

"I-I didn't know what to believe," she blurted out.

"Mother told Caro that it sounded as though you set a fancy table aboard your canal boat, but of course the idea seemed absurd."

"Laughable, huh?" His old insecurities returned.

He released her and ran his hand over his hair. Had the moon bewitched him into thinking he was good enough to bed Alexandria Paine? Heck, judging from her comments, she didn't believe him to be any more refined than the mules that pulled his canal boat. What the devil had he been thinking?

"Then when you brought us flowers," Alex continued, "well, I was thoroughly confused. About you and Caro. But now that I've gotten to know you, it doesn't—"

"Alex, hush!" Rush fisted his hands at his sides and stared at her. It was time he put an end to what he saw as becoming an impossible situation.

"Now that I've come to know you, it—"

"Alex," he said, "our being together is a mistake and not a good idea." He locked his fingers around her arm. "Come on. I'll escort you back to the dance."

"No," she said, jerking away from his grasp. "I don't want to go back. I-I thought you wanted to be with me. Besides, you—you were going to show me your scribblings."

Rush laughed, but it was a mockery of his true feelings. His protective shield snapped into place.

"Darling, as much as I'd like to show you everything, I don't think tonight is the right time." He tried again to take Alex's arm, but she sidestepped him then turned and started across the bridge toward the canal.

"Damnation," he muttered impatiently. "Where do you think you're going?"

She didn't answer him, but kept walking.

"Alex," he called, "it's not safe for you to go traipsing off in the dark alone. Besides me, there could be all kinds of unsavory characters waiting to pounce on you."

When she continued to ignore him, Rush had no choice but to follow her. "Dammit, Alex, you're the most stubborn female I've ever had the displeasure of knowing."

When he finally caught up with her, he yanked her around

to face him. Since nice wasn't working, he'd try mean. He hoped he could scare some sense into her.

"You realize that once we're on my boat, there'll be no sidestepping around. A man like me doesn't take a woman home to set up housekeeping."

Her chin came up in the same stubborn way that Caro's did, and like Caro she didn't cower. Instead, she crossed her arms against her chest and glowered at him. "I never cared much for housekeeping," she responded.

Damn, she was stubborn, but she was no match for Rush when he felt ornery. Besides, he was used to dealing with mules.

He tried another warning. "Once on board my boat, covering your bosom with your arms won't save you from the likes of me."

"Maybe," she responded, dropping her arms to her side and throwing her shoulders back, "I don't wish to be saved from the likes of you."

Her action made the pit of his stomach churn. Not even the darkness could disguise her lushly rounded bosom, especially to a man who had pressed her womanly softness into his male hardness less than a week ago.

Rush was close enough now that he could see the moon's reflection in her dark eyes. He looked deep into their depths, searching for the revulsion he had tried his darndest to put there. Instead, he saw amusement.

Amusement? Not possible, he told himself, but as he continued to study her, he saw the beginnings of a smile. That smile melted all his anger.

"Shucks, Alexandy, honey," he said on a softer note, "I don't think taking you to view my scribblings is the gentlemanly thing to do."

"Since when did you become a gentleman, Rush Duncan?"

"That's just it, sugar. You and I both know I'm no gentleman. But you, you're a fine lady whose reputation is at risk by being here with me."

"Don't you think I'm old enough to decide the fate of my reputation?"

She stepped nearer, stopping only inches away from him.

Alex tilted her head back, bringing her lips temptingly close to his—so close that he could kiss them if he wanted to.

He wanted to kiss her in the worst way, but he didn't dare weaken, so he stepped back. She dogged his steps. Finally, when she stood even closer to him than before and he could feel her warm breath fanning his face, he gripped her upper arms with his hands, forbidding any further contact. There was nothing he would have enjoyed more than taking her into his arms and kissing her senseless, but now wasn't the time. For them, there never would be a time, and he needed to dissuade her for both their sakes.

He flashed her his most charming smile. "You do realize, Alexandy, that it won't be your braids I'll be dipping in the inkwell if I take you aboard my boat."

Her gaze was riveted on his face, but instead of shrinking away from him, she laughed. "Rush Duncan, you always did have a way with words. I think it's time we see if you're as good as you claim you are, or if all your swagger is nothing more than a way to hide your real feelings."

Rush swallowed. He wondered if she realized how close she had come to the truth, but he also knew that now wasn't the time for him to reveal his weakness.

"Oh, I'm good, Goldilocks. So good that I'll have you howling at the moon before the night is over."

A twinkle warmed her eyes. "Is that a fact, now?" she asked, using his words. Then she had the gall to give him a come-hither smile.

"Damn tooting, it's a fact." He shook his finger at her. "And if you're not real careful you just might get more than you bargained for."

She captured his waving finger in her hand and brought it to her lips, surprising him even more. For a moment Rush thought she might put it in her mouth, and he knew all would be lost. His pecker was already as hard as river rock, and his willpower was eddying as swiftly as the Potomoc that flowed beneath them.

"Darling," he said, trying one last shot to be rid of her. She kissed the tip of his finger, making his lungs swell until they ached. It wasn't easy playing dirty with an angel, but she left him no choice. "A woman past her prime wouldn't know how to handle a man like me."

His words cut her to the quick, and the moment he said them, he wanted to take them back, but reason told him it was best to end this thing between them now before it went any further.

Her lashes dropped quickly, making her eyes unreadable.

Rush steeled himself for her exit. It was better this way. He studied her, committing her image to memory. He hadn't planned for the evening to end this way, but then how else could it have ended? They were too different to have a future together. No one knew better than he did that going forward was impossible, and for Rush there was no going back. At that moment, he knew he loved her, perhaps he always had.

"Your defense is good, Rush Duncan, but I don't buy it for a minute." With two hands, she clasped his hand against her chest. "I don't scare as easily as you would like," she said, her voice wistful. "As you so aptly put it, I am a girl past her prime—"

"Oh, Alexandy, you know I didn't—I was merely trying—"

"To scare me away," she finished for him. "But it didn't work. As you can see, I'm still here."

"But why?" Rush squirmed in place. "God, woman, you don't make it easy, do you?"

"Hush and let me speak. I knew earlier when I agreed to accompany you to look at your scribblings that I'd be doing more than looking at pretty pictures."

"Not if you were with a gentleman."

"I am with a gentle man. You're sensitive to a fault and tenderhearted, although you'd be the last to admit to having such qualities. Remember, I've witnessed your kindness first-hand in the way you treat Caro."

He was thankful for the darkness, because his face burned with heat.

"It's because of who you are that I decided to accompany you to your boat."

"Alex, you don't know what you're doing."

"You're wrong," she corrected. "I'm very much aware of

what I'm doing, so please don't make me beg.''

"Darling, I'd never make you beg for anything.'' Considering what he wanted to do to her, perhaps there were a few things he wouldn't mind hearing her beg for. With those images foremost in his mind, Rush teased, "Well, maybe just a small plea.''

Her smile deepened into throaty laughter. "Rush Duncan, you're still incorrigible.''

He winked at her. "I am at that.''

This time when she turned away from him and started moving across the bridge toward the canal, Rush followed her. Then he slammed to a stop and pulled her gently into his arms.

"Alexandy, you've got to be real certain about this, because I don't think I could stand knowing that you allowed me to ruin your good name, and that tomorrow you will have regrets.''

"There'll be no regrets, Rush Duncan, and I'll not be expecting any declarations of love. I'm a woman full grown and I am content with my lot, especially since I have Caro to look after. Since you're a man about town who wants no ties as well, I believe our little tryst is what we both need.''

"Darling, you sound like one hell of a businesswoman, but are you sure?''

"Remember, I'm Goldilocks, and what better wolf than you to make me howl?''

"Sugar, I believe you have your stories mixed up, but I want you to know that you'll be welcome in my bed anytime.''

RUSH'S REMARK ABOUT BED made Alex almost turn and run back toward town. *Lordy mercy, what's come over me?* Instead of howling like a wolf in heat, she felt more like bawling like a baby frightened out of its wits. *Whatever possessed me to be so brazen?*

The bridge was behind them now, and she stole a peek at Rush while they moved together along the canal path. What had brought her to this moment had nothing to do with good sense. He had bewitched her with his dark good looks and teasing manner, and those qualities had pushed her to be so brazen. Now she didn't know if she could go through with this. If she had any good sense left she would turn and run.

Alex took a deep breath, hoping to steady her quivering insides. The fresh air she drew in combatted her nervousness somewhat, but it didn't settle the arguments waging war inside her head. Arguments not unlike the ones Rush had presented her with before they had left the bridge.

No one knew better than Alex that if their tryst was discovered, her reputation would be ruined. No decent man would ever consider taking her to wife. And what about her poor mother? Alex could only imagine the shame she would have to endure because of her daughter's indiscretion. In her own mind, she was acting no better than Aunt Charlotte by agreeing to accompany a man unescorted to his home. Wagon or boat, they were both the same. The only difference in their situations was that it would be a canaller doing the defiling instead of a drummer.

Wrong, the voice inside her head corrected, *Rush did try to talk you out of accompanying him.* Perhaps Caro's father had tried to dissuade Charlotte as well, but like the aunt Alex had never known, she, too, was just as stubborn.

Beside her, Rush held her arm snuggled against his warm side, his fingers linked with hers. He walked the surefooted walk of a man with an objective—and she was the desired result. At least she was desired. Before tonight there had been no man who had claimed such an interest, barring the preacher, of course.

I've damned my soul to perdition, she thought. When she considered Rush's kiss, however, and the pleasure she'd enjoyed in his arms, Alex imagined that what she was about to experience would be more closely linked to heaven than to hell. Rationalizing, she decided she owed him for the kindness he had bestowed upon Caro.

Yes, that was it. She was paying back a debt. She was sacrificing herself for a good cause. Not being very good at self-deceptions, Alex knew she was lying to herself.

Rush Duncan had touched a cord deep inside her, making her want to be a desirable woman instead of a girl Leona

Whitley had claimed was past her prime. Was it wrong to want for one moment to feel that she was beautiful and desirable?

Rush is a canaller, she reminded herself. *A man with no roots, the kind of man you always said you'd never marry.*

Marriage! *No one had said anything about marriage.* Certainly not Rush. Alex's more rational side argued that their coming together would be nothing more than a pleasant experience: something shared between two people who were attracted to one another in the physical sense, but nothing more.

She *was* attracted to him, and he appeared to be attracted to her. Besides, two people as opposite as they were could never be anything more than friends. But then, allowing a man to bed her did go further than friendship, did it not? She marched beside him, her head high, her thoughts focused inward.

No, she finally rationalized, they would be acquaintances of a sort, but what name could she put to the *sort*? In truth, most of the time she didn't even like him—he with his blackguard ways. Except for tonight, of course; tonight she liked him in spite of, or maybe because of, his unprincipled behavior.

He walked beside her, his stride loose and unhurried. She could feel the heat of him radiating through the sleeve of his shirt. Alex exhaled a sigh. So moved was she by their close connection, she centered her thoughts on her surroundings rather than on Rush.

The moon silvered the towpath sand beneath their feet. As they walked between the river and the canal, it felt as though they were the only two people in the world. The boats tied up for the night appeared to be empty. Alex suspected that the crews were still away attending the frolic or passing time in one of the few taverns in town. Music from Bowstring's fiddlers floated to them from across the river, the sound joining with the swish of rushing water and the croaking of bullfrogs that had staked out space along the banks of both waterways.

They passed the house where Alex had lived with her parents until her father's death. She couldn't walk the towpath without feeling melancholy, and perhaps that was why she usually avoided this side of the river. It had been months since her last visit.

"Does it make you sad to come here?" Rush asked. His question took her by surprise. It was as though he had read her thoughts.

"It does," she answered, "but I have wonderful memories from the happy times to help combat the sadder ones."

"Well, it makes me sad, too, although I don't have many happy memories connected with Harpers Ferry." He squeezed her fingers. "I suppose if it weren't for Samson and your father's kindness, there wouldn't be any good memories at all. They both treated me as though I were someone."

"Of course, you were someone," Alex insisted. "Everyone is someone. How could they treat you any differently?" His reference to her father made her feel they had a common bond, because she had loved her father as much as life itself.

Rush laughed, but it sounded bitter instead of mirthful. "You do know about my past, don't you, Alex?"

"No, I don't suppose I do."

Alex knew only bits and pieces that she assumed were more gossip than truth. Like Leona Whitley's remark about his having bad blood. When Alex was a child, her father had told her that Rush lived with his mother and that the Duncans were very poor. She also knew that after his mother's death, Rush sometimes slept in Samson's storeroom behind the saloon.

Back then, she had never considered his situation as being tough, but tonight her heart went out to that orphaned boy who was now a man.

"Well," he said, "maybe I should tell you before this yearning between us goes any further."

Yearning, Alex thought. So that is what she should call this thing building between them.

He stopped walking. "Here's my boat."

Alex looked at the moored craft tied up well away from the lock. The name, *Chuck-a-luck,* was barely visible in the moonlight. If she hadn't heard Caro call Rush's boat by that name, she probably wouldn't have noticed the lettering. The boat appeared to be in good condition, no peeling paint visible, and the wooden decks were spotlessly clean.

Rush kneaded her fingers. "Are you sure you still want to do this?"

Without hesitating, she answered, "I've come this far, haven't I? That should be proof enough that I wish to stay."

"You're a brave woman, Alexandy," he whispered huskily. He smiled, and his teeth looked like ivory in the light of the moon. "If that's your decision, then the least I can do is see that we are as discreet as possible." Rush jumped aboard the boat, then grasped her waist with his hands. "Come on, darling, let's get you aboard." Lifting her up as though she weighed no more than a feather, he swung her away from the shore.

He didn't release her immediately. Instead, he carried her, his face almost buried in her bosom, to the shadows beside the boat's cabin. His muscular arms encircled her, and she expected his hot breath to dissolve the material of her new dress at any moment.

Then slowly he lowered her to the floor, sliding her down the length of his body. When her feet touched the deck, her knees felt rubbery, and she wasn't certain if her legs would hold her. Everything that was manly about Rush Duncan Alex discovered with her descent. His body was a composition of hard planes with rounded angles and one very defined protrusion below his belt. Her contact with him left her heart thumping, her head reeling, and with a hopeful longing to slide again. But it seemed she wasn't to be allowed a repeat performance, because Rush ended the sweet torment by releasing her and stepping away.

With a voice that revealed none of the runaway emotions she was experiencing, he asked, "Do you like buttermilk?"

"Buttermilk?" That was the last question Alex expected him to ask her, but what did she know about what one drank when taking part in a romantic tryst? "I-I like it sometimes," she answered, "especially when it's icy cold."

"A girl after my own heart." He grabbed her hand and pulled her to the opposite side of the boat.

Little did he realize it wasn't his heart that Alex was after, but more of the thrilling contact she'd just experienced in his embrace. She followed him obediently.

"Here it is," he said.

Alex stopped several feet away from him and watched as

he drew a line from the water. Attached to the line was a sealed gallon jug that thumped against the deck as he lowered it. Bending, Rush untied the container and lifted it, then he stood. ''What say we have a glass right now?''

Not waiting for her response, he was off again. This time he walked to the back of the boat and disappeared inside the cabin. Although he hadn't invited her to follow him, she assumed she was supposed to.

As she neared the doorway, a light suddenly chased away the cabin's darkness. Alex stepped carefully down the two steps to find Rush standing beside a table, putting the chimney back upon a lamp. Then he moved about the room, lighting several candles that were attached to the walls by sconces. Soon the interior glowed with warmth, and Alex gave the small space a thorough inspection.

The first thing she noted was that the cabin was impeccably neat, a fact that surprised her, considering Rush was a man who lived alone. The furnishings were sparse, but adequately filled the small space. They were of a much better quality than Alex had expected a canaller to own.

There was a small cooking stove and a rectangular oak table with two long benches made from the same wood on either side. A mason jar in the table's center held a fading bouquet of wildflowers. Pushed against one end of the table was a desk that had its own chair. On top of the desk stood a lamp, a green desk pad, a pen holder with pens, and wooden letter boxes that were filled with papers. What looked like a ledger lay open in the desk's center.

Her gaze shifted around the cabin. A man's leather chair with a matching ottoman sat in front of a wall with floor-to-ceiling bookcases where volumes of books were shelved.

Rush must have been watching her, because he said, ''I like to read.''

Beside the leather chair, a round table held a reading lamp, along with a stand containing a varied assortment of pipes. Before this moment, Alex hadn't considered the habits of the man she was with, but his home's interior revealed a side of Rush she never knew existed. A built-in bed wide enough for one occupied the space beneath the cabin's low hatch.

When her gaze skirted quickly over the berth, Rush added, ''And I like to sleep.'' This last information was accompanied by his most wicked grin.

She didn't want to think about what else he did in that bed, but wasn't that why she was here? How many other women had shared that same intimate space with him? Tomorrow her name would join their ranks, although Alex wasn't so certain she wanted to be lumped together with his other conquests.

He was a virile and experienced man. Hadn't Leona Whitley implied that no girl was safe within a foot of him after he'd reached puberty? Well, he was well beyond puberty now, and his reputation preceded him; but being with Rush no longer frightened Alex as it had earlier. Now that she had seen how he lived, her misgivings had all but disappeared. Those misgivings had been replaced with a growing curiosity to learn more about the real man.

''Now for that milk,'' Rush said, turning to retrieve two glasses from a cupboard. He thunked them down on the table beside the gallon jar. ''They're not of the finest crystal.'' Again, the mischievous look came into his eyes.

''Then I'm assuming they won't pass the fork test?'' After approaching the table, Alex picked up the glass.

''They're of the poorest quality, but they're functional.''

Lifting the glasses to their mouths, they both drank long and deep of the cold, creamy liquid, their eyes never leaving each other's above their glasses' rims. When they had finished drinking the milk, they returned the empty glasses to the table.

Rush laughed. ''You've got a milk mustache.''

''And you now have a white one,'' she countered.

They giggled like children before their laughter subsided into strained silence. They stared at one another, the air between them as charged as the current of a storage battery.

''Your cabin's nice,'' Alex said, hoping to clear the energized air.

''I modeled it after the cabin of my friend, Captain Steve. Aboard his ship I spent many comfortable hours in his living quarters.''

''This is the captain whose crew took up a collection for Caro?''

"That's right," he said. "You wrote him a thank-you letter, I believe. He appreciated your thoughtfulness."

"Then he received it? I wasn't certain that he would."

"I saw him on my last trip to Georgetown. He had just received your note."

Rush's fingers sought the top button of his shirt. Watching the very personal act made Alex's breath catch in her throat. She looked away, trying to act as though a man undoing his collar was an everyday occurrence in her life.

Rush must have picked up on her uneasiness because he dropped his hands to his side. "Hell, Alexandy, I'm only undoing the top button."

"Excuse me?" She tried to act as though she didn't know what he meant.

He was around the table in an instant. He stood so close to her that she had no place to go but backwards toward the bed, which was where he wanted her anyway, she supposed.

"I wasn't going to strip down to my birthday suit, if that's what you were thinking. Although I'll admit getting naked with you is top priority on my list of things to do at the moment. But I realize you need a little wooing before we get down to the hard stuff."

She gulped. The hard stuff he must be referring to was very visible beneath the buttons of his fly. When Alex realized where her gaze had lighted, her face burned with embarrassment. She yanked her eyes back to his, realizing her earlier courage had flown out the window.

"I-I thought you were going to show me your drawers—drawings?" she said.

He laughed then, a deep voluminous laugh that made his dark brown eyes sparkle like smokey topaz in the soft candlelight.

"Come here, sugar," he said, drawing her into his arms. He looked down at her. When he spoke, his voice sounded throaty, warm. "I promise you that whatever we do here tonight, I'll make it an enjoyable experience."

He kissed her. His kiss deepened, and he opened his lips. When she followed his example, his tongue slipped into her mouth. The touch was like moist silk. His breathing grew heavy, and his kisses became more urgent. He broke contact with a groan, then began trailing kisses over her face, to her ear, and down her throat to where the collar of her dress encircled her neck.

"May I undo your hair?" he whispered, pausing to draw in a shaky breath.

Unable to speak and knowing she had passed the stage of denying him anything, Alex nodded her head. He gently grasped her shoulders, turning her back to his front. The heat of him seared her backside, making breathing difficult.

She felt Rush remove the ribbon she had tied around the braided knot early that morning. His fingers trembled as much as her insides. Next he removed the pins that secured the long coil at her nape. Once the braid unrolled, Rush began raking his fingers through the woven strands to separate them.

She heard him sigh, then felt his warm breath against the back of her head when his lips brushed her hair. "Your hair is like sunbeams on water," he said, "and it smells like roses."

Rush pulled her hard against him, encircling her again with his arms. Alex could feel his body straining against hers. *This is heaven, not perdition.*

He continued to kiss her, settling her hair across her shoulder to allow him better access to the back of her neck. When his hands strayed upward to the front of her dress, a whitehot heat seared her core. His hands cupped her breasts, and the sweet contact was almost unbearable. He caressed her nipples with his fingers, and they reacted to his touch by turning into pebbly nubs.

Groaning, Rush turned her to face him again before trailing his lips where his fingers had been. Soon her dress posed too much of a barrier between them, and together they began working the buttons free from the tiny buttonholes.

Unbuttoned now to her waist with her skirt's placket open, Rush stared at her. Holding her eyes with his, he ran his fingers across the exposed roundness of her breasts beneath her camisole. Never moving his gaze from hers, he gently peeled her dress from her shoulders, then spread her hair around her shoulders as though it were a sheath of threads.

"God, you're beautiful, Alexandy," he said, "just as I envisioned you would be."

His eyes smoldered with fire. She watched them, knowing the flame in their brown depths was his need to possess her. With the pad of his finger he traced a blue vein barely visible beneath the skin of one breast. "Aw, shucks, Alexandy," he whispered, "we can't do this. You're too pure to be touched by the likes of me."

She clamped his hand against her breasts. When she finally had command of her tongue, she said, "You feel my heart beating, do you not? It's calling to you alone, Rush Duncan. You are a good and honorable man, and I can't think of anyone I'd rather be with like this than you."

When he spoke, his voice cracked with raw emotion. "My mother was a whore, Alexandria. I don't even know who my father was, and neither did she." His eyes were filled with contempt for himself. "I'm not worthy of taking such a precious gift from you."

Then, as though she were a child he was helping, he tugged the dress he'd peeled away earlier back upon her shoulders. "You deserve better."

Rush's words tore at Alex's heartstrings. Leona Whitley was not the only person who believed Rush had bad blood running through his veins; he believed the same about himself. His pain became Alex's. She had to convince him that his being born the bastard son of a whore didn't make him unworthy.

Alex pushed his hands away. "Stop this now," she said. Resting her hands on his shoulders, she forced him to look at her. "Don't even think such thoughts about yourself, much less voice them. Children aren't responsible for the sins of their parents, no matter what you believe. I want you, Rush Duncan. I want you to pick me up and carry me to that bed and do things to me that I never dreamed of before this moment."

When he looked away from her, Alex stepped closer and cradled his head with her hands. She stroked his hair that was still tied back with the piece of rawhide. Her fingers loosened the ends of the string, allowing the thick brown mane to tumble free around his shoulders. He looked up at her then. Alex smoothed his hair. It felt like silk beneath her fingers and smelled as fresh as summer sunshine. A more beautiful man she had never known, and she wanted him with every part of her being.

She teased him, wanting the carefree Rush to return. "You promised you wouldn't make me beg."

He looked deeply into her eyes, and that look drove its way into her heart like an arrow shot from a bow.

"Are you certain, Alexandy?"

"I've never been more certain of anything in my life."

"Then, my love," he said, catching her behind her knees and back. "This night will be one that neither of us will forget."

He carried her toward his bed. It was where she wanted to go.

16

RUSH FELT AS THOUGH he were dreaming when he carried Alex to his bed. Standing beside the mattress, holding her in his arms, he wondered how he could do justice to Alexandy, making love to her in a space that was barely large enough for him.

Gently he released her knees, helping her to stand. He kissed her lips, then her throat. To his delight, she stood unmoving, allowing him the pleasure of undressing her. He had never been granted such a gift.

"Christmas," he said, kissing her playfully on the nose as he began to peel away her dress.

"Christmas?" she asked. Her big brown eyes looked as though she thought he had suddenly taken leave of his senses.

"You, my sweet Alexandy, are the culmination of all the presents I never received as a child. A present wrapped in yellow gingham with buttons and bows, and whatever else you call those fancy underthings a lady wears."

"You're so silly," she whispered, borrowing Caro's words for a second time tonight.

She looked so delicate, almost ethereal, in the dim glow of the candles.

Alex sucked in a breath when her dress slid over her hips

to spread around her feet like the petals of a blossoming flower. She crossed her arms against her camisole, not because she was frightened of losing it, but because she was afraid its worn condition wouldn't measure up to the fancy underthings that a man like him must be accustomed to seeing on his ladies.

He bent forward and nuzzled her cleavage where her crossed arms made a vee. "Next the tissue," Rush teased. Straightening, he ran his finger beneath the ribboned strap of her camisole, not oblivious to its frayed edges that caught on his work-roughened skin.

Her hands covered the straps, blocking his finger's movement. Finally he managed to work his finger free to trail it lightly down the length of the strap where it fastened to her chemise. Her hands followed the movement, splaying across her breasts, covering the fabric.

"Holding back for the real surprise, are you?" Rush feared she had changed her mind.

Like a child, she shook her head no, but continued to cover the chemise's top with her hands.

Concerned now, Rush asked, "Are you having second thoughts, Alexandy?" He knew if she was he would live with her decision, but not taking her after seeing her like this would be the hardest thing he would ever have to do.

Groping for control, Rush asked, "So, my love, am I to be denied yet another gift?"

Her gaze dropped to her shoulders, then to her breasts, before seeking out his gaze. "No," she responded, alarmed. "It's just that my wrappings aren't as fancy as those you are used to seeing."

"I don't know, darling, they look pretty good from here." So good that seeing her made his skin tingle.

"You know what I mean," she responded. "All those fancy underthings that your other women wear."

"Other women?" Rush almost hooted, but when he saw she was serious, he bit back the urge to laugh. "Alexandy, although I doubt that you'll believe me, I assure you there haven't been all that many other women. In truth, you're the first one I've ever brought aboard this boat."

"But earlier you said—"

"Darling, I was funning with you. I figured if you were as nervous as I am, it would be easier to make a game of this thing we're about to do."

"Then their camisoles weren't of the finest lawn with frilly satin bows?"

"This conversation has a familiar ring, but last time I believe we were discussing plates."

Alex dropped her hands to the her sides. He could see her pulse beat at the base of her throat.

"Then my worn camisole doesn't offend you?"

"Offend me? Heck no, darling. You could wear a croaker sack, and I'd still find you beautiful."

She thought about this for a moment. "I'm glad," she said, looking relieved. "It's just that I didn't expect to be showing my underthings."

He stepped closer and tugged on the center of her camisole. "Does this mean I'm getting closer to being presented with my gift?"

She blushed. Clearing her throat, she said, "I'm glad that I'm the first woman you've brought aboard your boat."

"Shucks, sugar, you're the first woman I've *wanted* to bring on my boat." *You're the first woman I ever loved.* Rush grinned at his thought. Actually, she was. He had loved her since he was a lad, but it had taken him until now to realize it.

"That settles it, then," she replied.

Before he knew what she was about, Alex stripped away her camisole and drawers. Soon she stood before him as naked as the day she was born, except for her shoes. Her legs were long, her breasts high and firm, her waist thin, and her hips rounded. At the top of her long legs was a nest of curls a shade darker than her sunny-colored hair.

It took all of Rush's willpower not to lay her down right then and there and have his way with her.

As he studied her, his throat felt as though it had been stuffed with rags, and liquid-hot heat burned behind his eyes. Her beauty, or perhaps that she had chosen to share such an intimacy with him, made him feel close to tears.

"Santa came early this year," he quipped, trying to rein in his emotions.

Never taking his gaze from hers, Rush began to strip. When he, too, was naked, he moved toward her and urged her to sit on the narrow bed. With shaking fingers, he removed her shoes and stockings.

"It'll be a tight fit," he whispered, sitting down beside her. He kissed her while maneuvering her backward and encouraged her to lay down. He stretched out beside her, their fronts bonding from head to toe.

"It's supposed to be, isn't it?" Alex asked. "I mean, the first time?"

He chuckled at her response. Somewhere along the rocky road of his life he must have done something right. Why else would he have been granted the honor of being this woman's first lover?

"It may be uncomfortable," he cautioned her, not wishing to draw attention to her remark. He smoothed her hair away from her face. "But I'll try to make it as painless as possible."

The promise made, Rush got down to the serious business of paying homage to the special gift he'd been granted.

In all her wildest dreams, Alex had never imagined that being held and caressed by a man could feel so wonderful. Rush's every touch evoked a new sensation. He kissed her lips, and she kissed him back. When his mouth left hers to trail kisses down her neck to her breasts, she wanted it back. She wanted it, that is, until his hot tongue laved each breast, sending burning sensations spiraling to the very center of her being.

When his long fingers slid to her stomach then skimmed the nest of curls at the apex of her thighs, Alex felt she might die from the pleasure of his touch.

Soon his fingers moved lower, working similar magic on that secret part of her that had never been explored before. His touch made her writhe with a want that had no name.

Yearning . . . yearning . . . yearning, the voice inside her head repeated in cadence with her heartbeat. The air surrounding them felt almost tangible.

Rush's body was beautiful and so different from her own.

His was muscular and graceful as only a man's could be—
honed from steel. She gloried in the feel of him pressed inti-
mately against her, his satin-smooth skin sprigged with silky
brown hair.

The need inside her grew beyond boundaries. Then he was
above her, spreading her legs, his manly need undisguised in
his dark eyes and the rigid length of his man's body. As gently
as possible, Rush entered her with a deep thrust, and white
hot pain tore through her center.

He remained perfectly still.

"I'm sorry, my love," he whispered, his words as ragged
as his breathing. "It won't hurt anymore, I promise."

After a moment the pain subsided, and he began to move
inside her, making the yearning grow and spread. Alex locked
her legs around his hips taking him deeper into her womanly
place.

His thrusts became harder, deeper. Alex matched them, joining him in the dance of lovers where even the inexperienced
could excel.

The pressure built inside her, fusing with the peak of her
yearning before exploding into a thousand pieces as Rush carried them both over the edge. Colors as bright and varied as
the many patches of a quilt flashed against the darkness of her
closed lids, and Alex floated among them as though she were
suspended in a midnight sky.

Soon she opened her eyes. Above her, spent but smiling,
Rush stared into her eyes. "That was one heck of a ride, darling," he whispered, bracing himself above her with his elbows.

His lips found hers, and he sealed their joining with a
feathery-light kiss.

She stared back at him, feeling close to tears.

He must have sensed her confusion because he tried to
soothe her. "We were fine together, Alexandy," he crooned,
stroking her damp hair away from her face. "I hope I didn't
hurt you too much."

Alex wanted to tell him that he didn't, but the words
jammed in her throat. She had never felt so vulnerable. There
were so many things she wanted to share with him, such as

how wonderful she thought he was and how much she enjoyed their coupling, but her emotions were so raw that she feared if she spoke she would cry. So instead of speaking, she smiled weakly at him and said nothing.

He looked at her, his eyes revealing wonder. "No one has ever given me such a precious gift as you've just given me, Alexandy. I'll cherish it for the rest of my life."

She did weep then. Rush eased himself out of her and cradled her in his arms. Her tears seemed to make him uneasy. "Don't cry, darling," he soothed. "We'll sleep for a while," he said, pulling the sheet over them. "Then I'll take you home."

Home? Where was home for Alex now?

Long after Rush fell asleep, Alex lay awake, pondering that question. Tonight she had crossed into a territory that was as foreign to her as traveling to a new town would be. She had traveled to that new town with Rush, but she would return alone, for she had come to his bed not expecting any promises or commitments.

Her debt had been paid. Now they were even. What had he said when he talked about their coupling? *I'll try to make it as painless as possible.* Then why did her heart feel as though it was about to break?

∞

"JUMPING JEHOSHAPHAT," RUSH GRUMBLED, stabbing one leg into his trousers and almost losing his footing. He didn't have time to make his much-needed cup of coffee. He switched feet and stabbed the other leg into the remaining pants leg, then jockeyed the trousers up over his hips. Finding his shirt and shoes, he slipped into both. He had awakened about five minutes before with his limbs tangled with Alex's. After checking the ship's clock on the wall, he had maneuvered free of her embrace to get dressed. With daylight fast approaching, it was time to take Alex home.

Sometime during the night it had started to rain. Now the rain beat down on the boat's cabin with a steady, drumming vengeance. It appeared that the stormy weather covering Cumberland and parts further north had finally worked its way south.

"Damn," he grumbled again. The load of coal he was scheduled to deliver early in the week to the Georgetown terminus meant that he and his crew were in for an uncomfortable, soggy ride.

But now he had to get Alex home. He leaned across the bed where she lay sleeping and pushed aside several strands of golden hair that hid her face. The sight of her in the drowsy warmth of his bed reminded him again of how much he loved her.

Reflecting on last night's lovemaking, he chose not to awaken her immediately. In the soft light of dawn, made fainter by the overcast sky, she looked more beautiful this morning than she did last night, if that was possible.

Until he had actually possessed her, bringing them both to an ecstasy that a man and a woman could achieve together, Rush hadn't realized how deeply in love with her he was. Waking this morning with Alex in his arms had been as close to heaven as he knew he would ever get. Now, like an earthbound angel, Rush wondered after having experienced paradise if he could live without it.

"Alex," he called, gently shaking her arm. "You've got to get up, love. It's time for me to take you home." *Past time,* the voice inside his head reminded him.

When she rolled sideways and sent a small breath soughing through her lips, Rush was tempted to crawl back into the berth with her. Regrettably, he had fallen asleep last night after they had made love, causing him to miss out on loving her all night long. The delay in Cumberland had taken more of a toll on his body than he was aware of. That, along with their lovemaking, had drained him not only of his juices, but also his energy.

He was recovered now, and his desire to take her again was almost overwhelming. So strong was that desire, it almost made him forget the reality of their situation—especially the possibility of his crew returning to the boat early because of the rainy weather. Although none of his men was required to report before noon today, Rush couldn't chance it. He wanted to spare Alex the embarrassment of being discovered by his men who would know that she had spent the night in his cabin.

Also, there were the good folks of Harpers Ferry who might question her whereabouts if they discovered her out and about at daybreak, wearing the same clothes she had worn to the frolic. Tongues were always ready to waggle in this small town, and he knew Alexandy's reputation would be ruined.

He also had Stella and Caro to consider. He imagined they were both still in their dreams after last night's shindig, and Rush wanted to have Alex back home before they awakened. All of these reasons kept him from crawling between the sheets.

Falling on his knees beside the bed, he brushed her lips with a feather-light kiss. "Time to get up, sleepyhead," he whispered, gently shaking her again.

Her lashes lifted slowly, and she stared at him, disoriented. Then, realizing where she was and with whom, she grabbed the sheet, pulling it higher and anchoring it across her breasts with her arms.

Rush smiled at her. "You're safe," he teased. "As tempting as you are, sweetheart, I won't crawl back into the rack with you, because it's nearly daybreak, and I need to get you home."

"Daybreak?" She looked toward the windows. "But it's still so dark."

Rush pushed to his feet and began gathering her clothing that was scattered haphazardly across the floor.

"It will be light soon enough," he cautioned. "From the sound on the roof, I'd say it's raining catfish and bullfrogs."

"Raining?" She scooted backwards, holding the sheet over her, and leaned against the headboard. "But last night . . ." Her voice trailed off. "I must have fallen into a dead sleep because I never heard the rain until now." She listened. "Gosh, it is coming down."

He winked at her. "All that exercise made us both sleep like babies. Not exactly what I had planned for the whole night, but then you know what they say. 'The best laid plans of mice and men often go astray.' "

" 'Oft gang awry,' " Alex corrected. Still worrying with

the sheet, she swung her legs carefully over the edge of the bed and sat for a moment.

"It seems little Miss Hoity-toity has returned."

Alex didn't answer, but the look she shot him spoke louder than words.

After all they had shared last night, they were still hissing at each other like two sore-tail cats. Loving Alexandy would never be easy. In fact, it would be damned near impossible.

Rush resented her correcting him, but more importantly, he resented the tension building between them. If this was love, maybe he wanted no part of it.

Still battling for control of his earlier amorous longings, he felt overly sensitive as well. Rush had never been a morning person, or one who enjoyed jawing until long after his first cup of black coffee. Considering his circumstances this morning, he needed that strong coffee more than usual.

"However you call it, sweet cheeks," he said sarcastically. "Awry, astray, they both mean the same to me, and I believe you get my meaning." He found her camisole and tossed it at her. "Appears we both came out losers."

His attitude cut into Alex like a knife, but then what had she expected—pretty words and romantic phrases?

They had enjoyed themselves last night, or she imagined they had, but now that it was time to return to reality, Alex questioned if she had imagined the tenderness Rush had shown her. Gone was the gentle man who had made her feel both beautiful and special. In his place was the lad from her past, the same scoundrel who had shown up on her doorstep with Caro several weeks before. It was apparent that he had gotten what he wanted, what she knew every man wanted, and now that he had had her body, it was clear to her that she had been nothing more to him than a good roll in the hay.

Alex stood. Well, so be it. She hadn't entered into this liaison expecting a commitment. When Rush continued to stare at her, she asked, "Would you mind turning your back so I can get dressed?"

Her new yellow dress sailed through the air and landed at her feet. Seeing him treat it with such disregard only made Alex's anger grow.

"Are you going to turn around and give me a modicum of privacy, or am I to endure your philistine behavior while I dress?"

His gaze sparked with anger. "My uncultured behavior didn't seem to bother you last night," he retorted, "so I can't see why it makes much difference whether I watch or not. Besides, I've seen all of you, sugar."

"You—you are so crass," she responded. "If you won't turn around, I will."

She swung toward the bed, fighting to hold back the tears that his words had summoned. She stepped into her drawers, then slipped the camisole over her head and yanked it down over her breasts, scolding herself the whole time.

What a fool I was. Her emotions were in such a state, she groped for mundane thoughts. *Here I worried that my underthings were too ragged for him to see.*

Her underwear might be worn, she concluded, but at least it was unsoiled—clean. Not like the whores she imagined he usually bedded. Alex squeezed her eyes shut, trying to force away the liquid that built behind her lids, but a warm tear escaped. As it spilled over her cheekbone to slide down the side of her face, it turned cold, chilling her to the bone.

"Shucks, Alexandy, I don't want to fight," Rush said, coming up behind her. He turned her around, then encircled her with his arms. "But you are the most stubborn woman I've ever had the displeasure of knowing."

When he spotted the tear, Rush thought his heart would break. Hurting this woman was the last thing he wanted to do.

"I'm sorry, Alexandy," he said. "I never meant to be cruel." He kissed away the tear trail, then his lips moved over her mouth.

Alex willed herself not to respond. She remained in his arms, but stood as motionless as a straw-filled doll.

He pulled his lips away. "You make me crazy, you know? When I'm with you, I'm constantly warring with myself. Will you like me if I do this, then I worry that you won't, then I wonder if I should do that."

She tried to step away from him, but he wouldn't surrender his hold on her. "I liked you the way you were last night," she told him, "when you were kind and not hiding behind your usual armor."

Alex still believed Rush hid his true feelings behind his devil-may-care attitude, but what did she know? She knew that a man who carried so many demons was one she needed to stay away from. "This other you," she said, "I'm not so sure about."

He released her and shrugged. "What you see, darling, is what you get."

Alex scoffed, reaching for her dress that lay on the floor. She began pulling the yellow gingham over her head, disappearing for a few minutes as she struggled to find the armholes. Once she found them, the dress slipped over her bust and dropped to her waist. She began buttoning the tiny buttons.

"I guess that sums it up, sugar," she answered, using one of Rush's favorite endearments. "I don't want what I see."

After buttoning the buttons, she searched the floor for her shoes, amazed that she couldn't recall taking them off. The thought of what they had shared, and the discussion they were having now, only served to make her angrier.

"Last night we both had a good time together," she said. "You got to bed a lady, and I paid back my debt." She found her shoes and slammed her feet into them, forgoing her stockings.

"Fortunate for one such as me," he retaliated, then the meaning of her statement sunk in. "Debt?" Rush looked as though she had punched him.

"Yes, debt," she repeated. "We're even now. I've paid you back for your kindness to Caro."

"Paid me back?" It was Rush's turn to snort. "So that's what you were about? Sacrificing yourself for the good of the cause?" His gaze burned into hers. "I should have known that Alexandria Paine-in-the-ass wouldn't have lowered herself to sleep with the likes of me unless she intended to gain something from the doing. You martyred yourself."

Dressed now, she stared back at him, not denying his words.

"You always were a self-righteous, self-centered little brat. I can see you haven't changed a bit," he said.

Self-righteous. Self-centered? So that is how he really sees me. "I don't have to listen to this," Alex responded, stomping toward the door.

Rush moved to his desk. "Wait!" he shouted. He picked up a big envelope, then moved to stand beside her. "Here," he said, thrusting the flat paper container into her hands.

She looked from the envelope to his face. "What's this?" she asked.

"It's for your mother and Caro."

"For my mother and Caro," Alex repeated. "But what about—"

"You?" He sneered. "You got your present last night, darling."

Not giving her a chance to respond, he clamped his fingers around her arm and grabbed an umbrella hanging on the wall.

"Now, sweetheart," he said, ushering her out the door, "I think it's time I take you back where you belong."

17

ALEX SAT IN THE tub of steamy bath water, allowing her tears to flow in rhythm with the pounding rain outside the kitchen walls. After leaving the boat, Rush had accompanied her as far as the alleyway beside Samson's saloon. He had left her, along with his umbrella, soon after their arrival, with nothing more than an indifferent farewell.

When he had turned and walked away, Alex had wanted to call out to him, to tell him that their lovemaking had meant more to her than the obligation of debt she had claimed, but her feet had not carried her where her mind directed. Instead, as she stood watching his retreat, her feet had felt permanently rooted in the mud.

Alex buried her face in her hot, soapy cloth, the wretchedness of the night nagging at her. Was that all she had wanted to tell Rush? Dropping her head back against the rim of the copper tub, she searched the ceiling for an answer. *Only God was privy to what I wanted to tell him.* Whatever it was, He hadn't decided yet to allow Alex in on the secret.

She was thankful her mother and Caro were still in bed when she finally reached the house. Since she knew that sleep would be long in coming, Alex had chosen to bathe while the rest of the house was abed. Once the water was heated and the copper tub filled, Alex had slipped out of her damp clothes into the water, determined to wash all thoughts of Rush from her memory. But she had found it wasn't to be that easy. It would take more than soap and water to rid herself of Rush Duncan.

Rolling up the cloth, she placed it across her tear-stung eyes. Because her mother knew her so well, Alex wanted all traces of her unhappiness gone before she confronted her parent again. It would be difficult enough to convince her mother that her daughter hadn't changed radically in the course of a few hours—to keep her from learning that her only daughter was now a fallen woman.

"Why, why, why?" she moaned, despair oozing from every pore.

"Why what?" Caro asked. "And why are you taking a bath? Saturday was yesterday, you know."

She had been unaware of her cousin's presence until she had spoken. Wearily Alex considered her answer. "You know we take more than one bath a week, Caro," she responded, not bothering to remove the rag from her eyes. "I-I couldn't sleep. I felt chilled, so I thought a good hot soak would warm me up."

Caro moved closer to stand beside the tub. "You can't sleep if you don't come to bed."

Heaven forbid that I be allowed one tiny discretion.

Alex reasoned that it was true that God punished all sinners. Liars as well, she assumed, because she was about to add lying to her list of transgressions.

"I got in so late, honey," she answered, "that I decided to sleep on the parlor sofa so as not to disturb you."

Only the pounding rain filled the quiet that followed until Caro spoke. "How come you were so late? Where did you go? Aunt Stella and me, we couldn't find you when we got ready to leave the dance."

Not one ounce of mercy.

Alex finally answered. "I took a walk with Rush to the bridge. We were talking, and by the time I returned I suppose you and mother had already gone to bed."

Alex scooted down deeper into the tub, glad for the water's

soapy film. Otherwise her astute cousin might be able see last night's sin stamped upon her naked body.

"What about you, love?" she asked, hoping to take control of the conversation. "Did you enjoy dancing with Jamie? You certainly learned those dance steps quickly."

"It's like Rush said. I had a good teacher."

Alex almost sobbed aloud. *I had a good teacher, too.*

"Why do you suppose Rush never told me good-bye?" Caro asked. "He always tells me bye."

"As I said, honey, when he and I came back from our walk, you had disappeared. Do you recall what time you and Mother left the dance?"

Alex heard a chair being dragged across the floor toward the tub. If she knew what time they had left the party then she could firm her alibi in her mind.

"I'm not sure of the time, but it was late. Jamie and his folks left when we did. Once I got upstairs, I watched from the window."

"And you never saw Rush and me return?"

Of course Caro hadn't seen them return, because they hadn't. Should have, Alex mentally corrected, but didn't.

"Nope. Never saw you. Finally I got too tired to watch, so Snow and I went to bed."

Alex tried to sound upbeat. "We probably returned right after that."

"Maybe," she said. "Why you got that rag covering your eyes?"

"This rag?" Alex touched the cloth and squeezed the bridge of her nose. "I've got a small headache. I hoped it would make the pain go away."

"Your nose sounds funny, too."

"Does it?"

"Yeah. Like you got snot in it."

"Caro Swift, young ladies don't say snot," Stella Paine scolded from the stairs. "Alexandria, whatever are you doing bathing this early in the morning?"

When her mother had corrected Caro, Alex had jerked up her head. The rag had plopped into the water, and she was searching frantically for it.

"Yuck! Your eyes are all red and puffy," Caro announced.

"Soap, Caro, honey. When I washed my hair I got soap in my eyes."

"Boy, Aunt Stella, I'm worried about your daughter," Caro said, sounding more like an adult than a ten-year-old. "First she says she can't sleep because she's got a chill. Then she says she's got a headache, and now her eyes are all red and watery 'cause she got soap in them. What do you think, Aunt Stella, should we call the doctor?"

"Alexandria, are you ill?" Her mother stopped at the end of the tub and looked down at her daughter, her gaze questioning.

"Oh, for heaven's sake," Alex moaned. "A girl can't even take a bath without being interrogated." She shot up from the tub of water, grabbed the towel, and wrapped it around her. "If you two will excuse me, I'm going to get dressed." Then she practically leaped up the stairs, stopping only when she reached the landing and knew she was out of sight.

"What's wrong with her, Aunt Stella?" she heard Caro ask.

"I think she's got a bug, dear."

"Then are you gonna call the doctor like I said?"

"No, dear, not right away. Besides, I don't believe the doctor's got a cure for what is ailing Alexandria. We'll just wait and see how she does."

"Gosh, she sure is grumpy," Caro added.

Not waiting to hear her mother's response, Alex continued gloomily on toward the bedroom.

∽

RUSH HAD BEEN CORRECT in assuming his deckhands would come back to the canal early. When he returned after leaving Alex in Samson's alley, his cook had a pot of coffee brewing, and his men sat hunkered around his table, downing the last remains of their breakfast.

Most of the time, Rush didn't mind sharing his private space with his four-member crew. If the weather was bad as it was today, the men took their meals inside the galley. Otherwise they were served their food and would take it on deck to eat or to the hay house where they bunked. Everything that the canallers needed could be purchased at the many stores along the canal, both at locks and villages in the vicinity of the waterway. When the boat was underway, it was Rush's practice to have his cook serve breakfast daily. Their location en route determined what other meals were served.

Although the weather was horrible, Rush's mood was even worse. Company was the last thing he wanted. He wanted his coffee, his privacy, and a chance to ponder what had gone wrong between him and Alexandy this morning when everything had seemed so right as he'd drifted off to sleep last night.

On entering the cabin, he barked out an order. "We'll be leaving within the hour. Since it appears everyone is present and accounted for, I assume that means you're as anxious to be underway as I am."

"In this frog-choking rain?" one of his mule drivers asked.

"We thought you'd wait until the rain let up a bit, Captain," the other tender added. "Daisy and Petunia ain't too eager to get their arses wet."

Rush drew in a deep breath. "From the smell of this room, I think you could all use a good dousing. What whorehouse did you spend the night in?" he asked as he made his way to the cookstove and poured himself a mug of coffee. "The whole lot of you smell like a Saturday night whore."

"You know there ain't no such parlors in Harpers Ferry, boss. Only the Widow Margot, and she had so many customers last night, they was waiting in line for a poke." The man scratched his crotch. "That shindig in town had every boat between here and Cumberland and Georgetown stopping in for a little rest and relaxation."

"Most of us spent the night at the tavern up the canal a piece," the cook offered. "Damned near drowned getting back here this morning."

"The way you smell I thought you'd been dead for days," Rush answered.

"Aw, Captain, we don't smell that bad."

Rush took a long swig of coffee before he moved toward the door. "I want this barge moving within the hour."

At the stairs he set down his cup and donned the rain slicker and hat hanging beside the door. This done, he picked up the coffee again and sloshed back on deck. Grumbling, he walked to the mule shed. "A man can't even find privacy on his own damn boat."

He stood quietly, soaking up the warmth of his four mules that were as dry as newly diapered babies. The shed smelled of animal, hay, and rain—a hell of a lot better than his cabin smelled right now. Rush wondered fleetingly why the smell of hardworking men suddenly bothered him, when the scent hadn't bothered him in the past.

"Since you two are females of a sort," he said to Daisy and Petunia, "what do you think about a woman who allows you to bed her in order to pay back a debt? A debt," Rush emphasized, "that she didn't owe in the first place."

The mules continued chomping away on their breakfast, oblivious to their owner's ranting. The animals were more interested in eating and swishing away the flies that had taken cover from the downpour.

"I'm in one hell of a fix," he continued. "Caught in a trap of my own making. Never thought much about Alexandria Paine, one way or the other, during all those years I was away at sea. Then the moment I see her again, I'm that same frustrated lad of thirteen years ago. Only difference is, she is no longer that child. She's a woman full grown and ripe for the picking.

"So what do I do? I lure her to my boat so I can steal the damn cherry." He let out a snort. "I admit the cherry picking was never so good." Just thinking about Alexandy made his cherry picker as hard as a stone.

His coffee finished, Rush set down his cup and began stroking one of the mule's flanks.

"Out of my limits, that one," he said. "Too good for the likes of me. Besides, I've lived this long without a woman, I surely don't need one now. No, ma'am, you can't trust a woman with your heart, present company excluded, of course. You two gals are the only ladies I need in my life," he assured them. He turned to give the other female mule her share of affection.

"Alexandy and me, we're too different. I guess my family

tree is as distorted as yours, and that is why we get on so well together.''

"Captain, you in there?''

Rush silenced his tongue and acknowledged the mule tenders who ran into the shed. If they had heard the conversation he'd been having with the animals, they never let on.

"Just checking on the girls,'' he told them.

"The girls aren't going to be too happy when I take them out in this rain,'' one of the tenders said.

"They'll be fine. Won't you, ladies?'' Rush gave the animals an affectionate tap on their hindquarters. "You men, harness them up and head them out. We have coal to deliver.''

Leaving the shed, he ran back to the cabin. He would be glad to put some distance between himself and Alexandy, although leaving wouldn't put her out of his heart. Caro no longer seemed to need him, so he didn't have that obligation to contend with. Alex sure as the devil didn't want him. She had made her sentiments perfectly clear.

"Debt!'' Rush spit out the word.

Once inside the cabin, he removed his rain slicker. The room still stank of dirty men and fried bacon. Rush walked toward the bed and stopped beside it. Would he ever be able to look at that bed again without seeing Alex in it, looking as peaceful as a sleeping angel with her golden hair spread around her face like a halo?

Even now the image was so strong it made Rush feel as though someone had kicked him hard in the gut.

"Your punishment, Duncan, for taking a lady to bed. If Samson gets wind of what you did, you're liable to find yourself gelded.''

Disgusted, he swung away from the berth and stalked toward the table.

On the floor, lying beside one of the table legs, was Alex's yellow ribbon. He bent to pick it up, then cupped it in his palm. Running a finger over the satiny surface, he was reminded of the feel of Alex's skin. He buried his nose in his hand, sniffing for a trace of Alex's scent.

Roses?

"Mules,'' he said aloud, jerking his face away. He laughed

at himself, but the emotion didn't reach his heart.

"The latter I can better deal with."

Rush tossed the ribbon down on the table, grabbed his slicker, and headed back on deck. Maybe, if he was lucky, the rain would drown his sorrows.

∽

ON THE WEDNESDAY FOLLOWING the frolic, Alex sat upstairs with her mother, who had taken to her bed not long after the event, suffering from a bout of chronic rheumatism. The rain that had begun early Sunday morning still continued to fall, the steady gray drizzle showing no signs of ending. The dreary weather suited her, Alex thought. It mirrored her own dismal mood.

Her spirits had reached an all-time low, but Alex went about her daily routine as usual. Outwardly she resumed the role of her former self; inwardly she was no longer the inexperienced young woman who had gone willingly to Rush Duncan's bed.

She had just helped her mother bathe in warm salt water, and was now applying liniment made from hartshorn, laudanum, and unsalted butter to her aching joints. Her mother watched her speculatively as Alex helped her into her flannel night rail that the doctor had recommended she wear when he had dropped by earlier. The bath, the liniment, and the flannel against her skin would offer her mother a small measure of relief from the pain the troublesome ailment caused.

"You're a good daughter," Stella said, sitting on the edge of the bed.

Alex sent her mother a wary smile, then helped her to lift her legs and to lay back against the freshly plumped pillows. She pulled the quilt over her mother, making sure she was tucked in tight. This done, she moved about the room, tidying up. "I'll bring you some hot tea," she said. With her arms full of linen, she started toward the door.

"It's not tea I want, daughter." Her mother patted the edge of the bed. "I'd prefer conversation. Come. Sit. I think we should talk."

Talk was the last thing Alex wished to do. The last several

days, she had done everything in her power to avoid having this conversation, because Stella knew her daughter too well. The confusion and guilt Alex carried in her heart daily would be too visible to her mother's knowing eyes.

"I need to get these into the wash."

"The laundry can wait, Alexandria. What I have to say won't. Besides, you won't be hanging out sheets in this weather."

"Mother, please, I—"

Stella patted the bed again. "He's a good man, Alexandria, in spite of what you may be feeling."

Alex knew which man her mother referred to, but she pretended ignorance, hoping to skirt the topic. "Yes, Samson is a good man, Mother. I'm glad the two of you have found each other after all this time."

"Found each other? Mercy, child. I wasn't aware that we had lost one another. Friends, if they are true, remain so no matter what comes in between." She folded her hands on her stomach. After a moment she continued. "Samson is a fine man, and we enjoy each other's company. Maybe because we've reached a time in our lives when past events are easier to recall than the day-to-day ones. But it is not Samson's qualities I wish to discuss with you."

"Mother, I really need—"

"You need to hear what I have to say. Come," she called. "Spare this achy old woman a moment of your time. Please?"

"Mother, you're not old, so don't say that." Suspecting there would be no escape, Alex reluctantly dropped the pile of laundry on a chair and joined her mother, sitting beside her on the edge of the bed.

"Rush Duncan is a fine man, but I think you know that truth in your heart already. I truly believe that if you both would drop your misconceived ideas about what you think you want from life, you would realize you have already found it. I've seen the way he looks at you."

"Mother, don't be ridiculous. Being kind to Caro and hiring a detective to look into Charlotte's past doesn't make him a saint." *How does he look at me?*

"He's a canaller, Mother, a man with no roots," Alex reminded her. "He probably has so many lovesick females panting after him in every village along the C & O Canal that he's lost count."

Her mother smiled knowingly. "I know of one lovesick female, but the others I'm not so certain of."

Alex felt her face burn. She knew having this conversation would be a mistake. Already her mother's words proved it.

"Samson knows Rush better than anyone in this town. After all, he housed the lad after his mother's death. Eudora Duncan's sordid past left a lasting impression on that boy. From what Samson has told me—"

"Mother, you've discussed me and Rush with Samson?"

"We are dear friends, daughter. Yes, we've discussed our children only because we have their best interests in our hearts."

"Mother, I can't believe this." Alex jumped up from the bed. "You're no better than Leona Whitley with your matchmaking."

"Alexandria Paine, I'll not tolerate disrespect." Her mother's tone brooked no argument. "Now, sit down."

Alex hated herself for the outbreak, especially considering her mother's present health. "I'm sorry," she apologized. "I meant you no disrespect, or Leona Whitley either. It's just that everyone is always trying to marry me off."

"Alexandria, I'm not trying to marry you off to anyone. I just want you to consider your true feelings. Since the frolic on Saturday night, you've been grumpier than a bear and mooning like a lovesick female. Even Caro has noticed your foul temper."

Her mother's remark caused Alex to raise her brows. "Lovesick?"

"I'm using your own words, am I not?" When Alex didn't respond, she asked, "Did you not call those other females lovesick?"

"Yes, but the reference doesn't sound as ridiculous coming from my mouth."

"That, my dear, is a matter of opinion. Now, come here and sit down. It makes my neck ache to have to look up at you."

Alex moved to the bed and took the spot she had vacated earlier.

Stella continued. "Because of Eudora Duncan's history, I understand Rush isn't too keen on consorting with women, especially those of ill repute. Samson tells me Rush has never shown any inclination of a fondness toward any female but you."

"Oh, Mother, what does Samson know? Rush Duncan has been away from Harpers Ferry for years. He probably not only has a female in every village along the canal, but also one in every port in the world as well."

"Pshaw! That man guards his heart like a city under siege. As perceptive as you are, I can't believe you wouldn't have picked up on this. Trust me, Alexandria. Behind the devil-may-care attitude he shows to the world dwells a compassion as fine as any I've encountered."

"Maybe," Alex agreed. It amazed her that her mother had determined Rush's ruse as she had. Alex also suspected his deep compassion was a weakness he would rather not have.

"It's time you learn something of his past. I think it will make you better understand him."

"I don't want to understand him—"

"Hush, Alexandria, and listen."

Alex did as she was told.

"Eudora Duncan grew up here in Harpers Ferry, as I did. Her father, like so many men here, worked on Virginius Island. When Union soldiers occupied Harpers Ferry during the war, Eudora had the misfortune of meeting and falling in love with a Yankee solider, believing that they would someday be married.

"Theirs was a clandestine affair, one she kept from her family because of their southern sympathies. When the war ended, the man rode away from Harpers Ferry, breaking Eudora's heart and leaving her pregnant with his child. It was rumored later that he already had a wife and child waiting for him back home. The Duncans, on learning of their daughter's condition, disowned her. They moved away and forbade her to join them."

"Eudora stayed? Alone? But what did she do?"

"She went kind of crazy after her family left, but I guess you can't really blame her. She moved into a deserted shack outside of town. It was after Rush was born that she set up business. She became known as the town whore. People here might have helped her if she hadn't plied her trade. In short, they shunned her. No decent folks would have anything to do with her, and I don't suppose they were much nicer to Rush."

"Doesn't sound very decent of them, does it?" Alex asked, disgusted.

Recalling scenes from her childhood, she remembered now that the parents of her friends discouraged them from playing with Rush Duncan. But not Alex's father. He had always treated Rush fairly, regardless of his background. Rush had said as much last Saturday night.

"She was a fallen woman, Alexandria, especially after she openly began to sell her body. I suppose she went kind of crazy from heartbreak and loneliness, but it was drink that finally killed her."

"What about Rush?" Alex's heart cried out for the pain he must have suffered as a whore's child. "She did have him. If I had a child, I'd do everything possible to make a life for him, regardless of his birth. I certainly wouldn't drink myself to death and leave him an orphan."

"Perhaps you're stronger than she was, but who knows what we would do if we faced such a situation?"

After Saturday night, I could face such a situation. The possibility of her having a child hadn't occurred to her until now. Her mother continued talking, and Alex forced herself to listen.

"Samson said Eudora loved Rush in her own way. I understand Samson helped her out, giving them extra money, during those years before her death. Maybe that's why he took Rush in after she died."

At the moment, Alex was too angry to be tolerant of any man. "You mean, Mother, he paid Eudora for her services."

"Alexandria, don't be so quick to judge. I don't know what their relationship was and I really don't care. I do know a man has needs, and maybe she provided that for Samson along with countless other men in this town. I'm only revealing what I know of Rush's background. Most of what I've just told you, I've learned only recently from Samson. He told me after Rush brought Caro to us."

Alex considered her mother's words, recalling Rush's statement to her about his past. That he survived such an upbringing was amazing.

"I hope, Alexandria, that what I've told you will make you judge Rush less harshly. Lumping him with roustabouts because he chooses to make a living on the canal is wrong. Canallers are not all bad people."

"Mother, he's a wanderer. First a sailor, now a canaller. I've always said I wanted to marry a man like Father and not someone who spends every night in a different place. I want a permanent home like the one we had. Or this house with you and Caro. I don't want to spend my life living aboard a canal boat six or seven months out of the year."

"I'm not denying your father was a wonderful man. I was lucky that he wanted to settle in one place, and he loved this area as much as I did. But believe me, Alexandria, if he'd chosen to live in China, I would have followed him there, because I loved him."

"I guess I've never met a man I could love that way. Perhaps I never will."

"There is something else you should know. The money Rush gave us, claiming it came from that captain's crew, came out of his pocket."

"His pocket? But he said . . ."

"We both know what he said. Samson told me he wanted to give it to us because of Caro."

"We—I shouldn't have taken it—I'll have to give it back." Alex was stunned by this latest revelation. "He lied to me."

"We'll not give the money back, Alexandria. I promised Samson I wouldn't tell you, but I wanted you to know the type of man you're dealing with. He's a compassionate, caring individual, one whose friendship you shouldn't take so lightly."

"But I don't understand. Why would he give us the money?"

Stella sagged deeper into the pillow. "You think on it,

child. I'm sure you'll find the answer. Now I need to sleep. I'm very tired. But you remember that it's what is inside a person that counts for his real worth.''

Alex stood. She looked down at her mother, who had already drifted off to sleep. Alex settled the quilt more firmly around her mother before gathering the laundry from the chair and going downstairs.

The rain outside continued to fall, drumming a solemn dirge on the roof. As Alex walked down the stairs, she felt her whole world and everything she believed in had suddenly turned upside-down.

''My love,'' she whispered, ''however did you survive?''

18

TWO DAYS LATER THE rain continued to pour down on Harpers Ferry. Since floods were a way of life in the river-gap town, there was talk among the locals that a flood was imminent.

Stella was still confined to her bed, the infernal dampness impeding a swift recovery from her affliction. Her spirit never weakened, though, and she never complained, believing her condition to be one of life's hardships that one faced and endured. It broke Alex's heart to see her mother suffering, but she tried to keep up a good front for Stella's sake, even trying to display a happier mood she didn't feel.

The bad weather gave Alex plenty of time to think. She longed for those times when her biggest headache had been warding off Leona Whitley's matchmaking skills. Although Leona would never know her efforts were futile, Alex knew she would never marry. No decent man would want her once he learned of her indiscretion, and Alex had decided she would go to no husband's bed pretending purity, thus adding deceit to her growing list of sins.

After her and her mother's conversation, Alex had begun to think more favorably of Rush, considering the little kindnesses he had shown toward the three of them since his reappearance

in their lives. His generosity still puzzled her. She supposed it
sprang from his love of Caro along with his fondness for her
mother and his old friend Samson. It was as her mother said.
Rush had a very compassionate nature hidden beneath his hard
exterior, but then Alex had suspected as much.

Alone in the quilting workroom downstairs, she sat stitching
on Caro's quilt. Caro had spent most of the morning helping
her, but when Ella Hamilton and her two girls, along with
Jamie, had dropped by to invite Caro to their house for a visit,
Alex had gladly released the restless child. It was apparent
that Ella had more patience than Alex if she could tolerate
four rowdy youngsters on a day when the downpour would
keep them indoors.

She had just finished stitching around the appliquéd block
of the saloon when her gaze slid to the chest where Rush's
sketches had been propped at Caro's insistence. Her mother
had found them inside the envelope with the other information
Rush had sent home with Alex their last night together. The
envelope had contained the name and last known address of
the couple who had secured Caro's passage aboard Captain
Steve's ship in New Orleans. There was also a receipt for the
retainer fee that Rush had paid the detective agency, Cole and
Gate of Cumberland, Maryland, to trace Charlotte Swift's past.

In Alex's opinion, Rush had gone beyond mere friendship
with his generous gifts and his willingness to help them, but
no monetary value could be placed on the sketches he'd en-
closed. His scribblings, as he called them, were dearer to Alex
than the most priceless masterpiece. She viewed them now
through watery tears.

There were two penciled sketches; one labeled yellowwood
sorrel and the other blue-eyed grass. The man certainly had
gifted hands, in more ways than one, Alex reflected, but what
made the sketches so special was that he had titled one "Alexandy" and the other "Caro." Since he had already explained the significance of each wildflower, the sketches stood
as a personal reminder of the artist and the man—the same
person Alex couldn't shoo out of her mind no matter how hard
she tried.

Alex hated herself for the cruel words she had flung at him

their last night together, claiming that she had paid her debt in full. Until now, she hadn't realized how precious a gift he had given her—a part of himself that she believed Rush had never shared with another.

Was it possible what she felt for him was love? Heaven only knew how she ached for him and regretted the cruel things she had said. The thought brought on another bout of watery vision, and she blinked back the tears.

The front door opened, and Leona Whitley and her sister Rosellen scurried inside. Alex swiped at her nose and eyes with the back of her hand before she stood to face them, plastering a false smile upon her face.

"Ladies, whatever are you doing out in this miserable weather?" she asked. She moved to assist them with their umbrellas and to help them remove their wraps.

"We've come to sit awhile with dear Stella," Leona said, pushing her hair back in place once her kerchief was removed.

"How is your mother?" Rosellen asked. She removed her ever-present hat and hung it on the rack beside the door. The huge yellow blossoms on the hat's wide brim looked as though they had folded against the rain, but the hat's colorful presence brought a spot of cheer to the otherwise dreary day.

"Mother is better, but not well," Alex informed them. "If this rain would stop and the dampness dissipate, I know she would feel better."

"No chance of that anytime soon," Leona said. "This weather seems to have settled in for a while. As we speak, the rivers are rising. I understand the menfolk have begun to sandbag the banks of the Shenandoah. Not that their efforts will help if this deluge continues."

Leona looked at Alex. "You taking a cold, dear? Your eyes are red and watery."

"Pepper," Alex responded. "I got some up my nose earlier and I haven't been able to stop sneezing since."

"Does me the same way," Rosellen offered. "I see you're working on the quilt. My, my, doesn't it look nice," she said, bending closer to get a better look at the appliquéd square of the saloon.

"If this weather continues, we could get the quilting circle together and finish this quilt,'' Leona supplied. ''But without Stella in attendance, it just wouldn't be the same.''

Alex was in no mood for the ladies of the quilting circle, especially without her mother present. ''I'm hoping Mother will be better tomorrow, and we can make more definite plans. I suggest we wait and see how she feels.'' She moved toward the kitchen and toward the stairs. ''Come, ladies, I'll take you up.''

After leaving the three older women, Alex returned to the quilting room. The front door opened again, and in hustled Ella Hamilton with Caro and Jamie trailing behind her. Alex looked at the threesome, surprised they had returned so soon. Maybe Ella didn't have as much patience as Alex had first believed.

Caro jumped on one foot and then the other. ''We're going to the mill,'' she said, ''to buy flour.''

''In this weather?'' Alex asked.

''Yeah, Ma's flour has got weasels.''

''Weevils,'' Ella corrected, laughing. ''I thought I'd like to do some baking. In this weather, what else can you do? Besides, I've been promising the girls we could bake cookies. Mother dropped by the house and agreed to stay until I returned. These two insisted on accompanying me.''

''Lucky for your mother,'' Alex responded.

Suddenly the idea of baking appealed to Alex as well. For the last few days she had been like a slug, drained of all energy. The weather plus her mother's illness had kept her confined to the house. With Leona and Rosellen visiting, she could get away for a few minutes without leaving her mother alone.

''Maybe I'll walk with you,'' Alex said. ''I've needed to replenish our supply of flour since Saturday, but with Mother ill I haven't wanted to leave. The fresh air and exercise will do me good.''

''Wonderful,'' Ella said. ''We'd love to have your company, wouldn't we, kids?''

''Sure,'' both children answered.

In the entryway, Caro and Jamie shook like soaked puppies,

laughing when the rain sprayed off their rainwear, spotting up the windows.

"Since Leona and Rosellen are visiting Mother, I'll ask them if they wouldn't mind staying until we return from the mill. If they agree, I'll get my things and join you."

Several moments later, the foursome left the house with Snow the cat running beside them.

"Caro," Alex called, "you better take that cat home and close him inside."

"He wants to go with us," both children chimed.

"That means you'll end up carrying him before we return."

"That's okay, Alex," Caro answered. "Jamie and I will share carrying him."

"You remember that later."

The rain beat down on them as they walked along the sidewalk. Ella, Alex, and Snow fell in behind Caro and Jamie who ran ahead, stomping puddles and giggling, their umbrellas bobbing like windblown toadstools.

Yes, Alex thought, dragging in a lungful of fresh air. Already she felt better. She clutched the hickory-crooked handle of her umbrella, or rather Rush's umbrella, more firmly. A warmth spread from her fingers to her wet toes. For reasons unexplainable to Alex, the knowledge that the umbrella belonged to Rush made the dreariness of the day disappear somewhat.

∞

RUSH SAT ON THE train, and the premonition that had stayed with him since he had awakened this morning felt as bothersome as the rain pounding outside the glass window.

His early-morning visit to the Aqueduct Bridge in Georgetown had prompted him to take a train back to Harpers Ferry instead of returning with his boat. Crowds had gathered in the relentless downpour to watch the rising waters of the Potomac, which was swollen from almost a week's worth of rain. The Washington paper declared that areas as far north as Johnstown, Pennsylvania, were suffering from the endless showers, warning that flooding was eminent in and around rain-swollen rivers because of the downpour and the melting snows from higher elevations.

As the train chugged north, Rush caught glimpses from his window of the rising, angry-looking water.

"Alexandria," he said aloud.

His comment solicited a remark from the elderly gentleman who occupied the seat beside him. "Hail from that area, do you?" the man asked. "I'm from Arlington myself."

Rush only nodded to the older man, not wishing to encourage conversation. Too many thoughts were rattling around inside his head, keeping him from wanting to talk with a stranger.

Alexandria. His lips were silent this time when he said her name. Rush had done nothing but think about her since he left Harpers Ferry that rainy Sunday morning almost a week ago. Anger and hurt had snapped the barriers back into place around his heart, but as time and distance separated him from the woman he loved, Rush realized he could no longer deny his feelings or not act upon them.

He didn't want to live without her for the rest of his life. He never wanted it said that he hadn't at least declared himself to the woman he loved. Since the night they had made love, Rush had done a lot of rationalizing for both of them. One thing he had deduced from the excuses he made was that a lady like Alexandy wouldn't bed a scallywag like him unless she felt something more than what she had confessed.

A debt indeed. No woman used her well-guarded virginity to pay back a debt, especially a woman as proper as Alexandria Paine. She might not know it yet, but she loved him, too. Rush was going back to Harpers Ferry to make her admit it.

He knew that living with such a hard-headed woman wouldn't be easy, but it would be a site easier than living without her. Because he wanted her with him for the rest of his life and knowing her opinions of canallers and their wandering ways, he had considered how to get around that problem as well. But first he had to convince her that he couldn't live without her.

The train had just passed Point of Rocks. Here the railroad and canal parallelled the rest of the way to Harpers Ferry.

From the looks of the raging river below, Rush's eagerness to arrive in the river town doubled. Once again, he felt a premonition that something undetermined was waiting to happen.

∽

AS ALEX AND THE others walked along Shenandoah Street toward the footbridge that crossed the remains of the defunct Shenandoah Canal, she saw the gray structure of the mill in the distance. The Child and McCreight Flour Mill was one of the last operational buildings left standing on Virginius Island.

"You better pick up Snow," Alex told Caro. The street beneath their feet was fast becoming a quagmire.

The ground sucked at their shoes, making walking difficult. Caro scooped up the cat, having to juggle both umbrella and ball of fur to keep the rain off both of them.

Ella and Alex exchanged contemplative glances as they watched the rushing water sweep past. Down away from the bridge, she could see the sandbags the men had stacked along the banks. So far the bags appeared to be holding off the fast-flowing current, but if these rains kept up overnight, the bags, too, would be swept away to mix with the other debris that bobbed in the river like flotsam.

"Maybe we ought to forget the flour," Ella said, looking at Alex.

"I was about to say the same thing."

"Aw, Ma, come on," Jamie complained. "We've come all this way. We'll hurry and get the flour, then head home. What else you gonna do in this weather but bake?"

"Jamie, our stomachs aren't the most important things in our lives. We can live without cookies, but I'm not certain I'm up to tangling with that river."

"Ma, we're wasting time. Come on, please." He and Caro stopped at the edge of the footbridge and were about to run across.

"Caro, wait," Alex cautioned.

No sooner had she commanded her to stop than Snow took her order as a reason to escape. He jumped from Caro's arms and sprinted across the bridge toward the mill. Caro and Jamie chased after him.

"Y'all come back here now!" Ella shouted.

"We can't, we gotta get Snow!"

"Damn that cat, anyway." Alex started after the threesome, and Ella followed. Once they had crossed over the bridge, they looked toward the mill, the doors of which stood propped open.

"We're here now," Ella said. "We might as well get our flour and leave."

Caro scooped up Snow who had stopped running, and the five of them hurried into the building.

∽

THE TRAIN WAS ABOUT to approach the tunnel at Maryland Heights across the Potomac River from Harpers Ferry when Rush looked down in horror at the river and canal below. Where the Potomac and Shenandoah Rivers converged, the water rose with a speed that had been absent earlier. The fierce dash of the water's waves against the rocks filled with unidentifiable drift told him his worst fears had come true. Harpers Ferry was in the throes of a flood.

The train squealed to a stop, and the sharp sound of the brakes echoed off the walls of the tunnel. Rush jumped to his feet. He had to get off the train and to Harpers Ferry before the railroad bridge was carried away by the raging rivers.

People on board moved about restlessly. Men leaped to their feet, women whispered anxiously among themselves, and children squirmed and began to cry. Rush pushed past the steward who tried to stop him, but soon gave up when he realized he couldn't outmuscle him.

As Rush plowed forward, past the aisle filling rapidly with people, the porter announced with a megaphone, "Ladies and gentleman, please. There is no need to panic. We've been advised by the telegraphic dispatch that this train should not proceed to the station in Harpers Ferry because of flooding."

The noise inside the train grew, and the employee shouted again. "Ladies and gentleman, please! You must remain calm.

There is no cause for alarm. The B & O track sits well above the river, and we are safe from rising water. We have been advised that you should stay in your seats until we hear the extent of damage to the town, if any. Again, it will be only a short delay."

That was all the information Rush needed. He pushed through the forward door of the train car, wondering if he could make it through the next car's clogged aisle, and to the front of the train. People were moving around now in a disorderly manner.

Standing on the platform in between cars, Rush leaned sideways to look down the length of the darkened tunnel. The gray round light at the end forced him into action. He jumped from the train and began running along the tracks toward daylight.

Once outside the tunnel, he was glad to see that the railroad bridge still spanned the river, but below him where the rivers converged, they were fighting for space between the gorge. Trees rushed by in the impetuous torrent, resembling twigs being tossed about in the water's fury. A roof raced by with a man clinging to its peak. All manner of debris churned in the thrashing water. The C & O Canal and Lock 33 were completely submerged in water. The few canal boats he saw that had probably been tied up nearby were being tossed about in the rushing water like some giant's toy boats.

Fear for Alex and her family drove him further into the center of the bridge. He ran at full speed, uncertain what he might face once he reached Lower Town. For all he knew, the streets might be impassable.

As he neared the end of the bridge, he stopped to consider his next move. The wagon bridge that crossed the Shenandoah no longer spanned the river. It was gone. Only the tops of the cemented supports or piers remained.

Rush looked toward High Street and toward Samson's Tavern. After a moment, he broke into another sprint, having decided he would stay on the tracks until he was directly behind Samson's Tavern. Once there, he would take his chances with the street, using the alleyway beside Samson's to get to Alex's house.

The ground was higher here, but still lower than the tracks. Although he waded in ankle-deep water, he knew from having grown up in Harpers Ferry that the ground of Shenandoah Street and anything below it would probably be submerged in water before this day ended. In past floods, the water had risen as high as the second stories of the buildings that fronted those lower streets.

Samson's. The tavern only had a foot or so of water around its base. Rush dashed across the street.

"Samson!" he yelled, slamming through the front door. The tavern was empty of all sound.

Determining that no one was there, Rush kept up his pace. He dashed past the bar, through the storeroom, and out into the small yard that connected with the Paines' back entrance.

Rush took the stairs two at a time and nearly tore the door from the hinges when he pushed it inward. The kitchen appeared to be dry, as did what he could see of the front room. The rising water hadn't reached this far up High Street, and with any luck, he hoped it wouldn't. Finding no one downstairs, he took the stairs two at a time to the second level.

"Alex," he shouted. At the top of the stairs, he nearly knocked over Leona Whitley and Rosellen. They stood speechless, looking at him as though he were the devil himself come up from hell.

He grabbed Leona by the arm and asked, "Alex, Caro, Stella, where are they?"

She stared at him speechless, her mouth gaping like a fish. It was the first time he could recall seeing the woman at a loss for words.

"They're not here," Rosellen answered, then shook her head as though correcting her thoughts. "I mean, Stella is here, but Alex and Caro are not. They went with Ella Hamilton and Jamie to the Child and McCreight mill for flour."

"To the mill? For flour? What the hell did they do that for?"

Leona Whitley seemed to have gained her bearings, and she sputtered. "To get flour, stupid boy. To bake bread."

"There's a flood out there, in case you ladies aren't aware of it."

"A flood?" Leona croaked. "Oh, merciful heavens, Rosellen. A flood."

From a room at the back of the parlor, Rush heard Stella Paine call, "Rush, is that you? Please, come here."

On recognizing her voice, he pushed past the two older women and moved toward the room. Once at the door, he saw her. She lay in bed, her face pasty. Stella's appearance shocked him. The last time he had seen her, she had been dancing around the street in Samson's arms. She had looked so full of life then; now she looked as frail as death.

"Her rheumatism," Rosellen whispered. "Took to her bed last Sunday. Damp weather hasn't helped any. We're sitting with her to give Alex a break."

Alex.

"Find them, Rush," Stella said, trying to sit up. "I'm so worried. They've been gone too long. Did you say it was flooding?"

"You rest, Stella," Rush consoled, not wanting to reveal the truth of her worst fears. Everyone present knew that the mill was located on Virginius Island. "I'll find them and bring them home."

He spun around to leave. "You ladies stay here," he whispered, taking them back to the parlor. "The water is rising, but when I came in, it wasn't too high. If you stay upstairs, I'm sure you'll be fine. When I find Alex and Caro, I'll bring them back here."

Rush didn't wait for a response. He flew down the stairs and out onto High Street. The water was rising steadily. If they were still at the mill, Rush didn't want to contemplate what that might mean. Instead, he pressed on toward Shenandoah Street, then darted up the stone stairs leading to the Catholic church on the hill.

19

SOON AFTER ALEX AND her little party entered the mill,
they heard a terrible grinding sound. Everyone turned back
toward the entrance and watched as the small footbridge connecting them to the mainland was torn away. The fast-moving
current picked up the wooden timbers and scattered them like
kindling across the churning water that soon began to ebb
across the wooden floor of the building.

Alex exchanged a horrified look with Ella.

"Ladies, you best get upstairs, and fast," Mr. Perkins, the
mill hand, ordered. "I'm afeared ye're in for more than wet
feet, and lollying down here ain't gonna help matters."

Alex stood frozen in place, watching the water that rushed
around their feet. "Mr. Perkins, are we the only ones here?"
She looked expectantly around the room, then toward the
stairs.

"Which brings me to my own question, missy. What in
tarnation are you ladies doing out in this here weather anyway? Anyone with a lick of sense done deserted this space
hours ago."

"You're still here," Alex rebutted, wishing as soon as the
words were said that she could recall them.

It was rumored that Mr. Perkins fell into the category he'd

just described. After he lost his family in the flood of 1877, he hadn't been the same "upstairs," and she didn't know if she could blame him. He lived alone on the near-deserted island as a custodian for the mill.

"We came for flour to do our baking," she replied.

"Well, we got plenty of that." He took a basket from the counter and began plopping sacks into the space. When it was full, he shoved it toward her angrily. "Not that I think ye'll be doing much baking this fine afternoon, unless it's in hell. Now get up them stairs like I told ye and stay out of my way."

Alex glared at him. *Wonderful!* Cut off from the mainland with a crazy man as their protector. If they were looking for assurance or help from this quarter, they would have a long way to go.

A feeling of helplessness swept over her, but then her need to survive kicked in. She took a deep steadying breath, realizing that ultimately a person had only herself to rely on. After her father's death five years before, Alex and her mother had overcome much adversity. Alex was determined all of them would survive this as well.

"Let's get upstairs," she told the children, handing the basket of flour to Ella.

Ella ushered Caro and Jamie to the second level of the building. "We'll be fine," she assured them. "Someone from town will come for us soon, once they realize the footbridge is gone."

Jamie stood at a window at the far end of the building. "Hey, Ma, the footbridge ain't the only bridge that's gone. So is the wagon bridge." Caro joined him at the window. "I always wanted to see the ocean," he said, looking down at the tossing, swirling water that surrounded them. "You reckon this is how it looks?"

"Come away from that window, Jamie Hamilton. Worrying about how oceans look isn't our top priority." She looked to Alex for confirmation. "We all need to stay close together and remain calm. Maybe if we open that door and stand there where someone from town can see us, they'll know how to find us."

The four of them walked to the big floor-to-ceiling door in

the center front of the building. The planked door was shut now, but it was made to open and had once been used for loading and unloading supplies. Now a wooden rail was built across the opening, halfway up its height.

"Alex, do you think we should ask Mr. Perkins if we can open the door?" Ella asked.

The custodian had remained on the first level. They could hear him moving about downstairs, loud thumps accompanying his offkey voice as he sang verses from the hymn, "Amazing Grace."

"I don't think Mr. Perkins cares one way or the other what we do as long as we stay out of his way," Alex replied. She moved to the end of the heavy door, unlatched it, and began rolling it back across the wall. It moved surprisingly easy. Once it was open, a view of the opposite shore and town could be seen.

From their vantage point, it looked as though the river now covered all of Shenandoah Street. When the rivers flooded, it wasn't unusual for the water to rise to the second level of the buildings. The water was rising now, but not as rapidly as it had after the first surge that had carried the footbridge away. The rain continued to fall in a steady drizzle, but not the heavy downpour of the preceding days. Perhaps the worst was over, and all they needed to do was wait here. When the water receded, they could wade back to town safely, or wait until someone came in a boat for them.

"Look, Alex," Caro said, "there are people gathered on the high ground behind those buildings." She pointed to the area where the Catholic church stood. The high ground that backed up to Shenandoah Street had always been a lookout for townsfolk during floods. Sure enough, there were people lined up.

"Wave at them to get their attention," Ella said. The four of them began to wave.

Someone saw them, then everyone started pointing and waving and shouting. Alex searched the crowd. A longing deep inside her surfaced, and she searched each distant face, hoping to see one whom her heart believed could get them out of this mess. *Rush, are you there?* Then she wondered why such a thought had even occurred to her.

"We could swim across," Jamie told his mother.

"Don't be ridiculous. You can't swim in flood water. With all that debris, you'd be knocked unconscious and carried miles downriver."

"I told you I could swim, but I can't" Caro said. "I'd have to stay here alone."

"No one's swimming," Alex assured her.

It felt as though a million years had passed since she and her cousin had had the conversation about swimming, with Caro declaring she knew how to swim. They had come a long way since that moment, and the frightened, defiant child Caro had been no longer existed. This knowledge made Alex's heart swell with love.

She hugged Caro to her. "We're all gonna stay right here together until someone comes for us."

"But—but what if they don't, or can't?" her cousin asked. "Or what if this building falls before anyone can get to us?"

"Don't you worry, sweetkins. This building has survived a good many floods, and it's still standing. We're safe here."

With the look Ella sent her, Alex realized they both knew the soundness of her words. True, the mill had withstood one of the worst floods in Harpers Ferry history, in 1870 when most of the industrial island was destroyed. But should that be considered a plus or a minus? Alex wouldn't allow herself to think of the minus. Even now she could feel the floor vibrating beneath her feet, caused, she assumed, by the water rushing around the building's foundation.

"Tell you what," she said, pointing to a stack of flour and grain piled on the floor. "See those big bags of meal? Why don't you and Jamie see if you can drag some of them over here by the door so we'll have a place to sit. You think you can do that, sweetie?"

Happy to have something to do, Caro released Snow. The cat slinked down close to the floor, conveying in his stance the fear she believed they all felt but wouldn't reveal. Caro and Jamie skipped toward the bags and began to pull them across the floor to the space in front of the open door.

Downstairs something crashed against the building's wall. The sound of the thunderous noise echoed up the open stairwell. Caro dropped to the floor and began to cry, and Jamie looked as white as the sack of grain he'd been dragging. Both women vaulted across the room toward the children.

"It's all right, honey," Alex said, falling to her knees and cradling Caro against her. "That was probably just an uprooted tree." She smoothed Caro's hair away from her face.

"I'm scared, Alex. I don't like it here. I want to go home." She began to cry and buried her face in Alex's shoulder. "I want Rush to come and save us. Do you think he will?"

"Maybe he will, darling," Alex crooned, having had the same thought only a moment before. She knew the possibility of his coming to their rescue was not only impossible, but also improbable. He wasn't here, and considering the way they had parted when she last saw him, Alex feared his shadow would never cross her path again.

"Come on, love," she said. "Ella and I will help you pull these bags by the door. You'll see, everything will be fine."

"How come Mr. Perkins stopped his singing?" Caro asked once they were all settled upon the lumpy bags of grain.

"Maybe he no longer feels like singing," Alex answered. She didn't want to dwell on the absence of song now echoing up the stairs.

The foursome kept a weary vigilance on the crowd across the street. There was a lot of activity with people running to and fro. They thought they heard someone shout that a rescue had been planned, but as far as they could tell, the best anyone could do was wait and pray, and hope the water would soon subside.

෮

"WE CAN DO IT, Samson," Rush said, "I know we can."

Rush and Samson and a group of other men stood on a rise of ground near the old ferry crossing on the Shenandoah. Surprisingly, the flat-bottomed boat was still secured in place on a rise of overgrown branches beneath the heavy ropes that once ferried wagons and people across the river.

"All we need to do is get a rope out to the mill, secure it to the building, and use those poles and the rope to bring them back."

"The current will smash that old boat like kindling," one onlooker said. "I say we leave 'em till the water subsides. It's going down already."

"You saw the back end of the building tumble," Ham Hamilton said. He stood with the others, looking sick with worry since he had learned his wife and son were stranded on Virginius Island. "How much longer you think the rest of that old mill is gonna stand? We all know it's been through too many floods already."

"If you men will stay here on shore and help pull that rope once I get it attached," Rush said, "I'm willing to pole that boat out to the mill and bring those women and children back."

"I'm going with you," Samson said. "Once you hit that current, you'll need all the help you can get."

"Duncan, I'm going, too," Ham said. "With the three of us out there poling, it will be a lot easier to control that old flat tub."

The threesome looked at each other and nodded in agreement.

"Sure beats sitting here twiddling my thumbs and feeling helpless. My wife and son are out there, and I'm not too eager to watch them collapse along with that building. I say we get going while we still have time." He looked at Rush and Samson. "I'm curious, Duncan. What's your reason for risking your neck?"

Ham had seen him at the street dance and probably knew about his return from Ella, if not Caro. Samson watched him, waiting for Rush's answer. After a moment, he declared himself. What the heck, he thought, everyone would know soon enough anyway.

"The woman I plan to marry, if she'll have me, is out there with a very special little girl."

Samson slapped him so hard on his back, it almost knocked the breath from his lungs. "I just might get me them grandchildren after all," he said.

"If Alexandy is willing," Rush answered, "you just might at that, old man."

Rush laughed then—a laugh that started in the middle of his chest and lifted upward. He wasn't certain why he felt so damn good all of a sudden, especially considering the present situation. Whatever was the reason for the soul-lifting, he suddenly felt as though the weight of his past had evaporated, leaving him feeling almost invincible. It had taken him all his adult life to discover what had been buried in his heart—what he had wanted and yearned for and never admitted until now.

He wanted to love a special woman and have that love returned. Because he'd been denied a family as a child, he had claimed he never wanted one, but all those denials had been nothing more than him running from the truth. Well, he was through running. But he would swim if he had to to get to Alexandria Paine.

He turned to the men gathered around him. "What do you say, men? Are you willing to anchor this crate from shore?"

Someone among the crowd responded. "Aye, we are, sir. If the three of you are crazy enough to risk your necks to save them women and children, we'll help you any way we can."

"Then let's get this old tub afloat."

∽

ALEX SAT WITH HER eyes glued on the town that appeared so close, but in the reality of their circumstances, was so far away. Had the townspeople alerted her mother about her daughter's and niece's situation? Alex hoped they hadn't.

In her mother's present condition, the added stress could only make her worse. Even if she were well, there was nothing her mother could do to help them. Nothing, she supposed, that anyone could do, considering the ocean of water surrounding them. Their fate was in much greater hands than those of the mere mortals who watched from the opposite shore.

Uncertain of how long they had been trapped, she glanced at the gray light beyond the railed door. To Alex, it seemed like an eternity. Long ago she and Ella had run out of small talk. Now they sat silently, both caught up in their own thoughts, especially after Caro and Jamie had fallen into a restless sleep. Snow, too, had settled down. He was curled into an orange ball, snuggled between the sleeping children.

There had been no more song issued from Mr. Perkins downstairs. The women heard only the sound of rushing water and an occasional bump of flotsam thumping against the building. Alex suspected the worst had happened to Mr. Perkins. Maybe he had met his maker in the same way as his family before him. The thought made a shiver walk up her spine.

Would they have to stay here through the night? If so, how could she bear it? Already she was chilled to the bone. They all were. At least the rain had ceased falling. The steady drizzle had been replaced by a damp, gray mist that hung heavy over the river and the distant shore. Once night settled around them, she could only imagine the critters that might come out of hiding in the old mill, unsuspecting of the humans who invaded their territory. Everyone knew rats and mice loved mills. Alex didn't want to think of the other critters that might slither in, looking for a dry place to wait out the flood.

Her gaze landed on Rush's umbrella. If worse came to worst, she would beat the rodents away with it, using it as a weapon. The umbrella reminded her of its owner. Rush. Where was he, and wherever he was, was he safe? She hoped so. For a man who appeared to love life as much as he did, it would be horrible to imagine he had met an early end.

Tears pricked the corners of her eyes. She knew now that she loved him and realized that she might never have a chance to tell him how much. When had she started loving him? she wondered, then decided it was that first night when he had pinned her against the wall.

Alex thought of her mother's statement about following her father to China if he'd asked her to go. Her mother had loved Herman Paine enough to leave everything behind that she held dear in order to be with him. Alex knew now that if she were offered the same choice, she would do the same. It no longer mattered to her how Rush earned a living. Too late she had learned that it was the man she had fallen in love with, not his profession.

How could she have been so blind? Her tears felt warm as

they trickled down her cheeks. Rush had done nothing but
show his true character from the moment he reappeared in her
life, not only in his concern for Caro, but also for her mother
and herself as well. He had done little things that even now
she couldn't put her finger on, but they showed his kindness
just the same. Alex propped her arms on her drawn-up knees
and buried her face in the fold. *I love you Rush Duncan,
wherever you are.*

"Ahoy, there," a voice called from somewhere below them.
At first she thought she had imagined it.

But the others had heard the call as well. All four of them
were jerked into movement at the same time. They crawled
on their knees to the rail and looked past the wooden bars.

"Look, Ma, it's Pa!" Jamie shouted, jumping to his feet.

Ella jumped up as well and began waving. "It is, Alex, it's
Ham. He's with Samson and—"

"Rush!" Caro was now on her feet, standing beside the
others. She began jumping up and down as well. "I knew
Rush would come, Alex. I just knew he would save us."

"Rush?" Still on her knees, she strained to see past Jamie's
dancing legs and Ella and Caro's swaying skirts. "Rush is
here?" she repeated. "Surely you're mistaken."

Alex jumped to her feet, jockeying for standing space behind the rail. She stared down into the thickening mist.

The water was higher than she remembered. It still foamed
and pitched around the base of the building like a bubbling
stew in a cauldron, but in the midst of the fast-moving water
was a boat. She recognized it immediately as one of the old
boats that had for years ferried wagons and people back and
forth across the Shenandoah but were no longer in service.

Yet it wasn't the boat that fascinated her, but the man who
stood in its center, balancing himself with the long pole that
he had stabbed in the water. When his gaze snagged with hers,
he sent her that devil-may-care smile. "How you doing, darling?" he shouted.

Relief washed over her, accompanied by a white-hot flash
of desire so foreign to Alex that she felt it all the way to her
toes. Her eyes burned, and every nerve flamed with sizzling
awareness. This crazy enveloping longing was due to the won-

derful, handsome man who stood smiling up at her from the wind-tossed sea below.

Rush had come for her, even after all the mean and horrible things she had said to him. *He came for me.* To Alex his coming could mean only one thing—that he loved her as much as she loved him.

She slapped her hand over her mouth and nose, hoping to hide the sob that forbid her to respond. Caro looked up at her. "We don't need to be afraid no more," she told her. Noticing Alex's tears, she said, "Don't cry, Alex. Everything's gonna be okay now—now that Rush has come."

The next thirty minutes were a blur to Alex. Somehow the men in the boat managed to steady the small craft in front of and below the railing of the upstairs door. They wouldn't have been able to do it without the combined help of the men working the anchoring ropes on shore. There were times she believed the boat would capsize, and the men would drown, but the long poles they used moved the boat as well as anchored it against the tide. Soon they had more ropes tied and secured around the rail.

When the boat was secured against the building, Ham forded the railing. Once inside, he hugged and kissed Ella and his son, then did the same to Alex and Caro. He ordered them to stand back and began to tear away the railing with a crowbar that was passed up to him by Samson. Soon the rail was torn away from the door, and they were lowered in turn to the rocking, swaying boat.

There wasn't time for an exchange of words between Rush and Alex. She only had time to smile at both Rush and Samson before she was told to sit in the bottom of the boat and hang on. Alex sat huddled in the middle with the others, her arms around Caro, whose arms were around Snow.

Working as a team, the three men pushed the boat away from the building, and they began the perilous trip back to shore.

When the square bow finally bumped against what was left of the shoreline, Alex was too weak to stand or to move. Rush told her to stay put until the others reached the shore safely, and then he would return for her. When he did, he scooped her up in his arms and stepped off the boat. Instead of allowing her to stand, he held her in his arms.

"Alexandy, I've said it once and I'm saying it again. You are absolutely the most stubborn female I've ever had the displeasure of knowing. Why in heaven's torment did you decide to buy flour from that mill in such gosh-awful weather? I'll never—"

She silenced him with her finger across his lips. "I was wrong."

"You were?" He looked shocked, not anticipating her answer. "I can't believe you'd admit—"

"I love you, Rush Duncan," she said. Her eyes locked on him, taking in everything she loved about him.

Her words made him look like a little boy who was caught with his fingers in a candy jar and didn't know what to say.

Finally he responded. "And I you," he whispered huskily.

The crowd gathered around them suddenly went quiet. All eyes were centered on the couple.

Rush cleared his throat, figuring that now was as good a time as any to declare himself. In a voice loud enough to be heard by all, he asked, "Will you marry me, Alexandria Paine, and spend the rest of your life making me miserable— happy?" He winked at her.

Yes, yes, I'll marry you, Alex's heart cried. But then she remembered Caro. How would she feel about this relationship between Rush and her? She searched the crowd for her cousin, hoping she could speak privately with her.

Caro stood beside Jamie. They were tugging on Snow, trying to decide which one should hold him. If she had heard Rush's proposal, she didn't appear to be overly concerned.

Rush looked at Alex, waiting for her answer, and everyone else who had heard his proposal looked on and waited as well.

"Caro," Alex called. Jamie and Caro stopped tugging on the cat who was now stretched between the two youngsters. "Rush has just asked us to marry him. What do you say— should we accept?"

Her cousin looked at Rush then at Jamie. "You can have

him, Alex,'' she answered, ''because I'm going to marry Jamie.''

Everyone laughed.

Before Rush's lips met hers, Alex saw Jamie bolting away with Caro hot on his trail.

Epilogue

"DEARLY BELOVED, WE ARE gathered here in the sight of God and this company to join this man and this woman in holy matrimony."

Alex listened to the familiar words. It was two weeks since the flood. The rivers had risen to an unprecedented height of 34.8 feet, but, surprisingly, when the water had finally receded, there was little damage done to the town except for the filthy deposits left by the waters. The Shenandoah wagon bridge was destroyed, and the Child and McCreight flour mill closed for good.

It wasn't until later when Alex, Rush, and Caro had returned home to tell Stella they were safe that Alex had learned that a section of the backside of the mill had collapsed, and Mr. Perkins had been swept away by the current.

Several days later, he had reappeared in town. He had been swept several miles downriver. Those who told of his rescue said later that his grabbing onto a tree after the wall collapsed was what had saved him. It was his offkey singing of "Amazing Grace" that had led rescuers to his location. Alex believed that it was His amazing grace that had saved them all.

Today was her wedding day. The good reverend was to perform the service that would take place at Jefferson Rock.

Leona Whitley believed Alex was suffering shock from the trauma of the flood when she chose to hold her wedding in such a place, but Alex had been adamant about her choice, and of course Rush would have hung the moon in place of the sun if she had wanted him to.

They were gathered now—the bride in her yellow gingham dress, the groom in white shirt and black trousers, and the bridesmaid, Caro, dressed in a matching yellow gingham dress. Alex glanced at her small family, her eyes lingering on her mother who had recovered remarkably fast from her bout of rheumatism once the rain and dampness had disappeared. Then she looked at Samson who was Rush's best man. The tavern keeper looked quite the polished gentleman in his new Sunday suit.

Alex couldn't recall a time when she had felt so complete. She wished her father could have been with her today on this very special occasion, but she knew he was close by, smiling down on the proceedings from heaven, just above their heads. Maybe, she thought, Eudora Duncan was also watching the ceremony.

So many things had happened in the past two weeks since she and Rush had declared their love. A letter had arrived from the detectives informing her mother of what had happened to Charlotte once she'd left Harpers Ferry. She had married the tinker, Tyler Moore, who later deserted his small family, leaving them in Independence, Missouri. Charlotte had worked as a barmaid in a saloon in the town where the Oregon Trail began. In order to earn room and board for her and her baby daughter, Charlotte had kept the saloon clean and cooked meals in the kitchen instead of serving drinks to men as Stella had believed.

While working at the saloon, she had met and married Jack Swift, and they had joined a wagon train heading west, but got no further than the Nebraska plains where they had homesteaded land. Charlotte had given birth to a baby boy. Soon afterwards, the whole family, except for Caro, had died of cholera. After their deaths, a family called the Wormleys took Caro in. Later they had decided they didn't want her, so they sent her to her relatives back East, which had been Charlotte's last request.

Caro still wouldn't talk about that experience, but Rush had advised Alex not to hurry her. In time the child would tell them—and if she didn't, so what? Everyone agreed that there couldn't be a more well-adjusted ten-year-old.

Alex glanced down toward the canal and the house where she had grown up. After the flood it was rumored the canal would go into receivership and be run by the B & O Railroad. Rush had agreed to take a job at Lock 33 as lockkeeper once the canal was repaired. In the meantime, he'd been hired to help repair the broken locks in the area. This suited Alex fine, because most of the time he would be close enough to come home at night. He would lease his boat once the canal reopened, but for now it was berthed in Georgetown.

It was the perfect spot for a wedding, she decided, recalling her trip up here weeks before. Harpers Ferry was as Jefferson described it—a place of meeting—and here she, too, would meet with the man who had claimed her heart. On this very spot they were pledging their hearts and souls together for all eternity.

"I now pronounce you man and wife," the preacher said. "You may kiss the bride."

She looked up at Rush, and he looked down at her. His lips dropped to hers, and then he kissed her. Her heart soared with the swiftly moving clouds overhead.

Everybody cheered and gathered around the happy couple, then she felt Caro tugging on her dress. Alex turned to face her.

Stella stood beside Caro, her arm draped across her niece's shoulders. "Alex and Rush," Caro said, "I have a wedding present for you."

Together they watched as Caro unfolded the square of fabric that Stella handed her. Alex dropped down beside Caro to admire her gift. It was an appliquéd square not unlike the many already sewn together in Caro's quilt.

"I made it for you," Caro said.

Alex looked at the fine stitching. The square was of a family, and Alex recognized the members immediately. First there was a figure of a tall man with black hair, and standing beside him was a woman with a long, yellow braid. Another figure of a shorter woman, whom Alex knew had to be Stella, stood beside a little girl with a mop of curly black hair holding a marmalade cat.

"It's our memory quilt," Caro told her. "Now that we are a family, we can start one of our own."

Alex hugged her cousin to her, unable to speak because of the lump that had formed in her throat.

Rush spoke for her. "Caro, sugar, you couldn't have given us anything that we would like better." He clamped his arms around both of his girls, and together they started back down the hill.

"Come on, squirt," he said. "Let's go eat some turnips."

Everyone in attendance heard Caro's reply.

"Oh, Rush, you're so silly."

Author's Note

Research on a previous book led me to the C & O Canal that runs from Washington, D.C., to Cumberland, Maryland. I became intrigued by the villages and the people who worked and lived along the flatwater route. I wanted to bring some of that history to my readers, which is why I decided to set this book in Harpers Ferry, West Virginia.

Harpers Ferry sits in the river gap between the Potomac and Shenandoah Rivers and is probably best known because of the raid by the abolitionist John Brown on the U.S. Armory and Arsenal that took place there in 1859 before the start of the Civil War.

In 1944 the Harpers Ferry National Park was founded and is now an integral part of America's history. I hope this book will encourage you to visit and enjoy the beautiful preserved area.

Because of Harpers Ferry's location at the confluence of the two rivers, it is always at their mercy. Many floods have occurred throughout history, so it seemed essential that I put a flood in my book. The 1889 flood in Harpers Ferry did little damage and caused no loss of life. The flood did close the Child and McCreight flour mill on Virginius Island, and the Shenandoah Wagon Bridge was washed away. This same system of rainy weather also caused the flood that destroyed Johnstown, Pennsylvania, on June 1, 1889.

Caro's memory quilt is of my own imagination, but such quilts do exist and can be identified by other names, such as album quilts and friendship quilts.

I loved the telling of Alex and Rush's story, and I hope you enjoyed reading it. I love to hear from my readers. You can write to me in care of Berkley/Jove, 375 Hudson Street, New York, New York 10014, or E-mail me at ccotten-@mindspring.com.

Turn the page for a preview of
JILL MARIE LANDIS'S
latest novel,

Blue Moon

Coming in July from Jove Books

Prologue

She would be nineteen tomorrow. If she lived. In the center of a faint deer trail on a ribbon of dry land running through a dense swamp, a young woman crouched like a cornered animal. The weak, gray light from a dull, overcast sky barely penetrated the bald-cypress forest as she wrapped her arms around herself and shivered, trying to catch her breath. She wore nothing to protect her from the elements but a tattered rough, homespun dress and an ill-fitting pair of leather shoes that had worn blisters on her heels.

The primeval path was nearly obliterated by lichen and fern that grew over deep drifts of dried twigs and leaves. Here and there the ground was littered with the larger rotting fallen limbs of trees. The fecund scent of decay clung to the air, pressed down on her, stoked her fear, and gave it life.

Breathe. Breathe.

The young woman's breath came fast and hard. She squinted through her tangled black hair, shoved it back, her fingers streaked with mud. Her hands shook. Terror born of being lost was heightened by the knowledge that night was going to fall before she found her way out of the swamp.

Not only did the encroaching darkness frighten her, but so did the murky silent water along both sides of the trail. She realized she would soon be surrounded by both night and water. Behind her, from somewhere deep amid the cypress trees wrapped in rust-colored bark, came the sound of a splash as some unseen creature dropped into the watery ooze.

She rose, spun around, and scanned the surface of the swamp. Frogs and fish, venomous copperheads and turtles, big as frying pans, thrived beneath the lacy emerald carpet of duckweed that floated upon the water. As she knelt there wondering whether she should continue on in the same direction or turn back, she watched a small knot of fur float toward her over the surface of the water.

A soaking wet muskrat lost its grace as soon as it made land and lumbered up the bank in her direction. Amused, yet wary, she scrambled back a few inches. The creature froze and stared with dark beady eyes before it turned tail, hit the water, and disappeared.

Getting to her feet, the girl kept her eyes trained on the narrow footpath, gingerly stepping through piles of damp, decayed leaves. Again she paused, lifted her head, listened for the sound of a human voice and the pounding footsteps that meant someone was in pursuit of her along the trail.

When all she heard was the distant knock of a woodpecker, she let out a sigh of relief. Determined to keep moving, she trudged on, ever vigilant, hoping that the edge of the swamp lay just ahead.

Suddenly, the sharp, shrill scream of a bobcat set her heart pounding. A strangled cry escaped from her lips. With a fist pressed against her mouth, she squeezed her eyes closed and froze, afraid to move, afraid to even breathe. The cat screamed again and the cry echoed across the haunting silence of the swamp until it seemed to stir the very air around her.

She glanced up at dishwater-gray patches of weak afternoon light nearly obliterated by the cypress trees that grew so close together in some places that not even a small child could pass between them. The thought that a wildcat might be looming somewhere above her in the tangled limbs, crouched and ready to pounce, sent her running down the narrow, winding trail.

She had not gone a hundred steps when the toe of her shoe caught beneath an exposed tree root. Thrown forward, she began to fall and cried out.

As the forest floor rushed up to meet her, she put out her hands to break the fall. A shock of pain shot through her wrist an instant before her head hit a log.

And then her world went black.

One

Noah LeCroix walked to the edge of the wide wooden porch surrounding the one-room cabin he had built high in the sheltering arms of an ancient bald cypress tree and looked out over the swamp. Twilight gathered, thickening the shadows that shrouded the trees. The moon had already risen, a bright silver crescent riding atop a faded blue sphere. He loved the magic of the night, loved watching the moon and stars appear in the sky almost as much as he loved the swamp. The wetlands pulsed with life all night long. The darkness coupled with the still, watery landscape settled a protective blanket of solitude around him. In the dense, liquid world beneath him and the forest around his home, all manner of life coexisted in a delicate balance. He likened the swamp's dance of life and death to the way good and evil existed together in the world of men beyond its boundaries.

This shadowy place was his universe, his sanctuary. He savored its peace, was used to it after having grown up in almost complete isolation with his mother, a reclusive Cherokee woman who had left her people behind when she chose to settle in far-off Kentucky with his father, a French-Canadian fur trapper named Gerard LeCroix.

Living alone served Noah's purpose now more than ever. He had no desire to dwell among "civilized men," especially now that so many white settlers were moving in droves across the Ohio into the new state of Illinois.

Noah turned away from the smooth log railing that bordered the wide, covered porch cantilevered out over the swamp. He was about to step into the cabin where a single oil lamp cast its circle of light when he heard a bobcat scream. He would not have given the sound a second thought if not for the fact that a few seconds later the sound was followed by a high-pitched shriek, one that sounded human enough to stop him in his tracks. He paused on the threshold and listened intently. A chill ran down his spine.

It had been so long since he had heard the sound of another human voice that he could not really be certain, but he thought he had just heard a woman's cry.

Noah shook off the ridiculous, unsettling notion and walked into the cabin built over water. The walls were covered with the tanned hides of mink, bobcat, otter, beaver, fox, white-tailed deer and bear. His few other possessions— a bone-handled hunting knife with a distinctive wolf's head carved on it, various traps, some odd pieces of clothing, a few pots and a skillet, four wooden trenchers and mugs, and a rifle—were all neatly stored inside. They were all he owned and needed in the world, save the dugout canoe secured outside near the base of the tree.

Sparse but comfortable, even the sight of the familiar surroundings could not help him shake the feeling that something unsettling was about to happen, that all was not right in his world.

Pulling a crock off a high shelf, Noah poured a splash

of whiskey in a cup and drank it down, his concentration
intent on the deepening gloaming and the sounds of the
swamp. An unnatural stillness lingered in the air after the
puzzling scream, almost as if, like him, the wild inhabitants
of Heron Pond were collectively waiting for something to
happen. Unable to deny his curiosity any longer, Noah
sighed in resignation and walked back to the door.

He lingered there for a moment, staring out at the growing shadows. Something was wrong. *Someone* was out
there. He reached for the primed and loaded Hawken rifle
that stood just inside the door and stepped out into the
gathering dusk.

He climbed down the crude ladder of wooden strips
nailed to the trunk of one of the four prehistoric cypress
that supported his home, stepped into the dugout *pirogue*
tied to a cypress knee that poked out of the water. Noah
paddled the shallow wooden craft toward a spot where the
land met the deep dark water with its camouflage net of
duckweed, a natural boundary all but invisible to anyone
unfamiliar with the swamp.

He reached a rise of land, which supported a trail, carefully stepped out of the *pirogue* and secured it to a low-
hanging tree branch. Walking through thickening shadows,
Noah breathed in his surroundings, aware of every subtle
nuance of change, every depression on the path that might
really be a footprint on the trail, every tree and stand of
switchcane.

The sound he thought he'd heard had come from the
southeast. Noah headed in that direction, head down, staring at the trail although it was almost too dark to pick up
any sign. A few hundred yards from where he left the *pirogue,* he paused, raised his head, sniffed the air, and listened to the silence.

Instinctively, he swung his gaze in the direction of a
thicket of slender cane stalks and found himself staring
across ten yards of low undergrowth into the eyes of a
female bobcat on the prowl. Slowly he raised his rifle to

his shoulder and waited to see what the big cat would do. The animal stared back at him, its eyes intense in the gathering gloaming. Finally, she blinked and with muscles bunching beneath her fine, shiny coat, the cat turned and padded away.

Noah lowered the rifle and shook his head. He decided the sound he heard earlier must have been the bobcat's cry and nothing more. But just as he stepped back in the direction of the *pirogue*, he caught a glimpse of ivory on the trail ahead that stood out against the dark tableau. His leather moccasins did not make even a whisper of sound on the soft earth. He closed the distance and quickly realized what he was seeing was a body lying across the path.

His heart was pounding as hard as Chickasaw drums when he knelt beside the young woman stretched out upon the ground. Laying his rifle aside he stared at the unconscious female, then looked up and glanced around in every direction. The nearest white settlement was beyond the swamp to the northeast. There was no sign of a companion or fellow traveler nearby, something he found more than curious.

Noah took a deep breath, let go a ragged sigh and looked at the girl again. She lay on her side, as peacefully as if she were napping. She was so very still that the only evidence that she was alive was the slow, steady rise and fall of her breasts. Although there was no visible sign of injury, she lay on the forest floor with her head beside a fallen log. One of her arms was outstretched, the other tucked beneath her. What he could see of her face was filthy. So were her hands; they were beautifully shaped, her fingers long and tapered. Her dress, nothing but a rag with sleeves, was hiked up to her thighs. Her shapely legs showed stark ivory against the decayed leaves and brush beneath her.

He tentatively reached out to touch her, noticed his hand shook, and balled it into a fist. He clenched it tight, then opened his hand and gently touched the tangled, black hair that hid the side of her face. She did not stir when he moved

the silken skein, nor when he brushed it back and looped
it over her ear.

Her face was streaked with mud. Her lashes were long
and dark, her full lips tinged pink. The sight of her beauty
took his breath away. Noah leaned forward and gently
reached beneath her. Rolling her onto her back, he straightened her arms and noted her injuries. Her wrist appeared
to be swollen. She had an angry lump on her forehead near
her hairline. She moaned as he lightly probed her injured
wrist; he realized he was holding his breath. Noah expected
her eyelids to flutter open, but they did not.

He scanned the forest once again. With night fast closing
in, he saw no alternative except to take her home with him.
If he was going to get her back to the tree-house before
dark, he would have to hurry. He cradled her gently in his
arms, reached for his rifle, and then straightened. Even then
the girl did not awaken, although she did whimper and turn
her face against his buckskin jacket, burrowing against him.
It felt strange carrying a woman in his arms, but he had no
time to dwell on that as he quickly carried her back to the
pirogue, set her inside, and untied the craft. He climbed in
behind her, holding her upright, then gently drew her back
until she leaned against his chest.

As the paddle cut silently through water black as pitch,
he tried to concentrate on guiding the dugout canoe home,
but was distracted by the way the girl felt pressed against
him, the way she warmed him. As his body responded to
a need he had long tried to deny, he felt ashamed at his
lack of control. What kind of a man was he, to become
aroused by a helpless, unconscious female?

Overhead, the sky was tinted deep violet, an early canvas
for the night's first stars. During the last few yards of the
journey, the swamp grew so dark that he had only the yellow glow of lamplight shining from his home high above
the water to guide him.

•   •   •

Run. Keep running.

The dream was so real that Olivia Bond could feel the leaf-littered ground beneath her feet and the faded chill of winter that lingered on the damp April air. She suffered, haunted by memories of the past year, some still so vivid they turned her dreams into nightmares. Even now, as she lay tossing in her sleep, she could feel the faint sway of the flatboat as it moved down river long ago. In her sleep the fear welled up inside her.

Her dreaming mind began to taunt her with palpable memories of new sights and scents and dangers.

Run. Run. Run, Olivia. You're almost home.

Her legs thrashed, startling her awake. She sat straight up, felt a searing pain in her right wrist and a pounding in her head that forced her to quickly lie back down. She kept her eyes closed until the stars stopped dancing behind them, then she slowly opened them and looked around.

The red glow of embers burning in a fireplace illuminated the ceiling above her. She lay staring up at even log beams that ran across a wide planked ceiling, trying to ignore the pounding in her head, fighting to stay calm and let her memory come rushing back. Slowly she realized she was no longer lost on the forest trail. She had not become a bobcat's dinner, but was indoors, in a cabin, on a bed.

She spread her fingers and pressed her hands palms down against a rough, woven sheet drawn over her. The mattress was filled with something soft that gave off a tangy scent. A pillow cradled her head.

Slowly Olivia turned her aching head, afraid of who or what she might find beside her, but when she discovered she was in bed alone, she thanked God for small favors.

Refusing to panic, she thought back to her last lucid memory: a wildcat's scream. She recalled tearing through the cypress swamp, trying to make out the trail in the dim light before she tripped. She lifted her hand to her forehead and felt swelling. After testing it gingerly, she was thankful that she had not gashed her head open and bled to death.

She tried to lift her head again but intense pain forced
her to lie still. Olivia closed her eyes and sighed. A moment
later, an unsettling feeling came over her. She knew by the
way her skin tingled, the way her nerve ends danced, that
someone was nearby. Someone was watching her. An in-
stinctive, intuitive sensation warned her that the *someone*
was a man.

At first she peered through her lashes, but all she could
make out was a tall, shadowy figure standing in the open
doorway across the room. Her heart began to pound so hard
she was certain the sound would give her consciousness
away.

The man walked into the room and she bit her lips together to hold back a cry. She watched him move about
purposefully. Instead of coming directly to the bed, he
walked over to a small square table. She heard him strike
a piece of flint, smelled lamp oil as it flared to life.

His back was to her as he stood at the table; Olivia
opened her eyes wider and watched. He was tall, taller than
most men, strongly built, dressed in buckskin pants topped
by a buff shirt with billowing sleeves. Despite the coolness
of the evening, he wore no coat, no jacket. Indian moccasins, not shoes, covered his feet. His hair was a deep black,
cut straight and worn long enough to hang just over his
collar. She watched his bronzed, well-tapered hands turn up
the lamp wick and set the glass chimney in place.

Olivia sensed he was about to turn and look at her. She
wanted to close her eyes and pretend to be unconscious,
thinking that might be safer than letting him catch her staring at him, but as he slowly turned toward the bed, she
knew she had to see him. She had to know what she was
up against.

Her gaze swept his body, taking in his great height, the
length of his arms, the width and breadth of his shoulders
before she dared even look at his face.

When she did, she gasped.

·   ·   ·

Noah stood frozen beside the table, shame and anger welling up from deep inside. He was unable to move, unable to breathe as the telling sound of the girl's shock upon seeing his face died on the air. He watched her flinch and scoot back into the corner, press close to the wall. He knew her head pained her, but obviously not enough to keep her from showing her revulsion or from trying to scramble as far away as she could.

He had the urge to walk out, to turn around and leave. Instead, he stared back and let her look all she wanted. It had been three years since he had lost an eye to a flatboat accident on the Mississippi. Three years since another woman had laughed in his face. Three years since he moved to southern Illinois to put the past behind him.

When her breathing slowed and she calmed, he held his hands up to show her that they were empty, hoping to put her a little more at ease.

"I'm sorry," he said as gently as he could. "I don't mean you any harm."

She stared up at him as if she did not understand a blessed word.

Louder this time, he spoke slowly. "Do-you-speak-English?"

The girl clutched the sheet against the filthy bodice of her dress and nodded. She licked her lips, cleared her throat. Her mouth opened and closed like a fish out of water, but no sound came out.

"Yes," she finally croaked. "Yes, I do." And then, "Who are you?"

"My name is Noah. Noah LeCroix. This is my home. Who are you?"

The lamplight gilded her skin. She looked to be all eyes, soft green eyes, long black hair, and fear. She favored her injured wrist, held it cradled against her midriff. From the way she carefully moved her head, he knew she was fighting one hell of a headache, too.

Ignoring his question, she asked one of her own. "How

did I get here?'' Her tone was wary. Her gaze kept flitting over to the door and then back to him.

"I heard a scream. Went out and found you in the swamp. Brought you here—''

"The wildcat?''

"Wasn't very hungry.'' Noah tried to put her at ease, then he shrugged, stared down at his moccasins. Could she tell how nervous he was? Could she see his awkwardness, know how strange it was for him to be alone with a woman? He had no idea what to say or do. When he looked over at her again, she was staring at the ruined side of his face.

"How long have I been asleep?'' Her voice was so low that he had to strain to hear her. She looked like she expected him to leap on her and attack her any moment, as if he might be coveting her scalp.

"Around two hours. You must have hit your head really hard.''

She reached up, felt the bump on her head. "I guess I did.''

He decided not to get any closer, not with her acting like she was going to jump out of her skin. He backed up, pulled a stool out from under the table, and sat down.

"You going to tell me your name?'' he asked.

The girl hesitated, glanced toward the door, then looked back at him. "Where am I?''

"Heron Pond.''

Her attention shifted to the door once again; recollection dawned. She whispered, "The swamp.'' Her eyes widened as if she expected a bobcat or a cottonmouth to come slithering in.

"You're fairly safe here. I built this cabin over the water.''

"*Fairly?*'' She looked as if she was going to try to stand up again. "Did you say—''

"Built on cypress trunks. About fifteen feet above the water.''

"How do I get down?"

"There are wooden planks nailed to a trunk."

"Am I anywhere near Illinois?"

"You're in it."

She appeared a bit relieved. Obviously she wasn't going to tell him her name until she was good and ready, so he did not bother to ask again. Instead he tried, "Are you hungry? I figure anybody with as little meat on her bones as you ought to be hungry."

What happened next surprised the hell out of him. It was a little thing, one that another man might not have even noticed, but he had lived alone so long he was used to concentrating on the very smallest of details, the way an iridescent dragonfly looked with its wings backlit by the sun, the sound of cypress needles whispering on the wind.

Someone else might have missed the smile that hovered at the corners of her lips when he had said she had little meat on her bones, but he did not. How could he, when that slight, almost-smile had him holding his breath?

"I got some jerked venison and some potatoes around here someplace." He started to smile back until he felt the pull of the scar at the left corner of his mouth and stopped. He stood up, turned his back on the girl, and headed for the long wide plank tacked to the far wall where he stored his larder.

He kept his back to her while he found what he was looking for, dug some strips of dried meat from a hide bag, unwrapped a checkered rag with four potatoes inside, and set one on the plank where he did all his stand-up work. Then he took a trencher and a wooden mug off a smaller shelf high on the wall, and turned it over to knock any unwanted creatures out. He was headed for the door, intent on filling the cook pot with water from a small barrel he kept out on the porch when the sound of her voice stopped him cold.

"Perhaps an eye patch," she whispered.

"What?"

"I'm sorry. I was thinking out loud."

She looked so terrified he wanted to put her at ease.

"It's all right. What were you thinking?"

Instead of looking at him when she spoke, she looked down at her hands. "I was just thinking . . ."

Noah had to strain to hear her.

"With some kind of an eye patch, you wouldn't look half bad."

His feet rooted themselves to the threshold. He stared at her for a heartbeat before he closed his good eye and shook his head. He had no idea what in the hell he looked like anymore. He had had no reason to care.

He turned his back on her and stepped out onto the porch, welcoming the darkness.

Friends Romance

Can a man come between friends?

__A TASTE OF HONEY
by DeWanna Pace   0-515-12387-0

__WHERE THE HEART IS
by Sheridon Smythe   0-515-12412-5

__LONG WAY HOME
by Wendy Corsi Staub   0-515-12440-0

All books $5.99
Prices slightly higher in Canada